PENGUIN  CLASSICS

AFRICAN MYTHS OF ORIGIN

STEPHEN BELCHER was born in Cairo, Egypt, the son of an American Foreign Service officer, and spent much of his childhood in Africa and Europe. He holds a doctorate (Ph.D.) in Comparative Literature from Brown University, and has taught at the University of Nouakchott (Islamic Republic of Mauritania), the Pennsylvania State University (USA) and at the University of Kankan in the Republic of Guinea. He is the co-editor, with John W. Johnson and Thomas Hale, of an anthology, *Voices from a Vast Continent: Oral Epics from Africa*, and the author of *Epic Traditions of Africa*.

T0353928

African Myths
of Origin

Stories selected and retold by
STEPHEN BELCHER

PENGUIN BOOKS

PENGUIN BOOKS

Published by the Penguin Group
Penguin Books Ltd, 80 Strand, London WC2R ORL, England
Penguin Group (USA) Inc., 375 Hudson Street, New York, New York 10014, USA
Penguin Group (Canada), 90 Eglinton Avenue East, Suite 700, Toronto, Ontario, Canada M4P 2Y3
(a division of Pearson Penguin Canada Inc.)
Penguin Ireland, 25 St Stephen's Green, Dublin 2, Ireland
(a division of Penguin Books Ltd)
Penguin Group (Australia), 250 Camberwell Road,
Camberwell, Victoria 3124, Australia (a division of Pearson Australia Group Pty Ltd)
Penguin Books India Pvt Ltd, 11 Community Centre,
Panchsheel Park, New Delhi – 110 017, India
Penguin Group (NZ), cnr Airborne and Rosedale Roads, Albany,
Auckland 1310, New Zealand (a division of Pearson New Zealand Ltd)
Penguin Books (South Africa) (Pty) Ltd, 24 Sturdee Avenue,
Rosebank 2196, South Africa

Penguin Books Ltd, Registered Offices: 80 Strand, London WC2R ORL, England

www.penguin.com

First published 2005

024

Set in 10.25/12.25 pt PostScript Adobe Sabon
Typeset by Rowland Phototypesetting Ltd, Bury St Edmunds, Suffolk
Printed and bound in Great Britain by Clays Ltd, Elcograf S.p.A.

ISBN-13: 978-0-14-044945-7

www.greenpenguin.co.uk

MIX
Paper from
responsible sources
FSC
www.fsc.org   FSC® C018179

Penguin Books is committed to a sustainable
future for our business, our readers and our planet.
This book is made from Forest Stewardship
Council™ certified paper.

Contents

TRICKSTERS

PART II. STORIES OF KINGDOMS
AND PEOPLES

ANCIENT AFRICA

PEOPLES OF THE UPPER NILE AND
EAST AFRICA

KINGDOMS OF THE GREAT LAKES

CENTRAL EAST AFRICA

THE PEOPLES OF SOUTHERN AFRICA

THE CENTRAL ATLANTIC

FROM THE FOREST TO THE NIGER

THE PEOPLES OF THE COAST

THE MOSSI PLATEAU

LAKE CHAD AND THE
CENTRAL SUDAN

THE KINGDOMS OF THE
WESTERN SUDAN

THE PEOPLES OF SENEGAMBIA

THE SAHARA

Introduction

This book is an invitation to the worlds and the peoples of African mythology. It offers stories of animal-creators: Mantis, who made the moon from a feather coated with gall, or Ananse the spider who found the moon to settle a wager with the sky-god Nyame. Some stories, from the tropical forests, tell how chimpanzees once possessed arts and crafts, until humans stole them. For the most part, the protagonists are human. The stories tell of how their world was shaped and how their culture was established: by gifts from the spirits, through misadventure and accident, from conflict and rivalry. Some of the humans are exceptional by nature, such as Lianja who was born fully grown and armed to avenge his father. Others become so: Sunjata was a cripple during his childhood, until he rose to manhood and empire. The stories tell of migrations for all sorts of causes: to escape a monstrous crocodile, to escape the growing Ashanti empire, to escape a tyrannical father. The themes are as varied as the peoples who have created or adopted these stories as their narratives of origin.

Africans have occupied every type of environment on their landmass: deserts and fertile river valleys, mountain-slopes and swamps, the tropical forests and the savannah grasslands. They have adjusted their material culture and their social systems to the needs of the ecologies they exploit, as well as developing the technologies required to master their environment. Such diversification is hardly surprising; it was from Africa that humans dispersed, tens of thousands of years ago, into every habitable corner of our globe. But no other part of the world displays quite so much human variety as is to be found among the peoples of Africa. No generalizations are possible. Africa is home to some of the oldest human civilizations, and at the same time something close to the lifestyle of our stone-age ancestors has survived in isolated regions of the continent. The peoples of Africa speak thousands of languages, and each language represents a distinctive culture and way of life – comparable, perhaps, to those of the neighbours, but nevertheless individual and treasured by its people.

Visitors may come to know a corner of Africa quite well, but local understanding cannot always be translated to other contexts. Every place has – or had, for admittedly modernization is homogenizing the cultures of Africa – its own texture of local specificities and interactions. These specificities may stem from the physical environment, for example, the important difference, for farmers, between the *waalo* and the *jeeri* lands along the Senegal river (*jeeri* lands are flooded only when the river overflows its banks and leaves pools, isolated from the regular course; the richer *waalo* lands are the floodplain), or ways of cultivating yams, or the wide variety of palm trees and banana trees available in certain areas of eastern Africa. More often, and less visibly, they apply to the social environment, to the ways in which people interact and the rules which they obey (and which strangers too often break). The joking relationship which exists among many clans and peoples in west Africa (particularly in the Mande world, whose peoples look back to the medieval empire of Mali) would be an example: the occasionally shocking insults which are exchanged are actually an affirmation of an underlying shared social bond. They are also a recognition of a shared history.

IDENTITY AND THE PAST

This shared history is not the documented political history of academic discourse, transmitted through memoirs and monographs. Rather, it is a shared perception of the past, as translated through recognized stories (in many variants) about that past. Stories articulate the content of the past (who did what,

and when) and also its meaning: why certain events are important, what relationships they established, and how they connect
to the present world. The common past of groups is the subject
of this book. The past involved, however, is not the recent past
(the last two or three centuries), but one more remote. The
recent past is that of individual and documented history, and it
extends three or four generations back from the present of a
given speaker (perhaps more, in some special circumstances).
The group's past derives from a time much longer before that,
from an era associated with and comparable to the time of
creation in which the world took shape.

In Africa, the recent past (since 1800) has also been marked
by external disruptions: Islamic conquests in the interior, colonization and finally the transformations of modernization, and
even before 1800 many areas were put into turmoil by the
effects of the transatlantic slave-trade. Many of the older cultural configurations have become irrelevant, as lifestyles have
changed and the movements of peoples have erased the long-
established social alliances. But change does not completely
erase what has been inherited from the more distant past: language, names, relationships, a sense of place and of self. What
binds individuals into communities is not only the amalgam of
shared practices and activities, the daily routine that allows
reference to common experience, but also, often, a sense of
common origin derived from knowledge of the stories about
how the community came into being, how its institutions were
established, and how they are justified. Knowing these stories,
with something of their context and function, can be a key to
understanding the cultures from which they arose.

MYTHS

A story that explains origins and the root-causes of things is
called myth, and the word has acquired a tremendous range
of associations ranging through the religious, spiritual and
psychological domains. In the twentieth century the historical
element of myths is no longer much considered. We moderns

do not believe, as did the Greeks of old, that the infant Oedipus was really cast out with his feet bound, or that Orestes was pursued by a howling pack of Furies to the gates of Athens. We have substituted different modes of interpretation for the stories, viewing them largely as keys to self-improvement and spiritual growth, thanks to the work of Sigmund Freud, Carl Gustav Jung and Joseph Campbell. But in this collection of stories the historical element regains its importance, for it supplies the function that unites them. It might be more accurate to call these stories 'traditions of origin', leaving out the word 'myth', for that phrase captures the defining criteria: the stories describe cultural origins for the peoples involved, and they are 'traditional' – meaning that they have been handed down from one generation to another, although always with changes and adaptations to keep them relevant to their contemporary audiences. These are not necessarily the stories associated with spiritual cults or religious practice, although they may echo the same world view. Cult myths have their own functions and rules (some of the stories included here do count as cult myths, and may serve as examples of the type in distinction to the historical traditions of origin).

MYTHS AND FOLK TALES

We must also set these stories apart from folk tales, although there may be overlap in form and content. Almost every African culture distinguishes between the sort of tale that serves for entertainment and narratives possessed of higher value or meaning. The stories retold in this collection are not casual tales to be recounted in the dusk, as the family gathers around the last embers of the cooking fire to pass time before sleep calls them. Many thousand tales of this sort have been collected and published. Such stories, folk tales, are clearly patterned; they have defined beginnings and often moral endings, and they frequently include songs as part of the action. The purpose may be morally normative, and content may explain or reinforce social customs, but the tools are those of fiction, invention and style. A large number of these tales belong to the realm of animal fable – stories of the trickster Hare or Tortoise or Spider and many other characters – and many of them have an aetiological function, explaining the animal's shape or colouring or role in the creation of the world. But these often light-hearted stories do not have the cultural weight associated with the human actions of the past. They are a vehicle for the entertainment of adults as well as children, and they teach something of the culture's vision of the human condition. But they do not define the group. That is the function of myths of origin.

The stories told in this book are generally distinguished not by the artistry of their telling, but by their cultural importance. They might be the stories told by elders to young men and women during initiation rites, to teach the youth who they are and what their ancestors did. They might be the stories preserved by royal bards entrusted with the prestige of the lineage. They might be the accounts advanced in the course of judicial proceedings by clan elders, when discussing some tangled question of property rights or matrimonial obligations, or recounted in the privacy of chambers to explain some prohibition to a visiting anthropologist or historian. They are also the stories which people tell visitors to explain who they are, and how they differ from their neighbours. The content of the stories is generally known to everyone in the group, but not everyone in the group would feel entitled to tell the story, and it would not be considered a subject for ordinary narration (although the myths of one group may become the folk tales of their neighbours). For the group members, the information is often considered potent and possibly dangerous, best handled by specialists who have the knowledge and authority to dispense it. Artistic considerations of plot line and character are secondary to the importance of the content: the genealogies, the localities, the events that are commemorated in current ritual or that have shaped the current social practices.

Of course, some of the narratives are performed by specialists, and display a high degree of artistry and skill. These traits are not imitated or properly translated in these retellings of the stories, but readers who are interested might pursue the references to the royal traditions of Rwanda (Chapter 29), or to the epic traditions of the Sahel: the stories of Sunjata and the Bamana kingdom of Segou (Chapters 64 and 65) in particular offer rich versions available in English translation.

THE WORLDS OF THE MYTHS

When reading the stories, we should remember to respect specificities. The different myths resonate within particular cultures. The familiar interaction of humans and animals evident in the San hunter myths (Chapter 1) is not to be expected everywhere else; hunter-gatherers have a far more intimate relationship with the natural world than do the city-dwellers of Benin (Chapter 48) or Djenne (Chapter 62). The time of creation (usually by the gods) is often almost taken for granted, and the focus is upon the earthbound human activities of the primogenitors. These persons often possess divine powers, and can shape or name the world around them, but they are of a later generation than the deities who created the world, and their scope is narrower. For some groups, such as the Yoruba, the Buganda or the kingdom of Rwanda, the connection of humans with heaven is direct, because it establishes a divine origin to the royalty of the kingdom. Elsewhere, and particularly where peoples had contact with Islam, such a connection made will be to the lands of the east: to Yemen or to Mecca, or more rarely to pre-Islamic rulers of Persia.

Some themes are general to many cultures, and have been grouped in Part I of the book. Hunting was universal at one time, and even where societies have long been sedentary agriculturalists, hunters still enjoy a special esteem. Cattle are a generalized form of wealth, in the areas where they can survive (the major threat was sleeping sickness, carried by the tsetse fly), and are prized even by peoples who are not themselves pastoralists. And tricksters are found across the continent, fulfilling different functions. Among hunter-gatherer groups, the trickster is a sort of creator figure, who helps to shape the earth for human habitation, although not always perfectly.

Elsewhere, the trickster may retain that creative ability (see the stories of Ture or Ananse, Chapters 16 and 19), but is also clearly marked by human traits such as greed and occasional lust, despite his animal form.

READING THE MYTHS

How, then, should we read the myths? Answering this question leads first to a general discussion of the transmission process behind oral tradition – for Africa is the continent of oral tradition – and next to some specific observations about the texts (and see also Note on the Text).

A romantic (and discredited) view of mythology portrays the lore embedded in the narratives as the hallowed remnants of a far greater knowledge born in a bygone golden age, and handed down through the years as a dwindling heritage of that past. The logic is that of the myth of the golden age: at the time of creation, people were closer to their divinities and endowed with greater knowledge, and over time that knowledge has been lost. Despite our new appreciation of the history of the human species and its ascent into civilization, this view still has an appeal for many.

Study of the transmission of information in non-literate cultures does not support this vision of mythology. It is not that people do not respect their pasts. All peoples have strong feelings towards their ancestors, who shaped the world in which we now live. But in traditional societies, the effort involved in preserving the past must be balanced against the cost and the effort involved, and against its practical value. In the industrialized world, these costs take the form of libraries, archives, museums and other forms of information storage. They are relatively invisible. In non-literate economies, the costs are far more directly perceived: someone must make the effort to acquire, retain and transmit the information. Such work rarely contributes directly to the production of foodstuffs, and so, especially in times of famine, it is of secondary importance. Furthermore, the information is reconfigured with every new generation that learns it. Except in very rare cases (such as the Hindu Vedas), information in non-literate cultures is not preserved verbatim; it is reformulated and combined with new elements as they arise. Every teller changes the version he or she will pass on, preserving some details, altering some, and occasionally adding elements. The listeners of each new generation will understand and retain some parts better than others, and they in turn will adjust their own tellings.

What is transmitted, then, is what is relevant to the present of the tellers. Working with Trobriand islanders in the south Pacific, Bronislaw Malinowski termed this the 'chartering' function of mythology: traditions of the past are maintained to explain and justify the institutions of the present, and so they are a reflection of the present, rather than an image of the past (see his essays in *Magic, Science and Religion* (1954)). As conditions and institutions change, so do the traditions that explain them. This does not mean that material cannot be old, or that it cannot be accurately preserved. But it does mean that one must keep in mind the present function of traditions, and balance present interest against the probable evidence of the past.

These interpretations focus upon transmission as a passive process. There is also a creative aspect to the process of oral transmission and mythology: these stories are the ways in which the tellers hold their societies up for examination. They are a form of self-image, grounded in the 'present' of the societies that produced them, and they serve to identify the features which the society considers the most significant or problematic or informative about themselves. The traditions are thus a dialogue of the present with the past, in which the present seeks to find its roots in what is remembered, or invented, of the past. This interaction has a dynamic quality which is not so visible in literate traditions: Christians and Muslims, for instance, may believe that their past and their dogmas are fixed through the medium of their writings. For them, the dialogue occurs on the level of interpretation, as in debates on the truth of the Book of Genesis, the ongoing quest for Noah's Ark, and regional explanations of social practices such as polygamy. In oral tradition, the stories respond immediately to the issues that need to be addressed, and can serve as the basis for a group discussion.

Traditions change in the face of new cultural needs and new information. They define their legitimacy in new ways. In almost all the old kingdoms of the Sahel, noble families now claim a tradition of origin linking them with the Islamic world. In some cases, the tellers seem simply to have realigned an older story: arts and skills that once were brought down from heaven (down a vertical axis) are now brought from Mecca (across a horizontal axis), and figures such as the Prophet Muhammad become a source of blessings and laws comparable to the former sky-gods and demiurges. In other cases, families have adopted narratives: many groups tell a story comparable to that of Jacob and Esau, in which a younger brother by a trick obtains the inheritance due to the elder. The purpose of the story seems to be to confuse questions of primogeniture, or to acknowledge a certain weakness in the root legitimacy of a given lineage. Responding perhaps to intellectual movements such as the Afro-centrism of the Senegalese Cheikh Anta Diop and his followers, tales of an Egyptian origin have gained prominence in the latest interpretations of these traditions. John Thornton informs me that BaKongo traditions, for instance, may now include a claim to Egyptian origin, although this innovation is not reflected in the stories given in this book.

Christian missionaries (especially in the colonial period) had little trouble discerning echoes of their holy Scriptures in the narratives they heard, or in linking the sky-gods they encountered with the divinity they were promoting. Usually, though, they failed to acknowledge the role of Islam in disseminating stories from the biblical tradition. It is not widely recognized to what extent the Muslim narratives of sacred history are the same as the Judaeo-Christian stories, adopted from that source as part of the Muslim vision of a grand tradition of prophecy and cumulative revelation. There are occasional embellishments: in the Muslim tradition, for instance, Joseph marries Potiphar's wife, who has remained a virgin, after the death of her husband. Whether the stories are derived from Christianity or from Islam, however, the point should be made that they were adopted to serve a local purpose. Choice was exercised in the selection of the narratives, and in their adaptation. The process should not be seen as passive.

It is this dynamic and self-reflexive quality that makes myths such potent artefacts within their cultures, and that makes them such valuable keys for the observer from outside the culture. Through myths, people explore what it is to be human in their particular way, and both the implicit questions and the answers supplied in the stories have an appeal and an interest for all of us.

THE NARRATORS

As noted above, these stories are not to be considered as artistic creations, especially when retold in English. The reader must also remember that this collection is based on published and written sources, and so exists at some distance from the original narrations made to the men and women who have reported them for us. In many cases, we do not know who the informant was. For accounts before 1900, we depend largely on travellers and other such outsiders: priests visiting the kingdom of Kongo in the seventeenth century, traders on the Gold Coast in the eighteenth, and very often missionaries. There are some local African documents from the past, often written in Arabic – the *Tarikh es-Sudan*, written in Timbuktu in the seventeenth century, and many documents collected in northern Nigeria about the history of the region around Lake Chad (not counting, of course, the Egyptian and Ethiopian materials, which go back even further). From 1900 on, we have a growing number of accounts produced by African members of the groups, intended to preserve their history and to disseminate knowledge of their people: Sir Apolo Kaggwa, writing about Buganda, the Revd Samuel Johnson, writing about the Yoruba, Jacob Egharevba, writing about the city of Benin, and many others. In some cases, these might count as 'official' histories: Sultan Njoya of Bamun oversaw the collection of traditions of his country, and Mwata Kazembe XIV of the Lunda authorized his collection as well. From more recent times, we have a growing collection of texts, recorded in the field and published in translation or in bilingual form. Many of these texts are by specialized and highly skilled performers, and accurate transcriptions allow us to appreciate their artistry. In this collection, one of the narratives about Rwanda and several of the Mande stories were recorded from such performers, although it must be noted that the versions in the book are retellings, and not a reflection of the original presentation. But the resources are there for anyone who wishes to pursue this dimension of the narrative tradition. A student of the epic of Sunjata now has some forty transcriptions to consult, collected in the last hundred years, and the number increases each year.

GOALS OF THE COLLECTION

This book is intended to provide the general reader an accessible collection of myths or traditions of origin for a variety of the major peoples and historical states of the continent. The collection is representative, not comprehensive: a full collection would run to many volumes, for the two thousand and more groups upon the continent (and each of them offers variants in space and time). As much as possible, it looks to a conceptual period before the European conquest of Africa at the end of the nineteenth century, before the establishment of current national boundaries. The versions of the stories presented are generally the oldest versions available. When it has proved possible, versions from different time periods are given to illustrate how a story may change over time. Many stories have changed since they were first written down – readers might consider the different presentations of the figure of Oduduwa in the Yoruba myths – and some have been lost in the era of modernization. In that respect, the aim of the book is to create an image of the past, as seen from within the continent, as a sort of prelude to the history of colonization, modernization and independence.

ORGANIZATION

The organization of the book may require some explanation. It starts with general themes, found across the continent (hunters, cattle-herding, and the figure of the trickster). These stories have little to do with history or politics, and often the groups from whom they have been collected have almost no social structures wider than the family. But the themes in the stories do recur in the more localized and functional narratives, as do the characters. Hunters and tricksters abound in African mythology.

The core of the book is the series of narratives, beginning with stories from ancient Egypt (which are not to be considered historical, but as the oldest evidence for narrative traditions from Africa). The individual chapters are also gathered into groups, each of which has a short introduction; the goal is to assist the reader in recognizing regional patterns and relationships. Each chapter has a short introduction describing the people involved, and some of the stories in turn have their own introductory note. Information on sources and suggestions for further reading are found at the end of the book.

After the chapters on general themes, the narratives start with Egypt and Ethiopia because they are the oldest available, and then proceed, on a principle of contiguity, south along the eastern part of the continent, and then north along the Atlantic coast. In west Africa, there are some jumps because the concentration of peoples is so great that a linear progression became impossible. Instead, after treating peoples of the coastal areas (the Igbo, the Yoruba, the Akan-language groups such as the Ashanti and Baoule), the line moves back to the region of Lake Chad, so as to consider the various kingdoms and states of the Sudan (or Sahel) in an east–west progression. 'Sudan' in this context refers not to the modern nation of Sudan, but is an Arabic term: *b'lad es-Sudan* means 'the land of the blacks'. Historians use the term to denote the regions known to, and described in, medieval Arabic historical writings; the central Sudan was the region around Lake Chad (the kingdoms of

Kanem and Bornu, the Hausa states of northern Nigeria), and the western Sudan means largely the territory along the Niger river (the empires of Mali and Songhay). Another term used for the region is the Sahel, from the Arabic word for 'shore', through which the Sahara becomes a metaphoric sea separating the peoples north and south. The sequence ends in the Sahara, with Tuareg groups.

HISTORICAL BACKGROUND

Historical background for the specific regions and peoples is given in the part and chapter introductions; the basic themes are migration and the spread of languages. It may be useful here to provide a quick overview, and to point to some specific regions of greater complexity.

The history of the peoples of Africa can be inferred, to some extent, from the map of language distribution: it is the story of the expansion of the Niger–Congo family of languages from their homeland, lying to the east of the lower Niger river in what is now Nigeria and Cameroon. The speakers of the languages had developed various crops and had some knowledge of iron-working. One set of groups moved east and south from this homeland, and developed into the Bantu language family. Moving east through the savannahs, north of the great equatorial forest areas, some of the peoples reached the area around the great lakes of east Africa: this region is where all four of the language families of Africa met and traded cultures. The cluster of kingdoms found to the south of that region (Bunyoro, Buganda, Rwanda and others) offer some of the densest layers of mythological traditions to be found on the continent. The Bantu-speakers then turned south, through the fertile lands of the lake system, having acquired cattle. At the same time, other speakers of related languages were moving south-east from the common homeland, through the forests of central Africa; the two groups together, with all their descendants, are now known as the Bantu language speakers, and dominate all the southern third of the continent. Resident groups – largely hunters and gatherers – were assimilated or pushed out into marginal lands. The savannah region south of the forest became home to a number of related kingdoms – Angola, Kongo, Kuba, Luba and Lunda – whose interactions cut across the continent.

For western Africa, the pattern of migration is not so simple in terms of language, but must be read against the longer geological history of the region. Ten to fifteen thousand years ago, the Sahara was not a desert; it was a well-watered savannah across which many groups spread. As the climate changed, groups moved south, some moving into the forest as hunters, others clustering in the open lands where rainfall and river-flooding allowed agriculture. This region of open lands became the home of great kingdoms, which are known to us through their trade with the Mediterranean: Ghana, Mali, Kanem, Bornu and later Songhay. The lower Niger also witnessed a growth in population, but differing patterns of state formation: among the Yoruba to the west of the river, city-states with divine kings were the rule, while among the Igbo groups to the east there were very few chiefs and little central authority.

The other language groups, the Khoi-San to the south and the Nilo-Saharan in the north, essentially found themselves surrounded by the expansion of the peoples of the Niger–Congo family, and their languages now exist as isolated members of a once far greater family. The fourth group, the Afro-Asiatic, is found on the edges of the continent north or east of the Sahara.

While it tells us something of the movement of the peoples, language alone does not explain the spread of populations. For that we must look at the history of food-production and to aspects of technology such as iron-working. Africans have domesticated or adapted different crops in different regions: millets in the savannahs, rice in wetlands, yams and tubers in tropical zones, bananas (brought from the Indies) in east Africa. Iron made the practice of agriculture possible, allowing farmers to work the heavy soils. Agriculture in Africa has almost always been dependent on human effort; diseases such as the sleeping sickness (trypanosomiasis) have prevented the use of draught animals such as oxen or horses. The pattern of migration, particularly in the more recently settled southern half of the continent, has been one of the slow movement of peoples into new territories as their old fields became exhausted, or as their population grew high enough to limit resources.

As well as the internal history of migration, we must also acknowledge external factors, operating from the east and the west. From the east (symbolically speaking) came Islam, beginning in the seventh century AD, and Islam was also the vehicle of trade. For west and central Africa, it was a trans-Saharan trade made possible by the introduction of the camel in the first centuries AD; in east Africa it was a maritime trade carried by the seasonal monsoon winds. The trading world of eastern Africa included the entire basin of the Indian ocean. The island of Madagascar, off the southern coast of Africa, was colonized from Indonesia around 1,500 years ago; the Chinese were exploring until the thirteenth century. The principal commodities of trade varied by region: in west Africa, gold; in central Africa, slaves; and in eastern Africa, ivory and slaves, followed also by spices. The coasts of east Africa are marked by a fusion of the worlds of Islam and of Bantu Africa. North Africa became largely Arabic-speaking; the original inhabitants were pushed into the desert and demoted in status. The Sahel, the borderlands at the southern edge of the Sahara from Senegal in the west all the way to the Nile, for a long time served as the interface of sub-Saharan Africa with the rest of the world. Contacts through trade were supplemented by contacts through religion: at least two rulers of west African states made the pilgrimage to Mecca, a duty of Muslims, and uncounted believers of lower status followed them.

This relationship began to change in the fifteenth century, when the Portuguese began to explore the coasts of Africa and to establish new trade routes. The new trade became very unbalanced and largely destructive, for what Africa had to offer that the new traders wanted, besides gold, was slaves: human labour to assist in conquering the new worlds that had also just been opened. The effects of the Atlantic slave-trade which developed in the seventeenth and eighteenth centuries were disastrous; states formed to engage in warfare to capture slaves to buy weapons to make war . . . The resulting turbulence ended only with the European conquest of Africa at the end of the nineteenth century and the imposition of colonial rule. The colonial period (1890–1960 for most of the continent) brought forcible changes and modernization to the peoples of Africa. Most of the continent remains impoverished and underdeveloped in relation to the rest of the world. Independence has not, so far, fulfilled the hopes which its prospect had inspired, and in the last two decades the scourge of HIV/AIDS has threatened to undo much of what progress had been made. The picture of Africa presented in western media is bleak.

Against these grim external comparisons, one can set a more local picture of amazing progress in the past century. Julius Nyerere, father of Tanzanian independence, titled one of his works *We Must Walk While They Run*, referring to the great differential of means between the industrialized world and his own country, best known for its game parks. But the walk has been steady, despite the obstacles (which often include the new governments). The peoples of Africa are integrating with the modern world, while striving to balance the new with that part of the old which defines their identity. They do not wish to lose the human traits which characterize so much of their community life, and which ensure (or used to) that every individual exists in a network of relationships of support and obligations which gives him or her a meaningful place in the world. To that end, this book is an attempt to give outsiders some keys to the many worlds of African cultures.

A Note on the Text

There is no uniform set of sources from which to develop a collection of African myths. Although there have been numerous anthologies, collections and studies (those I found most useful are listed in the notes at the end of the book), none offers the scope and focus which are the purpose of this book: the traditions of origins of a significant number of groups across the continent, including kingdoms and stateless peoples. Consequently the nature of the sources varies tremendously.

The stories all come from published sources. I have retold them in my own words, aiming at a clear and engaging English narrative which gives the content and details that seem significant, but is not to be confused with an original source. For each narrative, I have consulted as many variants as I could find, in languages I could read, and have used them all in the retelling. I have not tried to reproduce an 'original' text or narrative style, although there may be some variation due to my understanding of the originals. In most cases, the versions I located were not 'original', reliable transcriptions with accompanying information on the circumstances of recording, but narratives assembled by missionaries, visitors and scholars, each reproduced in its own way, often with some expurgation or other form of transformation.

In some cases, particularly for the kingdoms of the Sahel, I have been able to use documents produced by Africans, in Arabic or in other languages, and translated by scholars such as H. R. Palmer (*Sudanese Memoirs*; see notes to Chapter 50) or O. Houdas (*Tarikh es-Soudan*; see notes to Chapter 61). This category would include more modern material: Sir Apolo

Kaggwa's history of the kings of Buganda is invaluable as a
written source created around 1900 by a member of the royal
court; and similar texts were prepared by Sultan Njoya of
Bamun, or Mwata Kazembe XIV of the Lunda. There is also
valuable modern scholarship: Christopher Ofigbo's *Ropes of
Sand* (see notes to Chapter 44) is an invaluable study of Igbo
historical traditions, and guided my own research.

Source(s) used in the retelling and suggestions for further
reading are given in Sources and Further Reading at the end of
the book.

List of Maps

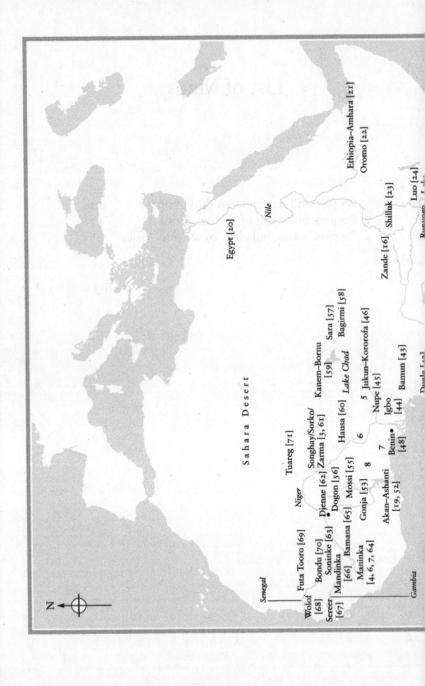

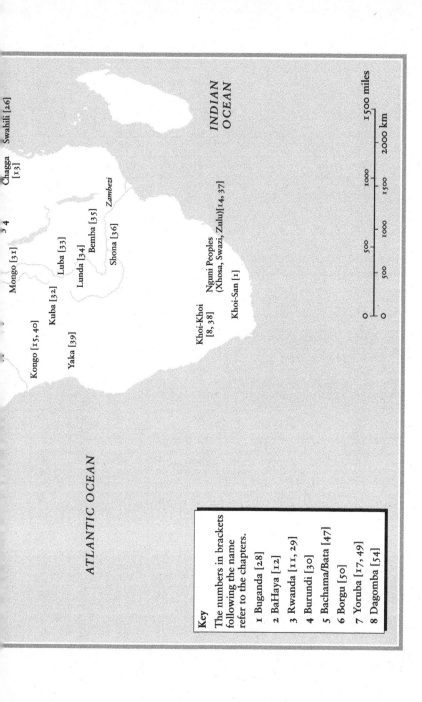

Mongo [31]

Chagga [13]

Swahili [26]

INDIAN OCEAN

Kongo [15, 40]

Kuba [32]

Luba [33]

Lunda [34]

Bemba [35]

Zambezi

Yaka [39]

Shona [36]

Khoi-Khoi [8, 38]

Ngumi Peoples (Xhosa, Swazi, Zulu)[14, 37]

Khoi-San [1]

ATLANTIC OCEAN

| 0 | 500 | 1000 | 1500 miles |

| 0 | 500 | 1000 | 1500 | 2000 km |

Key

The numbers in brackets following the name refer to the chapters.

1 Buganda [28]

2 BaHaya [12]

3 Rwanda [11, 29]

4 Burundi [30]

5 Bachama/Bata [47]

6 Borgu [50]

7 Yoruba [17, 49]

8 Dagomba [54]

PART I

SOME GENERAL THEMES

STORIES ABOUT HUNTERS

The original human lifestyle is foraging mixed with hunting. Humans have adapted to it, they are quite successful at it, and they find it satisfying enough so that the practice has persisted into the modern era, although in ever more isolated regions. In Africa, the pressures of population growth, agriculture and development have forced the few full-time hunting bands that remain into marginal territories which in many cases are no-where near as hospitable as their earlier habitats.

Africa offers a number of well-known hunting-gathering groups: the San peoples of southern Africa (once known as 'Bushmen'), the Pygmy groups of the equatorial forest zones, and, along the savannahs of the Sahel, various now-vanishing groups such as the Sorko and the Nemadi. Other less-well-known groups are scattered across the continent. It would be wrong to think of these groups as representing the ancestors of humanity, although they may have kept more closely to our ancestors' methods of subsistence. Just as much as any city-dweller of London or Tokyo, the surviving hunter-gatherer bands are the heirs of human evolution and development, and they have adapted their culture and practices to their changing environments in dynamic fashion.

For human groups to subsist entirely on the produce of the natural world requires a very low density of habitation (although in relatively fertile areas such as the central African forests or the regions of the great lakes the carrying capacity of the land may be much higher). With the higher population density allowed by agriculture, hunting becomes a subsidiary activity performed by individuals or groups who may or may

not be descended from separate hunting populations absorbed
by the larger mass of settled agriculturalists. While in southern
Africa the San groups were forced to flee from intruders, in
central Africa many Pygmy groups exist in a symbiotic relationship with their larger neighbours, providing hunting services in
exchange for the product of plantations (especially bananas).
Many of the settled groups such as the Mongo clearly survive
with a mixture of hunting and agriculture of some form. In
much of west Africa, however, the hunting groups have entirely
lost their ethnic identities; instead, we find hunting associations
or brotherhoods, set somewhat apart from the majority groups
of the culture. In some cases these hunting associations helped
to form the nucleus of kingdoms (see the story of Biton Kulibali,
in Chapter 65).

Hunting tends to be a male activity; foraging and the collection of vegetable foods is the female specialization. It is tempt-
ing to see some of the current divisions of labour practices in
Africa, where women keep gardens or mind fields, while men
engage in heavy group work such as land-clearing and the like,
as a reflection of this inherited pattern. Hunting is often a group
activity which serves to bond men together, but it is equally
often now a solitary activity. Among settled groups the hunter
is seen as an adventurer, bold and brave, daring to confront the
perils of the world outside the sphere of human order (not all
of the perils are physical). The hunter is also dangerous because
he deals in death and provides an entry into the human community for the forces of chaos which threaten the fragile stability of society. The members of specialized hunting groups are
reputed to possess unparalleled knowledge of the natural world,
in part because of their skilful exploitation of a far greater
variety of natural resources than is common among settled
populations. The hunter-gatherer's detailed knowledge of the
environment translates easily into the occupation of healer and
diviner, and in many cases hunters have turned to such practices
when hunting itself became impossible.

Because of these deep cultural associations and beliefs, hunters
count as mythical figures across Africa, and they occupy a
central place in the traditional lore of almost all the peoples of

the continent. This section offers a selection of stories intended to illustrate the range of practices: the first two chapters present stories from hunting-gathering peoples (the San of the southern plains and the Pygmy groups of the forests); the third represents a hunting group that is now part of a larger, sedentary society (the Songhay-speaking Sorko of the Niger river); Chapter 4 gives several version of the foundation myth of hunting associations from Mali, and Chapters 5 to 7 offer representative stories showing the figure of the hunter in west Africa. These last stories are very widespread across the cultures of west Africa, and it would be problematic to assign any definite ethnic or linguistic origin to them. Readers will also note the occurrence of hunters in many of the stories given in Part II (for example, Chapters 33, 55, 61, 65).

I

THE SAN PEOPLES OF
SOUTHERN AFRICA

*Around the edges of the Kalahari desert in the modern states
of South Africa, Botswana and Namibia, a large and diverse
number of hunting groups have survived into recent times with
something of their former culture and organization. They have
endured ecological competition from encroaching farmers,
occasional attempts at outright extermination by groups who
considered them subhuman, and the upheavals of modernization, and clearly few still live as did their ancestors of the
relatively recent past. But some have survived well enough
to support several generations of anthropologists engaged in
studying them, and so they are well documented.*

*The San peoples, as they are called in preference to the
derogatory 'Bushmen', generally subsisted in small, nomadic,
family-based groups, gathering together only in certain seasons
and under certain conditions of abundant food. Typically, men
wandered further from the camp while hunting; women and
children remained the core of the group. Modern analysis suggests that although hunting seems to have been the more pres-
tigious activity, the contribution of women's foraging actually
provided the bulk of the groups' food supply.*

*The San languages belong to the Khoi-San family, a very
diverse group marked by the use of clicks, that was once spread
across southern Africa (in the following stories, the signs '/'
and '=' indicate different click sounds). Despite the very small
populations involved, the surviving groups are fairly diverse
linguistically and culturally. The stories of this chapter are
taken from two groups: the first three were collected in the
mid-nineteenth century from the Maluti group near the Cape*

of Good Hope, which has now disappeared. The last two were
collected some twenty years ago among the Ju/hoan groups of
the Kalahari desert of Botswana. The stories deal with a time
before people, animals and other things had become set in
their final shape, and in some cases explain how that process
occurred.

THE BATTLES OF KHAGGEN

Khaggen, whose name means Mantis, was the first person. He
brought everything else into being: the earth, the sun, the moon,
the stars, the animals. He had a family: his wife, his son Cogaz,
a daughter, and other children as well. One day, after he had
scolded his daughter, she ran away and went to live among the
snakes. Their chief married her and she lived with them, but
she did not eat their food.

Khaggen sent his son Cogaz to fetch the daughter; he gave
his tooth to his son, to give him powers. Cogaz came to his
sister, and his arrival made some of the snakes very angry at
the intrusion of this human. But the chief told them to control
their anger, and that it was all right if a person came to visit his
sister. The sister prepared food for Cogaz, and then they both
tied bundles of grass around their legs. They left the snakes'
camp. Some of the snakes followed and tried to bite them, but
their fangs could not pierce the bundles of grass.

The chief of the snakes and some of his followers saw the
attacks made on Cogaz and his people. They knew that there
would be retribution, so they built themselves a platform and
climbed on it. After the bad snakes returned to camp, a flood
came down upon them and the waters rose very high on the
mountainside. Many snakes were drowned, but the platform
was high enough to save the chief of the snakes and his followers. Later Khaggen told them to stop being snakes and to
become human. He struck each of them with his walking stick
and they left their snake-skins on the ground and became
humans.

Khaggen later sent Cogaz to rescue another woman who had

been taken by giants with axes who were accustomed to kill women and pour out their blood. Cogaz took Khaggen's tooth and succeeded in getting the woman, and they started on their way back. Khaggen was worried and sent out a bird to bring news, but the first two birds he sent brought no news back; it was only the third bird, a black and white one, that reported that Cogaz was coming and that the giants were following him. When the giants attacked Cogaz, he used Khaggen's tooth and it made him a refuge built very high up, so he was safe from the giants. From this vantage, he would shoot poisoned arrows at the giants, so that some of them died. Then he played his flute so that they fell asleep. Khaggen decided that the giants were bad, and so he cut his sandals and his hunting bag into pieces and turned the leather fragments into wild dogs and sent them to chase the giants away.

Another time, Khaggen sent Cogaz out for wood with which to make bows. While Cogaz was alone he was captured by the baboons. When they learned he was getting wood to make bows, they decided that Khaggen planned to kill them, so they killed Cogaz and placed his body in a tree and danced around it, singing a song. Khaggen knew what was happening through his charms, so he went to the place of the baboons and found them dancing and singing. The song they sang was abusive of Khaggen, saying he only thought he was clever, but when they saw Khaggen approaching they changed the words. But Khaggen heard a little baboon child singing the original words, and he told them all to keep singing as they had done before, so they did. While they were singing, Khaggen took pegs from his bag and went behind each baboon and drove a peg into its behind, and then sent them to live in the mountains and eat baboon food. Then Khaggen brought down the body of Cogaz and with his magic he brought it back to life.

Later, Khaggen met an eagle collecting honey from a hive on a cliffside and asked the eagle for some. The eagle gave him a honeycomb and then told him he might have what was left on the rocks, but when Khaggen climbed up to lick the remaining honey he found that he was stuck and could not come down. He sent a message to his son Cogaz, asking advice, and Cogaz advised him to cause water to flow down the cliffside and to come down with the water. He tried it, and found he could do it, so he went up and down the cliff three times in the water. But while he was doing this the eagle came and tried to kill him, throwing spears at him, but the spears passed on either side or below Khaggen. Then Khaggen caused hail to fall down and kill the eagle. He returned home and told his son Cogaz what had happened with the eagle, and Cogaz warned him that these continual fights would lead eventually to trouble. But this was not the end of the adventures of Khaggen. He killed a woman who would throw men in a fire and eat them, and he killed a creature in the water that would drag people below by the feet, and yet others again.

KHAGGEN CREATES AN ELAND

Kwammanga, who was the son-in-law of Khaggen, threw away an old part of a sandal, which Khaggen picked up. He took it to a secluded place on the riverbank among the reeds, and placed it in the water. Every day he would come to the scrap of leather, the old shoe-piece, and rub it with honey. Quickly it stopped being a piece of a shoe and became an eland. But it was still very small. He would call out 'Kwammanga's shoe-piece' when he arrived, and the eland would come to him. This went on for some time; Khaggen would go and find honey and then take it to the eland and rub it on the eland's sides. The family began to wonder what was going on.

When the eland was getting large, Khaggen decided to bring his grandson Ichneumon, the son of Kwammanga and his adopted daughter, with him. When they came to the place in the reeds where the eland lived, Khaggen told his grandson to go to sleep. But Ichneumon did not fall asleep; he only hid his head under his cloth. When he thought his grandson was asleep Khaggen called out, 'Kwammanga's shoe-piece' and the eland came to him. It had grown very large. Khaggen rubbed it with honey and then it went away. Ichneumon sat up and called after it.

'What is it?' asked Khaggen. 'Why are you calling?'

'There was a person there,' said Ichneumon.

'No, that was not a person,' said Khaggen. 'It is just a piece of a shoe which your father threw away. It is nothing special.'

Ichneumon told his father Kwammanga about the creature he had seen in the reeds, and his father said they must go together to see it. When they came, the eland came to them. Kwammanga speared it and it fell down dead. He was butchering it when Khaggen arrived, bringing honey for the eland, and Khaggen scolded him for having killed the eland before he had been given permission. But Kwammanga said that they needed the food, the eland gave good meat, and Khaggen should simply gather firewood. But Khaggen continued to complain that they had killed the eland without consulting him; if they had brought him along and waited until he told them to kill the eland he would have felt much better.

He saw the eland's gall, where they had thrown it away. Gall is foul-tasting, and people consider it useless. Khaggen decided he would do something with it. When he approached it, the gall threatened to burst and cover him all over, leaving him foul-smelling and rank. But Khaggen was determined. So he hid his shoe in his bag and followed the others as they were carrying the meat back to their camp. Then he said he had lost his shoe, the string had broken, and he must go back and look for it. Ichneumon said he had put it into his bag and was simply planning something tricky, and Kwammanga said that Khaggen surely had seen the eland's gall and wished to do something with it. But despite them, Khaggen turned back and went to the gall. He pierced it, and the gall burst, covering him with mucus so that he could not see. He stumbled about, feeling the ground with his hands, and he found an ostrich feather; with it he brushed the gall from his eyes. Then he threw the gall-coated feather into the sky and told it to become the moon, and to give light at night, and that it should wane and wax again.

QWANCIQUTSHAA

Qwanciqutshaa was a great chief, in the same way that Khaggen the Mantis was a chief, but he had no wife. On one occasion, a woman was grumbling about the stick she had been given to dig up the ant larvae, because she said it was crooked. Her words made a baboon nearby very angry, because the baboon thought she was talking about its tail rather than her stick. So it threw stones at her and she ran away. The night before, she had dreamed that a baboon would come to marry a certain woman who had refused to marry Qwanciqutshaa, so she went to the woman and warned her about the dream and the baboon who had attacked her. So the woman sank into the ground and travelled a certain distance, and then emerged from the ground. She did this again and again, like someone swimming through water. When at last she came out of the earth, she was in the camp of Qwanciqutshaa. She found him there butchering some meat. He had just killed a small antelope. He was surprised to see the woman come out of the ground. He asked her why she had come, and she told him she was running away from the baboon. He asked her to help him wash up after his butchering. She brought water, but she spilled it; when he asked her why she had spilled the water, she explained that she was frightened. So Qwanciqutshaa hid her in his hair.

The baboon did come looking for her. It asked the people it met where she was but none of them had seen her. But it could sniff her trail through the ground, so it followed her trace until it arrived at Qwanciqutshaa's camp. There it demanded that Qwanciqutshaa hand over the woman to be its wife. But Qwanciqutshaa said he had no wife there. The two of them fought and the baboon was beaten. So Qwanciqutshaa told it to go off into the mountains and act the way baboons always do now, eating bugs and things like that. Then he took the young woman out of his hair and told her to go home.

After that, young men came and asked the girl to marry them, but she said she had fallen in love with Qwanciqutshaa because he had saved her from the baboon, and she would not marry them. So the young men became jealous and they contrived to poison Qwanciqutshaa by putting snake fat on the meat that he was roasting. When he felt himself poisoned, Qwanciqutshaa threw all of his belongings into the sky, and then he himself jumped into the river. He became a snake and swam through the waters. When he came near villages, women often tried to catch him, but he avoided them because women had caused his downfall.

But the woman he had saved was still there, and she went and prepared charms with canna, a herb. She baited a trail from the river up to her hut with magical foods. That night, the snake came out of the water and ate her charmed food, then returned to the water. The next night, it ate the food, and then it took out a mat and flew into the sky to collect the belongings that had been thrown there. The third night, the woman waited outside while the snake came, eating the magic foods laid in a trail, and then Qwanciqutshaa took off his snake-skin and went into her hut to eat the rest of the food. Then he fell asleep, and while he was asleep she climbed on top of him to force more food into his mouth. He woke up and struggled against her, and asked her why she was doing this, since she was the reason the young men had poisoned him. She said it had not been her fault or her wish to have him killed, and that she loved him. Then she rubbed the canna all over him, and the two of them remained in the hut for three days. Qwanciqutshaa underwent a ritual of purification with his new wife, then he took the canna and ground it up and spread it about. All the elands that had died came to life again. He and his wife lived there, in a small valley surrounded by cliffs. The only pass that led to it was blocked by a frigid mist so that nobody could come through to them. Eventually, though, they were reunited with his family.

THE MARKING OF THE ANIMALS

The following two stories were collected more recently among the Ju/hoan of the Kalahari desert, and according to the collector they are paired in the culture. The first story, based on fire, is a male-centred vision of the creation process that ordered the world as it is now, with the different species marked distinctively and assigned their roles as food animals, carnivores and scavengers. The second story features a watery milieu in which birth takes place, and is considered the female vision of creation.

The different people were together, all alike, with no distinctive markings or signs to identify them. They were sitting, talking about what they liked to do, and they decided to create something to make everyone different. They would put markings on the hides and shape the animals. They would give a name to each animal.

They lit a big fire, and of course the animals collected round it to see what it was. The first there was the zebra, who was all blank and colourless. Then they marked the giraffe. They marked the kudu. They took the *n/om* that they had made with the fire and began to brand the zebra, tracing stripes up and down all over the zebra's body. The giraffe was standing there, and so they called to the giraffe and it came and they marked it up and down, all over the body and the long, long neck. They branded the male kudu with stripes and curled horns, and they gave the female somewhat different markings. They shaded the wildebeest a sooty brown. They branded the gemsbok. As the animals stood there, having been marked, the people all admired their appearance, and some people tried to put the same markings on themselves, as they do today in the rituals named for the animals.

The hyena heard what they were doing, and thought it was the initiation that is practised today, when a boy becomes a man. This happens after the boy has killed a large game animal. He asked people what he should bring them to receive markings, and the people answered he should bring a small antelope. So the hyena went out and caught and killed a steenbok. When he brought it back to his camp, his wife told him he should cook the meat for his family and not worry about getting markings. He was a hyena, and he should recognize this and not try to act like something that was not a hyena. The people would not be kind to him. But he disregarded her advice.

He came to the people. Their children were watching, and as he arrived they shouted out that the hyena had come. The adults rebuked the children, for it is considered impolite to shout out people's names. One should use terms of respect that avoid direct mention of a person's name. But although they scolded the children, they had no intention of marking the hyena the way they had marked the other animals. They took the steenbok he had brought, and some of them immediately began to cook it on the fire. The others took a long iron rod and heated it in the fire.

The hyena was having doubts. His wife had called him a hyena, the children had called him a hyena . . . would the people make him something different? But the people called him, and told him to come near the fire and to lie down. He should spread his legs out and lie flat on his belly. He should not look while they were preparing to brand him, or the markings would not be properly fixed on him.

When the hyena was lying there, they took the iron rod that had been heated in the fire and rammed it up his anus, so that he jumped up and howled. His stomach convulsed and he sprayed faeces everywhere and then he ran off. As he ran, the people threw old bones at him. 'Go!' they called. 'You are a hyena, you should gnaw these bones. That is what you should eat.'

After the hyena had been chased away, they continued to mark other animals with the *n/om* that they had made from the fire. They marked the hartebeest and the little duiker and the gazelles. The kori bustard came and they marked it, but since the bustard was a bird they gave him feathers all over his body, and they adorned his head with a tuft of longer feathers that reached back. The python came and they marked her carefully all along her body, tracing delicate designs on the scales.

When they had finished they looked over all the animals they had marked and agreed that they had done good work. They agreed among themselves that the animals they had marked would count as meat animals, because they were so pretty and they had been marked individually.

THE PYTHON WIFE

The animals lived together. The kori bustard was considered a leader of the animals, and many of them wished to marry him. The jackal in particular admired his looks. No one was surprised when the kori bustard married the python, because she was so beautiful in her markings and her sinuous movements and her shiny skin. But the jackal was very disappointed, and found herself wishing that the python might die or disappear so she could take the python's place next to the kori bustard.

One day, the jackal and the python went down to the spring to get water. They saw that the berries on the *n=ah* tree that overhang the spring were ripe and ready to be plucked.

'Oh, let us get some of the fruit while we are here,' said the jackal, but when she tried to climb up the tree she slipped back down the trunk. So the python went up instead, although she was pregnant and heavy. She plucked the *n=ah* berries. She threw some down to the jackal, and some she ate herself. She worked her way around the tree, and then she approached out on a limb that hung over the water.

'I shouldn't go out here,' she said. 'The branch looks too thin.'

'But see,' answered the jackal, 'there are lots of perfectly ripe berries at the end. You can get out there; you aren't as heavy as I am. You don't need to worry. I can pull you out of the water if you fall in.'

So the python wound her way around the branch to the end where the berries were clustered, and the branch broke. She fell into the water and sank to the bottom.

The jackal went running home, delighted that the python had vanished and she could take her place. She went to the kori bustard's fire and sat down just where she had often seen the python sitting. The kori bustard's relatives came and said, 'Where is the python? Where is our beautiful sister-in-law?' But the jackal said nothing. So the relatives did as they usually did: they dipped a tuft of grasses in some fat and spread it across

the jackal's face. They did this to the python because it made
her skin glossy. But the jackal simply licked the fat off her face,
and the relatives laughed at her.

'You aren't our sister-in-law,' they said. 'You think everything is food.'

The jackal said nothing and waited until night-time. Then
she went to join the kori bustard at his sleeping place. But he
had not been fooled. Before nightfall, he had planted lots of
bone-headed arrows tipped with poison in the ground, buried
in the sand with the heads up. When the jackal came to spread
out the skin on which she slept, he made her spread it over the
concealed arrows. When she lay down, the jackal complained
that things were sticking into her from the ground, that there
were thorns under her. The kori bustard told her to be quiet,
that it was where she always slept and there was nothing to
bother her there. So the jackal lay there, until the poison from
the arrows killed her.

In the morning the kori bustard examined the jackal. The
poison had made her anus stick out, and he saw there were *n=ah*
seeds in her bowels, and he guessed that the jackal and the python
had gone together to a place where there was a *n=ah* tree, and so
he decided that his wife, the python, must be in the spring.

He went to the spring to look for the python, and although
he reached down, he could not feel what was in the spring. So
he called all the animals to help him. They came and gathered
around the spring. In the meantime, the jackal's little sister had
found the jackal lying dead, with the *n=ah* seeds sticking out of
her behind. She cried out to her grandmother that her sister
was there with *n=ah* seeds in her behind, and the grandmother
scolded her for speaking so loud about a private matter. The
grandmother came and saw that the jackal was indeed dead.
So the grandmother and the little sister cooked the jackal over
a fire and spent the day eating this big meal.

The animals at the spring were trying to reach down and find
the python. But none of them could reach far enough into the
water. Finally, they called the giraffe, who had the longest legs.
The giraffe stretched its leg down into the water, as far as it
could, and it felt something.

'The python is there,' said the giraffe. 'But I think she is not alone. There is something else there with her. I think perhaps she has given birth.'

'Then we must prepare for a newborn,' said the kori bustard, and he sent animals back to the camp to fetch mats on which to place the newborn, to make it a creature of the camp. Then the giraffe reached down again and this time the giraffe was able to bring up the python and the new baby she had borne while in the depths of the spring. The kori bustard greeted his wife joyfully, and his relatives surrounded her and the new child, and they all returned to the camp.

2

PYGMIES OF THE CENTRAL AFRICAN FORESTS

The central African forests, from the Cameroon east to Rwanda, are home to groups of people who have been legendary since antiquity: the Pygmies. Characterized most particularly by their small stature (1.2 metres) and by their nomadic lifestyle as forest hunters, they have excited the imagination of outsiders for ages (they are mentioned in Homer). At times they have been considered subhuman and confused with the chimpanzees who are their neighbours in the forests. They have reached different sorts of agreements with their larger human neighbours; often they serve as professional hunters. Equally often, however, they have been mischievous raiders of banana plantations and other agricultural resources. Their life, until the advent of modernization (and the effects of deforestation), seemed to visitors in some ways an image of Eden-like delight: the forests provided ample foods at most times, and Pygmies were seen as carefree children of an older era. While Pygmy groups live throughout the forests of Cameroon, Gabon, Congo (Brazzaville) and the Democratic Republic of the Congo (former Zaire), the major concentrations now appear to be in the eastern basin of the Congo river and in south-eastern Cameroon. Although they still live in association with the forest, the modern world is encroaching on their once isolated territory. The stories given below come from the Bambuti groups living west of Lake Kivu in the eastern Congo, and were collected early in the twentieth century. The term 'Pygmy' has recently come under criticism for its negative associations.

THE CREATION OF HUMANS

The creator, Khvum, lived alone in his village. He passed his time smoking, but he got bored. There was no one to prepare his food, or to share it. He decided to create people to keep him company. He went into the forest and collected many, many *nkula* nuts, so that they filled his game-bag. Then he returned to his village and went to the waterfront, where he had left his canoe. He got into the canoe and called his crocodile; the crocodile came, and he fastened a harness on it and told it to pull the canoe far out into the waters.

The crocodile swam far, far out, until there was nothing but water all around them. There Khvum told it to stop. He removed a nut from his bag and rubbed it in his hands for some time, then blew on it and threw it back towards the land, saying 'You shall be the first man.' The next nut, he called a woman, and so on until all the nuts from his bag had been sent back towards the land.

When he reached the shore, all the people were waiting for him in the village. He gave them their places, and for a time he lived with them there. It was a wonderful time.

WHY PYGMIES LIVE IN THE FOREST

Mungu created all people, and at first they lived together in one village, the Bambuti Pygmies with other groups such as the Babali. Mungu said they should go hunting, and bring their catch back to the village. The Babali went out, but failed to catch anything and returned empty-handed to the village. The next day, the Bambuti went out and succeeded in killing a pig. But they ate it on the spot, rather than bringing it back to the village. Mungu therefore decreed that they should no longer live in villages, but should live in the forest. But because Mungu was kind, he also provided them with many food-giving trees to sustain them in the forest.

HOW THE PYGMIES GOT FIRE

At one time, chimpanzees were human, but after conflicts with the other humans (particularly the Pygmies), they withdrew into the forest and took with them their specialized knowledge of such matters as growing bananas and fire. One day, a Pygmy came upon their village. They welcomed him hospitably, feeding him bananas and allowing him to warm himself by the fire. He came back again and again, and each time they gave him a good welcome.

One day, he appeared wearing a strange costume of pounded bark, with a long tail. He came at midday, while the adult chimpanzees were out in their banana plantations and only small chimpanzees remained in the village. The small chimpanzees greeted him, as they had seen their parents do, and they offered him bananas and sat with him next to the fire. They saw that his tail was lying close to the embers and risked catching fire. They warned him about this, but he said that it did not matter. He ate his bananas and sat there talking with them. Eventually, his tail did catch fire, and then he rose up and leaped around as though he was trying to put it out, and crying as though he was suffering from the pain. The small chimpanzees followed him, shouting and laughing at the excitement. When he reached the edge of the village, however, he suddenly dashed straight into the forest. The small chimpanzees shouted out in surprise and alarm, and some of the adults came running to learn what was happening. They quickly guessed that the Pygmy had come in this costume to steal fire, and so they ran after him. But they came too late; by the time they reached the human village he had already distributed his prize among the other households.

The chimpanzees reproached the humans for stealing the gift of fire, rather than paying honestly for it, but the humans cared nothing for that. So the chimpanzees returned to the forest. They gave up the practice of all the arts they had possessed, and lived like animals.

3

THE SONGHAY HUNTERS
OF THE NIGER RIVER

The fertile Niger river has long sustained specialized populations of hunters and fishers. These groups have become assimilated to the larger populations that settled around them, and have adopted their languages. On some parts of the river, Bamana-speaking hunters are known as the Bozo; further downstream, in the orbit of the former Songhay empire, they are called the Sorko. The first two stories given here were collected upstream from Timbuktu at the start of the twentieth century from a Songhay-speaking population known at the time as the Gow. Nowadays, the term 'Gow' in Songhay refers to a spirit-medium or healer (perhaps a natural extension of the hunters' knowledge of the secrets of nature, or a change in employment). The third story, of Fara Makan, has been collected in many versions through the past hundred years. The two heroes Musa Nyame and Fara Makan represent different populations along the Niger, but are nevertheless very similar. They also share some features with other regional heroes such as Sunjata. (For the Songhay, see also Chapter 61.)

MUSA NYAME AND THE HIRA

Musa Nyame became the leader of the Gow. He was the son of Nyame; his father was unknown. His mother had become pregnant after sleeping near the tree of the spirits. Soon after Musa's birth, Kuruyore, the leader of the Gow, prophesied that Musa would become their leader, but people did not believe him. For much of his childhood he was rejected and teased by the other children of the village; finally, he could not stand it any longer and he went to his mother. He demanded that she tell him who his father had been, and she sent him to the spirit tree. There, his father appeared to him and taught him all the secrets of the bush and of hunting and magic, so that Musa had no peer.

When he returned to the village, Kuruyore took off his cap, the sign of leadership, and offered it to Musa, for he could see how the boy had changed. Musa refused the cap, and the other hunters protested, but it was clear to all that Musa should now become the chief because of his knowledge and powers. But he continued to resist until he got the people to agree to one condition: they would eat their food only in the village. They would not take cooked food into the bush. All agreed to this condition, and Musa then became the chief of the Gow. He did still have to overcome a challenge from Ndermabe, who at one point led people into the bush and served them food, but he managed this with the help of his daughter.

At one time, while Musa was still young, a magical beast called a hira came and began to attack people working in their fields, so farmers were afraid and they called on the Gow to come and kill the beast. Kuruyore went first; he armed himself with his weapons and charms and marched out into the field. He found the hira and struck it; none of his weapons had any effect. The spearpoint turned, the arrows bounced back, and the hatchet made no impression on the hide. Then the hira turned on Kuruyore. It beat him and trampled him, so that his clothes were torn off and he was covered with dirt. Kuruyore just managed to escape with his life and crept home to the village.

The same thing happened to other notable Gow hunters: Modi and Ndermabe and Mandingne and Kelimabe and Kelikelimabe. All went out to meet the hira, and all crept back, naked, bruised and dirty.

At that time, Musa was courting Meynsata, and he could not be bothered to hunt a hira. But the villagers continued to complain, and Meynsata said to the women, 'Well, since the men have not done anything, let's go and kill this beast ourselves.' So the women all dressed in hunters' garments and left the village in a band. As they got further from the village, though, their cheerful banter fell silent. Finally they came in sight of the hira, and they asked Meynsata, 'What is that huge thing? Is it a building or a city?'

'No,' answered Meynsata. 'It is the hira.' And with that the women screamed and soiled their clothes and turned to run back into the village. Only one woman stayed with Meynsata. But when the hira rose and approached them, she too soiled her clothes, and she begged Meynsata to let her have her clothes. 'I cannot go back to the village in this way,' she said. Meynsata let her have her robe, while she kept her undergarments. So Meynsata was almost naked when she began her struggle with the hira.

First, Meynsata seized the hira and threw it to the ground. Then the hira rose and seized her and threw her to the ground. Then she threw it against some bushes. Then it threw her against some bushes. She threw it against a tree; it threw her against a tree. This went on for some time.

Meynsata's companion returned to the village and announced that the hira was killing Meynsata. She made a point of telling this to Musa, for it was known that Musa wanted to marry Meynsata. When he heard her, Musa took his weapons and went into the bush to find Meynsata and the hira.

He arrived and found the hira throwing Meynsata into a waterhole. It stayed on the bank as she swam back. Then Musa seized the hira.

'Stop, Musa!' called Meynsata. 'This is my hira! I am hunting him because you could not be bothered.'

But Musa did not listen to her. He threw the hira onto the ground and then cut its throat with his knife. He struck so hard that the blade went into the ground and stuck fast, and he could not free the arm that was holding the knife. He struggled, and then asked Meynsata to help him. She freed his arm. Then she struck the hira. It rose up and transformed itself into an elephant. Meynsata broke its neck. Then Musa struck the hira. It rose up and transformed itself into a lion. Musa broke its neck. Then Meynsata struck the hira. It rose up and transformed itself into

a hyena, and Meynsata broke its neck. Then Musa struck the
hira. It rose up and transformed itself into a leopard, and Musa
broke its neck.

'Musa, I am not afraid of you,' said Meynsata.

Musa slipped a chain over her neck, and she removed it with
a spell. Musa slipped another chain over her neck, and she
removed it with a spell. This happened a third time, and then
Musa slipped a very fine chain over her neck, and she could not
remove it at all. Meynsata could not remove this chain, though
she tried all the spells her mother had taught her. Then she
used the spells she had learned from her father and from her
grandfather, but they didn't work either. Then Musa pulled on
the chain in a special way, and her underclothes fell off.

'Stop, Musa! Do you want to kill me?' cried Meynsata.

On the way back they found a herd of elephants. Musa killed
many with his knife, while Meynsata seized others and knocked
them together. They left one alive. 'You will ride it to the
village,' said Musa, and he changed it into a camel and settled
Meynsata on its back.

The women cried, 'Meynsata has killed the hira!'

The men cried, 'No, no! Musa has killed the hira!'

When they asked, Meynsata said, 'Musa killed the hira, or it
would have killed me.' Later, Musa and Meynsata married.

KELIMABE AND KELIKELIMABE

Kelimabe and Kelikelimabe were brothers, 'same mother, same
father' as they say, and they lived together. Kelimabe, the elder,
was ugly. Kelikelimabe was wonderfully handsome. They lived
together and they hunted together.

Kelimabe married a woman from a different village. When
she came to his home and met his brother, she was amazed at
his good looks. After some time, she approached the brother
and begged him to be her lover, but he swore that he could
never be false to his brother. She did not give up hope, but
waited on opportunities when Kelimabe was absent. At such
times she would approach Kelikelimabe and continue her suit,

but he continued to resist her. Finally, one day she lured him into the bedchamber and tried to take off his clothes, while opening hers. He pushed her away and cried that she should not try to trick his brother like that.

'Come,' she said, 'just once, and I shall give you a hundred of every measure of value' (she meant cattle, sheep, chickens and other goods).

'Not if you gave me the whole world,' he cried, and he pushed her away.

He left the house and ran away. The wife sat in the room, and after a while she tore her clothes and undid the bed and overturned things to show the signs of a struggle. Then she sat in the room and wept until Kelimabe returned and found her. She told him that Kelikelimabe had tried to take her by force and that she had resisted.

Furious, Kelimabe rushed from the house and searched until he found Kelikelimabe.

'How did you dare to do this?' he cried.

'I did nothing!' answered Kelikelimabe.

'You tried to rape my wife!' cried Kelimabe.

'I did not,' answered Kelikelimabe. 'If she told you that, she lied.'

But Kelimabe did not believe him. He threw himself on his brother, and with his hunting knife he cut off Kelikelimabe's penis. Kelikelimabe fainted. Kelimabe rushed off into the bush and the night.

When he revived, Kelikelimabe said he would seek his brother. People asked what the problem was, and he told them how his brother's wife had tried to seduce him, and then had lied to Kelimabe and said he had tried to rape her. 'I must find my brother,' he said. 'He is my elder. I must find him.'

So Kelikelimabe went looking everywhere for Kelimabe. He asked in every village, at every farm, everyone he met along the paths, if they had seen Kelimabe. Eventually he came to a village in which there lived a rich chief who had one unmarried daughter. He had agreed he would let her choose her husband, and she had not yet found a man who pleased her.

Kelikelimabe asked in this village about his brother. A weaver who worked for the rich man told him that yes, he had seen him – he had come through the village the day before, saying he was travelling. Kelikelimabe sat with the weaver for a time, while the man offered him some drink. While they were sitting there, the slave-girl of the chief's daughter brought the weaver's shuttle, filled with thread (in west Africa, women spin the thread for the men who weave). The slave-girl was so struck by the beauty of the weaver's visitor that she sat there until late that evening, and when she returned her mistress was of course furious. But the slave said, 'Wait! I saw a young man, as handsome as the devil, at the home of the weaver. I couldn't stop looking at him. You should see him.'

So the chief's daughter went past the weaver's house and saw his guest, and she was smitten. She stopped and stared at him for fifteen minutes, just standing in the path in front of the weaver's home. Then she returned to her father and told him that she had seen the man she wanted to marry. She told him who it was. Her father told her he would take the necessary steps. The next morning, he sent a messenger and summoned Kelikelimabe, and when the young man arrived the chief told him that his daughter would like him to marry her.

'I cannot,' said Kelikelimabe.

'Why not?' asked the chief, but Kelikelimabe did not want to tell him the reason. The chief asked again, and told him that he would become a rich man if he married his daughter, but Kelikelimabe still refused. Finally the chief said that if Kelikelimabe did not marry his daughter, the chief would have him killed.

'Then kill me,' Kelikelimabe answered simply. But when the chief told his daughter what Kelikelimabe had said, the daughter said that he should kill her too. So the father tried again. He begged Kelikelimabe to marry his daughter. Kelikelimabe refused.

'Is it because of the girl?' asked the chief. 'Don't you think she's pretty?'

'No, she's very nice. I like her,' said Kelikelimabe.

'Then why not marry her?' asked the father, and he sent the village holy men to talk to the young man, and at last

Kelikelimabe agreed to marry the chief's daughter. He asked if he couldn't go and look for his brother before the wedding, but they would not let him.

The couple were married. There was a great feast, and many guests came. The young man and woman were left alone together. Kelikelimabe did nothing. He sat and looked at his wife. He said nothing. In the morning, she brought him some food and he ate it. 'That was good,' he said. 'Bring me some water.'

'At least you can talk,' she said. He continued to watch her, but he did nothing more. At the end of the day, he said he would like to go bathe in the river.

'We will bring you water here,' she said. 'Do you want it hot or cold?'

'No, I must go to the river,' he said. So she sent a hundred of her father's men with him down to the river to watch him bathe. He went into the river and swam out into the water and tried to dive down and drown himself, but he could not. He tried again, but he could not. He swam back to the bank and sat staring at the water.

A man approached him. 'You are afraid to drown yourself,' he said.

'No, not at all,' said Kelikelimabe.

'Then go and do it,' said the man.

'I can't,' said Kelikelimabe.

'You are afraid,' said the man. 'I know all about it.'

'What do you know?'

'You fought with your brother. He mutilated you. And now you're married and you can't do anything about it with your wife. Isn't that why you want to drown yourself?'

'Yes.'

'Well, I can help you. Tomorrow the Gow are going out to hunt a hira. Go and hunt with them. When they have made their kill, I will send a bird to you. You should take one of the feet of the hira. If you can bring it to me before the bird gets back to me, I will restore your manhood and you will be able to satisfy your wife.'

Kelikelimabe went back to his home. He told his wife he

needed the fastest horse available, and that he would go hunting with the Gow the next day.

The next day, he followed the Gow as they went hunting; he watched as they killed and butchered the hira. A bird flew up and screamed over them. Kelikelimabe asked the Gow if there was one of them with enough magic to stop the bird for a while, and promised a rich reward to the man who could accomplish this. A Gow named Fabekondoro said he could. He pointed his finger at the bird, and it hung motionless in the sky. Kelikelimabe took one of the hira's feet and raced his horse back to the village where the old man lived.

The old man greeted him. He told Kelikelimabe to undress, and then to follow him. They went into the bush, to a large tree. 'There is an assembly of spirits there,' he said. 'Do nothing and say nothing, no matter what happens. Do not answer greetings, do not answer insults.' They climbed the tree, taking the foot of the hira with them. They sat silent in the assembly, as the spirits commented on the sexless state of Kelikelimabe and the white hairs of the old man. When the assembly was ended, they climbed down the tree and went to the old man's house. The old man gave Kelikelimabe the choice of two male members, and although he admired them both, he could only take one.

Then he went home. He and his wife consummated the marriage; they were very happy. His wife became pregnant and gave birth to a boy, whom he named Kelimabe. Then Kelikelimabe said that he must go on his way and find his brother. His wife protested, but he said she should give him a month, and at the end of the month he would return.

Kelikelimabe went to Musa Nyame, leader of the Gow. He told Musa that he wished to go to find his brother. The other assembled Gow approved, and in turn they rose and addressed Musa in the formal terms a hunter would use.

'Musa, do you know me?'

'Yes, I know you, Fabekondoro. You are the greatest eater of the hundred and twenty Gow. You eat while walking, while sitting, while standing, while lying down, you eat on your back and you eat while running, you eat a hundred and twenty measures of meal, you eat a hundred and twenty animals.'

'Yes. I, Fabekondoro, will go to look for Kelimabe, and I will not return without him.' And another: 'Musa, do you know me?'

'Yes, I know you, Moti. You are the hunter without a spear, without a bow, without an axe, without a cutlass. When you shout, the animal that hears you dies. If an animal cries and you hear it, it dies. If you pass before it, it dies. If you pass behind it, it dies. If an animal smells your breath, it dies. I know you, Moti.'

'Well, I, Moti, will go to look for Kelimabe, and what I hunt I find.'

And another: 'Do you know me, Musa?'

'Yes, I know you, Kuruyore! You are the grandfather of the Gow! You are their chief. You came from heaven. Your people came from heaven. Your boat came from heaven. Your magic hat came from heaven.'

'May my name be forgotten among the Gow, if I do not bring Kelimabe back.'

So the next day they all went off together to find Kelimabe. They searched through the villages and were told that people had seen him, and then they followed the direction they were given. After three days, they found an old man who said, 'Yes, I know where Kelimabe is. He is in the Kiekie wood, where he has married the daughter of a great tree spirit. I met him once when I was walking through the wood, and he asked me for news of his brother, saying he had mutilated him and run away, and he did not know if his brother was dead or alive. But I had no news to give him. But while we were talking his wife was becoming furious, for she was afraid I would take her husband away and she wished to kill me. If you wish to find him, you will have to deal with her. But don't tell them that I told you. Do not mention my name.'

So they went into the forest. They found Kelimabe's tree. But then his spirit wife appeared and attacked them, and they all ran away, even Kelikelimabe. The wife chased them to the edge of the wood and returned home. There she found Musa Nyame, who had captured her husband. He was sitting by the tree. The wife attacked him, but he avoided all her blows.

'I can't use my weapons,' he said, 'for you are a woman. Meynsata would laugh at me.'

So he slipped a chain over her. She slipped out of it. He tried again, and then a third time. But the third time he used a slender little chain, and she could not escape this one.

Meanwhile, the Gow were saying that Musa had been killed, and Meynsata was complaining of the shame, that Musa had not fulfilled his vow to return with Kelimabe. She summoned the women to follow her to the Kiekie wood. Then she flew there. She found Musa sitting in front of his two captives.

'Kelimabe does not want to return,' said Musa.

'Why don't you want to return?' asked Meynsata.

'They will kill me for what I did,' said Kelimabe.

'I ask you to return to the village,' said Meynsata.

'I will return only if Kelikelimabe comes here,' said Kelimabe.

So they called Kelikelimabe. He came and greeted his brother, and his brother greeted him. Kelimabe said he realized his wife had lied, and Kelikelimabe said the damage had been made good, and he told his older brother how he had followed his trail, asking after him, until he was caught by a young woman who made him marry her, and what had happened after that. And so the two brothers were again on good terms. Kelimabe returned to the village, where Musa Nyame had Kelimabe's first wife killed, in case Kelimabe took her back and she caused another disaster.

FARA MAKAN AND FONO

Fono thought he was the greatest of the Sorko river-hunters. Every day he would spear three hundred hippopotamuses and send his people out to fetch the meat. But an envious woman once told him that his equal lived up the river, and so Fono made enquiries and learned about Fara Makan, of whom many stories are told. He learned also that Fara Makan had a daughter, Nana Miriam, and so he decided to ask for her hand in marriage. But the emissary he sent to Fara Makan returned with bad news: Fara Makan foretold great misfortune from such a union, and so would not allow it. Fono decided to try himself, without relying on an intermediary, and so he travelled downstream to the territory of Fara Makan.

As Fono approached, Fara Makan knew why he had come, and prepared a courteous refusal. But Fara Makan's daughter saw Fono and fell in love with him, and she went to her father and begged him to allow her to marry the stranger who was coming. Very hesitantly, Fara Makan agreed, for he really could not refuse his daughter anything, but he knew in his heart that this action would bring misfortune. Still, he laid upon her a strong prohibition: that she should not reveal to her husband any of the hunting secrets she might have learned as his daughter. She agreed to this. Then the two were married with a great feast.

Fono and Nana Miriam lived in Fara Makan's town for some time. One day, Fara Makan and Fono went fishing together. Fara Makan returned with baskets of fish and loads of hippopotamus meat, but Fono did not catch anything that day. He returned disappointed and ashamed to his home, where Nana Miriam did what she could to console him. This happened again and again, each time the two of them fished together, and Fono became most depressed. He complained to Nana Miriam, and she let slip, at last, that Fara Makan's success was due to the hunting magic he possessed, and that without it, Fono would never be able to match her father.

After that, Fono began to bother his wife to reveal what she might know of her father's magic to him. She held out as long as she could, caught in this conflict of father and husband, and finally decided that she should teach Fono what she could. So she taught him the river magic her father had taught her, and he learned it well.

The next time Fara Makan and Fono went fishing together, Fono was the one to catch all the fish and to spear the hippopotamus. Fara Makan caught nothing, and he knew quite well why this had happened: his daughter had broken her promise and revealed his secret magic for river-fishing to her husband. At the end of the day, they turned their boats back to the town and landed at the riverbank. Fara Makan immediately hurried

away to Fono's house and broke in. As soon as he saw his
daughter, he killed her, and then he dressed a slave-woman in
her clothes, telling the woman to impersonate Nana Miriam.
He took his daughter's body away.

Fono returned home and called out his wife's name. The
slave-woman answered, 'Ah, Fono!' and he knew at once that
it was not his wife. He brought the woman into the light and
saw that she was not Nana Miriam, and he guessed what had
happened, for Nana Miriam had told him of her promise to her
father.

The next day Fono went and called Fara Makan to go out
fishing with him on the river. As soon as they were out of sight
of the village, they pulled out their weapons and prepared for
battle, each standing in the prow of his boat. Each hurled
spears. The spears struck the water or the gunnels of the boat,
but did not touch the adversary. They shot arrows, which
bounced harmlessly away. The struggle continued in this way
for some time, until Fono felt himself weakening and feared
that Fara Makan would get the better of him. So he turned his
boat and sent it down the river, so fast that the water grew
white at the bows. Fara Makan sent his boat after the fleeing
Fono, equally fast. Fono left his boat and ran ashore; Fara
Makan leaped from his boat and followed. Fono ran until he
was out of sight, and then turned himself into a stalk of millet.

Fara Makan came running after him, and then paused when
he could see no man running before him. He looked carefully
around, and then saw the stalk of millet growing. He turned
himself into a hen and began to peck at the millet seeds. Fono
became a man and ran away. Further on, he became a small
watercourse. Fara Makan followed him to the watercourse,
then turned into an elephant and began drinking up the water.
Fono became a man and ran away. Further on, he became a
tamarind tree. Fara Makan came up and stood in the shade of
the tree and called his name, 'Fono!'

Hearing his name, Fono became a man again. But when he
met Fara Makan's gaze, he changed into a monkey and ran
away.

Some people say that Fara Makan defeated Fono and re-

turned home, others say that he died in the pursuit, and others
again say that the two of them are still chasing each other along
the banks of the Niger.

4

THE ORIGIN OF HUNTERS'
ASSOCIATIONS: SANEN AND
KONTRON OF THE MANDEN

*Across west Africa, hunters among sedentary populations have
formed associations. In the Manden, the world of the old empire
of Mali, such associations may date back to the Middle Ages.
The patron deities of the modern Malian (Mande) associations
are two figures, female and male, named Sanen and Kontron.
Mande hunters' associations exist from the Gambia into Côte
d'Ivoire, and share a good deal of their story-material; the
myths of origin, however, vary considerably, as seen in the
following examples. Hunters' associations nowadays serve
more of a social than a practical purpose; most of the big game
has been wiped out over the years and there is little left to hunt
in much of this region. The associations, however, cut across
the other lines of division (status, family) in the society and
serve as a force for social and cultural cohesion.*

FIRST VERSION

Sanen was not born; she came into being by herself. She bore a
son whom she named Kontron. They had no country, for they
lived in the bush between the boundaries of countries and
peoples. They belong to everyone. Kontron became a great
hunter and brought down every kind of game. He never married. He remained a virgin. One day, his thigh began to swell;
it grew larger and larger over the following days until he could
no longer stand the pain. He cut the swelling with his hunter's
knife; out came a baby girl who grew rapidly into a young
woman. Hunters are uncertain if she was his unborn twin or a

daughter, nor do they know how the two of them first united – in mutual attraction or in violence. But they became husband and wife. Sanen and her son Kontron remain the divinities and models for hunters.

SECOND VERSION

Kontron was a great one-eyed hunter. He was married to Sanen, but she had never seen him. He came to her at night, and during the day he was invisible to her. She wondered what her husband was like, and talked about the matter with an old woman. The old woman said she could help Sanen see her husband, and gave her a medicine to put in his food.

She did so that night, and Kontron ate it with his dinner. In the morning, she saw him and was astounded to see that he was one-eyed. That day, Kontron called all his apprentices and led them out into the bush. He seated himself on a termite mound, and said to them:

'Listen carefully to what I say, for after today you will have no more opportunities to learn what I have to teach.' He began to expound the secrets of the hunters' lore: how to dispel the dark powers that are released at the death of an animal, how to keep themselves pure so that animals would not sense them and flee or attack, and much else. As he spoke, his body sank into the termite mound, and as his head vanished he stopped talking.

His apprentices did what they could: they dug up the termite mound and transported it to the nearest crossroads, which is a site that has remained sacred to hunters since that day. Then, confused and perturbed, they returned to town.

Sanen, when her husband failed to return, transformed into a bird and vanished into the bush. Kontron's dogs also disappeared. Thereafter, the apprentices started a cult to Sanen and Kontron, and made offerings at the termite mound.

THIRD VERSION

In a time of great drought, two hunters were crossing the bush. After two days, they were almost dying of thirst and so desperate for water that they would stop at nothing. They met a young woman with a baby on her back, carrying on her head a calabash of water.

'Please, give us some water,' begged the hunters, but the woman refused, for her water was barely enough for herself and her child. The hunters renewed their entreaties, but she continued to deny them. Then they became crazed. They seized her calabash from her head, and first one and then the other hunter drank his fill. Then they poured the water out for their dogs. The mother watched in horror. One of the hunters took her baby from her back and dashed it on the ground; the dogs furiously threw themselves on it and devoured it. Then they fought over the last remaining scrap, and one of the dogs killed the other.

The hunter whose dog had been killed protested, and with his axe broke the skull of the surviving dog. The other hunter then shot an arrow into his friend's chest. Then he took a second arrow and stabbed himself to the heart. The woman had watched in horror as this bloody scene took place. When the two hunters lay still she roused herself, maddened by the death of her child, and began to pound their remains with rocks, screaming curses at their still bodies.

The sky-god came down and asked her why she was not satisfied. He had repaid the death of her child with immediate and bloody vengeance. But the woman could not accept vengeance in the place of her child, and she continued to curse them. But the sky-god brought the hunters and their dogs back to life.

The hunters stared at each other, realizing that something marvellous had just occurred. And fearing that they might again become so estranged and lost to decency as to commit such crimes again, they bound themselves with a great oath. This, they say, is the origin of the hunters' association, in which all hunters are brothers and bound to respect each other, and which unites its members regardless of rank and wealth in the brotherhood of those who walk in the wilds.

5
HOW HUNTERS LEARNED ABOUT MAGIC

This and the following stories are taken from various groups in west Africa, where they are widely distributed as folk tales. They express the transformations of the figure of the hunter as the majority of the population become sedentary farmers. Hunters are the adventurers who leave the safe human world and bring back the wealth of nature; they are also intermediaries between the spirits of the wild and other humans. The belief is widespread in Africa that the arts of human culture were gifts from the spirits (sometimes they were stolen), and hunters are perceived as the usual beneficiaries. Hunters serve thus as culture heroes – figures who helped to establish the people's way of life. This story comes from the Fon of Benin (see Chapter 51). Vodun is the Fon term for a deity; transplanted to the New World, it became 'voodoo'. Fa divination is a Yoruba practice (see Chapter 49).

A hunter was in the bush when he heard the sound of drums and dancing. He went to see what was going on, and he saw the *agbui*, bush spirits shaped like rats, holding a dance. He watched the dance and he listened to their songs, and so he learned something of the history of the world: how first there were the trees, and among them the tree whose seeds are used in *fa* divination, and then humans and then the animals. And of all the animals, the bush rats said they were the oldest. After them came the lion and the leopard and the other great beasts of the earth, and then came the birds such as the eagle and the hawk, and then the beasts of the water such as the crocodile and the fish. All these creatures were sent by Mawu, who is the great goddess of the sky.

At that time people had no medicines and they suffered always from sickness. There was a hunter whose wife had leprosy. He was hunting in the forest, and he came upon a mound of earth. The mound was inhabited by an *azizañ*, a spirit of the bush. The *azizañ* spoke to him and offered him a cure for his wife's disease, and the hunter accepted it happily. He took the leaves he was given (although he turned his back and never saw the *azizañ*) and used them to wash the sores of his wife, and she was cured.

People naturally learned that the hunter's wife had been cured, and people who suffered from diseases then began to come to him and ask him to find a cure for their ailment. The *azizañ* had told the hunter that if he wished for more cures he should return to the mound of earth and explain the problem. So when people came to the hunter, he would lead them into the bush to the mound where the *azizañ* lived and they would tell the *azizañ* of their suffering, and they would receive a remedy.

Word reached the king of that country that a hunter had a means for treating sicknesses, and that it involved a spirit who lived in a mound of earth. So the king went to the mound, taking with him an offering of a goat, liquor and palm oil. He told the *azizañ* that in his land they had no means of curing sicknesses, and asked the *azizañ* to provide him with remedies. So the *azizañ* gave the king of the country many of the *vodun* who are now worshipped there such as Sagbata, Agé, Dañ and others, and the king took them back.

6

THE ANIMAL BRIDE I:
THE CHANGED SKIN

*The hunter's relationship with the natural, non-human world
is expressed in a variety of ways, and is often translated, for
the purposes of the story, into sexual or marital terms. The
story of the hunter who falls in love with a transformed animal
occurs around the world. The west African versions are generally tragic. They express an impossible alliance, an irreconcil-
able pairing. But the fruits of the union of the human and the
animal worlds can often be valuable for humans; one version
of this story makes it another myth of origin for the Mande
hunting deities Sanen and Kontron, who are the children of the
hunter and his antelope wife.*

A hunter was in the bush when he saw a beautiful woman
washing herself in a pool. He watched her from the bush for
some time without approaching her, and he saw that when she
finished her bath she didn't dress in clothes, but put on a skin
and changed into a graceful antelope. He made a note of the
place and promised himself that he would return. So when he
was hunting in that area, he would steal up to the pool, hoping
to see her again. One day he was rewarded: there she was. This
time he slipped up close until he could take her skin and hide
it in his hunter's bag. Then he approached the woman and they
talked. After some time he told her that he had taken her animal
skin, and begged her to come home with him and to become
his wife. She agreed, on one condition: he must never threaten
her with fire. He agreed. They went back to his home and lived
happily for some time, although people wondered where the
hunter's wife had come from: she had no family in the village,

and no one had ever seen her before in the region around. The couple had children, and the children began to grow up.

At last, though, the couple quarrelled, as married couples so often do. In the course of the quarrel, the husband seized a burning stick from the cooking fire and waved it at his wife. Without a word she went into their hut and seized her animal skin from under the roof where it was hidden, and returned to the bush in her antelope form.

Her departure left the hunter maddened, almost crazy with grief. He began to hunt ever more fiercely, filling the pots of the village with an abundance of game. One day he saw and shot an antelope. He brought it home and set it to cook. But his children refused to eat that meal. He ate it by himself, and that night he died.

In other versions of this story, the wife agrees to join the hunter if he promises never to reveal her animal origin, or to remind her of it. But he tells someone – perhaps his first wife or a relative – and in the course of a quarrel the other person, or the hunter himself, brings up the wife's origin and she runs away. In one version, when the antelope sees the hunter preparing to shoot she waves her legs, the hunter lowers his gun and they talk. They are reconciled and the wife comes home.

7
THE ANIMAL BRIDE II: SIRANKOMI

The hunter's relations with the animal world are far more often expressed in terms of antagonism. The story of the animals' attempt to learn the hunters' secrets through seduction by a disguised animal is extremely widespread in west Africa, and is found among many language and culture groups. The means by which the hunters escape vary with their powers. In some cases they are masters of magic, able to transform themselves. In others, the secret of their success is the use of dogs, and then the animal seductress turns her efforts to the destruction of the dogs (but the dogs are still able to rescue their master). The belief that one must master another's secret knowledge to defeat them is common in Africa, and occurs in historical and epic narratives as well as in folk tales. The name 'Sirankomi', used in this retelling, is taken from Malian versions of the story (the Manden – see Chapter 64).

A child was born who was clearly destined to be a great hunter: when Sirankomi could barely crawl he would stalk the animals around the house, and when he began to wander away from home he would return with small prey. When he was old enough, he became a hunter's apprentice. He learned the secrets of the bush and the magics necessary to protect himself from the angry ghosts of the animals he killed and from the hostile spirits that one sometimes encounters away from the houses of humans.

Then he became a hunter in his own right, and his promise was fulfilled: he was extraordinarily successful. Never did he come home empty-handed; his game-bag was always full or on his shoulders he carried the carcass of an antelope, or often a quarter of meat from some animal too great for him to carry alone. Day in, day out, he set forth and returned to fill the village larders with so much meat that the villagers smoked what they could not eat at once.

In the bush, the animals were becoming worried because every day Sirankomi killed some of them and their numbers were dwindling. They could see the day coming when Sirankomi would have killed them all, leaving the bush empty and lifeless. They set aside their differences and met in council to discuss what they might do.

'Every day, Sirankomi kills an animal,' said the hare. 'Often he kills more than one. Soon there will be none of us left.'

'True,' agreed the koba antelope. 'None of our tricks works against him. He sees us wherever we stand in hiding. He follows our trails no matter what we do.'

'True,' agreed the buffalo. 'And we are powerless against him. I have tried to catch him as he crept up on us; I have circled around to come up behind him, and then he escaped me. Always he has some trick.'

'We must do something,' said the elephant. 'But what?'

'We must learn his secrets,' said the hare.

'Indeed,' agreed the lion. 'If we learn his secrets, he can no longer hide and we can catch him in the bush.'

'How shall we learn them?' asked the antelope.

'One of us must go in disguise to learn them from him,' answered the hare. 'He is a man. He will not be able to resist a beautiful woman. So one of us must become a human woman and go to Sirankomi and learn the secrets of his power, and then bring him into the forest where we can kill him.'

'I shall go,' said the hyena. 'I will stay in his compound and help with the cooking and the food, and I shall learn his secrets.'

'No,' said the hare.

'I could go,' offered the warthog.

'I do not think you could become a beautiful woman,' said the hare.

'I will go,' said the buffalo, and on reflection all the animals agreed that she possessed the necessary magic to become a beautiful woman.

So the next day, as Sirankomi returned from the hunt, he met a woman on the path to the village: a lovely woman, more beautiful than any he had ever seen. Her lips were darkened, her teeth shone, her hair was woven into braids. Over her shoulders she wore a blouse of silk with rich embroidery, and it slipped now from one shoulder, now from another, showing a smooth and lustrous skin. Tight around her hips she wore a many-coloured cloth that shone and caught the light as she moved.

'Good evening, woman,' said Sirankomi as he approached her from behind.

'Ah, hunter,' said the woman, as she turned and smiled. 'You must be Sirankomi, the great hunter whose fame has spread across the villages of the Manden. I have come to find you, Sirankomi, because of your fame and your prowess.'

They walked together into the village, and what had begun so pleasantly continued well for Sirankomi. When they came to his house, the woman looked at him. 'Ah, Sirankomi,' she said, 'won't you be a good host? Won't you invite me in to share your meal? Are you the sort of man who talks to women only on the path?' And so Sirankomi invited her in and made her comfortable. He offered her water to wash and then tea, and they sat talking while the food was prepared by Sirankomi's relatives. They ate together, and Sirankomi saw little of the meal, because he was lost in the eyes of the woman from the path. He did not see what she ate, whether it was much or little, or whether she pushed aside the meat-sauce to eat only the *to*, the flavoured millet paste.

Night fell, and the other members of the household went to their rest, and Sirankomi and the woman stayed talking to each other until all was quiet.

'Ah, Sirankomi,' said the woman, 'do you wish to keep me in the courtyard all night?' So Sirankomi invited her into his private chamber, and they retired. There she leaned towards him and smiled, and he sat beside her and placed a hand upon her shoulder.

'Ah, Sirankomi,' said the woman, 'is this how you would treat a woman? I have come all across the Manden to find you, and can I be sure you are truly Sirankomi the hunter, master of

the secrets of the bush? Can you show me that you are Sirankomi? Tell me a hunter's secret, so that I may be reassured in
my quest.'

Sirankomi hesitated, for a hunter's secrets may mean life or
death to him, and he knew he was a master without equal. But
then he looked at the woman and saw the flash of her eyes and
her teeth as her mouth opened in a warm smile, and he hesitated
no more.

'What secret shall I tell you?' he asked. 'Shall I tell you of the
lion's movements, the hare's hiding place, or how the hyena
finds its food? Shall I tell you how the beasts of the bush meet
under the full moon, and of their dances?'

'No, Sirankomi,' said the woman, 'for those are little secrets
which all can learn. Tell me something of the power that makes
you Sirankomi, the great hunter of the Manden. Tell me how
you can go into the bush and come back alive, where other men
fall prey to the lion and the leopard and the buffalo.'

'Ah,' said Sirankomi, 'that is indeed a question.' And he
paused. But the woman leaned forward again, so that he could
see only her face and he felt her sweet breath upon his cheeks.
'But I shall tell you, my guest, since you have asked this of me.
Indeed, there are dangers in the bush, and the animals sometimes lie in wait for me, but every time so far, thanks to Sanen
and Kontron, I have escaped them.'

'And how do you do this, Sirankomi?'

'I have mastered transformations,' said Sirankomi. 'When I
see I am in danger, I change myself.'

'Ah,' said the woman, and she breathed deeply. 'And into
what do you change yourself, Sirankomi?'

'Into different things,' said Sirankomi. 'An anthill or a termite
mound, perhaps.'

'An anthill,' said the woman. 'And then?'

'A stump,' said Sirankomi. 'There are many in the bush.'

'A stump,' said the woman. 'And then?'

'A large tuft of elephant grass,' said Sirankomi.

'Ah, elephant grass,' said the woman. 'And then?'

But Sirankomi never answered that question, for his mother
interrupted him. She told him later she was just going to get a

cup of water and passed by his hut and heard them talking. She called out to him, 'Ah, Sirankomi! Do not tell all your secrets to a one-night woman! Be careful, hunter!' And her words reminded him of the value of caution. But the woman from the path asked him no more questions that night; the two stopped talking and passed the night together.

The next morning, the woman asked Sirankomi to accompany her some distance on the way and he agreed. He went to fetch his hunting gear, his weapons and his magic controls, but she scoffed at him and asked whether he really thought he would need all that to accompany a woman, so he left it in his chambers and accompanied her empty-handed.

They followed the path out of the town and past the fields, and then past the area where people gathered firewood and on into the really deserted areas where Sirankomi was accustomed to start his hunting. 'Where are we going?' he asked the woman, and she answered, 'Just a little bit further, where my kinsmen live and they will take care of us.' On they went, and still further, and they came to lands which Sirankomi knew – of course, a hunter knows all his territory – but not so well as others. 'Your kin are not so close after all,' commented Sirankomi, and the woman answered, 'Ah! Is the great Sirankomi tired by a little walk?' and so Sirankomi said no more.

Eventually they came to a great baobab tree at the edge of a clearing, and the woman turned to Sirankomi and said, 'This is the place.'

Sirankomi looked around and saw nothing. 'What sort of place is this?' he asked, and then he was answered as all the animals came out from their hiding places to attack him. There he saw the lion and leopard with claws and fangs, and the elephant, its ears fanning and its trunk raised high, and buffalo with their mighty horns lowered in a charge, and every animal that he had ever hunted showing what weapons they had. He looked about him and ran around the baobab, and he had just time to change himself into a small anthill before the animals came rushing around.

'Where has he gone?' shouted all the animals, and the buffalo-woman who had brought Sirankomi into the bush called, 'He has changed himself! He has become an anthill! Find it!' The warthogs came to the fore, their broad snouts and tusks ready for the job, and they snuffled through the scrub until they found a small anthill not too far from the baobab. They set to work, and Sirankomi quickly changed himself.

'There is nothing in the anthill,' said the warthogs, and the buffalo-woman called, 'Then look for a stump! He has changed himself into a stump!'

This time the elephants came up, their trunks snaking through the grass, and whenever they found a stump they set their tusks to work and uprooted it. Sirankomi had just time to change again and become a tuft of grass a bit further on.

'There is nothing in the stumps,' called the elephants, and the buffalo-woman cried, 'Then he has become a large tuft of grass! Tear up the grasses!' and all the animals went to work.

Sirankomi had time for his last change, and he became a small whirlwind and danced away from the animals. Meanwhile, they continued to tear at the grasses, calling to the buffalo-woman for help, but she could offer them no more advice. So Sirankomi blew himself home, and in this way escaped the trap of the animals.

There are many versions of this story. In some, Sirankomi, or the hunter, is successful because he is helped by two wonderfully skilful dogs. The woman who comes from the animals tricks him: sometimes he ties up the dogs when he accompanies her, sometimes he even kills the dogs to offer her a special meal. But when he does this, his sister or his mother collects the bones and the skin and sets them aside.

The next day, when the woman leads the hunter into the bush, the hunter is lost without his dogs, and he is forced to escape up a tree and there he waits and watches while the animals assemble to knock it down and capture him. He has time for one quick magical message which reaches his home, and his sister or his mother then releases the dogs, or treats the skin and bones with a remedy which brings them back to life, and the dogs rush into the bush to save their master. They succeed, and the hunter comes home somewhat wiser.

Some versions also say that the hunter then assembles his apprentices and leads them into the bush, and there they discover the city of animals. They wait in ambush, and in the morning, as the animals are going off to their various occupations, they begin a slaughter from which few animals escape, to avenge the betrayal of hunters' secrets.

THE CATTLE-HERDERS

There is still disagreement among archaeologists and other specialists on when, how and why humans domesticated their animals. By the available evidence, the people living in what is now the Sahara desert domesticated a local breed of cattle some 7,000–10,000 years ago. Sheep and goats, now widespread across the continent, were introduced from the Middle East some time later, and camels even later, after the period of the Roman empire. The presumption is that humans accustomed to follow the herds of wild cattle in their seasonal migrations eventually domesticated them; the question is why, for hunters in general have a varied, healthy and adequate diet.

It is association with cattle, rather than other forms of livestock, that really defines the pastoral lifestyle in Africa, and one can distinguish two separate modes of cattle management. Across the Sahel, the savannah that forms the southern edge of the Sahara, there were many specialized groups who lived by herding, following their cattle on a seasonal course of migration through the grasses that appeared with the rains. From the Atlantic east to Lake Chad, this group is primarily composed of fractions of the Fulbe; in eastern Africa (Somalia, Sudan, Kenya) there is much greater ethnic and linguistic variation: near the Nile, the Dinka and Nuer pasture their cattle on floodplains; the Oromo peoples circulate through Somalia, and in Kenya the Maasai are among the best known of the pastoral groups.

From the great lakes down into South Africa, in those areas where the absence of the tsetse fly permits cattle-herding, a different pattern developed. There, cattle coexisted with agriculture, *and constituted a form of wealth and social prestige. It was claimed, locally and later by Europeans, that cattle-herding peoples invaded and conquered local groups, and ownership of cattle remains a mark of aristocratic distinction. The claim was reinforced by physical differences between the populations: the cattle-herders, typically, were tall and thin, and the locals much shorter (for example, the Watutsi and the Hutu of Rwanda). Discussion of this question has been complicated by the 'Hamitic' hypothesis, the belief on the part of the first European administrators that the conquering groups were 'Hamitic' (that is, lighter-skinned northerners) who defeated the darker-skinned autochthons; the Hamitic thesis has long since been abandoned. Throughout this southern cattle-herding belt, cattle serve as a currency: brideprice, in particular, is calculated in terms of cattle, and cattle constitute the preferred form of tribute, sacrificial offerings and chieftainly wealth. This combination of practices is so consistent and widespread in this zone that anthropologists have coined the term 'cattle complex' for easy reference.*

8

KHOI-KHOI CATTLE
STORIES

The Khoi-Khoi (see also Chapter 38) live in Namibia, Botswana and western South Africa. They are closely related to the San hunting groups (the language family is known as Khoi-San), but separated from them at some point, probably in the last five hundred years, when they acquired cattle and stopped being hunters. The first of these two stories was collected in the mid-nineteenth century; the second is much later. Heitsi-Eibib is the culture-hero of the Khoi-Khoi.

THE TWO MEN

Two men were living together in the bush. One was blind. The other practised hunting, wandering around the land in pursuit of the game. One day, he found a hole in the ground from which animals were emerging. He told his blind friend of this hole and led the man there; the blind man was able to touch the animals, and he turned to the hunter and told him that these animals were not ordinary game animals, such as antelopes and zebra and gemsbok, but cattle with their calves.

The blind man then found himself able to see, and he made a fence from poles and thorny branches. He herded the cattle into this enclosure, and in this way became their master. He took to anointing himself with fat and oils, as the Khoi-Khoi did until recent times, to make their skin glossy and sleek.

The hunter came and admired the cattle. He asked how the man had been able to capture them, and the man told him to use an ointment of fat and oil. But he told the hunter he must heat it up before applying it to his body. The hunter warmed the ointment, but when he began to spread it over his skin he found it too hot, and so he was unable to complete the process. He abandoned the idea of capturing cattle for himself. Since that time, the Khoi-Khoi have lived with their cattle while the others lived by hunting in the bush.

HEITSI-EIBIB AND THE KING
OF SNAKES

In his travels, Heitsi-Eibib came into the land of the snakes. Their king possessed cattle, the only cattle that were known at that time. Heitsi-Eibib and the king of the snakes became friends, and after a time Heitsi-Eibib asked the king of the snakes for some cattle. The king agreed to give Heitsi-Eibib some cattle, if he would perform some services. Heitsi-Eibib agreed to this. He helped gather poles and branches to make a kraal for the cattle. He helped build the kraal, planting the poles and weaving the branches between them. He brought water for the cattle. He collected firewood.

In the evening, when the fire was lit, the king and Heitsi-Eibib sat near it together. The king had said nothing about the cattle he was to give to Heitsi-Eibib, and Heitsi-Eibib had realized that the king did not want to give him any cattle, and that he would think up all sorts of services and tasks for Heitsi-Eibib to put off the time when he would have to do so. So Heitsi-Eibib spoke to the king, and challenged him. Each of them should jump over the fire. So they began to dance around the fire, and after several rounds Heitsi-Eibib leaped through the flames and landed on the other side. The snake king coiled himself and then tried to launch himself over the fire, but he landed in the middle of the flames and quickly died. This is how Heitsi-Eibib got cattle for people.

9

FULBE STORIES OF CATTLE

The Fulbe (singular: Pullo, also known as Fula, Fulani and Peul) have historically been cattle-herders in the savannah zones across west Africa, and between the Atlantic ocean and Lake Chad their nomadic groups are to be found everywhere cattle may survive. Many Fulbe have settled down across this belt, forming distinct sedentary communities in areas such as the Futa Tooro (Senegal–Mauritania; see below, Chapter 69), the Futa Jallon (highlands of Guinea), Wassulu (in Mali), Liptako (Burkina Faso) and throughout northern Nigeria and Cameroon. These settled communities are also almost all associated with Islam, and in the eighteenth and nineteenth centuries many of them embarked on religious wars of conquest and conversion. In northern Nigeria, particularly, Fulbe religious militancy led to the conquest of the Hausa city-states by Fulbe dynasties and the establishment of the Caliphate of Sokoto. In modern times, the nomadic Fulbe have lost much of their former freedom of movement. They live in much closer association with the farmers whose fields are fertilized by the cattle grazing on the stubble. The herders often work for hire, tending other owners' cattle. The stories represent something of this geographic range: the story of Tyamaba is found from Senegal to Niger; the Muslim account was collected in northern Nigeria, and the story of the first cow in Mali.

TYAMABA, THE GREAT SERPENT

A woman gave birth to twin offspring. One was a normal boy whom she named Ilo. The other was an egg, and she kept the egg in her chamber until it hatched out a snake. Some people say the snake had ninety-six wondrous scales, one for each of the recognized colour patterns of cattle. She raised the boy normally, but she kept the snake hidden, first under a little dish, and later under an overturned pot. She fed the snake various things: milk, and sometimes small animals such as chicks. The snake grew, the boy grew, and time passed. The mother became old and died, leaving the care of the snake to his brother.

The snake was now so big that the brother built him his own small hut, set apart from the others, and every day the brother brought him a bowl of milk. Some people say it was goat's milk, others that it was milk from cows which appeared with the snake. The snake warned his brother that he should not marry a woman with very small breasts, for if such a woman were to see him he would have to leave.

But the brother fell in love with a woman who had very small breasts, and after a time he married her. He built a high wall around the snake's hut, so that it would be difficult to see him. Things went well for a time, but then the wife began to wonder why her husband went every day to visit a small hut, carrying with him a pot of milk. She asked an old woman, and the old woman suggested she should wait until her husband was away; then she could stand on an overturned mortar and peek over the wall, to be sure it wasn't another woman in there. So the wife waited for a few days, and then, when her husband was away, she took her mortar and turned it on end right next to the high earth wall, and climbed up on it and peeked over. She saw the snake sunning himself outside his hut. The snake saw her. He knew that the prohibition he had laid on his brother had been broken.

The snake swelled up. He knocked down the door and burst through the walls, he was so big. He began to slither away from the homestead, down towards the swampy areas by the stream.

Ilo came back and found the signs of the snake's departure: the breach in the wall where the gate had been, the empty hut. He saw the traces of the snake's path and followed him, running in his haste to catch up with his brother. It was night when he came to the swampy area where the snake had gone, and to his surprise Ilo found himself surrounded by cattle. The snake spoke to him. 'These are my water cattle, Ilo,' he said. 'Cut yourself a stick of ñelbe wood and begin to touch the cattle. Each cow that you touch will remain with you, to give you milk and make your wealth. The rest shall come with me into the water. The prohibition has been violated, and I must leave you.' And with that, the snake began to move through the swamp towards the deep-flowing currents of the great river beyond it, and the cattle, lowing in the darkness, gathered and followed him.

Frantically, Ilo cut himself a stick, and that stick has become the emblem of the Fulbe herdsmen to this day. He rushed into the herd, touching cattle left and right, and those he touched turned aside from their course towards the river and moved backwards. And the snake, followed by all the cows which Ilo did not touch, slipped into the waters of the great river and vanished.

Ilo was the ancestor of all the Fulbe herdsmen.

A MUSLIM VERSION FROM NORTHERN NIGERIA

Muhammad sent disciples to west Africa to bring Islam to the peoples there. One man was named Yacouba, and he married a king's daughter. She had four children, two legitimate and two illegitimate: people knew they were not Yacouba's children because they did not talk in Arabic or in their mother's language, but instead used a quite different form of speech: Fulfulde, their own language. So eventually Yacouba rejected his wife and the two illegitimate children. He performed a divination, and then wrote out a Koranic talisman and placed it around his wife's neck, and sent the three down to the river, saying that there she would find her lover and the children would find their father.

When they came to the river, a handsome man came out of the water and greeted them. He told the children he had a gift for them: he would give them cattle, which before then were unknown. But thereafter they must follow the cattle in the bush; they could not live in villages, but must wander from place to place. He said that when the cattle began to come from the river, the children should walk away without looking back, calling 'Hai, hai, hai', for if they looked back the cattle would stop coming out of the river.

So the children turned and walked away, calling out 'Hai, hai, hai', and a flood of cattle followed them. But eventually one child looked back, and the cattle stopped coming out of the water.

THE FIRST COW: WHY FULBE
ARE HERDSMEN

The first cow appeared in Masina, in the floodplains of the middle Niger delta; she appeared with her calf, and a Labbo, a woodworker, was the first to see her. He watched her grazing and then saw her disappear into the water. He came back the next day with two friends, a Pullo and a Bambado. Among the Fulbe today, the Pullo is the nomad and the Bambado is a musician. They saw the cow appear, followed by her calf, and they watched the animals grazing on the fresh shoots of grass. They decided they would try to catch her, and so they set up a trap baited with clumps of grass on the path they saw the cow taking. The next day they caught her in their noose, and after a considerable struggle they were able to subdue her. They tied her in one place, and after some time the calf which had run away returned to its mother.

After they caught it, there was some question who would take care of it. The Labbo had his woodworking business to take care of – he carved calabashes and made bowls and utensils for people. The Bambado was something of an idler who preferred strolling around and passing the time of day with people to any regular activity. So the Pullo was the one who took care of the cow. He brought her food and water and he watched over her carefully. He even imitated the calf one day, sucking at a teat to see what the milk tasted like. He found it delicious.

The other two, co-owners of the cow, caught him at this treat one day and asked him what it tasted like. He squeezed some milk into a bowl and gave it to them to taste, and they too found it delicious. Thereafter it was agreed that each of them would get a bowl of milk in the morning. But the two co-owners let some days pass without coming for their milk, and although the Pullo dutifully collected it into calabashes for them, it seemed to be going to waste sitting there, and likely to spoil. Still, when they did finally come and ask for their milk, he showed them the calabashes he had saved for them, expecting his friends to be disgusted by the stale milk. But he was amazed to see them smacking their lips in pleasure at the new taste of curdled milk, and when he asked what was so good they let him taste this new product.

After some time, the Pullo realized that he was the only one taking care of the cow, and so he decided to steal away so he could enjoy the fruits of his herding by himself. He slipped off one day and found himself a campsite some distance away from his friends' dwellings, in a place where the grass was green and fresh and there was good pasturing for his cow and her growing calf. He made musical instruments for himself, and he would sit playing to his animals as he watched them graze.

But his friends noticed his absence, and after some time they went looking for him. It took them a month or two to locate his campsite, and they found him one evening sitting with the cow and calf nearby, playing a tune on the stringed instrument he had devised and singing to the cow. They paused for a moment, struck by the beauty of the scene, and then they greeted the Pullo, and he, after a start, returned the greeting and invited them in. They asked him where he had been. He said he had been worried about the cow and wanted her to

have fresh grass, especially since the calf was now growing and
eating as well, and needed tender new shoots, and he thought
that the new spot was doing well. He also thought that the cow
might be pregnant, for he had seen her in the company of a
male that came out of the waters near where they had found
her. He said nothing about having wanted to take the cow away
from them.

The two friends agreed that the cow looked very well. Then
the Bambado asked the Pullo to let him have the stringed
instrument he had been playing, for he did not think he could
live without that music. 'What can I give you for the instrument?' asked the Bambado, and the Pullo hesitated, not thinking to ask a price for something he had made. 'I shall give you
my share of the cow,' said the Bambado, 'but on condition that
periodically you shall give me one of its male offspring which
you won't need for milk.' Surprised and delighted, the Pullo
immediately accepted the offer.

'And I shall give you my share,' said the Labbo, 'for I see
that you know how to take care of these animals. But I too
shall ask a condition: that I may have milk whenever I ask for
it.' And naturally the Pullo agreed to this price.

Since that time, the Pullo gives milk freely to the Labbo and
periodically gives a bull-calf to the Bambado, since to withhold
their price would bring disaster down on the herds that have
grown up since that original bargain. And the Pullo is the one
who leads the cattle to their grazing grounds and lives with
them, and knows them.

THE MAASAI OF EAST AFRICA

The Maasai are probably the best known of all African pastoralists, since their pasturing grounds abut many of the most famous game parks of east Africa and they count as one of the tourist attractions. They are considered the quintessential cattle-herders, and, by repute, to be Maasai is to be a cattle-herder: to live and travel with the cattle, defending them from lions and other predators (hence the distinctive large shields and long spears), living on milk and blood drawn from the necks of the living beasts. But in fact the specialized pastoralists are a small part of a larger group of Maa-speakers, and throughout their range, in the plains between the Kenyan highlands and the coast, stretching south into Tanzania, there is considerable variation in patterns of cattle-ownership and herding practices. Maasai who have lost cattle to drought may be forced to settle down for a time until their herds are rebuilt (and in the past, warfare was another means of winning or losing cattle), and at all times the nomads depend on the farmers for grain. The stories below explain why it is the Maasai who own the cattle, rather than other peoples. Both stories were collected around 1900.

THE ORIGIN OF CATTLE

Naiteru-Kop, one of the gods of the Maasai, walked the earth at the dawn of the world and he found it already held some inhabitants. He found a Dorobo (a member of a hunting people, also known as Okiek), a snake and an elephant living together. After Naiteru-Kop had passed by, the Dorobo found a cow in the bush and took it as his property. After that, the Dorobo would take the cow out into the grasslands to watch it feed, and then return to the homestead that he shared with the elephant and the snake at night.

The snake often sneezed, for it crawled in the dust which was trampled by the man, the cow and the elephant, and when it sneezed it sprayed its venom in the air. The elephant did not feel anything, its hide was so thick; but the man became very uncomfortable and developed rashes. The Dorobo complained to the snake, and the snake answered that the sneezing was not its fault, but happened because of all the dust around their camp. That night, while the elephant and the snake were sleeping, the Dorobo took a cudgel and crushed the snake's head. Then he cast the snake's carcass in the bush. The elephant asked after the snake in the morning, and the Dorobo said he had no idea where the snake had gone. From his manner the elephant guessed that the human had killed the snake. But they continued to live together.

A season of rains came, turning the grass green and covering the land with small puddles in which the Dorobo's cow could drink. But after the rains had passed the waterholes dried up until there was only one left. This was the elephant's favourite spot; it was the elephant's custom to graze upon the tall grass, harvesting it by the bushel with its trunk, and then to go down to the waterhole and loll in the water and the cool mud. During the rainy season, the elephant gave birth to a calf, and the two of them would do this together.

When the rains had ended, the Dorobo could find no other water for his cow than the elephant's waterhole. He asked the elephant not to muddy the hole, so that he could water his cow, but the elephant answered that its custom had always been to enjoy the hole and it did not wish to change. So in secret the Dorobo made an arrow, and then one evening he shot the elephant and it died. When the mother elephant died, the calf went away: the older elephant had warned it about the Dorobo and how the man had killed the snake, and now the man had killed the elephant. The calf went to another country.

There, the calf met a man, a Maasai named Le-eyo, and they talked. The elephant calf told the Maasai why it had run away from the Dorobo who had killed the snake and the elephant to protect himself and his cow. Le-eyo said he wished to see this man, and so the elephant calf agreed to show him the way. They went back to the camp. There, the Maasai was very surprised by the hut the Dorobo had built: it was built on end, so that the doorway looked up at the heavens. While they were standing there, Naiteru-Kop called out to tell the Dorobo to come out the next morning. Le-eyo heard the message, and so the next morning it was the Maasai and not the Dorobo who went to learn what Naiteru-Kop wished to tell him.

Naiteru-Kop gave Le-eyo instructions, and he followed them carefully. He built himself a large enclosure, and to one side he built a little hut of bent branches and grasses. Then he searched the bush and found a thin calf. He took it back to his enclosure and slaughtered it. But he did not eat the meat. Instead, he spread out the calf's hide and piled the meat upon it, and then he tied it up into a great bundle. He built a very large fire in the centre of his enclosure, and when it was roaring he lifted the bundle of the calf's meat and threw it into the fire. Then he hid in the hut. As he did so, the clouds gathered thickly overhead and thunder rolled over the plains.

While the man was hidden in the hut, a leather cord dropped from the heavens and cattle of all sorts began to come down the cord into the enclosure. They descended until the enclosure was filled and they were bumping against each other to make space. One of them then put its foot through the wall of the Maasai man's hut, and he cried out in alarm and surprise. At the sound, the cattle ceased coming down the cord from heaven. Naiteru-Kop called out, and Le-eyo went out to answer his call. 'These are all the cattle you shall receive,' said Naiteru-Kop, 'because by your cry you have stopped them coming. But they shall be yours to tend, and with them you shall live.'

Since that time, the Maasai have herded their cattle. The Dorobo have become hunters, using clubs and bows and arrows to kill their prey. When people who are not Maasai own cattle, the Maasai presume that the cattle have been stolen from Maasai and try to reclaim them.

*

Later, Naiteru-Kop told Le-eyo what to do in the case of death:
the body should be disposed of, and he should say, 'Man, you
have died and shall return. Moon, you shall die and not return.'
But the first person to die was a child, not of Le-eyo's family,
and so when Le-eyo took the body into the bush he said, 'Child,
you have died. Do not return. Moon, die and then return.' So
the child did not return, and the moon began to wax and wane.
Later, one of Le-eyo's own children died. He took it into the
bush and said, 'Child, you have died and you shall return.
Moon, you shall die and not return.' But Naiteru-Kop spoke
from the sky and said that he could not change matters now;
what he had said at first would be the rule for humans.

When Le-eyo was close to death, he called his children and
asked them what they wanted of his belongings. One son
answered that he wanted a share in all his father's wealth. So
Le-eyo gave him cattle, goats, sheep and grain. The younger
son answered that he wanted only the fan which his father
always carried under his arm. His father smiled at that, and
promised him that because he had chosen well he would always
have power. So the younger son became the ancestor of the
cattle-herding Maasai, while the older son's descendants are
considered to be inferior.

WOMEN AND THE CAMPS

An old man had three children: a son and two daughters. The
son was made responsible for the family's cattle. There came a
time of warfare with neighbouring peoples, and so no one dared
leave the group or take the cattle far to graze or to find the
salt-licks which the animals loved. After some time, the animals
began to suffer from the lack of salt, and so the son decided
that he would venture out to the salt-lick. The elder daughter
accompanied him. The brother told the younger sister that if
she saw a great smoke, it would be a sign they were safe. He
and his sister then established a small camp. During the day,
the sister stayed in the camp while the brother tended the cattle
in the bush.

After some days, though, the brother noticed odd footprints in the enclosure he had made of thorns and branches, and he guessed that while he was in the bush, men had come to visit his sister. But the sister told him nothing of this. So the next day, the young man drove the cattle off as usual, but then circled back in secret and spied on the cattle-pen. His suspicions were justified. After he left, warriors from the enemy group came from the bush and approached his sister; clearly, they were on terms of intimacy. As they left, she told them to stay nearby and listen for her voice: when her brother was busy milking the cattle she would begin to sing, and they would then be able to seize his cattle.

The brother took the cattle back into the bush, and at the end of the day he returned to the enclosure. But he did not take his weapons to the shelter, as was his custom. Instead, he laid them on the ground near him in the enclosure. Then he fetched the gourds and began to milk the cattle. As he did so, his sister came out of the hut and began to sing. Immediately, one of the enemy leaped over the thorn-fence. But the brother was expecting this; he had seized his spear, and the enemy died immediately. Another man leaped the fence; he too was killed. The brother killed five men before the others fled.

He then collected firewood and burned the bodies of the enemy. The smoke rose high, and far away his younger sister saw it. She announced to the family that her brother had signalled that he was safe, and so the family moved out to join him at the salt-lick.

There was discussion of the behaviour of the elder sister. Her father immediately found her a husband, because he said that it was frustration that had made her betray her brother. Since that time, women have been free to come and go at the warriors' camps, because it seems safer to allow them the liberty than to attempt control.

THE GREAT LAKES I:
THE ORIGIN OF CATTLE
(RWANDA)

The highlands between the great lakes of the Rift Valley have been compared to an earthly paradise. The altitude moderates the equatorial heat and draws ample rainfall, the volcanic soils are fertile, and humans have settled there and prospered. The kingdoms of the region are treated individually below (Chapters 27–30: Bunyoro, Buganda, Rwanda, Burundi), but cattle are sufficiently important for representative stories from this region about the origin of cattle to be given as well as other stories of cattle. These stories are part of larger dynastic narratives, and were collected in the early twentieth century.

Gihanga was one of the first kings of Rwanda, and he is said to have invented the making of vessels and containers from wood and gourds. He travelled, and married two women from different places; the first gave him a daughter, Nyirarucyaba, and eventually the second wife also became pregnant. Gihanga provided for his wives by hunting. When he returned from the hunt, he would give to each of his wives in turn the hide of his kill. But one day he brought home the hide of a cerval, beautifully spotted. Both wives wanted the skin and began to fight over it. The daughter, Nyirarucyaba, ran to the aid of her mother and struck the second wife, who was still pregnant, with a sharpened stake. She pierced the belly, and the woman died. But the child was saved: it was a boy and they named him Gafomo because he had been born before his time.

Nyirarucyaba feared her father's anger and so she fled into the forest. There a hunter found her and gave her shelter, and eventually they married and Nyirarucyaba bore him a child.

One day, as she was walking near their camp, she saw a cow feeding her calf; she was able to get close and to taste some of the milk that had spilled, and she found it delicious. After some thought, she caught the calf with a rope of braided vines and led it to her camp; the cow followed quietly after it. Her husband, the hunter, at first refused to drink the milk, but eventually was brought to do so when he was sick.

After some time, Nyirucyaba learned that her father was sick, and so she decided to take him some of the marvellous substance she had discovered. She did so, and he recovered immediately. He pressed her to give him the cow, and she agreed only after he had threatened to kill her husband and child.

Gihanga discovered where the cows came from: they came out of a lake. He prepared his men to go and capture all the cows, but diviners warned him that he should send away his son Gafomo, who might spoil the enterprise. So he sent Gafomo off on an errand while everyone else prepared to go down to the lake. But Gafomo secretly turned back and followed them to the lake-side, and there he climbed a thorny tree known as a *mushubi*.

The cows began coming out of the lake to graze on the grass, and men caught them with braided ropes and led them quietly away. Then came the bull of the herd, and seeing it Gafomo was frightened and called out from the top of his tree. The bull turned back into the lake, leading the rest of the cows with him, and the men were not able to get all the cows they wanted. At that time they renamed Gafomo after the tree in which he had sat, and his name became Gashubi.

Gihanga then allotted portions to his children, and he named Kinyarwanda to be king after him. When Nyirucyaba came and asked what her share was to be, Gihanga told her that she and her descendants could come to the king as he was being enthroned and demand milk, and he would have to provide her with milk.

Kinyarwanda later decreed that women should not milk cows, because the squatting position was obscene.

THE GREAT LAKES II: THE
STORY OF WAMARA
(BAHAYA)

*The BaHaya live on the south-western shores of Lake Victoria
(Victoria Nyanza), and in former times were divided into
several principalities or kingdoms (Kiziba, Ihangira, Usswi).
Much material from their traditions of origin is shared with
neighbouring peoples (Kintu is the central figure), proof of a
common origin at least for the ruling dynasty and their idioms
of power. The BaHaya are also noted for their iron-working.*

A jackal came at night and yapped around the compound of
King Wamara, disturbing his sleep, and so Wamara and his two
principal chiefs Irungu and Mugasha went out hunting for the
animal. They quickly started it from the bush, and then their
dogs pursued it as it led them on a course which ended in a
cave. Following the trail, Wamara, Mugasha and Irungu found
themselves in an underground world, a place they had never
seen before. This was the land of Kintu, who rules beneath the
earth. Kintu ordered the strangers to be brought before him,
and then greeted them politely. He asked them where they had
come from and who they were, and Wamara answered.

Then Kintu offered them food. Fearful, Wamara ordered
Mugasha and Irungu to taste it first. Kintu's servants brought
banana beer and goat-meat; Mugasha was unable to stomach
this food and threw up, but Irungu tasted it, found it delicious,
and recommended it to his king.

Then Kintu's servants brought in a *kitare* cow, one of the
beautiful long-horned cows with a brilliant white coat, attended
by a maiden who milked her before the visitors. Kintu offered
them the milk; Wamara told Mugasha not to bother tasting it,

because he trusted Irungu's opinion. Irungu drank a bit from the bowl and then told his king, 'Of all that we have been offered here, this is the best.' Wamara tasted the milk and fell in love with the cow.

Kintu expressed surprise that they did not have such provisions in their world above the ground, and then invited them to stay. For nine days they remained in Kintu's caves, and during that time Mugasha wandered through Kintu's domains and saw his people cultivating fields and growing different crops; he collected the seeds of the different crops that he encountered. Kintu, meanwhile, assembled a herd of cattle and goats, and when the time had come for Wamara to return to his kingdom, Kintu offered to send the livestock up with Wamara, on condition that Wamara send back the servants, including the maiden who attended the *kitare* cow, and that he should not forget to thank Kintu for the gifts.

They returned home, and found some of the followers still waiting outside the cave. Then they returned to the court. Mugasha set about planting the seeds he had brought with him, assisted by his wife. Wamara shared the milk from the cattle with his household, and showed his wives how to anoint themselves with butter so that their skin glistened. He would sit admiring the *kitare* cow, the pride of his herd, and the servants heard him say, 'I should die if I lost her.'

But despite his love of the cattle, Wamara forgot to give thanks to Kintu for his gifts, and beneath the earth Kintu became impatient. Eventually, he asked his servants which of them would go to punish the humans for their forgetfulness. Rufu, death, presented himself. He would go and remind the humans of their debt.

But when Rufu came to Wamara's court, Wamara's men beat him mercilessly with sticks and he was forced to flee. Wherever he hid, they found him and beat him, until he came across the maiden from Kintu's land who watched over the cow. She took him beneath her wrap and hid him inside her vagina, and so he escaped the pursuers.

Later, he came out and seized the opportunity to drag the *kitare* cow into a swamp so that it drowned. And then people remembered what they had heard Wamara say, that he would die if ever he lost the *kitare* cow. Wamara went with his followers to the swamp and threw himself into the morass; Irungu and the other servants followed him.

After their deaths, Wamara, Mugasha and Irungu became *bachwezi* spirits watching over humans. Mugasha in particular is associated with the lake and its storms, but he is also thanked for the food he provided for people.

13

THE CHAGGA OF EAST
AFRICA: MURILE

*The Chagga are a farming people who live in Tanzania in the
region at the foot of Mount Kilimanjaro, and nowadays they
are known mainly for growing coffee. Their story of Murile,
collected early in the last century while the region was still a
German colony, can serve to illustrate an appreciation of cattle
from a people that was not marked strongly by pastoralism or
by the 'cattle complex'. One might compare Murile's transformation of a yam into a child with Khaggen's transformation of
a leather scrap into an eland (Chapter 1).*

The boy Murile was the eldest of three sons. He assisted his
mother when she went out to gather colocasia roots (a sort of
yam) which they were going to store and then plant in their
fields. One day they dug up a particularly fine root, and Murile
told his mother that it reminded him of his youngest brother.
The mother laughed at the idea, but Murile found that the
image of the root stayed in his mind. Some days later, he slipped
into the storeroom and removed the root; he found a hiding
place for it in the hollow of a tree-trunk. There he sang a spell
over it and poured water upon it. The next day, when he
returned, he found that the root had become a little child.

He fed the child in the hollow of the tree from his own share
of the family's food; he would scrape a handful or two into a
small bag which he kept hidden at his side, and then eat one or
two more mouthfuls. But he himself started to suffer from his
limited rations, and his mother began to worry about him. She
asked his younger brothers what he was doing, and they told
her that he always put a part of his food into a small bag. She

asked them to find out for her what he was doing with this food, and so they watched him more carefully and soon discovered that he was taking the food to a tree-trunk in the bush. They told their mother, and one day she went to the tree-trunk and found the child in the hollow. She had no idea where this child had come from, but she saw it as a threat to her own son Murile, since he was suffering from a lack of food on the account of this child. So she killed the child and returned to her camp.

That evening, after dinner, Murile slipped away again with the share of food which he kept for his root-child. But when he came to the hollow he heard no noise, and when he looked inside he found the child lying lifeless on the ground. At first he could not believe that it was dead; he lifted it and called to it. He sang a song over it. But the body remained limp. Then he wept for a long time. It was late that night when he returned to his parents' camp.

The next day he broke out weeping again as they sat together in the morning, and his mother asked him what was the matter. He answered that it was the smoke from the fire burning his eyes. She told him to move to another side of the fire. But tears continued to stream down his face, and eventually she told him he should move away from the fire entirely. He took his father's small stool and sat down at the end of their cleared space.

He began to sing. He sang to the stool on which he was sitting, telling it to carry him up higher than the tree-tops, higher than the clouds. The stool lifted off the ground and Murile rose into the air. His younger brothers saw him and shouted. His mother came and cried out, calling on him to return to the ground. He shouted back that he was going away and he would never come back. His father called to him. Neighbours and relatives, drawn by the noise, came and called to him. To all he gave the same answer: he was going away and he would never return.

The stool carried him into the air until he reached the land above the clouds. He got off the stool and walked for some way through empty lands of trees and bushes until he met some people cutting grass to serve as thatch. Murile asked them

where he was, and they said they had no time to speak to idle
hands. So Murile joined them in their work and cut several
bundles of grass which he bound up with vines. Then the people
told him he was in the land of the Moon, and that the Moon
had a great palace, and they pointed him in the direction of the
palace. Murile walked on, and a bit further he found young men
cutting saplings to serve as a base for the thatch roofs. Murile
helped them, and they pointed him on his way. Closer to the
settlement he found fields, and there he helped the people who
were setting and watering beds, and others who were hoeing the
weeds. After the fields he came to the well, and he helped the
water-carriers by carrying a pot back into the kitchen area.

The women who were preparing the food invited him to sit
and join the meal when they fed the workers, and so he sat
down with the other men. To his surprise, the food was not
cooked. There were roots and bulbs, such as he ate at home,
but although they were sliced thin they were still raw. There
were thin strips of meat laid over the pounded grain, but these
too were raw. Murile wondered at this, and after the meal he
asked the head cook if that was the only way they knew to
prepare their food. The cook answered that it was.

'I know a different way,' said Murile. 'Give me some tubers
and some meat, and I shall show you something new.' The cook
agreed and gave Murile the foodstuffs. Murile went behind the
palace and collected some dry wood and some tinder and laid
out a fire. Then he made himself a fire-starter from several
pieces of wood: the base and the twirling shaft, and a small
bow whose string was looped around the shaft. He sawed with
the bow for a short time and soon the tinder began to glow and
smoke, and after that the dry wood caught on fire. Murile
roasted the tubers in the coals and then grilled the meat on
sticks. He brought the meal back to the cook who tasted it and
cried out in delight and amazement. The cook immediately
hastened to the Moon to offer him this new delicacy, and
Murile followed after.

The Moon was delighted with the new foods, and promised
Murile any reward he might wish for the secret of its preparation. Murile asked for such wealth as was available, and he

was given cattle and goats and sheep, as well as several wives. He settled in the Moon's palace and lived there for some time.

After many years, he felt a longing for the earth and his family. So he thought how he might manage a return. He had told his family that he would never return, but such promises can be changed. He decided to send a bird as a messenger to announce his return. The bird flew down to Murile's family and sang to them about his imminent return, but the people did not believe the words of a bird. Nevertheless, Murile set out. His wives and much of his wealth remained in the land of the Moon, but he took some boys to help him drive a great herd of cattle and goats before them. They walked and walked, for the path down to the earth was much longer when there was no flying stool to carry a body. After some time Murile began to feel tired. He was walking near his finest ox, a beautiful bull with great horns and a sleek coloured hide. The bull saw that he was tired, and spoke to him. The bull agreed to let Murile ride on his back if Murile swore that he would never touch the bull's meat, and Murile readily made the promise, for he had no intention of ever using the bull for food. So Murile was riding a bull when he reached his parents' camp.

They welcomed him joyously, for they had never expected to see him again and here he had returned bringing great wealth with him. He settled with them, giving strict instructions that the bull who had served as his steed must be kept in safety until the end of its days, and that its meat should never be used as food.

He lived with his family on earth for many years, and in this time the bull became old and slow. One day, without consulting his son, Murile's father decided that the bull's time had come and he slaughtered it. They cut up the meat and held a great feast. Murile realized that they were eating the meat of the bull which had helped him, and so he abstained from the meal. His mother noticed this, and became concerned that her son was not getting the nourishment he needed. She did not accept his reasons for not eating the meat of the bull. So she saved some of the fat and later prepared a dish of cooked grain in which she used the fat as seasoning.

As soon as Murile took a mouthful of the dish, the food spoke to him. 'You have broken your promise,' it said. 'You said my meat would never touch your mouth.'

'Mother,' cried Murile, 'you have given me the meat I forbade.' But his mother simply told him to be quiet and to finish his meal. So he ate another mouthful, and yet another. But with each mouthful, his body sank further into the ground until he was completely swallowed up by the earth. So he disappeared, leaving his cattle and goats as wealth for his family.

TRICKSTERS

The trickster is one of the most popular mythological and folkloric figures in the world, and Africa is richly endowed with trickster tales. The figures themselves are often animals – the tortoise, the hare, the spider – but their appetites and failings are invariably human. Trickster tales have a moral dimension: tricksters exemplify the consequences of thoughtless or disobedient behaviour. The tales also have an expressive function: they speak to that which is real and human in us, rather than what is ideal and perhaps unnatural; they express the human reality, often in a comic and thus more palatable tone.

But tricksters also have a more serious purpose and nature. The trickster and the culture-hero often overlap, if they are not identical. The 'trickster-transformer' is a world-shaping demiurge whose shifts and contrivances overcome immediate dangers while leaving consequences for humans to face in later times. Tricksters are also often associated with the systems of established world order that underlie divination systems (such as the Ifa divination system in west Africa), and they serve as the interpreters of the messages from that system. They thus explain possible mistakes in the content of the messages, protecting the system itself; more significantly, they can control the system by exploiting loopholes and bending rules. Thus, they add an element of disorder and unpredictability to the world: features which we all know by experience are present in our lives. Because the trickster can see past (or through) the rules, the trickster is also creative. The trickster is rarely intentionally so; the benefits of the trickster's inventions are usually accidental afterthoughts. But they remain real.

14

UTHLAKANYANA, THE
ZULU CHILD TRICKSTER

*Uthlakanyana is an excellent example of the hero-trickster who
gets into trouble through a lack of self-control or an inability
to foresee consequences, but whose ingenuity and considerable
powers solve his problems and benefit his people. Many of
Uthlakanyana's adventures are reported of other figures, and
although this story is taken from Zulu traditions, in the south
of Africa, it can be considered representative of the type across
the continent. This story was collected in the mid-nineteenth
century.*

Even before his birth, Uthlakanyana amazed his family: he told
his mother when he wished to be born, so that she cried out in
amazement and all the men of the kraal came to see what was
the matter. At his birth, Uthlakanyana cut his own umbilical
cord with his father's spearhead and then announced his arrival
to the world. Such an unusual beginning promised extraordinary deeds, and Uthlakanyana fulfilled that promise. He is
remembered not for his strength, but for his cunning, his ten-
acity and his small size, which evoke the mongoose, killer of
snakes.

As a child he was greedy and often tricked his family out of
their food, taking it all for himself. When they no longer posed
a challenge he decided to go out into the world. He came across
a bird-trap set by a man-eater, and as he was fond of birds he
removed them and ate them. Later, he came across other traps
and again removed the birds. But this time he got caught: the
man-eater had realized that someone was taking his birds from
his trap and so had laid sticks coated with birdlime around the

traps. Uthlakanyana walked unawares onto the sticks and so
was caught. But when the man-eater came, the wily boy persuaded the ogre not to eat him immediately, but to take him
home and let his mother cook him. Uthlakanyana claimed that
if he were not cooked properly he would taste bitter, and the
man-eater would have no pleasure in chewing his bones. And
besides, he should have the birdlime washed off.

The ogre agreed and took his prize to the home where he
lived with his mother and small brother. They washed him and
laid him out that night, and in the morning the ogre told his
mother to cook Uthlakanyana while he and his brother went
off hunting. First, though, at Uthlakanyana's request, he put
the boy on the roof of the hut to dry in the sun, before being
cooked. But Uthlakanyana really wished to be able to see in
which direction the ogres went to hunt.

When the ogres were out of sight, Uthlakanyana called down
to the old woman and said that he was dry and ready to be
cooked and she should bring him down from the roof. As she
filled the pot with water and placed it on the stones over the
fire, he proposed a game: he should boil her a bit, and then she
should boil him. Since he seemed to know how things should
be done, she agreed. He put his finger into the water after a
time and said, 'Yes, it is ready for boiling now. You must put
me into the pot and boil me for a time, and then I shall come
out and it shall be your turn.' She agreed, and put him into the
pot. He sat there for a time and then told her it was time for
her to come into the pot. He helped her undress; when she
observed this was not proper, he reminded her that he was to
be cooked and eaten, and so was only food. He didn't count
for anything, and her nakedness would not matter. Before she
got in, however, he added wood to the fire. Then he put her in.

The water began to boil and she began to feel scalded. 'Let
me out,' she called, 'the water is scalding me!'

'That can't be true,' he said. 'If you were really scalded you
wouldn't be able to talk at all. You are lying.' After a while,
though, she stopped crying out. He looked into the pot and she
was there, boiled and dead. 'Now you truly are scalded,' he
said, and he stirred the pot. Then he dressed himself in her

clothes and swelled out to fill them, and lay down on her mat and waited for the two other ogres to return.

They came back in the evening, and without rising Uthlakanyana told them to feed themselves from the pot where their game had been boiling all day. They reached in and one of them pulled out a hand. 'This looks like our mother's hand,' said the younger ogre, but Uthlakanyana protested and said the younger ogre was cooking his mother in his thoughts. But when they pulled out another limb, the ogre repeated the thought. Again, Uthlakanyana protested. Then he slipped out of the house and escaped, shedding the mother-ogre's clothes as he went. At some distance from the house he called back to the man-eaters and told them what they were really eating, and then he raced away. He came to a river, too deep to cross easily, and changed himself to a stick by the path. The ogres pursued him and came to the river. There the trail of footprints ended. 'He must have leaped across,' said the older man-eater, and in frustration he picked up the stick lying there and threw it across the river.

Some time later, Uthlakanyana came across the den of a leopardess, in which there were two cubs. He waited until the mother returned with her prey, and when she prepared to kill him, he addressed her and promised to take care of her children while she went off hunting, and to build them a shelter, if she would only spare him and share her food. So she agreed. At the start of his duties he would bring the cubs to be suckled. But he brought them one at a time, where before the mother had suckled both together. He would hand her a cub, and then when she returned it he would hand her the other.

The next day the leopardess went off hunting, and Uthlakanyana busied himself building the shelter. He made it with a narrow door and a long passage through the back, leading to a small hole, and at the end he left four spears. And then, to reward himself, he ate one of the leopard cubs. At the end of the day the mother returned with a small deer. Uthlakanyana prepared the deer for dinner, and the leopardess asked for her cubs. Uthlakanyana handed her the one, and it suckled for a time, and then he took it back, and then he handed it to her again. Then the two adults ate the deer. Uthlakanyana went back into the shelter, and then crawled quickly down the passage, for he knew the leopardess would recognize that he had killed the cub. But he counted on the narrow door to delay her while he escaped. That is how it happened: the leopardess had trouble squeezing through the door, and when she got in she found only one cub: the other was missing. So she knew that Uthlakanyana had killed her other cub and escaped down the passage. She followed him. But when he reached the end, Uthlakanyana had fixed the four spears to block the entrance, and when the leopardess reached them they pierced her and she was dead. So Uthlakanyana was able to eat the other cub and then the mother as well.

Further on, Uthlakanyana met another ogre. This one possessed a drum made from a calabash, but although Uthlakanyana greeted him politely as a kinsman, the ogre refused to recognize any relationship and wouldn't let him use the drum. So Uthlakanyana went on ahead and found another man-eater living in a house. The man-eater was working on a skin, and after Uthlakanyana had greeted him he suggested they should flap the skin. They did so and it made a great noise, and in answer the ogre with the drum who was coming that way beat his drum. The ogre living in the house took fright at the noise and ran away, and Uthlakanyana was left to await the drum-bearing ogre. Uthlakanyana asked his name, and he said he was 'Eat-all, who consumes bushes of wild greens and swallows men whole'.

The drum-bearing ogre took possession of the now empty house, but since Uthlakanyana said he had been living there the ogre allowed him to continue, on condition that he watch the house carefully and prevent the former owner from returning. Then he went off hunting. But Uthlakanyana also went hunting; he took a sack and went into the fields. He found a snake; he caught it and put it in his bag. He found wasps; he caught them and put them in his bag. He found scorpions; he caught them and put them in his bag. He filled the bag with all sorts of biting and poisonous animals and brought them back to the kraal. He placed them just inside the doorway.

When the ogre returned, Uthlakanyana told him he was

worried about the large size of the doorway; it offered no security. But the ogre told him not to worry, that the large doorway was all right. But that night Uthlakanyana sneaked out of the house and fetched staves and limber boughs and with them he made the doorway quite narrow, so that he could pass through easily, but the ogre might find it difficult. In the morning he called out to the man-eater, and the man-eater came to the door of the kraal and wished to come out, but he could not, for Uthlakanyana had made the doorway too narrow. So the ogre called to Uthlakanyana, and the boy told him he should take the sack that he had left inside the doorway and open it, and he would be able to get through the door. But when the man-eater opened the sack, all the poisonous and biting creatures that Uthlakanyana had placed inside it came out and bit and stung and pierced and jabbed him and he began to cry out and then he swelled up and died and the creatures ate him.

So Uthlakanyana gained possession of the calabash drum, and later he retrieved a flute he had made earlier, from the iguana which had stolen it. Then he decided it was time to return to his mother. On the way he found some *umjanjan*, a root, and he took it back. At home he asked his mother to cook the *umjanjan* while he took his instruments to a wedding dance. His mother did so, and when it was ready she tasted it to see if it was all right, and it was so good she could not stop herself: she ate it all.

Uthlakanyana returned and asked his mother for his *umjanjan*, but she had to admit that she had eaten it all. He complained that she had taken what was not hers, and so in exchange she gave him a gourd to carry milk. He left his home and went out.

On the way he found some boys trying to milk their cow. But they had no pot to hold the milk; it had broken. So Uthlakanyana said they might use his gourd if they also gave him some milk. But one of them broke the gourd while they were milking the cow, and Uthlakanyana complained that they had deprived him of his gourd, the gourd his mother had given to him after she ate the *umjanjan* that was his while he was away at a wedding dance. So the boys gave him a small spear.

Further on, he met some other boys trying to cut meat. They had no knife, and so they were using the rind of a sugar cane. He told them they might use the cutting edge of his spear if they gave him some of their meat, and they agreed. Each cut off a piece of meat. But the last boy to use the spear broke the haft. Uthlakanyana complained that they had broken his spear, the spear given to him by the boys who had broken his gourd, the gourd his mother had given to him after she ate the *umjanjan* that was his while he was away at a wedding dance. So the boys gave him an axe, and he went on.

Further on, he met some women collecting firewood, but they had no tool to cut the wood. He told them they might use his axe. So each of the women cut some wood, enough for one load, but the last woman broke the axe. They told Uthlakan-yana and he complained that they had broken the axe, the axe given to him by the boys who had broken his spear, the spear given to him by the boys who had broken his gourd, the gourd his mother had given to him after she ate the *umjanjan* that was his while he was away at a wedding dance. So the women gave him a blanket and he went on.

Further on, he met two young men; they were sleeping naked on the ground. He offered them the use of his blanket and spent the night there with them. But during the night the young men rolled back and forth, each pulling at the blanket to cover himself, and in the morning the blanket was so worn and torn that it could not be recognized. Uthlakanyana complained that they had ruined his blanket, the blanket given to him by the women who had broken his axe, the axe given to him by the boys who had broken his spear, the spear given to him by the boys who had broken his gourd, the gourd his mother had given to him after she ate the *umjanjan* that was his while he was away at a wedding dance. So the young men gave him a shield and he went on.

Further on, he found some men hunting a leopard. They had cornered it and were trying to get close enough to spear it, but they could not because of its sharp claws. So Uthlakanyana offered them his shield and they took it, and with the shield they were able to get close enough to spear the leopard and kill it. But in the last struggle, one of the men twisted the shield and the handle broke. Uthlakanyana complained that they had broken his shield, the shield given to him by the young men who had ruined his blanket, the blanket given to him by the women who had broken his axe, the axe given to him by the boys who had broken his spear, the spear given to him by the boys who had broken his gourd, the gourd his mother had given to him after she ate the *umjanjan* that was his while he was away at a wedding dance. So the men gave him a large war-spear.

And with the war-spear he went home. Later he had many more adventures.

15

STORIES OF MONI-MAMBU
OF THE BAKONGO

The stories of Moni-Mambu are told among the eastern BaKongo of the Congo. The BaKongo are known for their early contacts with the Portuguese and their powerful kingdoms with complex political history (see Chapter 40); Moni-Mambu comes from the periphery of that culture, from a world of forest villages and small chiefs. The stories of Moni-Mambu are adapted from a collection published in 1940.

Moni-Mambu's parents met when his father saved his mother from some ghouls. She had gone out fishing with some other women, but when they paired up in teams she was left alone. A man who was really a ghoul came from the bush to help her, and they caught lots of fish. At the end of the day, when she divided their catch, the ghoul refused to accept its share and demanded that she try again and again. Meanwhile, other ghouls were coming out of the dusk and joining them. When the chief came, they said they would eat her.

Luckily, a young man was hidden in a tree above this gathering, and he had a calabash of palm wine. Just as things were getting critical for the woman, he dropped the calabash on the head of the chief ghoul, and they all ran away. He came down out of the tree, brought the woman and all the fish home, and they became man and wife.

When Moni-Mambu grew up, he went off on adventures. He came once to a village where there lived two brothers, born of the same mother, who had never quarrelled. One was a fisherman, the other a palm-wine tapster. Moni-Mambu learned this when he was bathing in the river and enquired about the fish-traps he saw.

In the middle of the night, Moni-Mambu got up and took a *lukamba* (the strap used by climbers to allow them to walk up the tall and slender trunks of palm trees) and climbed up the palm trees. He took down the calabashes that had been hung there to collect the palm wine, and brought them all down to the river. There he placed the calabashes at the ends of the fish-trap lines, where little baskets held the captured fish, and he removed the baskets with all the fish that had been caught. Then he went back into the forest, and climbed the palm trees and hung the fish-baskets where the calabashes had been.

The next morning, the elder brother went off to draw palm wine and the younger went off to tend his fish-traps. And by the river, the young man asked himself, 'Who could have replaced my fish-baskets with these calabashes?' And meanwhile, the elder was also wondering, 'Who could have replaced my calabashes with these fish-traps?' When they met in the village, each blamed the other and they quarrelled.

Moni-Mambu came out while they were fighting and mocked them. 'You said you never quarrelled,' he called, 'and yet with a simple trick I have made you fight each other in the village square!' And after taunting them some more, he went on.

One day he came to a village where women were harvesting peanuts and he greeted them. The rules of hospitality required them to offer him food. So the women called to Moni-Mambu, and one of them told him that at her house she had some peanut-stew simmering, and if he wished he could go and eat it with her children for lunch.

Moni-Mambu asked, 'Really, I can go and have the peanut-stew with your children for lunch?'

'Yes,' said the woman. 'Go and eat it with the children.'

So Moni-Mambu went to her hut and found the peanut-stew and the children. They ate the peanut-stew together. And when they finished the stew, Moni-Mambu roasted the children and ate them for lunch.

When she came back from the fields, the woman was horrified and called all the other villagers. They assembled and argued late into the night. She complained that Moni-Mambu had eaten her children, and he replied that he had only done what she told him to do. 'She told me to eat the stew with the children for lunch,' he said, 'and that is what I did.' And when the woman admitted that she had said that, the village eventually agreed that Moni-Mambu was not to blame and they let him go.

Another time he came to a village where they were planning a hunt. The chief was hungry for meat, and so he declared they would have a big round-up of the game; the entire village would go out and beat the bush and drive the game to the hunters who lay in wait. And he warned any witches who might wish to try to kill humans to be off, and he activated his magics against any witchcraft. And the chief welcomed Moni-Mambu, saying that Nzambi-Mpungu (the BaKongo name for God) must have sent him, for his skill at shooting was well known and he could be placed to shoot the game.

The chief took Moni-Mambu to his station and gave him a rifle and ammunition, and told him to shoot everything that came along: 'Everything, I say. I don't care if it has feathers or scales or fur or not, just shoot it. The only things I want left in this bush are snails and millipedes.' Moni-Mambu questioned this order, but the chief repeated his command. 'With or without fur or feathers or scales, edible or not, I want you to shoot it.' And so the hunters all agreed.

Then the chief went off and organized his villagers for the drive, and they lit fires, and the chief called on his magics to bring them success in the hunt. As the villagers drove the game on, each thought he or she should seize something then, because if they waited until the spoils were divided out in the village they wouldn't get so good a share. The fire spread and the game ran, and at the other end Moni-Mambu was shooting away at everything he saw. If a fowl came by, he shot it, if a lizard came by, he shot it, if a snake came by, he shot it. Then when hunting dogs came by, he shot them, and then he shot the hunter and he shot some children. And he shot the chief's favourite wife, the one with six heavy copper bracelets.

The other hunters heard Moni-Mambu shooting, and one of them went to see what was going on. Moni-Mambu shot him too, but another hunter realized what was happening and saw the heap of Moni-Mambu's victims. He brought word to the village. They went out and brought Moni-Mambu back.

Moni-Mambu said he had only obeyed the chief's instructions, but the chief did not accept that answer. He ordered his men to kill Moni-Mambu.

So Moni-Mambu said, 'Very well, but it is useless to kill me with a rifle. In my land we are born with protections against bullets. If you want to kill me, you must drown me in a fish-trap. Then I will get taken up into the sky. But if you try bullets or a knife, it will be useless. You must build a large fish-trap, big enough to hold me, and carry me to the river and throw me in.'

So they built the fish-trap out of bamboo and vines and raffia, and then they tied up Moni-Mambu and carried him off towards the river. But the river was quite a way off, and Moni-Mambu was heavy. Halfway there, everybody got hot and thirsty, and so they put Moni-Mambu down and went looking for good drinking water. But there was none nearby and they went further and further away. Meanwhile, Moni-Mambu was thinking to himself that he had to get out of this fish-trap.

Along came a party of traders from a neighbouring people. Moni-Mambu addressed them, 'Hey, who is the chief among you?' The traders pointed him out, and Moni-Mambu announced that he was the ritual specialist for anointing kings, and he was waiting by the path because the time had come to anoint their chief and make him a true king. Their chief said he would like that very much.

'Then take me out of this magic fish-trap and untie me,' said Moni-Mambu, and the men did so. 'Now you must get in,' said Moni-Mambu, 'and you will be taken to the river and dipped, and when you come out of the water you will wear the regalia of kings and all men will respect you and hail you as a great chief. We shall go and wait for you in the village while the spirits do their work.'

Then Moni-Mambu took all of the chief's trade goods, and he and the others went down the path. When the men who had been carrying Moni-Mambu returned from drinking, they were a little bit surprised to find a different man in the fish-trap, but they knew how cunning Moni-Mambu was and they thought he might simply have disguised himself. So they took the trader and threw him in the river.

Moni-Mambu eventually got married, but after the wedding he would just stay at home doing nothing. His wife complained that he never went hunting and never brought home meat, but was content with the manioc and the greens which she cooked for him. Eventually she told him he had to go hunting. Moni-Mambu went into the bush and saw an antelope. He shot it, and the antelope fell down. But when he went to fetch his catch, the antelope's tail and skin came away in his hand and the antelope itself got up and bounded away.

'Oh, antelope!' called Moni-Mambu. 'What will your wife say when you come home naked?'

'Oh, Moni-Mambu,' answered the antelope, 'what will your wife say when you come home with an empty hide and no meat as sauce to the manioc?' And the antelope ran away and Moni-Mambu ran after it. The antelope jumped over a stream, but Moni-Mambu fell in and was washed downstream. He came out in the village of his in-laws.

They gave him peanuts and a yam to grill, and he went and sat by the fire grilling his food. His nose began to run and drip onto the food. He told his nose to calm down, and wiped it with a leaf. He put the leaf with the snot down next to him, saying, 'Wait, and I'll take you back when I've eaten.' And he continued grilling his yam and peanuts.

A dog sidled up and seized the leaf with the snot and ran away with it. Moni-Mambu seized a burning stick from the fire and threw it at the dog. It fell onto the thatched roof of his in-laws' house and burned it down. His in-laws sent him to gather the materials for a new house and gave him a machete. Moni-Mambu went to work along the stream and cut down a tree or two and some reeds, and then the machete fell in the water. While he was searching for it, a crocodile seized him. But an osprey taunted the crocodile, and when the beast came to the surface and opened its mouth to reply, the osprey seized Moni-Mambu and flew off with him.

One day, Moni-Mambu came to an abandoned village and found a skull. He asked the skull what had killed it, and the skull answered, 'What killed me? What doesn't kill people? We die in the water, we die of disease, we die of hunger . . .' Moni-Mambu went on his way, with a shudder of fear. He came to a fork in the road and after some hesitation made his choice. He came to another village where the elders were gathered, talking.

'Oh, elders,' said Moni-Mambu, 'back there in the abandoned village I met a talking skull.'

'That's a lie!' said some, and others asked, 'Will it talk to us as well? Will it answer our questions?' And Moni-Mambu answered, 'Yes, of course it will.'

'And if it doesn't answer, what should we do?'

'In that case, you should kill me.'

The elders went to the abandoned village and found the skull. They questioned it, but it said nothing. They came back and told Moni-Mambu that he had lied and he should die. They were preparing to beat him to death when the chief arrived. They waited and told the chief everything that had happened, and the chief listened. Then he said, 'Nzambi-Mpungu sees all and knows all. Moni-Mambu is very cunning, and he has killed many people and escaped from many traps. Will he escape today?'

Moni-Mambu asked for some water, but the chief said no. Then he told a young man to fetch a spear from his house, and when the young man returned the chief told him to stab Moni-Mambu. So the young man did, and Moni-Mambu died. But they did not bury him.

16

TURE, THE ZANDE
TRICKSTER

The Zande live in western Sudan and the Central African Republic, between the waters of the Nile and the waters of the Congo, in a region of savannah and what are called 'gallery forests' growing along watercourses. Their recent history has been marked by turmoil: they were the victims of slave-raids by the Arabs of the Sudan in the nineteenth century. While the Zande territory was divided into kingdoms, central authority was very weak, and the typical pattern of settlement was for individual householders to strike out and set up a homestead. While they have knowledge of agriculture, they also exploit the natural resources of the region (fish, game, termites), and their mythology shows strong similarities with the stories of the Khoi-San and other foraging peoples. Ture, their trickster figure, is the subject of a wide cycle of stories, many of which are also told of other tricksters. Ture is a spider, but his behaviour is entirely human and the stories do not really exploit his animal form. These stories were collected in the first half of the twentieth century.

TURE RELEASES THE WATERS

An old woman used to grow fine crops of yams, which she served to the people who came to work for her. But she never gave the people water while they were eating the yams, and so they would choke on the dry starch. If they did not die of thirst, she would kill them with a big knife while they were choking.

Ture heard about this woman and realized she was hiding

the water from people so she could kill them. He decided to go to work for her and receive yams to eat, but he made some preparations. He searched all around her home, until he found the water she had dammed up and hidden from people. He filled a gourd with this water, and then he cut a long hollow reed which would reach into the gourd when he hung it on his shoulder, and from which he could drink the water. Then he went to work for the woman.

After he had worked some time, she told him to come and eat. She filled a large pot with water and began to boil her yams. When they were cooked, she served them to Ture. While he was eating, she fetched her large knife and sat watching him, waiting for him to choke. Ture ate the first yam, and when it caught in his throat he ducked his head and sipped water through the reed. He finished the first yam, and the old woman brought him a second, and then a third, until he had eaten all the yams in the pot. The old woman was amazed at him for eating all these yams and yet not choking.

As he was finishing the last yam, he began to pretend to choke, and the old woman came running up with her knife, ready to slaughter him. But then he leaped up and ran away from her, towards the place where she had dammed the water. She called after him not to go that way, that he was running into the area where she left her excrement, but he did not listen. He ran on, and she followed, until he came to her dam. Then he fell against the dam and broke it, and the water spread all over the fields and ran down in streams. In this way Ture spread water over the world.

TURE SETS FIRE TO THE BUSH

Ture went to visit a clan of people to whom he was related and who worked as blacksmiths. They had forges, and they made iron and shaped it into tools. At that time, other men did not know of fire. So Ture went and worked for his relatives; they set him to working the bellows, and he pumped up their fires for them. When the day was ended, Ture told his relatives that the next day he would dance for them. That night, he made himself a costume of old and frayed bark-cloth, using lots and lots of cloth so that it wrapped about him and dangled behind him in all directions.

The next morning, he worked on the bellows for a time until the fire was burning strongly, and then he told his relatives the time had come for him to dance for them. He put on his costume of bark-cloth, and then danced around the forge several times. Finally, he went and danced into the forge, and he leaped over the fire. The strips of cloth dangling behind him trailed over the coals and caught fire. His relatives, the smiths, tried to put out the smouldering bark-cloth, but they could not: it was too dry and frayed. The flames spread around the cloth as Ture danced away from the forge. And then Ture ran out of their village into the bush, and the flames spread from the cloth to the grass, and that stopped the smiths from following Ture.

Ture stopped then and sang a song to the fire, so it would know who he was and what its place should be, and then he went on and brought the fire to other people.

TURE'S WIFE AND THE GREAT BIRD NZANGINZANGINZI

Nzanginzanginzi was a monstrous bird which would swallow people when they passed by. It lived on top of a high hill, so it could look all around, and when it saw people it would fly down and swallow them. It swallowed all sorts of people, everyone who went by.

The bird lived along the path that ran from Ture's house to that of his wife's mother. One day, Ture's wife Nanzagbe ground up some meal to take to her mother. She piled it into a bowl, and then on top of the bowl she placed a millipede. She then set off on the path to her mother's house.

Nzanginzanginzi saw her coming. He flew off his hill and came down to her, singing,

> 'I see you coming, I see you on the path,
> I shall swallow you.'

Ture's wife said nothing, but the millipede on top of the meal in the bowl sang a song in answer to Nzanginzanginzi:

> 'No, no, you must let her go,
> No, no, she loves her mother,
> No, no, you must let her go.'

The bird tried again when Ture's wife had passed its hill and was coming to her mother's village, but again the millipede sang a song to answer it and it turned away. So the bird left her alone and she was able to continue on her way to her mother's house. She gave her mother the meal, and she placed the millipede at the bottom of a pot. But after they had eaten, her mother poured scalding water into the pot and the millipede was badly hurt – not killed, but burned and weakened. When Nanzagbe saw this she was distressed, and she told her mother she did not think she could escape the bird this time.

She started on her way, with the millipede in the bowl she carried, and Nzanginzanginzi saw her coming and flew down to eat her. Again, he sang a song:

> 'I see you coming, I see you on the path,
> I shall swallow you.'

But the millipede had enough strength to answer it and to sing:

> 'No, no, you must let her go,
> No, no, she loves her mother,
> No, no, you must let her go.'

So it let her go on. But after she had passed its hill and was coming to her own village, it flew down again and sang its song. But by this time the millipede had died, and could not answer Nzanginzanginzi. So the bird ate Ture's wife.

When Ture heard that the bird had eaten his wife he was

greatly distressed. He went to consult the oracle, and he was so upset that he knocked the oracle from its place. But then it gave him an answer: it told him to forge many little knives and to carry them with him on the path, and to let the bird swallow him when it came down, and in this way he could save his wife.

So Ture went home and forged the knives, and then he went out on the plain before the hill of Nzanginzanginzi. And the bird flew down to him and sang:

> 'I see you coming, I see you on the path,
> I shall swallow you.'

And Ture said, 'Please do.' So the bird swallowed him in one gulp: it put its head down, closed its beak, and then raised its eyes to the sky and Ture went tumbling down its throat.

When he came inside the bird, he found his wife and all those people whom the bird had swallowed still alive, and so then he took all the little knives he had forged and brought with him and distributed them, and told the people to cut at the bird's guts. When the bird felt this, it began to sing a song in pain, and when Ture heard the bird singing he told the people to cut harder and faster. And so they continued cutting at the bird's insides until it died and fell down, and then they continued until they had cut through its belly and could come out of the bird. So all those people escaped.

TURE DANCES

Little Dog followed his mother when she went into the bush to collect the termites on the night they swarmed from the termite mound and could be gathered for food. But he did not assist his mother in her work; he lay on the path they had taken. And so Ture, who was also going to gather termites with his bag and his broom and his torches, did not see Little Dog on the path and he stumbled over the dog who lay there. And Little Dog then sang a song about Ture stumbling over him, and he said that Ture was dancing.

Ture did not see it was Little Dog, and he asked himself what he had stumbled over that sang like this. And so he stumbled over it again, to hear it sing. Again, Little Dog sang his song, and Ture listened carefully and enjoyed it very much. And so he threw away his equipment into the bush, and stumbled over Little Dog again and again, and danced with delight as Little Dog sang his song.

But after a while, Little Dog's mother finished gathering her termites and she came back to the path and took her child with her back to their home. Ture finished his dance and came back to find Little Dog, but could not, and then realized that because he had spent his time dancing he had missed the opportunity when the termites were swarming out of the mound to gather them and store them up for good eating. He could not see where he had thrown his equipment, so he took his torches and while he was looking for his gear, a dry bush caught fire and then while he was running to avoid the fire he fell into a stream.

So he went home wet and tired, clutching sticks, hoping to convince his wife that rain had come on him and prevented him from catching the termites. But when he came to his home and knocked on the doors for them to let him in, they were not deceived. His two wives had gone out and they had collected many termites in bulging bags. They did not believe his story. They told him he had wasted his time dancing when he should have been collecting the termites, and that he was wet only because he had fallen into the stream. Because he had been so foolish, they would not let him have any of their termites.

TURE AND HIS INNARDS

A certain man had a special magic, an oil he used to rub on his belly and then his belly would open. He would pull out his innards and wash them, and then he would tuck them back in and rub his belly with the oil and it would close up.

Ture came upon this man once as he was travelling about,

and was amazed to see him take out his inner parts and wash them. He expressed his admiration and astonishment, and begged the man to teach him the secret, promising to pay a rich price. But the man was generous, and he showed Ture the secret for nothing. He took the oil and rubbed it on Ture's belly, and Ture's belly opened up so he too could wash his intestines. And as he did so, Ture gloated over the way his innards now would be clean, but those of the women at home were filthy. 'Ha!' he exclaimed, 'I shall really be able to mock them now, with their messy innards.' And when Ture had washed his intestines, the man rubbed more oil on his belly and it closed up again. Then the man gave him a small supply of the oil in a horn, and Ture went on his way home.

He paused several times along the way to rub his belly with the oil and to take out his inner parts and to examine them. And one time, as he had pulled them out, a wind came and blew over the horn and all the oil was spilled on the ground, and Ture was left with his innards hanging out. He did not know what to do. He tried various medicines and potions, but none of them worked. He tried the dung of various animals, which is known to possess magical qualities, but it did not help to restore his belly. And during all this, of course, Ture's inner parts were being baked by the sun and the heat and drying out and it was quite painful. Ture began to cry out loud in his pain, calling out and crying what had happened to him.

The man who possessed the magic heard Ture and said to himself, 'I should have known that Ture would make mistakes. Now I must go and help him.' So he brought his medicine and some water with which to wash Ture's ailing innards, and then he rubbed the oil on Ture's belly so that Ture was able to replace the parts inside himself.

Ture did not wish to wash his innards any more.

TURE AND HIS MOTHER-IN-LAW

One day, Ture's mother-in-law came to visit her daughter. She came just at the time the termites were swarming, and Ture and his wife were preparing to go to their mounds to collect the termites. Ture and Nanzagbe owned two mounds, one close to the village and another some distance off in the bush. They prepared the torches and the bags they would need, and then they discussed how they would divide the work. It was agreed that Nanzagbe would tend the mound close to the village, while Ture and his mother-in-law would go to the mound further away.

Ture and the mother-in-law made their way to the second termite mound. The termites were not yet swarming. Ture built a fire and they sat beside it, waiting for the termites. After a while, Ture spoke to the mother-in-law. 'We are far from the village, and there are hyenas and other dangerous animals about. You should not sit so far from me.'

So the mother-in-law moved next to him by the fire. The night wore on and it became late; they lay down to sleep on the bags they had brought to carry termites.

'You should not turn away from me,' Ture said to his mother-in-law. 'If you face away from me, an animal might come and bite your face.' So the mother-in-law turned towards Ture. After some time, the fire died down. They had no more wood. Ture spoke to his mother-in-law, 'Now I am cold. Let me share a corner of your wrapper; it can cover the two of us quite well.'

With the cloth over them, their bodies were in contact. After a time, Ture began to caress the mother-in-law, and when she made no response he began to have intercourse with her. She responded then; she enjoyed it. They kept up their love-making all the rest of the night.

While they were busy, the termites swarmed out of the mound and flew away. Ture and the mother-in-law had no termites to bring home. But his wife Nanzagbe had caught many sacks of termites; she fried some up when her mother returned and offered the dish to the two.

As he was eating, Ture's penis called to him, 'How dare you eat termites, when you let all the termites at the other mound escape because you were sleeping with your mother-in-law?'

'You are lying!' cried Ture to his penis, but his mother-in-law's vagina spoke, saying, 'You know it is not a lie. You let the termites escape while you were amusing yourself with me.'

Nanzagbe was furious and seized her pestle; she chased Ture and her mother out of the compound.

ESHU OF THE YORUBA

Eshu is only one of the Yoruba tricksters; there is also the tortoise Ajapa. But Eshu, or Eshu-Elegbara, as his fuller name goes, occupies a special place because of his association with Orunmila, the god or orisha *of Ifa divination (see also Chapter 49). Eshu himself is also an* orisha. *Like the Fon Legba (see Chapters 18 and 51), to whom he is closely related, Eshu works to introduce the unpredictable into an orderly system; this can cause trouble at times, but it also can help (as in the second story below, when Eshu helps Orunmila escape a destined death). The following stories were all recorded around 1960.*

ESHU'S KNOWLEDGE

At the time of creation, the various *orisha* went to their Father's house to receive their powers. At that time, Eshu had no possessions or farm to delay him, and so he arrived first. He stayed and helped the Father as he carved the various beings that would fill the world; he did not get impatient, but he stayed and stayed for sixteen years, helping the Father. Other *orisha* would come and stay for four or eight days, waiting until the Father assigned them a post and duties, then they left and returned to their homes or farms. Eshu did not leave. He learned how the Father shaped humans: how he made hands and feet and eyes. Eshu learned everything. So finally the Father told him to go and take his place at the crossroads. He said that everyone coming to see him should give Eshu a gift, and everyone leaving should give him a gift. So Eshu became wealthy, and he said, 'Lazy men live by their wisdom; only fools do not know how to manage their affairs.'

ESHU, ORUNMILA AND THE SERVANT OF DEATH

Agbigbo became a servant of Death; his task was to carry the coffins in which Death placed those he had killed to their houses. One night, Orunmila, the *orisha* of Ifa divination, dreamed of death. The next day, he consulted the Ifa oracle and was told what offerings to prepare. He collected the materials for the sacrifice and carried them to the shrine of Eshu.

Agbigbo was sent with a coffin to the home of Orunmila. Along the way, he met Eshu sitting outside his shrine. Eshu asked him what he was doing with the coffin and Agbigbo told him it was intended for Orunmila. Eshu asked him what he would take to leave Orunmila alone, and Agbigbo said that he could be persuaded by the gift of a rat, a bird and some other bush-meat. Eshu said that he had all these things, for they had been included in the sacrifice Orunmila had left with him. He gave them to Agbigbo, who put the coffin on his head and went his way. As he left, Eshu commanded that he should never be able to put the coffin down. And this is the mark of Agbigbo to this day: he is a bird with a large tuft of feathers on his head, indicating the coffin he carries.

ESHU PARTS TWO FRIENDS

Two men were very close friends and had sworn that nothing would part them. Their compounds were next to each other, their fields lay on opposite sides of the road out of the village; they were always together. At one time, they consulted the Ifa oracle, and were told to make a sacrifice to Eshu, but they did not. And so Eshu punished them.

One day, he came walking down the road between their fields. His hat was red on one side, white on the other. After he had gone, one friend spoke to the other and mentioned the white hat. The other corrected him: the hat had been red. The first was sure the hat was white. The second knew it was red. They argued about it and finally began to fight. When they stopped, they went back to work in the fields.

Eshu came walking back in the other direction. This time, the man who had seen the white side saw the red and the man who had seen the red saw the white. Each went to apologize to the other. But when the first said the hat had been red, the second thought he was mocking him. Again, the discussion led to blows, and their families had to come and help them back to their compounds.

The families spoke to the men, and reminded them how close they had been, and asked why they had come to fight in this way. They said there must be an underlying cause, and so the two friends consulted Ifa again. They learned how Eshu had set them against each other, and so this time they made the prescribed sacrifice to Eshu and appeased him. They remained friends after that.

LEGBA OF THE FON

The Fon of Benin (formerly Dahomey) established the kingdom of Abomey in the seventeenth century (see Chapter 51); they later came under the domination of the Yoruba state of Oyo at the end of the eighteenth century, and from them they took a number of ritual elements, and particularly the practice of Ifa (Fa) divination. Legba, the trickster figure, is similar to the Yoruba Eshu; he has also become important in the Caribbean practice of vodun, because, as the intermediary of humans and gods, it is he who enables believers to be possessed by their divinities. This story is retold from a version collected in the 1930s.

Many stories are told of Legba, and he serves many purposes in the complex Fon pantheon. It is said that he was the youngest born of Mawu, goddess of the sun, and so she favoured him and gave him the gift of all languages, so that he serves as the linguist or spokesman for the gods; all who would approach a god must do so through Legba. Another story says that he was given this post because he, alone of the gods, was able to play a gong, a bell, a drum and a flute, all at the same time and while dancing. Legba is also the servant of Fa, the deity of divination, although the representations of this situation vary. One story says that Fa is personified by the female Gbadu, who has sixteen eyes around her head and sits atop a palm tree looking out over the world; each morning, Legba climbs the tree and opens her eyes according to her instructions. Children of Gbadu were the first Fa diviners in the world, by a dispensation of Mawu. Legba is also said to have caused the war between the sky and the earth at the beginning of time, and then to have effected the settlement by which the people on earth may request rainfall from the sky.

One complex story illustrates Legba's qualities. At one time, he and his siblings Minona, a female deity who protects women, and Aovi, a god who punishes those humans who disrespect the gods, formed a funeral band and went about the country playing music for funerals. They heard of a funeral for a great man, and so they went there to perform. At the funeral they encountered several other persons. King Metonofi (it is said he ruled the land of the dead) was there, displeased because he had married his daughter to the king of Adja and he had proved impotent with her. The king of Adja's son was there, because he had come to consult Fa, the spirit of divination who was also Legba's master. And Fa himself was there, because he was needed. Fa could not speak by himself; he required Legba's assistance to express himself.

The king of Adja's son came and told Fa about his father's troubles with Metonofi's daughter, and Fa told him he could supply a powder that would enable his father to consummate his marriage. He then told Legba to give the prince some of the white powder which he kept in his sack. But Legba gave the prince a red powder instead, that removed potency, rather than the white one which restored it. Then the funeral went on, and Legba's band played its music so that the mourners could dance.

The three siblings were paid in cowrie-shells, the currency of the time, and they left the town and stopped at a crossroads to divide the shells. But the shells would not divide evenly: there was always one left over, and the three could not decide what to do with the remaining shell, or who should get it. Finally, a woman came by and they asked her what to do. The woman answered that she thought the eldest child should receive the last cowrie, and so Minona should have it. But Legba and Aovi were furious at this answer, and so they killed the woman and threw her body in the bush. Legba, always lecherous, then slipped off and lay with the corpse.

Another woman came by, and she said that the middle child should receive the extra cowrie. She was killed by Minona and

Legba, and again Legba lay with the corpse. A third woman came by, and she was killed when she said the cowrie should go to the youngest. Legba lay with her body too.

Then Legba created the figure of a dog, and made it move and speak, and sent it to the three siblings. They asked it what to do with the cowrie, and the dog answered that they should give it to the ancestors. The dog dug a hole and buried the cowrie, and the three siblings were satisfied. They went home. Since that time, the dog is respected among humans.

Meanwhile, people began to complain to King Metonofi and to Fa: women had been killed, and the powder Legba had given the prince, which was supposed to restore potency, had instead made men impotent. The king sent for Legba, and he ran away to the home of his in-laws. As it happened, his father-in-law was away at the time, and so Legba slept next to his mother-in-law and in the middle of the night they lay together.

The next morning, the king's men caught him and brought him to face his accusers and their charges, among whom he could now also count his father-in-law who accused him of adultery. First they asked about the three women who had been killed, and Legba explained that it was always a pair of siblings who killed them, not he. He also explained how he had solved the problem by creating the dog, and he produced the figure of the dog.

King Metonofi was very impressed by Legba's ingenuity, and so he declared that Legba would be given a special responsibility to watch over people. Minona he ordered to go become a guardian of women, and because Aovi was so violent, Metonofi charged him with enforcing respect for the gods.

Then Legba's father-in-law spoke his complaint, and Legba had to admit that he had slept with the woman, but explained that it was a mistake because she had been lying where his wife normally lay. But Metonofi and the other people were not satisfied with this explanation, and so they ordered that Legba was not to live in houses with people, but must always be found in the open spaces such as crossroads, and this is why shrines to Legba are generally placed at crossroads.

Finally, they heard the case of the king of Adja and the

complaint that Legba had given men the red powder instead of the white. Legba simply denied this. He said the red powder was perfectly good. But he had changed the colours of the powders: he mixed the white powder with blood, so that it became red, and he mixed the red powder with white clay, so that it became white. When the people said Legba had given them the red powder, Metonofi ordered Legba to take some of it himself.

Then came the question of the marriage of Metonofi's daughter. Metonofi built a hut and placed his daughter inside it, and then said the men of Adja should attempt intercourse with her. One by one they tried, but none succeeded. Then Legba said that he would accomplish this task. He asked for drums to play when he entered the hut, and then he danced in and lay with the daughter, who was a virgin. Then, still erect and with blood on his penis, he danced out of the hut and showed everyone what he had accomplished.

Metonofi then said that Legba should marry his daughter, but Legba said that instead she should marry his master, Fa, and he gave her the name Adje, which means cowries. At the wedding, Legba mixed the good powder in with the palm wine which was served to all the guests, and so the men of the country recovered their potency.

ANANSE THE SPIDER, OF
THE ASHANTI

*Ananse is the trickster-hero of the Ashanti of coastal west Africa,
in modern Ghana (see Chapter 52). He is not quite a god, but he
has done a good deal to shape the world, and for the Ashanti he
owns all stories (we learn why in the second story). In form, he is
a spider, although he is also very human in behaviour and charac-
teristics; as a story-figure, he is related to a variety of other
animal-shaped (theriomorphic) tricksters found around Africa:
Nden-Bobo, the spider of Cameroon, Kamba the tortoise of central east Africa, Leuck the hare of Senegal, and others. Ananse
also travelled with African slaves, and he appears in Jamaican
folklore as Aunt Nancy. The first story was reported by a Danish
traveller in the eighteenth century; the other two are retold
from a collection made at the start of the twentieth century.*

THE STORY OF NANNI

*Perhaps the earliest reported story of Ananse dates to the
eighteenth century, in Ludewig Rømer's* Reliable Account of
the Coast of Guinea *(1760). Rømer was a Danish trader, part
of a multi-national European community along the Gold Coast,
and much of his work concerns trade conditions. But he also
reported what he understood of African affairs and culture,
and his story of Nanni shows clear links with the modern
narrative traditions.*

At the beginning, the spider Nanni assisted God in creating
humans. The spider wove stuff, and God used the spider's

weaving to make humans. Nanni expected the humans to recognize her part in their creation, but humans turned instead to
oracles and fetishes. So Nanni took a little bit of the stuff that
was left over and made another being, just like herself. She
taught this being trickery. For instance, people would sacrifice
chickens to the oracle. But the little Nanni learned from his
mother that he could eat the meat of the chicken, and sacrifice
only the feathers and bones, reassembled to resemble a live
chicken.

The younger Nanni lived with people. He married and had
a large family. One time there was a famine, and Nanni did not
have enough food stored up for his wives and children. But he
knew his neighbour, a hunter, had a large store of beans which
he had gained by selling the meat of animals he killed. The
hunter was often away from home, in the bush, and during that
time he had instructed his children to keep the beans dry and
free of pests by laying them out in the sun and turning them.

Nanni went one day to the hunter's home and greeted the
children. Their father was away, and they had laid out the
beans. At first, they thought Nanni had come to steal beans and
they watched him carefully to make sure he did not pick any
up. But he reassured them, telling them he had only come to
play a new game with them, a dance he had learned and which
he thought they would enjoy. In the dance, he threw himself
about on the ground and rolled about, and it happened at times
that he rolled over the beans. The hunter's children did not
realize that Nanni had coated his body with gum, so that he
was sticky all over, and they did not notice how many beans
stuck to his body. When he had finished dancing, Nanni showed
the children his empty hands and to reassure them that he had
not taken handfuls of beans, and then went home. In this way
he was able to provide food for his family for some time.

But the hunter returned home, and noticed that he had fewer
beans than before. He suspected Nanni, especially after his
children told him how Nanni would come and play the game
of dancing and rolling on the ground with them. One day the
hunter only pretended to go into the bush and in fact hid quite
close to his home. He saw Nanni come and dance, he saw

Nanni roll on the ground over the beans, and he saw Nanni
leave with beans sticking all over his body. So he leaped from
his hiding place, seized Nanni and cut off Nanni's hands with
his great knife. Then he brushed the beans from Nanni, and
sent him on his way.

Nanni returned home, hiding his lack of hands, and announced loudly from the centre of the compound that since
food was so scarce he would feed only the children, and he
would feed them privately, in his own hut. One by one, the
children were brought into the hut, and there he threatened
them until each agreed to say he or she had been fed. But after
three days the secret got out; the children told the mothers they
had not been fed, and the mothers discovered that Nanni had
lost his hands. They determined that they would leave him,
since he could not provide for them any more.

Nanni ran out, ahead of them on the path, and scraped
together a bundle of firewood. He pulled a cloth over his head,
so they would not recognize him. When the wives and children
came by, he asked them where they were going. They answered
that their husband Nanni was no longer able to provide for
them, and they were seeking another home. 'Ha!' said the
disguised Nanni. 'You will not find one. I have had twenty
wives, and have sent nineteen away because they did not please
me. Who will take the lot of you in these times?' But the wives
ignored him and continued down the path.

Nanni ran ahead of them again, and found a place where he
could pretend to be fishing. When the wives reached him, he
asked where they were going. As before, they explained they
were leaving their husband Nanni. 'Ha!' said Nanni the fisherman. 'No one will take you. I have cast off forty-nine out of
fifty wives. Times are hard. You will find no home.' But the
wives ignored him and continued down the path.

This happened again, and the wives began to discuss whether
they had really chosen the right course. They decided that they
should perform a divination at the nearest fetish. So they went
there. Nanni had concealed himself in the shrine, and when the
wives put their question to the fetish Nanni answered that
they should go home at any price, because they faced certain

destruction elsewhere. So after much discussion, the wives returned home.

But at the compound, Nanni held the door shut against them. He refused to readmit them until they had agreed not to question his authority, and that they would take over many household tasks and provide many services to him.

HOW ANANSE GOT THE STORIES
FROM THE SKY-GOD

This is perhaps one of the best-known and best-loved stories of Ananse, collected in the Ashanti heartland at the beginning of the twentieth century.

Ananse the spider went to Nyankopon the sky-god and asked to buy the stories which the sky-god owned. The sky-god asked, 'Why should I sell them to you?' and Ananse answered, 'Because I shall be able to pay the price.'

The sky-god told him, 'Men have come from powerful towns, offering to buy the stories, but they could not pay the price despite all their men and their wealth. You are a simple man without a chief, without a clan. You say you can pay the price?'

Ananse asked, 'What is the price of the stories?' The sky-god answered, 'The only price I will accept is for you to bring me the python, the leopard, the bush-spirit and the hornets.' Ananse replied, 'I shall bring you those things, and in addition I will bring you my own mother.'

'Then bring them,' said the sky-god.

Ananse went home and told his mother about his bargain, how he asked to buy the stories of the sky-god and the price the sky-god had asked of him: the python, the leopard, the bush-spirit and the hornets. 'And,' he admitted, 'I told him I would throw you in with the price.'

Then the spider asked his wife how they might get hold of the python. His wife told him to cut a length of bamboo and some vines and to take them down to the stream. Ananse cut them and went down to the stream, muttering furiously to himself as he went. 'Of course he's longer than it is! How could it be longer? He can't be shorter! He must be longer! It must be shorter . . .'

The spider passed by the python lying in the sun, and the snake heard the muttering. 'What are you talking about?' asked the python.

'My wife has argued with me,' said the spider. 'She says that this bamboo is longer than you are, and I say she is a liar. It could not be longer than you.'

'Measure me,' said the python.

Ananse laid the bamboo by the python's body, and the snake straightened out its coils. 'Stretch yourself,' said Ananse. The python stretched himself.

'I can't tell,' said the spider. 'When you stretch at one end, you move away from the bamboo at the other. If I could fasten the bamboo to you, so that it didn't move, then I could tell.'

'Then tie me to the bamboo,' said the python. Ananse tied the python's tail to the bamboo.

'Now stretch yourself again,' said the spider, and the python strained himself to be longer than the bamboo. As he was stretching, the spider coiled the vines up his body until he was tied completely to the bamboo. And then the python couldn't move.

'Heh!' said Ananse. 'Now I have caught you, and I shall take you to the sky-god as part of the price of the stories.'

So Ananse took the python up to the sky-god, and the sky-god admitted that he had paid a part of the price. 'And what remains remains,' he said.

Ananse came down and talked with his wife. 'Now let us get the hornets,' he said, and his wife suggested that he get a gourd and fill it with water.

He took his gourd into the forest, until he found a nest of hornets, and then he began to splash water about, particularly on the hornets' nest. He held a large leaf over his head, as though to shelter him from the rain.

The hornets buzzed, thinking it was raining.

'Ah,' said Ananse. 'Why don't you take shelter from the rain inside this gourd?'

'Thank you, Kwaku Ananse,' said the hornets (Kwaku is a term of respect that has become part of Ananse's name), and they buzzed out of their nest and into the gourd. Quickly, Ananse stopped up the mouth of the gourd with a leaf. 'Heh,' he said. 'Now I have caught you, and I shall take you to the sky-god as part of the price of the stories.'

He took the gourd up to the sky-god. 'What remains remains,' said the sky-god.

Ananse came back and talked to his wife. 'Now for the leopard,' he said.

'Dig a hole,' said his wife. 'I understand,' said Ananse. He went into the forest and found the tracks of a leopard. There he dug a very deep pit and covered it over. He went back to his hut for the night. The next morning, as the sun was beginning to show, he went along the path to his pit and found a leopard in it.

'Heh!' said Ananse. 'Little brother, what has happened to you? Surely you were drinking too much last night and so you fell into this hole in the dark. Such is the price of foolishness. I would let you out, but you would then simply hurt me and my children.'

'Oh, no,' said the leopard. 'I would never hurt you if you let me out.'

'Well,' said Ananse. He placed two sticks in the pit, far apart, so the leopard's paws were spread as he tried to climb them. And then Ananse pulled out his knife and hit the leopard as soon as his head reached the top of the pit.

The leopard fell back in, and Ananse pulled him out with a ladder. 'Heh,' he said. 'Now you are mine, and I shall take you to the sky-god as part of the price of the stories.'

He brought the leopard to the sky-god. The sky-god took the leopard and said, 'What remains remains.'

Ananse went home. He carved a large wooden doll, the size of Ananse himself. He drew the sap from trees – gummy sap that did not dry. He coated the doll with the glue. Then he pounded yams and made some food. He put some in a bowl and some in the doll's hand. He took the doll and the bowl of food into the bush, and placed it at the base of a great tree where spirits lived. He tied the doll to the tree.

A spirit came by and saw the bowl of food. 'May I eat?' asked the spirit.

Ananse moved the doll's head to say yes.

The spirit ate from the bowl of food and then thanked the doll. But the doll did nothing. The doll did not answer.

'Ah!' said the spirit to another spirit. 'This person told me to eat and I ate, and now when I have eaten and I return my thanks this person says nothing at all. What sort of a person is this?'

'It is a bad person,' said the other spirit. 'You should slap the person's face.'

So the spirit slapped the face of the doll, but its hand stuck to the glue. 'My hand is stuck to the person's face,' the spirit called.

'Then strike the person,' answered the other spirit.

The spirit struck the doll with its left hand. The left hand stuck too. Then the spirit kicked the doll. One leg was stuck. Then the other, and finally the stomach.

Ananse came out from behind the tree. 'Heh,' said Ananse. 'Now I have caught you, and I shall take you to the sky-god as part of the price of the stories.'

Ananse went home with the doll and the spirit and called to his mother. 'Come, mother,' he said, 'for I have the last part of the sky-god's price, and I wish you to go along as well in exchange for the stories.'

He took the doll and the spirit and his mother and carried them to the home of the sky-god. When he arrived, he greeted the sky-god. 'Here is the bush-spirit,' he said, 'which is part of the price of the stories, and here also is my mother whom I said I would bring. Have I not paid the price?'

The sky-god called his council together and they talked. 'Kings and cities have come,' said the sky-god, 'but they could not bring me the price of the stories. But Ananse has paid it. I told him to bring me the python, the leopard, the hornets and the bush-spirit. He has brought me the python, the hornets, the leopard and the bush-spirit, and he has also brought me his mother. Surely he has paid the price and the stories are his? Surely we should praise him?'

So they all praised Ananse.

'Ananse,' said the sky-god, 'now and for ever, I give you my stories. I take them and I give them to you with my blessing. No longer shall the stories be the stories of the sky-god, but they shall be the stories of Ananse.'

And so they are. All stories today belong to Kwaku Ananse.

ANANSE AND THE CORNCOB

This story was told among the Krachi, close neighbours of the Ashanti, who preserved their independence from the powerful Ashanti kingdom thanks to a celebrated shrine. The theme of the story – the successive exchanges – is widespread in Africa and around the world (see, for instance, Uthlakanyana, Chapter 14 above).

At the start, the sky-god Wulbari lived close to man; he lay next to Mother Earth. But in this condition, he was so close to man that problems came about, and now he has moved far away. There were a number of reasons for this. When the women pounded their millet or their yams, their long pestles would poke him. The smoke from the kitchen fires got in his eyes. Men would wipe their hands on him, because he was so close and handy. But the worst of all was an old woman, who cut bits from him each night to thicken her soup.

Wulbari removed from men and went to live with the animals. For a time, all went well. Then one day Ananse the spider asked Wulbari for a corncob. 'Certainly,' said Wulbari. 'But what will you do with one corncob?'

'For one corncob,' said Ananse, 'I will bring you one hundred slaves.'

Wulbari did not believe him.

But Ananse went down to earth onto the road from Krachi to Yende. That evening, he got to the town of Tariasu, and there he asked the village chief for lodging. At night-time, he went to the chief again.

'I have another question,' he said. 'I have here the corncob of Wulbari. He is sending it to Yende, and I must keep it safe on the journey. Where can I place it for the night?'

The chief said he might hide it in the thatch of the roof of the chief's house, and so Ananse left it there.

But in the middle of the night, Ananse got up and took down the corncob and threw it to the chief's chickens. The next morning, he asked for the corncob – and they found it in the yard, all eaten and pecked at. So Ananse complained loudly about his loss and the insult to Wulbari, and to compensate him the people of Tariasu gave him a large basket of corn.

Ananse carried the basket out of town for some way until he was so tired he had to rest. He put the basket down and rested in the shade, until a man came by with a chicken. Ananse greeted him and they talked, and Ananse admired the chicken, and the man said he would sell it. So Ananse traded the large basket of corn for the chicken, and the man carried off the basket and Ananse went on his way with the fowl.

That night, he came to Kpandae, and he went to greet the village chief and to ask for a night's lodging. And he also asked for a very safe place to keep his chicken, which belonged to Wulbari and which was being sent to Yende and had to be kept carefully. So the people put the chicken into a small coop and all went to bed.

But Ananse got up in the middle of the night and took the chicken from the coop and crept out of the village. There, he sacrificed the chicken, but he saved some blood and feathers and marked the door to the chief's compound with them. Then he washed his hands and went back to bed.

The next morning, he asked for his chicken, and it was not there. Ananse began to yell and complain. They had broken their promise! He would lose his job! They showed no respect for Wulbari! Where was his chicken? Everyone was there, and then Ananse pointed out the blood and the feathers on the chief's door.

There it was. And while they were talking about it, a small boy brought in the body of the chicken which he had found at the edge of town. Clearly, the chief was guilty: he had broken his trust, he had stolen the chicken.

The people begged Ananse to intercede, to hold away the wrath of Wulbari. Could they make up for the loss of a chicken? Would another chicken – or lots of chickens – be enough?

Ananse thought that maybe some sheep would be enough to avert the anger of Wulbari.

'We will give you sheep,' cried the villagers. 'How many do you want?'

So Ananse left the village with ten sheep. He reached the town of Yende, and paused for a while outside the town to let the sheep graze. While he was resting, a crowd of people came towards him, wailing. They were carrying the corpse of a young man, and after Ananse asked them, he learned they were returning him to his own village for burial.

Where was this village, Ananse wanted to know, and was it far away? Yes, it was far away, answered the mourners.

'Well,' said Ananse, 'if you carry the body that far it will rot and spoil.'

'True,' they agreed.

'It would be better,' said Ananse, 'if you let me take the body. In exchange, I will give you these ten sheep.'

This was a very strange bargain, but after they thought about it the mourners agreed that it was a good idea. So they left the corpse with Ananse and took the sheep back.

Ananse waited until it was late at night, and then he picked up the body and went into the town to the compound of the great chief of Yende. There he begged for a small place to sleep for the night, for him and his companion.

'I am Ananse, from the court of Wulbari,' he said. 'My companion is the son of Wulbari, but he is young and tired from the long journey today. He is already asleep. We wish only to lie down as soon as may be.' The people of Yende were delighted to have such distinguished guests, and they quickly got ready a hut with two beds. Ananse put the corpse in the bed and arranged the sheet so he seemed to be sleeping.

Then Ananse went outside, where the people greeted him lavishly: pots of food and drink. Ananse took a bowl into the hut, saying it was for the son of Wulbari, but he ate it all himself. Then the people asked him if they might sing and drum

and dance in honour of their distinguished guests, and Ananse
replied that of course they should sing and drum and dance.
The son of Wulbari would sleep through it all: he slept very
soundly, and in the mornings Ananse sometimes had to beat
him to get him out of bed.

When morning came, Ananse said they should continue on
their way. So he asked some of the chief's children, who had
been dancing with him, to wake up the son of Wulbari. If he
did not get up, said Ananse, they should beat him. So the
children went into the hut and tried to wake up the young man.
They pushed him and pulled him, and finally they began to beat
him. He did not wake. They went to Ananse, and he told them
to hit harder. So they beat the body again.

Then Ananse said he would try to wake up the boy. He went
into the hut and called Wulbari's son by name. He shook him
and pushed him and pulled him, and then found . . . that the
boy was dead! Ananse screamed and everyone in the compound
came running.

There was Ananse. There was the body of the son of Wulbari.
There were the chief's children who had beaten the son of
Wulbari to death. The people were appalled, and they were
certain that the sky-god would destroy their village instantly.
The chief came and offered to kill his children. He would kill
himself and his family and burn his compound. He would offer
gold and silver.

Ananse said that the shock was too great, that he could not
think. For that day, they should do nothing. He would consider
what they should do. The people should bury the boy, and
Ananse would think of a plan.

So the town of Yende gave a funeral to the young man's
body.

Then the town sat in silence, waiting for Ananse to come up
with a plan.

Ananse sat all day beneath a shade-tree in the chief's compound, thinking. In the evening he called the chief.

'I cannot blame the village for the death of the son of Wulbari,' he said. 'I will return to the court of Wulbari and take
the blame upon myself. But he may not believe my word alone.

You must send people with me to bear witness to what I have done. Send one hundred young men with me.'

The chief and the people of the town were delighted with this solution, and so they chose one hundred of the finest young men of the town and sent them with Ananse to the court of Wulbari.

When they reached the court of Wulbari, Ananse showed him the young men, and told him how he had gotten them all from a single corncob. Wulbari was greatly pleased and confirmed Ananse in his court position and gave him names of honour.

Later, however, Ananse began to boast of his cleverness and to say that he was smarter even than Wulbari. Wulbari heard him say this one evening, and became angry at Ananse for these words. So the next day he called Ananse and told him to bring him something. He did not say anything more.

Ananse thought and thought all day. In the evening, Wulbari laughed at him. 'You said you were more clever than I. Now you must prove it.'

The next day, Ananse went away from the sky to find the something. He stopped a bit away from Wulbari's court, and he gathered all the birds he could find. He took one feather from each of them, and then he wove all the feathers into a marvellous and strange cape such as had never been seen before. He went back to the court of Wulbari and put on the cape. He climbed into the tree near Wulbari's hut. Soon, someone noticed this peculiar being, and called attention to it. Wulbari asked what it was, and people could not tell him. Not one of the people there could tell him what kind of a bird this was.

Ananse might know, suggested an animal, but Wulbari said that he had sent Ananse on an errand. What was the errand, all the animals asked, and Wulbari laughed. 'I have sent Ananse to find something,' he told them.

So of course the animals wanted to know what something was, and eventually Wulbari told them. 'By something,' he said, 'I mean the sun, the moon and darkness. Ananse has said he is as clever as I. If he can bring these things back, then perhaps he is.'

All the animals laughed with Wulbari, and they agreed that it was unlikely Ananse would be able to guess what Wulbari wanted and to bring it back. Then they went back to their various businesses. When they had all dispersed, Ananse came down from the tree and took off the cloak of feathers and left the court again.

He went far away, for a long time. Who knows where he went or what he did? But he found the sun, and the moon and darkness. Some say the python kept them in its belly; others say other things. But Ananse found them and put them into his bag and he brought them with him back to the court of Wulbari.

He walked up late one afternoon, and Wulbari greeted him.

'Well,' said Wulbari. 'Have you brought me something?'

'Yes,' said Ananse. He opened his bag and let out the darkness. Everything was black. No one could see anything anywhere. Then Ananse reached into the bag and pulled out the moon. A little light came back into the world, and people could begin to see again. Then he reached into his bag and pulled out the sun.

Those who were looking directly at Ananse when he took the sun from his bag became blind. Some were not looking straight at the sun, and their sight was only partly harmed, and others were looking away. They were not harmed.

So it is that blindness came into the world because Wulbari asked Ananse for something.

PART II

STORIES OF KINGDOMS AND PEOPLES

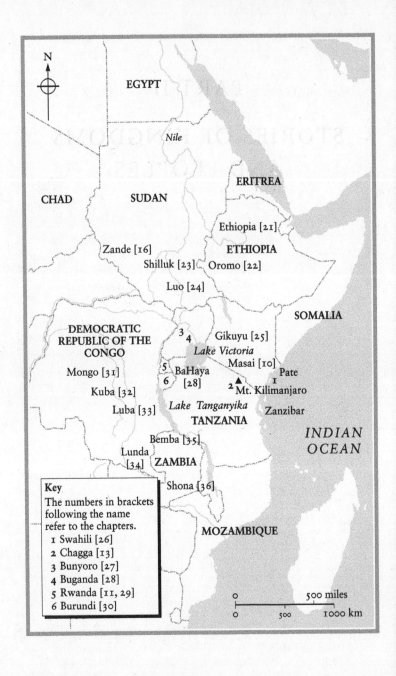

N

EGYPT

Nile

ERITREA

CHAD   SUDAN

Ethiopia [21]

Zande [16]   ETHIOPIA

Shilluk [23]   Oromo [22]

Luo [24]

SOMALIA

DEMOCRATIC
REPUBLIC OF THE
CONGO

3 4   Gikuyu [25]

Lake Victoria

5   BaHaya   Masai [10]   Pate

Mongo [31]   [28]   1

6   2 Mt. Kilimanjaro

Kuba [32]

Luba [33]   *Lake Tanganyika*   Zanzibar

TANZANIA

INDIAN
OCEAN

Bemba [35]

Lunda

[34] ZAMBIA

Shona [36]

Key
The numbers in brackets
following the name
refer to the chapters.
1 Swahili [26]
2 Chagga [13]
3 Bunyoro [27]
4 Buganda [28]
5 Rwanda [11, 29]
6 Burundi [30]

MOZAMBIQUE

0   500 miles

0   500   1000 km

ANCIENT AFRICA

Almost no records exist of local cultures prior to the Middle Ages for most of the continent. North Africa was an important part of the classical world, colonized first from Phoenicia and then integrated into the Roman empire, but its possible relations with sub-Saharan Africa have been effaced by the later Islamic conquest. Egypt and Ethiopia represent the oldest indigenous literate cultures on the continent. A significant gap in time and space separates these two cultures from the rest of Africa; the distance is compounded by the difficulties of crossing the desert out of Egypt and the passage of the mountains which shielded Ethiopia from Muslim conquest. In Islamic times (from the seventh and eighth centuries on), an active trade in various commodities and the Muslim practice of pilgrimage to Mecca did multiply contacts.

EGYPTIAN STORIES

While early Egyptian culture sprang from African roots, the question of the continuities across time and space remains a methodological challenge. For the past two or three thousand years, Egypt has been far more closely tied to the Mediterranean world than to the distant lands on the upper Nile. To identify two-thousand-year-old influences in oral tradition seems an impossible task. Nevertheless, the assertion of a continuity from ancient Egyptian culture to modern Africa is a central tenet in some visions of African history, and particularly in the Afrocentric movement derived from the works of the Senegalese historian Cheikh Anta Diop. The following selection of stories, taken from early Egyptian literature (3000–400 BC), is offered as evidence for possible narrative parallels and thematic agreement with the stories recorded in more recent years in sub-Saharan Africa. In the Middle Ages, Egypt was an important passage for Muslim pilgrims travelling from sub-Saharan Africa to Mecca, but the dominant culture by that time was almost purely Islamic.

THE CONTENDING OF HORUS
AND SETH

The best-known myth of the death of Osiris and his resurrection by Isis is actually a late Greek version, reported by Plutarch after the cult of Isis had become something of an international phenomenon in the Mediterranean world. The image of Osiris *before that time was somewhat different. For Egyptians, judging by the surviving literature, it was the question of the succession to Osiris that mattered most – a question whose theological relevance can easily be understood in terms of the system of divine kingship: how could a divine Pharaoh die, and who then could succeed him? This version of myth is reported from the New Kingdom (c. 1000 BC), but may be older.*

The story of the death of Osiris is well known: how his brother Seth grew jealous of his power and his popularity and plotted to kill him, and so contrived a coffin made to the measure of Osiris which he produced at a feast, inviting the guests to see whom it might fit. When Osiris lay in it, Seth and his helpers fastened the lid shut and threw it into the Nile. But Isis, the wife of Osiris, searched long for her husband and found the coffin where it had come to rest near the town of Abydos. It was then that she lay with her dead husband and conceived her son Horus. But Seth later came upon them and seized the body of Osiris and scattered it in parts over all of Egypt, and he sent messengers to try to slay the infant Horus. But Isis again searched and found all the parts of her husband's body, and later she cured her son of the poison which afflicted him. So Horus became an adult and went before the gods of Egypt to demand his father's inheritance.

Seth argued that he, rather than Horus, should rule Egypt, for he was the brother of the dead king; he was a man of experience and wisdom and a tried warrior who was responsible for guarding the ship of Ra as it sailed through the nightlands where monsters lay, while Horus was young and callow and had never been tested. After some discussion the gods agreed to send a message to Neith, goddess of the sky, asking her judgement. Thoth the scribe drafted and wrote out the letter. Neith's reply was that Horus should receive the realm of his father. But Atum refused to recognize this reply as valid and refused to consent to Horus' enthronement.

The discussion continued, and Isis began to lose her temper. The gods decided to continue their talk in a place without her, and withdrew to an island in the Nile. But Isis, ever resourceful, changed her appearance, bribed the boatman and so came onto the island. There she took the appearance of a beautiful young woman and walked past Seth as he sat by the riverbank. Seth walked with her for a time, drawn by her beauty, and they talked. She told him she was a young widow; her husband had died, and she had a small son. But the son could not get his father's cattle and fields, because a stranger had come into the village and claimed that those possessions were his by right.

'How can a stranger claim a father's property while the son yet lives?' asked Seth, drawn into her story.

'Indeed,' said Isis. She resumed her own appearance and called the other gods to witness that Seth had spoken a judgement against himself. But again Seth disputed the decision and claimed that the circumstances of the two cases were entirely different.

Finally, the gods decided that the two contenders should meet in combat. After some negotiations, Seth and Horus took the form of hippopotamuses to fight in the river. The gods assembled and watched as the two mighty beasts roared and rolled in the water, slashing with their tusks and attempting each to drown the other. Isis, meanwhile, watched anxiously, armed with a harpoon, for she was determined that her son would not lose this battle. But it was difficult to tell the two hippos apart, especially as they rolled over each other in the foaming water. One of them seemed to be winning, and although she was not certain, she thought it was Seth. The harpoon darted out and pierced the thick hide. But it was Horus, not Seth, and he bellowed in pain and reproached her as she hastily removed the harpoon and did what she could to quickly heal the wound.

She watched closely again, and then stabbed. This time she had caught Seth. She pulled him close to her, and he turned and spoke, reminding her that she was his sister and should not be guilty of his blood. Swayed, she released him and he returned to the combat. But Horus had followed the action, and his mother's interference had gone too far for him. He left the water, seized an axe, and chopped off her head. She later replaced it, of course, although there are also statues of the headless Isis in Egyptian temples.

Then Horus, appalled that he had tried to kill his mother, rushed into the wilderness and fell asleep under some bushes. Seth, following his trail, came upon him as he slept and blinded him. But the next day, as Horus wandered aimlessly, unable to find his way, the sometimes-merciful Hathor came to him and poured milk in his eyes and restored his vision.

Horus returned to the gods and resumed his suit against Seth. The gods determined that they must consult a final authority, and sent a letter to Osiris who had become the ruler of the underworld, the land of the dead. Osiris' reply was decisive: if they did not grant the inheritance to his son, he would return from the land of the dead with his hosts of dead spirits, and there would be no peace for the living.

So Horus became the ruler of Egypt after Osiris.

CHEOPS AND THE MAGICIANS

This linked set of stories (an early example of the frame-tale) was recorded around 1800 BC. On one level, it counts as popular literature: the narration of wonders associated with an earlier king whose wondrous monument surpassed all others. On another level, however, it marks a transition, for it tells how King Cheops (or Chu-fu) learned that another dynasty would supplant his own. It serves thus as an after-the-fact justification for that succession, and this sort of mechanism is widely encountered in dynastic legends of origin.

Cheops, king of Upper and Lower Egypt, sat with his sons as they told him tales of the great wise men of old times, and he decreed cult offerings of beer and oxen and grain to the memory of those men. His son Khephren rose and said, 'I would tell you of a wonder that occurred in the time of your predecessor, Nebka of the Third Dynasty. It shows the powers of the priest Webaoner. He was married, but his wife had taken a lover to whom she sent gifts. She would meet her lover in a garden-house on Webaoner's estate, near the water, and before a tryst she would tell the caretaker to clean the garden-house and to prepare it for a visit. Then she would come and spend the day eating and drinking and sporting with her lover who would come through the water to meet her.

'The caretaker went to Webaoner to tell him how his wife was misbehaving. Webaoner opened his chest of ebony and gold and made his preparations. He fashioned a small crocodile of wax, about fifteen centimetres long. Over it he read a spell, so that if someone bathed in the crocodile's waters the beast would seize him. Then he gave the wax crocodile to the care-taker and told him to wait until the lover had gone into the water, and then to cast the wax figure in after him. So the caretaker returned to the gardens with the wax crocodile.

'Some time later, the wife again sent to the caretaker and instructed him to clean the garden-house and to prepare it for a visit. And then she came and met her lover and they spent an agreeable day. At the end of the day, the lover left his mistress and went to the water, and the caretaker threw the wax croco-dile in. At once it grew twenty times as large, and it seized the lover and carried him under the water.

'Webaoner stayed at his duties in the royal court with Nebka, king of Upper and Lower Egypt, for seven days, and during this time the lover was held under the waters, unable to breathe. After seven days, Webaoner approached King Nebka and bowed, and invited the king to come and behold a marvel. His Majesty accompanied Webaoner, and they went across Webaoner's estates to the garden-house and the water near it. Webaoner called out to his crocodile, and summoned it to bring forth the lover, and the crocodile did so. And when he was laid on the banks, the lover breathed again. The king was frightened of the crocodile, but Webaoner spoke words over it, and again it became a figure of wax, fifteen centimetres long. Then Webaoner explained who this man was, and why he had set the crocodile to catch him, and the king said to Webaoner and to the crocodile: "He has done wrong. He is yours. Take what belongs to you."

'Webaoner placed the wax crocodile on the ground and spoke, and again it grew twentyfold and it seized the young man and carried him into the depths of the water. Later,

Webaoner had his wife burned, and her ashes were thrown into the river.

'This', said Khephren, 'was a marvel that occurred in the time of King Nebka.' Cheops decreed offerings of food and drink for his forefather and for his forefather's priest, the wise Webaoner.

Then Baufre rose to tell of a marvel that had occurred in the time of Cheops' father Snefru. One day, King Snefru was bored. He summoned Djadjaemonkh the learned priest to his chambers, and asked him to suggest a distraction. Djadjaemonkh told the king that he should go down to the lake in his gardens, and equip a boat with maidens chosen among the beautiful women of his palace to row it, and in this way he would find distraction.

So the king ordered the boat to be prepared with oars of ebony and sandal-wood. He ordered twenty women, dressed in netting, to take the oars, and boarded the boat. The royal party rowed about the lake, and the words of the learned priest were fulfilled. The king found his ennui dissolved. But one of the maidens knocked her hair with an oar, and a charm of blue stone which she had been wearing, in the shape of a fish, fell from her hair into the water. In her distress at the loss she stopped rowing. The rower behind her stopped, and then all the rowers on that side and then all the rowers entirely. When the king dreamily asked why the boat had stopped, the women all looked at one another, and finally one answered that it was because one of them had stopped and then the rest followed suit. So the king asked the maiden why she had stopped rowing, and she said, 'A blue charm shaped like a fish fell from my hair into the water, and I was distressed and so stopped rowing.' And the king told her, 'Be easy in your heart. I shall offer you another charm when we return to shore, and your loss shall be made good.' But the maiden wept, and when he asked she admitted that she would not be satisfied: she must have her own charm.

Then the king turned to the learned priest Djadjaemonkh and asked him what they should do. The priest went to the side of the boat. He recited his charms, and the waters parted, piling up on either side, and so he was able to descend to the bed of the lake, although it was twenty-four feet in depth after it had parted, and there on the lake-bottom he found the fish-shaped charm belonging to the maiden and so he returned it to her. The maiden regained her cheer, the king was pleased, and he rewarded the priest with rich things.

'Such, oh king, was a marvel that occurred in the days of your father Snefru,' said Baufre, and Cheops ordered that offerings should be made to his father and to Djadjaemonkh, and so it was done.

Then Hardedef rose, and he told King Cheops that while these marvels of the past were all very well, there was a living man named Dedi who might match them. Dedi lived in a village, eating prodigious quantities of meat and drink. Dedi, said Hardedef, could reattach a severed head and perform other wonders. So Cheops ordered Hardedef to bring Dedi to the Pharaoh's court, and Hardedef equipped a boat and set off on the river to the village of Dedi. He found the old man lying at home, tended by his servants. Descending from his sedan chair, Hardedef greeted Dedi politely and invited him to the palace of the king. Hardedef raised Dedi up with his own hands and led him to the boat, and so they embarked along with Dedi's pupils, and sailed on the river to the royal palace. When they arrived, Hardedef sent a messenger to announce his return to his father King Cheops, and to inform him that the great magician had arrived.

When they came before King Cheops, the king greeted Dedi with respect for his age and wisdom, and told him that a report had come that Dedi could reattach a severed head. And Dedi said that he could perform this action. So the king proposed that they should bring in a prisoner who had been condemned to death, as a subject for Dedi's magic, but Dedi refused, saying the magic was not to be used in this way. So they brought in a goose and chopped off its head, and then they laid the head on one side of the throne room and the carcass on another, and Dedi stood between them. He closed his eyes and muttered his spell, and the two parts of the goose came together and the head joined onto the neck, and the goose rose and cackled and waddled through the room. Then they brought him another bird, and he did the same, and then a great ox, and again he restored the ox's body and head and made it rise and walk.

Then the king asked Dedi if he could help them find the hidden chamber of Thoth, where lay the magics that would ensure the stability of his reign, and Dedi reflected for some time, lost in thought. Then Dedi answered that it would not be Cheops who uncovered the chamber of Thoth, but that would be accomplished by the three sons of Redderet. And King Cheops naturally asked who Redderet might be, and he was told that she was the wife of a priest of Ra at Sakhbu. Then King Cheops became saddened at the thought that the three sons of Redderet, not his own sons, would rule after him. But he appointed a rich living for Dedi and ordered him to be taken into the household of Hardedef.

Redderet was indeed pregnant, but when she gave birth she had a difficult labour, so that out of compassion Ra of Sakhbu ordered the birth goddesses to attend her and help her through. The goddesses, in the guise of musicians, presented themselves to Redderet's husband, but he told them he did not want music, because his wife was in labour. Then they offered their services, claiming that they had skills in birthing. So he brought them to his wife. Isis knelt before her, Nephthys stood behind, and the other two goddesses did what they could to ease the birth. The first son came out, and Isis said that he would rule the two kingdoms. The goddesses cut his umbilical cord, wrapped him and laid him aside. A second son was born in the same way. Again Isis said that he would rule the two kingdoms, and they cut his umbilical cord, wrapped him and laid him in a bed. Then a third son was born. Again Isis foretold that he would be a king and rule over the two kingdoms, and they cut his umbilical cord.

The goddesses left Redderet and told her husband that his wife was safe and that he had three sons. He gave them bags of grain as payment, so they might make beer, for he thought they were musicians and entertainers. They took the bag, but then thought to themselves that they must perform some marvel as a token that the three sons would be kings in their time. So they created three golden crowns and placed them in the bags of grain. Then they caused some rain to fall and they returned to Redderet's house to ask the husband to keep the grain dry under his roof until they returned to claim it. Then they placed their seals upon the bags and departed.

Two weeks later came a great feast day. Redderet consulted with her servants on their stores and provisions for the feast. She asked what they had to make beer, and the servants told her they had no grain except for that which the husband had given to the musicians who had helped with her childbirth. After some thought, Redderet told the servant to use that grain to make beer in preparation for the feast and they could purchase more before the musicians returned to claim their grain. So the servant broke the seal on the bags, and was amazed to hear the sound of music and singing coming from the bags, such music as is played in the Pharaoh's court to honour the ruler of the land. She reported this to Redderet, who came into the storeroom. She listened carefully in a different part of the room, but heard no music. Then she touched the bags left by the musician goddesses. The music played clearly, and Redderet realized this was a sign that her sons would be honoured as kings. She was proud and delighted and later told her husband.

But some time later, Redderet punished the serving-woman for some misdeed, and the woman swore that she would tell the king how Redderet had borne three sons who would become kings. But on her way to Pharaoh's house, she knelt down to drink at the water's edge, and a crocodile burst from the river, seized her and carried her off. She never delivered the message. So King Cheops never heard of the sons of Redderet, although in time they came to rule and established the fifth dynasty of those who ruled over Egypt.

THE TWO BROTHERS

This old story offers many elements which are to be found later and elsewhere; the false rape accusation is widespread (see Chapter 3), and so also are the motif of the heart preserved outside the body, the hair which causes the king to fall in love, and the trickster who becomes the child of his enemy. The story seems to be based on a local myth, and echoes many of the migration legends which will be found later; the fraternal bond especially is a theme in migration legends.

Anubis and Bata were brothers. After the death of their parents they lived together, and the elder, Anubis, cared for the younger Bata as would a father, feeding and clothing him. Bata in turn served his brother in the fields, ploughing, sowing and reaping or watching the cattle according to the seasons. Because he was dutiful and kindly, the cattle took to him. They would indicate to him where the best pasture was to be found or anything else they needed. Therefore the brothers' herds were the finest in the region.

Anubis had a wife, but she began to turn her eyes on her husband's brother. It was not only his kindness and gentleness with the animals, but also his strength: once, having come to fetch seed for planting he carried off five bags on his shoulders. She watched his back beneath the load as he returned to the field. One day, when she knew her husband would be absent she spoke to Bata and invited him to lie with her, promising that he would not suffer from it and she too would reward him as did her husband. But Bata was enraged by her infidelity and reproached her, and said he would speak no more of this. Then he went his way with the cattle, and avoided the house that evening.

But the wife worried that he might mention her offer to his brother, her husband, and so she practised a ruse: she smeared her face so that it appeared she had been beaten, and she ate herbs to make her stomach ill, and she lay in the dark of the house, doing nothing to prepare the evening meal. When her husband returned and found her, he was at first worried for her

health. He asked what had happened, and she said that Bata
had approached her and asked her to lie with him. When she
refused he had beaten her about the head and the body so that
she was sick.

Her story infuriated Anubis, and he determined to kill Bata.
He took his spear and waited behind the door of the cow-shed
to slay his brother when he returned. But as Bata approached
the cow-shed, driving the cattle, the leading cow turned back
and warned him that danger awaited behind the door. So he
immediately turned and ran away. Anubis followed, bran-
dishing the spear, but Bata prayed to the god of justice, and the
god made a river flow between the brothers.

The next morning, speaking across the river, Bata asked
Anubis why he had tried to kill him, although they were
brothers and Anubis stood to him as their father and mother
who had died. Anubis asked why he had tried to sleep with his
wife. Again, Bata called upon the god of justice to assure the
truth of his words, and swore that he had made no such attempt.
But Anubis did not believe his oath. Outraged that his brother
trusted his unfaithful wife over his faithful brother, Bata cut off
his penis and threw it in the water. Then he told his brother
what he intended to do, and what course of action Anubis
should take if he wished to make amends.

He went away to the Valley of Cedars and made himself a
fine house. He tended the land so that all the plants flourished
and the valley was beautiful enough to draw the gods in admiration. The god of justice suggested to Khnum the potter, who
makes the babies that are placed in women's wombs, that he
should fashion a wife for Bata who lived there alone. Khnum
agreed, and made the loveliest woman in the land to be Bata's
companion. But the seven Hathors who preside at childbirth
prophesied that she would come to a bad end.

Bata was entranced with his new companion and devoted
himself to pleasing her and making her comfortable, and he
revealed all his secrets to her: how his heart was preserved at
the top of a cedar tree and it was the secret that might control
him. He also warned her not to go near the sea, for since he
had lost his penis he had no power over the waters.

But she disobeyed him and walked on the shore. The waves tried to seize her as she fled up the beach to the trees. She escaped them, but one lock of her hair fell into the waters. The waves carried it to the home of the Pharaoh of Egypt. There by the water's edge, servants found it glistening. Because it was so fine and lovely, and because it gave off a sweet smell, the servants brought it to their supervisors, and in turn the supervisors brought the lock to the lords of the household, and they in turn brought it before Pharaoh. Pharaoh summoned his wise men, and they told him whose hair it was and where he should find her. So he sent men and chariots over the sands to fetch the woman. She came willingly, delighted at the thought of consorting with the Pharaoh of Egypt.

When Pharaoh asked about the man with whom she had lived, she made light of Bata and told Pharaoh how he might be destroyed: by cutting down the great cedar tree in whose flower he kept his heart. Pharaoh sent men to perform this task, and Bata, lying in his home mourning his lost woman, died. And Pharaoh made the woman a princess.

Anubis realized his brother had died when the tokens which Bata had foretold came about. So he travelled to the Valley of Cedars and found Bata's body. Then he sought his brother's heart among the cedars. One year he searched, and then a second, and a third, and finally in the fourth year, as he was beginning to despair and weary of this fruitless task, he came upon the fruit of the cedar and knew it was his brother's heart. So he returned to Bata's fine home, where the body still lay, and he placed the heart in a container of water and went to sleep. Overnight, the heart drank up the water and was restored to life, and the body of Bata regained its colour and his limbs moved. In the morning, Anubis found his brother's body revived, and the heart lost in the water. He gave his brother the heart's water to drink and so the heart was replaced where it should be.

Then Bata told his brother that he would become a bull, which Anubis should deliver to the Pharaoh. So Anubis did so, and was richly rewarded for the fine animal which he brought to the ruler of the land. Bata seized an occasion when his former woman came by and told her he was still alive. The princess was disturbed and went to Pharaoh, and after pleading asked him for a favour, which he was happy to grant her. She asked to be allowed to eat the liver of the bull which he had just received. Reluctantly, Pharaoh agreed, and sent men to slaughter the bull.

When they did so, two drops of the bull's blood spurted from its neck and landed on the ground on either side of Pharaoh's door, by the posts of the gate to the great house. Very quickly two great trees sprang up on either side of the door. The next morning the servants informed Pharaoh that two trees had grown up overnight by his gate. Pharaoh was very pleased and made an offering to them, since clearly this was the work of the gods.

But when the princess next passed near the trees, they whispered to her that they were Bata, whom she had twice tried to kill, as a bull and as a man. The princess was disturbed and grew fearful, worrying what the trees might do against her. When an occasion came, she again asked Pharaoh for a favour, that he would make her furniture from the wood of the great trees by his gate. Pharaoh agreed and sent craftsmen to cut down the trees and saw them into planks and pieces suitable for furniture, and the princess went to watch. As she was watching, a chip of the wood flew into her mouth, and she swallowed it unawares, and immediately she became pregnant.

A son was born to her, and after many years, when Pharaoh died, the son became Pharaoh in turn, and then he summoned his wise men and told them he had information to impart. He told them how he had been Bata, falsely accused by one woman, and three times betrayed by another, and how he had escaped her and become Pharaoh. The wise men pronounced a judgement against her and she was punished. Bata summoned Anubis, who still lived, and made him a prince to rule after him.

THE TREASURE OF RHAMPSINITUS

This story, first told by Herodotus (c. 450 BC), became wide-spread during the Middle Ages through Arabic popular literature. It is now part of world folklore. The thief offers certain affinities with trickster figures found south of the Sahara.

King Rhampsinitus had a great treasure in silver, and determined to build a storehouse in which to keep it. He summoned a master-builder and ordered him to prepare the treasury, and allotted him the men and materials for the task. The master-builder set about his work, and soon the new treasure-house was built and the king moved all his store of wealth into the new edifice.

The builder had planned for the future of his sons: at the back of the building, facing onto the street, there was a stone carefully contrived so that it could be removed and replaced with no sign of its disturbance. On his deathbed, he told his sons of his device, and left them to enjoy parts of the king's treasure. The two sons made their way to the back of the treasure-house, found the movable stone and entered the treasury; there, they filled bags with silver coins, and then escaped, replacing the stone as they had found it.

The ease with which they obtained this wealth made them profligate. Very soon, peering into their bags, they found that they needed more silver. They returned to Rhampsinitus' treasure-house and replenished their store. Some time later they again felt the need for another trip. Eventually, King Rhampsinitus was informed that some of the containers of silver in his treasure-house were unexpectedly empty. He realized that a thief must have found his way into the treasure-house. But there was no trace of the thief's passage; the seals on the door were unbroken and the guards were trusted, so he did not suspect them. He guessed there was a secret passage. He consulted his advisers, and they in turn contrived traps which they set in the treasure-house to catch the marauder.

Soon after that, the builder's two sons needed more silver

and so they returned to the treasury. They entered and filled their bags, and then one of them was caught by the trap and found himself unable to break free. Desperate, he instructed his brother to kill him and cut off his head, so he would not be recognized. Seeing no other recourse to preserve their family, the other brother obeyed. The next day, the king found a thief in the treasure-house, but it was an unidentifiable corpse. Clearly his associate had escaped.

The purpose in cutting off the head was evident: to avoid recognition, to protect the family. The king reasoned that the thief would be mourned, and so ordered the guard to march the corpse around the town, keeping alert for any undue signs of grief among the onlookers. Eventually, the grim procession passed by the builder's house, where the two brothers lived with their mother and wives. Seeing the corpse, all felt the anguish of grief and began to weep. The soldiers, hearing the sound of wailing, became suspicious. The surviving brother perceived the danger, and immediately dropped his brother's young son into the well in the courtyard, so that when the soldiers entered to investigate the wails, they found a scene of chaos as all ran back and forth to retrieve the infant. Satisfied with this explanation, the soldiers withdrew.

Rhampsinitus then ordered that the body should be exposed by the city gate, to shame the family. The mother, widow of the builder, reproached the surviving brother and demanded that he retrieve his brother's corpse. The young man loaded two donkeys with wineskins and led them out past the city gate; as he passed the guards, one donkey broke free of his lead, while wine began to pour from wineskins on each of the donkeys. The young man raced back and forth in confusion, apparently uncertain whether to try to catch the loose donkey or to stop up the pouring wine, and the soldiers, watching, laughed at his antics until he turned and began to curse them for lazy and useless good-for-nothings. Then one soldier caught a donkey, and he was able to stop the flow of wine, and the other soldiers summoned him to withdraw his curses. After some discussion, he offered them a bag of wine, which they willingly took and drank, and since that one went so fast he gave them another, and then another, until the entire party of guards lay drunk by the road. Then the thief brought down his brother's corpse, loaded it on one of the donkeys, and led the animals home.

Growing desperate to catch the thief, the king ordered his daughter to assist him with a new trap: she would go down to a public house and offer herself to whichever man told her of the cleverest and most wicked thing he had done; when the thief came (as the king was sure he would), she would seize him and summon the guards who would be waiting nearby. The news of this challenge was spread around the town, and of course the young thief heard of it and decided to take it up. But he made his preparations before he went to see the princess.

He was admitted in due course, and sat for a while telling her how he had robbed the treasure and rescued his brother's body, and the princess realized that he was the man her father sought. She seized his arm and cried out for the guards, but he pulled away: it was not his arm she held, but the arm of a corpse he had taken from the graveyard. So he escaped again.

Rhampsinitus was so impressed by such ingenuity that he announced a pardon for the thief: these were talents he wished to have in his service, and their worth outweighed the crimes that had been committed. So the young man came forth and was rewarded with a post in the king's court, and also married the princess.

ETHIOPIA

*Ethiopia was the home of ancient cultures such as Axum and
Meroe, contemporary with Pharaonic Egypt. It was also closely
linked with the cultures of South Arabia, Yemen and Sa'ba,
lying across the Red Sea as it narrows. The introduction of
Christianity, in the first centuries AD, gave Ethiopia a new
identity, visible in the legend of origin of the Solomonid dynasty
which claims continuity from the time of Solomon, through
Solomon and the Queen of Sheba, to the present. This legend
is recorded in the* Kebra Negast, *the 'Glory of Kings', which
recounts the origin of the dynasty. The book was most probably
composed in the Middle Ages, after 1200, at a time when
Christian Ethiopia was being forced to fight against Muslim
challengers (such as Mohammed Gragn in Chapter 22). This
section also includes some stories from non-Amharic subjects
of the kingdom of Ethiopia which were recorded early in the
twentieth century.*

SOLOMON AND THE QUEEN
OF SHEBA

A very long time ago, the land of Ethiopia lay under the oppressive rule of a serpent which exacted sacrifices and tribute from
the people. A man came from another land and lived with the
people. He saw their plight, and he determined to end the rule
of the serpent. He killed a goat, slit open its stomach, and
stuffed the carcass with poisonous herbs. Then he sewed up the

carcass and offered the slaughtered goat to the great serpent. The serpent devoured it, fell into a torpor, and died. The people made the man king, since he had delivered them from the serpent, and he married. His only child was a daughter, Makeda, and on his death the people made her queen. She became the celebrated queen of Sheba.

At that time, which was also the time of the glory of Solomon, there was great trade across the Red Sea and merchants came from the land of Sheba to Jerusalem. These merchants admired the glory of the city and the wisdom and prudence of Solomon, and they took the report of his accomplishments back to their land. Makeda, the queen of Sheba, ruled alone and had not married.

Those reports of the glories of Solomon's reign intrigued the queen of Sheba, and she determined to visit him. She ordered ships loaded with the wealth of her lands, to offer as gifts to the great king, and with a great retinue she travelled to Jerusalem. While they were there, Solomon instructed her in his faith and his belief in the one true God, and convinced her of the truth of his words, so that she took him as her teacher.

After a time, she determined to return to her home, and the heart of Solomon sank, for he was a great lover of women and she was beautiful among all women, dark and comely. So he offered her a banquet, in which the different courses were heavily spiced or flavoured with vinegar, but there was nothing to drink. Then it was agreed that they should sleep in the same room, but she asked him to swear that he would not take her by force, while he made her swear that she would take nothing of his by force. And so both lay down in their beds, and Solomon pretended to fall asleep.

In the middle of the room was a table, and on it a bowl with clear water. Makeda could not sleep, because of the thirst that was on her from the spicy foods, and when she thought Solomon was asleep she rose to drink from the bowl. But he was awake and watchful, and he also rose and reminded her of her oath. She asked him to release her from the oath, so she could drink, and he agreed on condition she release him from his oath. After she had drunk they lay together and he knew her.

That night, Solomon dreamed of a sun that shone bright over his land, but then departed and shone over the lands of the Nile and the land of Sheba, while another sun arose of the people of Judah in Israel, but the people of Israel mistreated it and killed it and held it of no account, although it rose from the tomb and brightened the whole world, especially Ethiopia and Rome.

In the morning, Solomon gave a ring to the queen of Sheba, saying that if she should carry his seed and it should prove a boy, she should send the child to him with the ring as token. The queen returned to her own land.

Her son was born and grew up and asked about his father, and she replied that she was his mother and his father, and twice he was satisfied with this answer. But the third time he did not accept it, and so she told him the truth and he set off for Jerusalem to see his father.

When Bayna Lekhem came to Gaza with the merchants, the people of Gaza wondered to see a man so like to their king, and the word of this marvel travelled throughout the land and reached Jerusalem and the ears of Solomon. Solomon called the captain of the guard and ordered him to bring this young man to him. Bayna Lekhem came and stood before Solomon in the presence of the nobles, and Solomon admired him and said he resembled not Solomon, but his father David in the days of his youth. And when Bayna Lekhem offered the ring as a token of his birth, Solomon put it aside for he had already acknowledged the son beyond possible doubt, such was the resemblance between them.

After a time, Bayna Lekhem asked of his father that he should be allowed to return to his homeland with the command that hereafter women should no longer rule, but men should rule instead. Solomon hesitated, for he wished to make Bayna Lekhem his heir, but Bayna Lekhem answered that Solomon already had a son born of his wife, but that Solomon and his mother had not married properly. Solomon answered that his own father David had not properly married his mother Bathsheba, but at length he consented. It was Bayna Lekhem who had craftsmen create a duplicate of the Ark of the Covenant, and he stole the true Ark, leaving the duplicate, and brought it into Ethiopia where it still remains. Solomon discovered the substitution and pursued Bayna Lekhem, but his army turned back when they were told that people had seen Bayna Lekhem and his people travelling at an extraordinary pace, and that their feet and the wheels of their carts did not touch the ground.

THE SEPARATION OF THE DARASSA
AND THE JAM-JAMO

This story is a clan-legend, collected at the start of the twentieth century. The Darassa and the Jam-Jamo were subject to the government of Ethiopia; the Guji were their neighbours within the same administrative district in the south-west part of the kingdom.

The Jam-Jamo were ruled by a king named Uraga who had imposed tribute on their neighbours, the Darassa and the Guji. He was hated for his severity. At that time, the Darassa had no money or livestock with which to pay the tribute, and so they were forced to give Uraga slaves: a young man and a young woman, each year. If they failed in their tribute, Uraga would make war on them. From fear of his army, the Darassa made no settled houses, but lived in trees and came down at night to drink.

There was division among the Darassa. Some leaders wished to resist Uraga, others feared war and argued against it. After a time, the leaders calling for resistance won the day; they began to withhold the tribute they had paid until that time. Uraga brought his army into the land of the Darassa and called a parley; he asked why they had not paid the tribute, and they replied that their children were too dear to them, and that they wished only for each side to live as they wished. They did not want war, and they were tired of living in trees. But Uraga was not persuaded. A conflict began, and the Darassa were victorious.

The leader of the Darassa travelled into the land of the

Jam-Jamo, who had suffered from the war, and came across a great pool of blood. He asked what this pool was, and he was told that it was the blood of Uraga. Then the Jam-Jamo asked him to intercede with the other Darassa leaders to bring about peace. 'For a time, we were in power,' they said, 'and now you have the upper hand. But these are the fortunes of war. Let us put our enmity behind us.' The leader agreed, but later word came to the Darassa that some among the Jam-Jamo were planning to renew the war. So they marched into the territory of the Jam-Jamo and drove many of them south, where that fraction of the people took the name of Uraga Jam-Jamo.

HOW RULE PASSED FROM WOMEN
TO MEN

This is a story of the Darassa, collected in the 1930s by European researchers.

In the early days of the Darassa, there were very few women, and so the men were forced to do all the household tasks: they fetched the firewood and drew the water and minded the gardens, work which is now done by women. The rulers were women, the officials were women.

Ako Manoya is the name of the woman who was the last queen among the Darassa. She had named no heir apparent from her followers at the time, although she was childless. She governed alone, giving orders to the officials and hearing their reports and inspecting their works. During this time, the men were beginning to grumble about their tasks and the way in which they were forced to serve the women. The leader of the men was married; he had a beautiful wife. But he also had a mistress, and the mistress revealed his sedition to the queen. The queen summoned the wife and told her that she knew how her husband was subverting the men and plotting against her rule.

'He must die,' said Ako Manoya. 'How he dies is your choice.

If you bring me his head, I shall make you my heir and you shall rule after me.'

That night, the wife served a big meal to her husband, so that he fell asleep after dinner. Then she took a knife from the kitchen and cut his throat, and when he was dead she cut off his head. She took the head to the queen in the morning, and was named the heir apparent to the realm.

The loss of their leader disheartened the men for a time, but then they reorganized. They decided that the queen must die, and they selected the time, place and means. The queen would have to leave the town for a festival, they knew, and so they dug a pit along the road, a deadfall trap. They covered the pit with branches and leaves, and then over the leaves they strewed earth and clay. When the day came and the queen left the town, the men crowded about her on the road so that she was forced to walk over the pit, and she fell in.

Furious, she pronounced her last words: she would be the last queen of the land. Then the men buried her in the pit. They also wished to stone the heir, the young wife, but she climbed into a tree and clung to it, and so instead they killed her with spears. Since that time, men have ruled.

PEOPLES OF THE UPPER
NILE AND EAST AFRICA

*South of the Ethiopian mountains and north of Lake Victoria
is a region of savannahs bounded by desert, crossed in the west
by the Nile, which also forms the sudd, a great flooded plain
and swamp that is the home of cattle-herding populations such
as the Shilluk, the Dinka and the Nuer, and their neighbours,
the Luo. To the south are groups belonging to the Bantu language family: the Gikuyu and the Swahili in Kenya, the kingdoms of the lakes in Uganda (see Chapters 27–9). This region
is where a number of migrating groups came into contact with
each other. All the language families of Africa are represented
here; here the Bantu-speakers of eastern Africa acquired cattle
before beginning their migration south along the Rift Valley. It
has never been unified (and Somalia today remains completely
anarchic) or marked by powerful kingdoms.*

THE OROMO OF SOUTHERN ETHIOPIA

The Oromo are a group of peoples, linked by language and institutions such as the age-grade system, in the southern regions of Ethiopia, western Somalia and northern Kenya. Through much of their history, they were dominated by their northern neighbours, the Amhara of Ethiopia, but they formed some small kingdoms in their territories. However, they were never unified as a people; their many lineage divisions were more important than any of the political units. Their current emergence and national spirit is a response to modern political conditions. They have also been called the Galla (perhaps from gada, the word for their age-grade system), but that term is seen as pejorative. The stories in this chapter were all collected in the early twentieth century by European researchers.

THE FIRST HUMANS

A man fell from the sky down to earth. As he wandered over the empty land, he came across footprints very like his own, and he followed them until he met another human. The other human looked very much like him, but there were differences: he had a penis growing from his finger, and the other human did not. She had a vagina placed under her right arm. They walked on together until night fell, and then they lay down next to each other. They caressed each other, and he moved his hand under her arm, so that the penis entered the vagina. They found this very agreeable and determined to remain together.

The woman became pregnant. Her body swelled up, and at

first she worried what disease might be afflicting her. But she could find no remedy for her condition. One day, when the swelling had become so great that she thought she could no longer bear it, she felt movement and something began to emerge from her vagina. It was a small human, and it was followed by eight others. (The woman at some point became embarrassed at the placement of her vagina under her arm, where all eyes could see it, and besought Waqa the sky-god to move it; he placed it in her groin, and then moved the man's organ to match it. It is not said whether this happened before or after she first gave birth.)

The nine children were divided into five boys and four girls. When they grew older, four of the brothers married the four girls; the oldest son, however, had no mate and had to wait until one of his nieces grew old enough for him to marry.

One day, while their father was asleep, his covering slipped off his body, revealing his private parts and his legs. One of the sons laughed at this, another closed his eyes, another turned away his head, and a fourth ran away, never to return. Only the eldest, who was devoted to his father, went up and pulled the covering back over his legs and body. The eldest was in the habit of bringing his father a bundle of firewood each day, for as the man had become old he needed the warmth of the fire in the evenings.

As the father felt his death approaching, he decided it was time to pass on to his preferred son, the eldest, the knowledge which Waqa had given to him when he came down from the sky. So he told the eldest to come to him the next day. But the youngest son, the one who had laughed at him, overheard his instructions. The next morning he came bearing a bundle of wood, as his brother always did, and convinced the dim-sighted old man that it was indeed the eldest son there. So the father allotted to him his destiny: he would be richer than the others, he would dress in white, and he would rule over the others. The youngest son then slipped away to the waters and began to swim away. In the meantime, the eldest son returned and learned of the trick which had deprived him of the inheritance his father had intended for him. But the father reassured him: there was still something he might receive, and the father bestowed upon him the riches of the earth, crops and cattle, and promised him many wives. The son tried to call back the youngest brother, who was by then far across the waters, but he would not return.

The youngest son, who had crossed the water, became the ancestor of Arabs and Europeans. The eldest became the ancestor of Oromo groups such as the Konso and the Borana. The second son became the ancestor of the Gabra, a group who has camels and do not practise Islam. The third became the ancestor of the Muslims. The fourth, the one who had run away, became the ancestor of the Shangalla.

THE ADAMITES OF THE KINGDOM
OF GUMA

The kingdom of Guma arose at the start of the nineteenth century, one of a cluster of small kingdoms in a region known as Gibe. This story was recounted by Loransiyos Walda Iyasus in the early years of the twentieth century; the teller warned that such traditions of the Oromo kingdoms of southern Ethiopia were being lost, as the conquest by the Amhara had effaced the importance of such chronicles and the old men who knew them were dying out. The story itself, however, is older than the kingdoms of Ethiopia; it recalls the Epic of Gilgamesh, and serves as evidence for the long-standing connections between the cultures of Ethiopia and those of southern Arabia.

The line of the Dagoye ruled Guma, until the time of King Sarbo. In his days, some hunters of the royal court went out into the woods that lay at the edge of their lands, and there they witnessed amazing deeds performed by a man whose name was Adam. Adam lived among the buffaloes that wandered in the woods; he drank from their milk and ate of their flesh, and he lived in a cave whose entrance he blocked with a huge stone. He was so mighty that the first hunters fled at the sight of him.

They sent a master hunter to observe this man and see how he lived.

The master hunter went out and spent several days concealed in the woods, watching the behaviour of this wild man. Then he came back and made his report. The wild man, he said, lived from the buffalo. He would follow the buffalo, and then seize one and throw it to the ground, and then he would slay it with a knife. He carried the carcass easily back to his cave, rolling aside the great boulder with one hand, and then he ate the entire buffalo, save for the entrails, the head and the horns.

The master hunter was led before the king, who questioned him. The king found this story hard to believe, and so he sent other men out to observe the wild man, promising that if the story was true the master hunter would receive a rich reward; otherwise, he would be killed as a liar. The hunter led a party of twelve men into the woods. As soon as the men saw Adam, they fled in fear, but after a time they thought of the report they would give the king, and so they turned back again to stay watching Adam. So they were able to see Adam come out for his daily hunt; they saw him seize a buffalo and easily slay it; they watched him devour it, leaving only the head and horns and the entrails. They saw him catch a mother buffalo, followed by a calf; he tethered its legs with vines and then drank from its milk until he was satisfied. Then he released the mother buffalo with her calf. They saw him roll aside the boulder and enter the cave to sleep.

They returned and reported to the king what they had seen. Sarbo gathered his warriors and went out to seize this wild man. This time, they found the man milking an elephant cow, and they were aghast. They waited until he had retired for the night, and attempted to roll aside the boulder from his cave. They could not. So the king ordered them to return.

On his return, one of the princesses of the royal house came before him and told him that she would be able to bring the wild man back to the court. The king questioned her; she answered only that she would find a way. She asked for food and fire, and for guards to watch her and protect her from the beasts, and promised that within seven days she would return with the wild man.

The guards accompanied her into the woods, and then they hid. She sat near the boulder which blocked Adam's cave, until he returned with a buffalo on his shoulder.

'What is this I smell?' he asked.

'It is the smell of man,' she answered, and he went into the cave. He devoured the buffalo he was carrying and then went to sleep. The next day he went out again, and seized a buffalo in the woods and devoured it. Then he came back and seized the woman and lay with her.

In the morning he went out. The big buffalo were too fast for him; he was only able to seize a small one. He ate it and then returned. This time, he brought the woman into his cave and spent the night with her there.

The next morning, he could not catch a buffalo at all. All he caught was an antelope. Now he was finding it difficult to move the boulder that blocked his cave, and he was forced to leave it ajar. After another night with the woman, he could only catch a gazelle, and of that he ate only half. The woman talked with the guards and told them to come the next morning; they would be able to capture the man at that time.

They did so, and brought the man bound before the king. The king gave him a house in the town, and he took the princess of the Dagoye as his wife. He acquired the weapons of a warrior and followers, and after a time he came to King Sarbo and challenged him to battle. In the battle, King Sarbo was slain, and so the people agreed to be ruled by Adam.

It is said that Adam made the people of the kingdom of Guma convert to Islam.

THE STORY OF MOHAMMED GRAGN

This story is not necessarily a tradition of origin, as Ahmed Gragn was a historical figure: the leader of the Muslim Oromo attack on the Christian empire of Ethiopia in the early sixteenth century. But the elements presented in this shortened version

*are not historical and one might compare Mohammed Gragn
with other heroes such as Liyongo (Chapter 26).*

The empire of Ethiopia was strong, and peoples beyond its
borders were forced to pay it tribute. It happened that a young
Muslim woman from Harrar was sent with the cattle that her
father owed in tribute, because he himself had fallen sick
and was unable to make the voyage. When she came into the
Ethiopian territory, she delivered the cattle to the king's representative, and the tally was noted by a young priest. The
priest was struck by the beauty of the young woman, and she
too found him extremely attractive; that night they met and
spent the night in passion. The priest left her before the dawn
light, but instead of his white headcloth, he put her blue shawl
over his hair. He appeared in the church, and was immediately
denounced. He refused to admit where he had been and why
he happened to have a Muslim woman's scarf upon his head,
but the church leaders felt that it was clear he had been consorting with a woman of the enemy faith and he was stoned to
death.

The woman returned to her home, and some time later gave
birth to a son, Mohammed Gragn. He grew at an extraordinary
pace, and in less than two months was fully grown. He tested
his strength by wrapping his arms around a tree and uprooting
it; in his hands, the tree changed into a heavy sword. So armed,
he began his war against the Amhara. He was immediately
successful, and men flocked to join him. The king of Ethiopia
sent a messenger to him, asking why he was making war upon
the Amhara and who he was. The answer he got was a riddle:
'Fearless as my father, cunning as my mother!'

Trying to understand these words, the king sent for his steward. The steward was married to one of the most beautiful
women in the country. He told the steward that he would give
him half the kingdom if he brought him, the king, the head of
his wife. But that night, as the steward gazed upon his beautiful
wife in her sleep, he could not bring himself to do the deed.
The next day, the king summoned the wife and made her the
same offer. The next morning, the wife appeared, with her

husband's head in a basket. Her reward was less than had been promised: the king ordered her buried alive. He began to fear his enemy, who combined the fearlessness of a man with the cunning of a woman.

But it was a woman who brought down Mohammed Gragn, after he had overrun several provinces of Ethiopia. He married a princess of Gondar, and she arranged for him to bathe in some hot springs. There he was ambushed by warriors of Gondar and killed.

23

THE SHILLUK OF
SOUTHERN SUDAN

*The Shilluk live along the upper Nile, in the modern republic
of Sudan. It is a flat and wet region subject to seasonal flooding.
They share the pastures with their neighbours, the Nuer and
the Dinka, and their livelihood comes from herding (cattle,
goats and sheep) and agriculture. The Shilluk formed a kingdom, and the ruler was in theory descended from their hero
Nyikang, but in the nineteenth century that kingdom was practically destroyed by slave-raiding expeditions led by the northern Arabs. The Shilluk form of 'divine kingship' attracted early
ethnographers who were interested in the theoretical question
and also in possible connections with the royal institutions of
Egypt, but the notion has not stood up over time. The Shilluk
language belongs to the Nilo-Saharan family, while Coptic is
part of the Afro-Asiatic family. This retelling of the story of
Nyikang is based on accounts collected in the early twentieth
century by researchers and missionaries.*

Jouk the creator made a great white cow which emerged from
the waters of the Nile and then gave birth to human children,
of whom the last was Okwa. Okwa once saw two maidens
come out of the water on the riverbank and desired them. They
had beautiful long hair like humans, but in the bottom half of
their bodies they were crocodiles. Okwa tried to approach them,
but they escaped. After several attempts he caught them. They
called to their father, who emerged from the water. Their father
was human on the left side and crocodile-shaped on the right.
After some discussion he agreed to give his daughters to Okwa.
　The elder was Nyakay, and she gave birth to Nyikang and

several other children, a boy and three girls. The younger, Ungwad, gave birth to a son named Ju. And by a later marriage Okwa fathered Duwat.

Nyikang and Duwat were the principal contenders for rule when Okwa died. After a fierce struggle Nyikang and his siblings left the country. As they left, Duwat threw a digging stick at Nyikang, and told him to use it to bury his people. Nyikang went south along the river, and there Nyikang found a wife, by whom he had a son named Dak. There also he made himself a kingdom. He made humans out of the crocodiles and hippopotamuses. When the new people had produced children, he caused the parents, the transformed animals, to die, so that the secret of their origins would remain hidden. At that time humans and crocodiles were friends, since they were relations through marriage; children would climb on a basking crocodile and all would call her familiarly 'my grandmother'. But one day Nyikang's son Dak killed the offspring of the crocodile, and then he roasted and ate them. When the crocodiles went looking for their offspring, Dak said he had cooked them. Then Nyakay's mother complained to Nyakay that her human offspring had killed their crocodile cousins. From that time it comes that crocodiles remain in the water and kill humans when they try to cross the river or when they come to drink, and humans will kill crocodiles when they find them outside the water. Nyakay resumed her crocodile form and returned to the waters; she has not died. Humans do not make offerings to her; she takes what she wants.

Dak made other enemies in Nyikang's new kingdom. He competed with his cousin Dim. Dim hid fire away, so people could not cook; Dak retaliated by making all the people blind. Then Dim succeeded in holding back the rain. Dak make Dim's cattle blind until the rains fell again on his field: thus he made enemies of his uncles. Fearing what would happen if Dak ruled after Nyikang, the uncles plotted to kill Dak during a dance ceremony. Nyikang was informed of the plot and made a wooden figurine representing Dak, and Dak placed some of his possessions about it. The uncles came, stabbed the figurine, and ran off. Nyikang mourned the death of his son and engaged in all the appropriate customs: for four days all the people of the village stayed inside, and then they gathered to end the mourning by singing and dancing. When the uncles came out, Dak reappeared and the uncles ran off in terror.

Nyikang moved to another land, and settled. In one place, he came against the sudd, the great swamp of the Nile, where the passage was blocked. But an albino man offered himself as a sacrifice. Nyikang speared him, the sudd broke up, and they were able to pass through. Every time he settled in a new place he would sacrifice a calf. Eventually Nyikang's cow decided to run away; she did not want to keep losing her offspring. She left Nyikang's territory and came to the land of the sun and joined the herds of the cattle of the Sun. Nyikang sent Ojul the hawk to find his cow, and Ojul found her among the cattle of the Sun. But when he asked Garo, son of the Sun, about Nyikang's cow, Garo denied that there were any strange cows among his herds. So Ojul returned to Nyikang and told him what he had found, and Nyikang sent his son Dak with an army to retrieve the cow.

Dak came against Garo; Garo was very tall and wore heavy silver bracelets. Dak defeated Garo and took the bracelets. But the army of the Sun rallied and defeated Dak and his men; they lay on the field. Nyikang came himself to the battle; he struck the Sun with an adze, so that it was wounded and fled into the sky. Then Nyikang sprinkled water over the dead and touched them with the silver bracelets, and they came back to life. Then Dak and the other men drove the herds of cattle back to the Shilluk country.

After Nyikang, Dak ruled in the Shilluk country, and then other kings. The lineage of Nyikang is still of importance in the annual movements of the cattle from one pasturage to another, because the cattle must get across the river and are then in danger from the crocodiles. But the descendants of Nyikang maintain a kinship with the crocodiles, and so they will intercede to allow the herds safe passage.

THE LUO OF SUDAN
AND UGANDA

*The term 'Luo' or 'Lwoo' covers a number of groups who are
the southern extension of the Nilotic (or Nilo-Saharan) family
of languages; the groups are found in the southern Sudan, and
northern Uganda and Kenya, where they interacted with other
populations to help form the rich cultures of this fertile area.
The Luo contribution seems to have been principally cattle, a
form of subsistence which they share with the northern groups
such as the Shilluk, the Nuer and the Dinka. Luo lineages
took over the kingship in Bunyoro (forming the Bito dynasty).
Elsewhere, however, the groups do not seem to have formed
centralized states. The stories are retold from versions collected
in the twentieth century by missionaries and by a Ugandan
scholar.*

THE ORIGIN OF DEATH

When humans went down to the earth and spread out in their
various livelihoods, Death began his work among them and
they died all over. Nsasaye, looking down from the sky, took
pity on them and sent down a message that if they would
furnish him with a sacrificial offering of pure white fat, he
would stop the ravages of death.

As by then all the people had lost a loved one to Death, they
quickly agreed to accept the terms of Nsasaye's offer. They
chose the fattest ram and cut it up; they carefully cut out the
rich fat from the haunches and the tail and wrapped them
carefully in leaves and the hide so that they would stay clean.

Then they contrived a great pole which stretched from the earth up into the sky, and they selected a messenger to climb the pole: the chameleon.

On the way up the pole, however, the chameleon's feet broke open the package as it swung from its strap on his shoulders, and the feet also soiled the fat. So when it presented the offering to Nsasaye, Nsasaye saw only a bruised and sullied packet of dirty fat. Outraged, he decreed that death would continue to afflict humans.

THE SPEAR AND THE BEAD

This story appears to be the central myth of origin of the Luo peoples, explaining their division and distribution, and numerous versions have been collected. The story also appears in clan legends of the Baganda.

The woman Nyilak became pregnant and gave birth eventually to three sons: Nyabongo, Gipir and Gifol. She lived with her husband and her sons, and they grew up. Nyabongo eventually went off to other parts; he passed into Bunyoro and established the Bito dynasty there. Gipir and Gifol stayed with their mother, herding cattle and raising vegetables and millet on the floodplains.

At that time, Gifol possessed an ornate spear which was used in rituals and which he considered a sign of his chieftainship. He would often leave the spear in front of his house while he was off working in the fields or with his cattle. One day, an elephant approached the gardens and broke through the hedge of euphorbia bushes and then began to eat the crops. Gipir heard the noise and raced to drive the elephant off; on the way, he seized a spear and when he came to the garden he drove the spear into the elephant, heedless of the danger to himself. In agony from the wound, the elephant turned away and rushed out of the garden and into the bush, and it took with it the spear, still driven into its flesh.

Then Gipir realized that he had used Gifol's spear. When

Gifol returned and learned what had happened, he was furious. Gipir offered to purchase a new spear, at any price: he would give all his cattle, he would hunt and bring skins and tusks. But Gifol was insistent: he must return Gifol's own spear, for no other would do. They argued for several days, but there was no resolution; Gifol would not accept any substitute or any excuses for the loss of his spear.

Finally, Gipir went off, following the elephant's track into the bush. He took some food and water, for he knew the elephant might have gone far, no matter how serious the wound in its side. He travelled for days, avoiding the lions and packs of hyenas, and finally came into a thick forest which was the secret home of the elephants. He did not have much food left by then. But at the edge of the forest he found a small hut, and in the hut an old woman, ugly and deformed, who sat over a cold hearth and an empty pot. She raised her head as he approached, but from the movements of her eyes he could tell that she was almost blind and did not really know where to look for him.

'Hello, mother,' he greeted her. 'I can see you are hungry, and I need some shelter for the night. Will you let me stay in the hut tonight? In exchange, I will share with you what food I have brought.'

She wheezed an agreement, and so he fetched some firewood and built up the fire; then he cooked all his remaining food and gave a generous portion to her. They each ate, and then they retired to sleep in different parts of the hut.

In the morning, the old woman looked dimly at her guest. 'Tell me why you have come here,' she ordered, and so Gipir explained how an elephant had raided their garden and he had driven it off with the first spear that came to hand, and how his brother was insisting that he must have that very spear back. The old woman listened to the story, and then told Gipir what he might expect in the forest. She made him promise that he would return to her when he had finished.

He made his way under the great trees. Soon, he met an elephant and the elephant asked him what he was doing there in the elephants' forest. He explained that he had lost a spear and had come to fetch it. The elephant asked some questions about how the spear had been lost, and then agreed that they might have it there in the forest. He led Gipir further under the trees, and they came to an open space where the ground was covered with spears lying about.

'Here,' said the elephant. 'If we have your brother's spear, it will be in this place.' Gipir began to look through them, amazed at the number and variety of spears. All had been thrust at elephants; all had been carried off. Some were rusty with blood and age; some were long and thin, while others were wide-bladed. Finally, treading delicately through the pile of weapons and ever conscious of onlooking elephants, Gipir found Gifol's spear which he could recognize by the shape of the blade and the ornamentation that had made Gifol so proud.

'This is my brother's spear,' he said to his guide, and they made their way back to the edge of the forest. There he found the hut of the old woman again; to his surprise, the elephant who accompanied him bowed down to her and called her 'Mother of Elephants', and reported that their visitor had found what he sought.

'It is well,' said the old woman, and she waved at the elephant, although she still seemed not to be able to see where it was. 'And for you, stranger, I have another gift,' she said, and she pointed Gipir to a small bag which lay on the ground. When he opened it he found it contained a collection of marvellous beads of all sizes and colours and designs, beads such as had never been seen before in their land, beads which surpassed all the ornaments of all the women he knew. He thanked her warmly for the gift and then made his way home.

It was very satisfying to return Gifol's spear to him; it was also rewarding to show the precious beads to his wife and see her amazement and delight, and then the pride she felt at the thought that she would now be able to wear jewels that had no equal.

A few days later, Gifol's wife came with her infant son to see Gipir's wife and admire the beads. Gipir's wife had sorted them into several small calabashes, and she spread them out before Gifol's wife so she could appreciate the variety of beads her husband had brought. The baby also was entranced with the bowls and crawled up to see them. Then, while the women were distracted discussing a possible design, the baby picked up one lovely bead and put it into his mouth. Before his mother could remove it, he had swallowed the bead. Highly embarrassed, Gifol's wife took him home, leaving Gipir's wife to tell her husband how one of the beads had been lost.

Gipir was furious. He marched over to his brother's compound and demanded the immediate return of the bead which had been given to him by the Mother of Elephants. Gifol asked him to understand that it was only a small child, that no harm had been meant, and that he would pay any amount of cattle or other wealth to make up for the loss of the bead. But Gipir was insistent: Gifol must return Gipir's own bead immediately, and no substitute would be acceptable.

'Give me a bit of time,' said Gifol. 'If the child ate the bead, it must pass through and we can return it in due course.' At length, Gipir agreed to allow them three days. During those three days, Gifol summoned a medicine man who administered purgatives and emetics, and they carefully examined the child's stools, soaking them in water and searching for the bead. But it did not emerge. At the end of the third day, there was no other choice: they killed the baby and opened its stomach, looking for the bead. They found it, washed it off, and returned it to Gipir.

After that there was no peace in the land. Eventually, the brothers agreed that they should separate. Gipir led his followers to the Nile at a place called Wang-wat-Lei and he told Gifol that they would cross there and take the lands on the other side, leaving Gifol the lands on the east of the Nile. Gipir then prayed, and the waters of the Nile parted. They marched across the river-bed, and in the middle Gifol and Gipir together drove an axe into the ground to mark the division of their lands.

A SHRINE OF BAKA AND ALELA

*This story is associated with a shrine, but is actually an expla-
nation of how a particular lineage became the guardians of the
shrine rather than a myth of the shrine's origin.*

Two brothers, Atiko and Weli, lived near each other, each
with his own household. Atiko's wife became pregnant, and
eventually gave birth. But instead of human babies, she gave
birth to two lion cubs. Weli was most disturbed by this, for he
considered it unnatural, and when Atiko asked him to provide
a sheep to be sacrificed to commemorate the birth of his
nephews, Weli refused. Atiko had to go out to find his own
sacrifice before it was too late, and the only thing he caught
was a grasshopper.

The two lions grew up and spent a great deal of time in the
bush, hunting animals. They always brought large carcasses to
their parents, and so Atiko had a rich store of meat which
he shared with his followers, and they naturally increased in
number. However, things did not go so well for Weli, and
eventually he became so poor that he had to go and ask his
brother for some meat. The two lions had just left Atiko the
carcass of a duiker (a very small antelope), and Weli asked
Atiko if he might have a small portion of the meat.

Atiko refused. He reminded Weli how he had refused to
provide a sacrificial animal for the birth of his nephews, so that
Atiko had been forced to honour them with a grasshopper.
Atiko would not share the meat, brought by those sons, with
the brother who had not fulfilled his own obligations.

Weli eventually left the country. Atiko became ever more
prosperous. He and his sons and followers travelled, and came
eventually to the village of Pakwaca, where there was the shrine
of Baka and Alela, which were the names of two hills nearby.
There the meat they provided made him so popular that the
people overthrew the old chief and chose Atiko to rule over
them and he became the guardian of the shrine.

THE GIKUYU OF KENYA

The Gikuyu are a Bantu-language family group living east of Lake Victoria; they apparently moved there from the north-east, where they were in contact with Luo and Galla groups with whom they shared some social institutions such as age-grades. The Gikuyu are essentially agriculturalists, although they also keep sheep and goats; typically, homesteads are placed along ridges and farming is done in the valleys below. They now constitute the politically dominant group in modern Kenya largely because of their numbers; in pre-colonial times they were not organized into larger polities. This retelling is based on versions collected in the first third of the twentieth century, most notably by Jomo Kenyatta who much later became the first president of independent Kenya.

At the beginning, the Mogai established the world and divided it up. He set Mount Kenya as a place for him to rest while visiting the world, and as a sign of his works. He created a man named Gikuyu, and he brought Gikuyu to the top of the mountain and showed him the lands about the mountain and how beautiful they were. He pointed out to Gikuyu a grove of fig trees, and told him that he should settle there when he came down from the mountain. And he told him that in times of need he should sacrifice and look towards the mountain.

When he descended, Gikuyu found that the Mogai had created a woman for him. Her name was Mumbi. The two of them set up their household and lived well together. They had many children: nine daughters. Gikuyu was disturbed at the absence of sons, and so he turned to the Mogai and the Mogai

answered him, prescribing a sacrifice: Gikuyu should take a
lamb and a kid from his flocks and sacrifice them at the great
fig tree in the grove near his homestead. The blood and the fat
of the animals should be smeared on the tree; the meat should
be burned as an offering to the Mogai. So Gikuyu took his wife
and daughters and performed the sacrifice, and then they lit a
large fire and made the offering to the Mogai. Then Gikuyu
and his family returned to their home. Later, as the Mogai had
instructed him, Gikuyu returned to the tree, and there he found
nine young men.

He brought the young men home, and they were greeted as
is proper: a ram was killed to provide meat, and the young men
were taken to the water where they could wash. All ate the meal
together and the night passed quietly. In the morning Gikuyu
talked to the young men about marrying his daughters, and he
insisted that they might marry only if the young men agreed to
live at his homestead and to be ruled by their wives. The young
men accepted his conditions. The daughters also were happy to
be married, as they had come of age, so the ceremonies took
place and each couple established their dwelling around the
homestead of Gikuyu. They took the collective name of Mbari
ya Mumbi (the Family of Mumbi) in honour of the mother.

Time passed and the generations multiplied. Gikuyu and
Mumbi died, leaving behind many grandchildren and great-
grandchildren. As the people multiplied, they found they could
not all belong to the same group, and so they divided the
people, descendants of Mumbi, according to her daughters and
established nine clans or descent groups. The women, through
whom descent was traced, continued to rule.

It is said, however, that their rule became oppressive and
unjust. They fought unnecessary wars, and they were not content with a single husband, although they would execute men
for committing adultery. The men were continually humiliated,
and they became indignant and plotted a rebellion against the
women. But this would not be easy, because at that time the
women were stronger than men, and they were more skilled
with weapons of war. So, on reflection, the men decided their
revolt could succeed only if the women were all pregnant. They

set a time in which to concentrate their efforts, and then they
launched their campaign, doing all they could to please the
women and to bring them to their beds, and the women were
pleased with the attentions and agreed, not realizing that this
was the men's plan.

The men then waited for six or seven months, to see the
results of their first efforts, and they were not disappointed:
most of the women were pregnant, immobilized by the advanced
stage of their condition. And so the men revolted, and the women
could not resist. The men became the heads of families, and
polyandry gave way to the new system of polygamy in which
one husband had several wives.

The men also tried to change the names: they renamed the
Mbari ya Mumbi and called themselves the Mbari ya Gikuyu.
But when they wished also to change the names of the descent
groups taken from the nine daughters of Mumbi, the women
refused. The women told the men that if the names of the first
mothers were removed, they would refuse to bear any more
children. Cowed by the protest, the men agreed. So the nine
clan names perpetuate the memory of the daughters of Mumbi.

26

THE SWAHILI OF
THE COAST

Some fifteen hundred years ago the Swahili were a small group of agriculturalists and fishermen living on the northern end of Kenya's coast, at the mouth of the Tana river and on islands not too far from the shore. They proceeded to become the dominant group of traders along the coast, settling islands and coastal towns as far south as Mozambique: Mombasa, Kilwa, Pemba, Zanzibar, Malindi, Sofala. They began converting to Islam six or seven hundred years ago, and are now wholly Muslim. Little remains of their pre-Islamic traditions or beliefs. The name 'Swahili' is itself Arabic, meaning 'people of the shore' (sahel, in Arabic), but is rarely used by the people themselves, who instead refer to their place of origin. In the last two centuries their language, Ki-Swahili, has become the principal lingua franca of eastern Africa. They began using Arabic script to record documents in Swahili as they converted, and there is now a sizeable corpus of Swahili literature, some of it translated from Arabic and other languages and some of it of local composition. The two stories given here mark their double heritage: the story of the poet-prince Liyongo is the principal surviving example of the pre-Islamic culture of the Swahili, while the story of the foundation of the town (and kingdom) of Kilwa shows how they incorporated Islamic elements into their traditions.

LIYONGO FUMO OF SHAHA

Liyongo was the son of a king, and extraordinarily talented. His strength was legendary, his skill with the bow was great, and he was a gifted poet. But he did not become king. His mother was a secondary wife, and so his brother Mringwari, born of the principal wife, became the ruler of Shaha instead. The two brothers eventually quarrelled, and Liyongo went into exile.

It was most probably before this period of exile that emissaries from the Oromo peoples along the Somali coast came to visit the Sultan of Pate. While they were waiting for their audience they heard people speak of the prowess of Liyongo. They asked the Sultan about Liyongo, and the Sultan sent for him. Liyongo said he would come immediately, and he packed a bag with those items he considered necessary. He also hung three great horns about him. Then he set off. The trip that had taken the messengers two days he made in half a day, and he arrived at the edge of the town in mid-afternoon. He took one of his three horns and blew such a mighty blast that the horn split in half. In the Sultan's court, the Oromo visitors were startled and asked what the sound had been. The Sultan told them that no doubt Liyongo was on the outskirts of the town. Soon, a second blast from a horn (and again, the horn broke in two) told them that Liyongo had come to the city gates, and a third announced that he had arrived at the Sultan's palace.

He was quickly admitted and brought before the Sultan and his guests. There, he emptied the bag he had brought from his home: a mortar, a pestle, a large sack of grain to pound, a large iron pot, the three stones upon which to rest the pot, and for good measure a small millstone. The Oromo visitors were amazed at the proof of his strength, and said to themselves that they must form an alliance with such a man, for his strength and his appearance convinced them that he was also a great warrior. So they asked the Sultan to serve as their intermediary, and he negotiated a marriage settlement. When the Oromo returned to their home, Liyongo accompanied them, and there he married the woman they had chosen for him. She quickly became pregnant, and in due time she gave birth to a son. As the boy grew, everyone agreed that he resembled his father in appearance and in strength.

But Liyongo returned to his home before the boy was grown, and his return caused trouble. His brother Mringwari was very popular as a ruler – people admired Liyongo for his skills, but did not trust his judgement – but he found so extraordinary a brother a challenge. Liyongo also may have shown signs of ambition, since he counted the Sultan of Pate and the clans of the Oromo as his allies. At any rate, Liyongo left his home. But he could not go to Pate – he had managed to make an enemy of the Sultan as well, somehow. So he took refuge on the mainland, living with groups of hunters in the bush. Word came to the hunters that there was a price on Liyongo's head, and they were tempted by the thought of wealth. But they did not dare to attack Liyongo openly, because they knew that he would kill them all without a second thought. So they devised a trick. On the pretext of a meal during which each guest took it in turn to climb a palm tree that had an edible nut, they planned to have him climb the tree and to kill him while he was unarmed and relatively helpless at the top of the trunk. But Liyongo avoided the trap. When it was his turn to bring down the nuts for the meal, he took his bow and arrows and simply shot the nuts down from the tree.

He understood that he was not safe with the hunters any more, and so he returned in hiding to live with his mother on the island of Pate. There the Sultan's men caught him and put him in prison. He was held for a time, and his mother learned where he was jailed. She prepared food and sent it to him with her slave-girl. Little of the food reached him – the guards would take the choice portions and leave him the coarse bread and perhaps some gruel.

The Sultan then announced that Liyongo was to be killed, and asked him if he had a last request. Liyongo asked that they provide the music for a marriage ceremony at the time of his execution, for he had composed several well-known marriage songs. Then Liyongo taught his mother's slave-girl a new song:

the song told his mother to prepare food for him, and to place a metal file into the loaf of coarse bread. The message reached his mother, and the file reached Liyongo. The night before his execution, the town began the wedding celebration he had requested, with lots of drumming and loud singing. The noise masked the sounds that Liyongo made as he cut through the iron bars of the window with the file. In this way, he escaped.

Other attempts to kill him failed, and the Sultan became convinced that Liyongo had magical protection. He remembered the son Liyongo had fathered among the Oromo, and had the lad brought to Pate. There the Sultan won the boy over with the promise of wealth and a good marriage, if only the boy could help him get rid of his father, who had become an outlaw troubling the kingdom. The boy was convinced.

The youth left Pate and went to the town on the mainland where his father was living in exile. He explained who he was, and Liyongo was delighted that his son had come to join him. Over time, the youth won his father's confidence, and discovered that the Sultan had indeed been correct: Liyongo was protected by magic, and ordinary weapons would not harm him. But he was vulnerable. Eventually, Liyongo revealed that a copper spike could pierce his navel and kill him. Even as he revealed this information to his son, Liyongo showed his suspicion: he told the boy that the information would not do him any good, and that if he attempted to betray his father he would have a bitter reward.

The son acquired a copper spike, and one day, summoning all his resolution, approached his father, who was sleeping soundly after the noonday meal. He drove the spike into Liyongo's belly and then fled. Liyongo felt the wound, and rose to his feet. He took his weapons and strode towards the town nearby. When he reached the well at the edge of town, where the women used to come and fetch the drinking and cooking water, he knelt down on one knee and drew his bow until the arrow's head touched the bow. There he remained, ready to shoot but motionless, for he had died.

Later in the afternoon, the women came from the town to get their water for evening use. They saw Liyongo, his bow drawn, an arrow ready to shoot, and they quickly turned back. They told the townspeople that Liyongo had set himself up by the well, and that he was ready to kill the first person to approach it. For two days no one dared go near the well, and the entire town began to suffer from thirst. Finally, Liyongo's mother determined to approach her son and to learn the reason why he was keeping the people of the town from their water. When she got close to him, she realized he was dead. He is buried in Kipini.

As Liyongo had foretold, his son did not profit from the treason. The Sultan of Pate turned him out, since he had betrayed his father. He returned to his mother's people, but they were disgusted by his deed and refused to welcome him back. He died in misery.

THE FOUNDATION OF KILWA

Kilwa lies to the south of the Swahili coast, in modern Tanzania. This retelling combines two accounts of the town's history. Both are nineteenth-century manuscripts, but their editor believes that one text may have been composed around 1520; the second is late nineteenth century, collected when the region had just come under German control. The stories given are very similar; the earlier text includes details on the motive for the departure from Shiraz which are absent from the later text (and which closely resemble the Islamic tradition of the fall of the city of Saba in southern Arabia). Historians do not entirely credit the claim to a Shirazi (Persian) origin, but note that the claim marks the eldest and best-established Swahili families along the coast.

The first ruler of Kilwa Kisiwani, the island, was Mrimba. He was a hunter, and he discovered that at low tide it was possible to walk from the mainland to the island. He led his people there and they settled on the island, leaving it to hunt on the mainland as the tides allowed.

Husain ibn Ali, the ruler of Shiraz, dreamed that destruction was coming to his city: he dreamed of a rat with an iron snout digging holes in the city walls and weakening them so much that they collapsed. He determined to leave Shiraz, but did not want to reveal his premonitions. So he staged a confrontation with his oldest son: at a public banquet the two of them began to argue more and more heatedly. Eventually the son began to revile his father in the foulest terms, and then stormed out of the hall. The ruler turned away from his people and withdrew into his apartments. Later, he announced that his shame was so great that he would leave the country. The people offered to bring him the head of the son who had insulted him, but he refused: such was his bitterness that the sight of the land made him ill. So he equipped ships and sailed down the coast of Africa. It is said there were seven ships, and each ship founded a town along the coast.

The ruler came to Kilwa Kisiwani, and reached an agreement with Mrimba that allowed him to settle there with his people. He gave Mrimba rich gifts of beads and other trade-goods, and Mrimba gave him his daughter as a wife. The settlement prospered, but Husain was uneasy at the coexistence of the two peoples, each under a different ruler. So through his wife he suggested that his father-in-law should withdraw to the mainland, because it was not good for him to meet daily with the father of his wife. Mrimba agreed, but asked for compensation. One account says he wanted enough cloth to circle the island, the other that the cloth stretched from the island to his new habitation. Husain provided the cloth, and Mrimba led his people to the mainland.

But Mrimba planned to come back. Husain and his people suspected this, and so at low tide they dug at the coral and the sands that formed the bridge to the island, until there was a channel deep enough to stop an army. When Mrimba did decide to attack the newcomers, his force was stopped by the waters. Later, Muhammad, the son of Husain and Mrimba's daughter, became ruler of both communities.

KINGDOMS OF THE
GREAT LAKES

The region lying west of Lake Victoria is a fertile and densely populated highland running between the lake and the mountains. It is also the crossroads of a number of cultural strains: hunters and gatherers (including the fishermen of the lake), pastoralists, and agriculturalists who benefited from early advances in iron technology. Archaeology has revealed peoples with advanced knowledge of iron-working some 2,000 years ago in this region. Speakers of Bantu-family languages entered the region some 1,500 years ago from the west. Bananas were introduced from the Indies in the eighth or ninth century, and now form a staple crop. There have been many kingdoms in the area, founded through conquest, migration and fission. Many of the smaller kingdoms seem to have been formed by princes from the royal houses of the larger kingdoms, although it is also possible that ruling dynasties claim such a family tie as a form of legitimation. In many cases, the ruling dynasty represents a foreign clan, usually associated with cattle-herding, and cattle remain the symbol of wealth and prestige. In the early twentieth century, outsiders interpreted this pattern as evidence for invasion and conquest by 'Hamitic' peoples from the north and also as evidence for the superiority of lighter- over darker-skinned peoples; this biblically inspired theory of racial identity has been abandoned.

The kingdoms of the great lakes area were prosperous and complex; their oral traditions were rich and well preserved, and were also written down in many cases soon after contact with missionaries and colonizers (although the missionaries brought their own bias to the material). Bunyoro, Buganda, Busoga,

*Ankole, Kitara, the BaHaya kingdoms of Kiziba and Kyami-
twara, Rwanda, Burundi – the list could be extended. The
traditions of these kingdoms overlap in numerous ways; the
kingdoms of Uganda share a recognition of different eras of
rulers: the Tembuzi, the Ba-Cwezi and later dynasties. The
Ba-Cwezi in particular appear as demi-gods, responsible for
the establishment of human culture and institutions, whose
influence is perpetuated through spirit-mediumship, and certain
figures of the Ba-Cwezi such as Kintu and Wamara recur from
one area to another. The following narratives are only a
sampling of the wonderful material available.*

THE KINGDOM
OF BUNYORO

*The kingdom of Bunyoro is a Buganda kingdom, founded
relatively early (fourteenth to fifteenth century) on the highlands lying north-west of Lake Victoria. Following the rule of
the Ba-Cwezi, of which part of the story is narrated below, the
Ba-Bito dynasty, recognized to be of Luo origin (see Chapter
24), established itself, and through them royalty became associated with cattle-ownership. In the eighteenth century Bunyoro
declined as the kingdom of Buganda, lying closer to the lake,
expanded. The following episodes are retold from an account
made by a missionary at the start of the twentieth century.*

RUHANGA

At the beginning, there were Ruhanga the creator and his
brother Nkya. Nkya complained that it was dull, and Ruhanga
had done nothing of what he promised. So Ruhanga separated
heaven and earth. Then he made the sun from a stone. When
Nkya was frightened by the sun's brightness and feared burning,
Ruhanga made the clouds to cover the sun. Then he made the
moon to lighten the darkness. And the two of them lived on
the earth. Earth and heaven were close in those days; heaven
was held up by a tree, a pole and an iron bar.

Nkya complained to his brother that the sun was too hot,
and so Ruhanga made plants and trees for shade. Then Ruhanga
went up to heaven to see how things were; when he washed
himself and threw out the water, it fell on the earth and caused
rain. Nkya complained that the rain made him cold, and so

Ruhanga devised a shelter for him, and then made him tools with which to cut branches and do the other work for building homes. Ruhanga then filled the world with animals and other living things, and he gave his brother Nkya domestic animals to live with him. Later he gave Nkya cattle to provide milk, and when Nkya asked for more solid food Ruhanga supplied gourds and other fruits and showed him how to cook them. But Ruhanga warned his brother that the stomach would rule humans.

Nkya had four sons, of whom the first was Kantu (little thing) but the others had no names. Ruhanga said he should send the three nameless sons across the valley to visit him, and he would give them names. They came to his house and he let them sit while he prepared certain items which he took to a crossroads that they would pass on the return journey. Then he gave each of the boys a pot of milk and told them to take it home. They left, and at the crossroads found baskets containing cooked food, tools, strips of oxhide and the ox's head. The eldest immediately began to eat, but the two brothers rebuked him, and so he took the tools that were farming implements. The second brother took the strips of oxhide, and the third took the ox head.

They came home and told their father what they had done, and he, too, rebuked the eldest for eating other people's food. Ruhanga then appeared, and told the boys to guard their milk pots during the night, and not to drink it as they had eaten his food. So they settled down with their pots. In the middle of the night the youngest jostled his pot slightly and some spilled out; he begged his brothers and they replaced most of it. Before dawn the eldest turned in his sleep and spilled his pot and all the milk ran out. Although he entreated his brothers, they refused to help him, because he would need much too much milk.

At daybreak Ruhanga came to the three sons and examined their pots. He asked what had happened to the milk, and they explained why the first was empty, why there was some milk missing from the second pot, and why the third was almost full. And then Ruhanga told Nkya that he had found names for the three boys. The first he named 'Servant', because he had taken

food and eaten it on the open road, and because he could not
keep the milk he had been given. So he should have a master to
watch him. The second he named 'Herdsman', because he had
taken the tools of the cattle-herder and had spilled no milk.
The third he named 'King', because he had taken the ox head
and he had the most milk.

When their elder brother, Kantu, heard this, he was angry
because Ruhanga had not considered him when assigning places
in society, and so he said he would oppose the order that
Ruhanga had set up and bring destruction and strife into the
world.

Hearing that, Ruhanga told Nkya to come with him, and
they left the earth which had become corrupt and withdrew to
heaven, pushing away the tree and the poles which had joined
the two. The iron bar fell down and broke into many small
pieces, so it is now spread over the world to be used in tools.

KING BABA

Baba was the grandson of Nkya, and became king after his
father Kakama Twale disappeared under the evil influence of
Kantu. People were prosperous under his rule, and so Kantu
became jealous. He went to Ruhanga and asked that he remove
the desire to eat from people. Ruhanga did so, and without the
desire for food no humans did anything any more: they let the
cattle wander, they did not visit each other or talk, they just
sat. King Baba realized that this condition must be due to
Ruhanga. Kantu perceived that thought and reported to
Ruhanga that Baba thought ill of him in his heart, and Ruhanga
became angry. So he released hunger and disease and death into
the world. The first to die was the child of the king, and naturally at first the people thought that he had fallen asleep, and
they wondered why they could not wake him. Then Baba sent
a message to Ruhanga telling him how they could not wake up
the boy. Ruhanga was sorry, knowing the boy had died, and at
first he wanted to limit death, so that after four days the body
would live again, but Nkya told him it would be better if people

died for good. So Ruhanga sent a reply to Baba and told him to bury the child.

In his grief over the loss of his son, Baba cried out and cursed the land, and Kantu caught him and took him away in the same way he had taken Baba's father.

KING ISAZA

Several kings followed Baba, and then a very young man named Isaza came to the throne. He immediately dismissed all the elders who advised the king, and said that as he was young, he would be advised by young men only. But he eventually changed his mind.

One day, when hunting, he killed a zebra, and admired the beautiful patterns on the skin. He determined to make the skin into a garment, and he had it sewn tightly around him. For a time, his new costume was spectacular and all admired him. But then the skin shrank as it dried, and it tightened upon the king's body and he began to feel constricted. He asked his friends what he should do, but they were little help. They told him that kings made a fine spectacle, but that kingship had its discomforts, and so he should simply endure the pain as the price of his splendour. But then the hide shrank further. The king began to have trouble breathing, and then fainted. His companions did not know what to do at that point; they could not cut the skin away without also cutting the king's flesh. So they wondered, and found no solution.

Word of the king's plight came to the elders who had been banished, and they decided they should help the king in spite of his foolishness. So they fetched Isaza and threw him in a pond of water so that he was almost completely submerged, and they would not release him even when he revived and complained. Isaza thought they were trying to drown him. But after a short time the wet skin began to stretch. The constriction of his chest eased and he could breathe freely. Then the old men withdrew him from the water and cut off the skin. In gratitude for their service, and recognizing his earlier errors,

Isaza decreed that property should thereafter be held by the
elders in families.

ISAZA AND THE KING OF THE
UNDERWORLD

Nyamiyongo, king of the underworld, decided to try to form
an alliance with a king on earth, and sent messengers to Isaza.
They came and asked the king to show them six things: that
which brings the dawn, that which falls short, that which binds
water, that which causes kings to turn, that which has no wit,
and that which ends sorrow. But they did not tell the king
what these things were. The messengers withdrew, and the king
consulted with his advisers. But they could not make out the
riddles of the messengers. Isaza summoned wise men from all
the region, but none could explain these things. But one day,
as his queen came worriedly from the consultations of the
ministers, she talked to her maid and told her of the challenge
from Nyamiyongo, and in a moment the young maid said that
she could solve the riddle for the king. So the king and his
ministers met with the maid, and she showed them what it
meant. She had a baby placed on the king's mat, and the baby
crawled about and dirtied the skin and overturned a water
container. There, said the maid, is that which has no wit. Then
she showed them a dog with a tobacco-pipe and fire: the dog
could not light the pipe, but sat there. There, said the maid, is
that which falls short. Then she filled a pot with water and set
it boiling, and then placed in it some millet, and after a time
the millet had absorbed the water. There, said the maid, is that
which binds water. Then she led them outside and showed them
a cock. There, she said, is that which brings the dawn. Then a
cow lowed nearby, and the king turned to see it. There, said
the maid, is that which causes kings to turn. She told them also
of that which ends sorrow, but that secret has been forgotten.

So the king's counsellors showed the maiden's items to the
messengers of Nyamiyongo, and the messengers of Nyami-

yongo explained their king's desire for an alliance with an earthly ruler. The king proposed that they should become blood-brothers, each eating a coffee bean soaked in the blood of the other. But Isaza was wary of this offer, and so gave the bean to a servant, rather than eating it himself.

But Nyamiyongo learned of this deception, and was humiliated to think that he had formed an alliance with a human servant. So he planned destruction for Isaza. First, he chose the most beautiful and deceitful woman in his court and dressed her in wonderful finery. Her name was Nyamata. She came to Isaza's court and easily won his attention and then his heart. He wished to send messengers to her kinsmen to formalize their relationship, but she refused that. She wished him to come with her, but he was not willing to leave his kingdom. But she persisted. One day, however, they were together when the herds of cattle were brought in from pasture, and the king stood admiring them and didn't even notice when Nyamata went from his side, and hardly heard her when she called him. Then he said he could not come, because he wished to watch the cows being milked. Realizing that she could not compete with his cattle, Nyamata withdrew into the underworld. There she gave birth to a son.

Nyamiyongo had discovered his weapon: he sent a pair of magnificent cattle, bull and cow, to Isaza, and Isaza took them and loved them. He spent all his time with them, even bringing them into his hut at night. But one night the cows vanished. The next day he went hunting them across the land, and he found their horns sticking up from a bog. He leaped in to try to pull them out, and found suddenly that he had fallen through the earth and was in the underworld.

There he was brought before Nyamiyongo, and while at first he was treated well, eventually Nyamiyongo reproached him for having tricked the king of the underworld into an alliance with a servant. Then Nyamiyongo gave the cattle to Isaza, as well as his wife and child who were there, and told him he was free to leave: but Isaza never found the way out of the underworld, and so was forced to wander there. This was the end of the kings who were gods.

28

THE KINGDOM
OF BUGANDA

The kingdom of Buganda developed in the eighteenth century in the areas immediately north-west of Lake Victoria, in regions where the heavy rainfall made banana-cultivation very rewarding but also made cattle-ownership difficult because of the insect-borne diseases. The expansion of Buganda in the nineteenth century also led to the spread of the story of Kintu into neighbouring areas such as Busoga (north of the lake) and BuHaya, to the south-west. This was the kingdom still in power when the English penetrated the area at the end of the nineteenth century; it was then divided between Muslim clans, who wished to retain some independence and particularly to maintain the slave-trade which had brought prosperity at one time to the royal house, and the Christians who considered themselves the victims of that trade. These episodes are retold from an account made by a member of the royal family at the end of the nineteenth century and later translated in English.

KINTU

The first man in Buganda was Kintu; he came into the country with one cow and lived from the cow's milk. That was all there was to eat. A woman named Nambi came down from heaven and saw Kintu and fell in love with him. When she returned to heaven she told her father Ggulu that she wished to marry the human, but he opposed the match. He said they should test Kintu, and so he sent his sons down to steal Kintu's cow. Kintu was now without his accustomed food. But he explored and tried various plants and was able to find enough things to eat. Then Nambi, seeing Kintu's cow among her father's herds, realized that her family was harming the man and determined to help him get his cow back. She went down and brought Kintu back to heaven.

When Kintu appeared in heaven, Ggulu decided that he should further test the man his daughter desired. They put Kintu into a house and then cooked a meal large enough for a hundred people. They brought this to him and told him he should eat it all as proof of his powers; if he left any they would kill him. So Kintu sat and ate as much as he could, but there was still a great deal left over. He looked around the hut and found a hole, and so he began putting the food down the hole. Thus he was able to dispose of the meal. Then he covered the hole so that it was invisible, and put the empty containers outside.

Ggulu found it hard to believe that Kintu had eaten all the food, and decided there must be other tests. He gave Kintu a copper axe and told him to cut firewood from the rocks. Kintu went, wondering what he should do: the copper was certainly not strong enough to break rock, and would only dent the edge or bounce back when he struck the rock. But he found a rock that was flaking away by itself, and so he was able to collect a certain amount of stone chips which he gave to Ggulu. Ggulu set him another test: Kintu must collect a pot of water, but he could not draw it from the well; it must be dew. Kintu placed the pot in a field and wandered about, wondering how to solve this problem, but when he came back he found the pot full of water (he guessed Nambi had helped him), and so he took it to Ggulu.

Ggulu decided at this point that Kintu was indeed an extra-ordinary person, and perhaps deserved to marry his daughter and to get his cow back. But as a last test, he told Kintu that he must pick his cow from among Ggulu's herds, in which there were many cows just like Kintu's. As Kintu was waiting for them to collect the herds a bee flew up to him and spoke, telling him to watch on which cow's horns it settled; that would be his own cow. So he watched the bee as they drove one herd by him; the bee didn't move, and he told them his cow was not in that herd. A second herd was brought, but again the bee did not move. Then a third herd was brought before him, and the bee flew out over it and settled on the horns of a cow. 'This', said Kintu, 'is my cow,' and he went to separate it from the herd. The bee flew on and landed on another cow. 'That', said Kintu, 'is a calf from my cow,' and he fetched it also, and again with two other animals. Ggulu agreed at this point that Kintu was clever enough to marry his daughter, and so he summoned Nambi and told the two of them they might marry. But he also told them they should collect their gear and leave immediately, and not come back, or else Nambi's brother Walumbe, Death, would wish to come with them.

They set off, leading the cattle and also sheep, goats and chickens, and carrying plantains and other food-plants. But a little way off Nambi remembered the millet she used to feed to the chickens and said she must go back for it. Kintu argued against this, reminding her of Ggulu's warning, but she insisted she must fetch her millet. So she went back, and although she tried to hide, Walumbe saw her and demanded that she let him come with her. Kintu was very displeased when he saw Walumbe, but there was no way to get rid of him, and so they continued on their way.

They settled and Nambi planted the plantains and soon had a large grove of plantain trees. She and Kintu had many children. One day Walumbe came and asked Kintu to give him a daughter to work as his cook. But Kintu refused: 'What shall I tell my father-in-law if he asks for his granddaughter?' he asked. Walumbe went away, but came back again another time, and again Kintu refused. 'In that case,' said Walumbe, 'I shall kill them.' But Kintu did not know what he meant, for at that time no one had died.

Later, one of Kintu's daughters died, and afterwards others, too. Kintu went to Ggulu to tell him what Walumbe was doing, and Ggulu reminded him that he had been warned. But after Kintu had pleaded, Ggulu agreed to send down another of his sons to help and to drive off Walumbe. So Kaikuzi came down and greeted his sister and then his brother, and told Walumbe that he had been sent down to bring him back to heaven. But

Walumbe refused to go without his sister. He escaped from Kaikuzi and fled away. Kaikuzi spent much time trying to catch Walumbe, but Walumbe succeeded in escaping. Finally, Kaikuzi decided to make one last attempt. He told everyone to stay in their houses and not to go outside for several days, until he told them it was all right, and he also warned them not to cry out or make any signs. And so he hunted freely over the earth looking for Walumbe. Walumbe had in fact emerged from the earth where he had hidden, and Kaikuzi was very close to catching him. But some children had taken their goats out to graze. When they saw Walumbe, they cried out in fear and Walumbe immediately withdrew back underground. Kaikuzi saw what had happened and decided that was enough. He told Kintu that the children had ruined his plan, and that he was tired of hunting Death. He would return to his father's house. Kintu thanked him, and since that time Death lives on earth and kills people freely.

KINTU'S KINGDOM

Having settled on the earth with Nambi and their possessions, Kintu began to travel around Buganda. They lived in many different places, and they established their children at those sites before they moved on. Kintu fought one war during this time, against a king snake named Bemba who lived on Naggabali hill. As he was preparing for war, a tortoise offered to assist him and he accepted. The tortoise went with his followers to the snakes and told them he was a medicine-man who controlled a power against death. At night, he said, his head and limbs would disappear, reappearing in the morning, and this was the secret of their eternal life. That night, all the tortoises withdrew their heads and limbs into their shells, and brought them out again in the morning. So Bemba the snake was fooled and told the tortoise to cut off his head that night, so that he might have the secret of life. That night the tortoise and his followers cut the heads off the snakes and then sent word to Kintu that the enemy had been defeated.

When he was old, Kintu went on a tour of his lands. On his return he found that his wife Nambi, daughter of Ggulu, had been unfaithful to him. Kintu's minister, Kisolo, had caught the man involved and locked him up, but did not tell Kintu immediately because he thought the king was too tired from the travels. But Kintu learned of the event and became furious with Kisolo, interpreting the minister's silence as guilt. While Kisolo was explaining why he had waited to tell the king, Kintu speared him, and Kisolo ran away. Later Kintu sent for him, but on the way back Kisolo died of his wounds. Ashamed, because he was the first man to kill another, Kintu himself vanished. His oldest son Mulanga refused to become king, as he knew his father had not died, and he also vanished. So they appointed a younger son, Chwa Nabakka, king.

LATER KINGS

The son of Chwa Nabakka, Kalemeera, feared very much that his father would vanish in the same way that Kintu and Mulanga had done, and so he was obtrusively watchful of his father. His father devised a plan to have him sent to the court of a relative, the king of Bunyoro. While he was in Bunyoro, Kalemeera and King Winyi became close friends, and Kalemeera was allowed to sleep in the same dwelling as the king's chief wife, Wanyana. He went further, and seduced Wanyana. She became pregnant. When he learned this, Kalemeera talked to an adviser, and the adviser found a way out. He went to King Winyi and told him that he had performed a divination and learned that one of the king's wives had committed adultery and was pregnant. The king should send her away, building a special house outside the palace, and never look on her again. When the baby was born, it should be thrown into a clay pit. These measures would ensure the continued prosperity of the kingdom and the king's rule. King Winyi agreed to these measures. The guilty wife was secluded, but the child was not killed. Kalemeera later left Bunyoro, but died on the return to his father's palace.

Chwa, meanwhile, vanished in the same way as his father had done. The chiefs then chose one of the ministers to rule them for a time, and then another, but they were dissatisfied. Then they heard of the son of Kalemeera who was living in Bunyoro: his name was Kimera.

Kimera was invited to rule in Buganda. After consulting with his mother and other advisers he agreed. He built his own capital, away from the old settlement of Ganda, and he organized the royal court and appointed the ministers and ritual specialists. Later, he heard his mother had died, and he buried his umbilical cord which until then she had guarded.

He died as a consequence of an expedition against Busoga. He appointed his son Lumansi as general to lead the expedition. But Lumansi died of an illness on the way out, and so the army returned. Lumansi's son Tembo was told that Kimera had caused Lumansi's death, and so he determined to kill his grandfather to avenge his father. He did not have many opportunities, but one day he found Kimera alone, hunting in the bush, and killed him with blows from a club. Tembo then became king. He ruled with his sister Nattembo. Two of his children committed incest, and he himself died mad.

THE KINGDOM OF RWANDA

The oral traditions of the royal house of Rwanda reach back to the fifteenth century. The kingdom was a highly centralized state in a small, mountainous and fertile area, and the people were divided into two major groups: the Wa-Tutsi, who considered themselves the aristocratic, pastoralist conquerors of the region, and the Hutu (associated with the Pygmy Twa groups) who became the subordinate and agriculturalist class. This social division has persisted into modern times with very tragic results; each group has seized opportunities to massacre numbers of the others, most recently in 1994. The promise of Rwanda, rich in resources and human potential, has been stunted as a result. The oral traditions of Rwanda have been very systematically collected over the years, and constitute one of the treasure-stores of traditional African culture, but the events since independence in 1962 have all but erased their meaning and value. The following narratives retell the story of the establishment of the kingdom (over the reigns of several kings) as narrated by Clement Gakanisha, an official historian of the royal house, recorded in the 1950s, and a more popular version recorded by a missionary at the start of the twentieth century.

A ROYAL VERSION OF THE ORIGIN OF
THE KINGDOM

King Shyerezo kept diviners who would use his spittle when performing their function; they would give the saliva to the animal who was to be sacrificed, and then they would examine the entrails. He had a wife, Gasani, who for many years had not borne a child, and Gasani had a serving-woman. One day the serving-woman came to Gasani and told her the diviners had sacrificed an auspicious ox. The two women watched for the opportunity, and then stole the heart of the *imana* (a word for sacrifice; Imana is also the name of the sky-god). Then they placed the heart into a pot and covered it with milk and closed it up. They hid the pot, and the serving-woman told Gasani that in nine months she would show her the reason for these actions. But every day, Gasani should pour fresh milk into the pot.

At the start of the tenth month, Gasani asked her serving-woman what to expect. The woman waited a few days, and then told her to open the pot. Inside, Gasani found a baby boy. She took him out, washed him off and fed him. She sent a messenger to her husband, who had gone away, to tell him that a son had been born, and to request the customary gifts. But Shyerezo did not believe the child was his: his wife had been so long childless, and they had ceased their relations. Shyerezo told his servants to go and kill the child. But Gasani and the servant prevented them.

When Shyerezo came home some time later, he went to see the child whom his servants had not killed. He found a beautiful and noble baby, perfectly made by Imana. He realized he could not kill the child. They named the son Sabizeze and raised him with the other royal children. After some years, other children started to call Sabizeze a bastard, claiming he did not know his father, although Shyerezo had acknowledged him. Sabizeze decided to leave home with his older brother Mututsi and their sister, to avoid conflict over his paternity.

They went off into the region of Umubari, where Kabeeja

ruled, taking with them chickens and sheep and cattle and egrets, as well as some tools. They settled there and built homes. After some time the followers of Kabeeja found them there and asked them who they were, and they explained.

After a while, the two brothers noticed that their pairs of animals had all reproduced. They debated what to do. Sabizeze said they should marry their sister: after all, the animals were brother and sister as well, and they had produced young. But Mututsi refused to marry his own sister. So Sabizeze married the sister and she had many children, boys and girls. Finally, Mututsi asked his brother for a bride. Sabizeze suggested that Mututsi should go across the valley and settle there, building himself a house; then he should return, introducing himself as the Umwega from the other side of the valley. Mututsi did so, and Sabizeze gave him one of his daughters as a bride. Since that time the descendants of Sabizeze and the descendants of Mututsi the Umwega exchange women in marriage.

They lived in the land of Kabeeja, and Kabeeja was the one who assigned portions of land for cattle-pens and homesteads. Kabeeja died under unusual circumstances. His diviners, the Ubukara, had foretold his death in various ways: one said he would break his neck while getting a drink, another that he would be burned in a house, a third that he would die from a maiden's spear, and a fourth that he would fall in a river. But he died in all these ways; none of the diviners was better than another at consulting the spirits.

Kabeeja went hunting one day during a drought. On the way home, a torrential rain caught them and they sought shelter. They saw a homestead and rushed towards it. A maiden was there, weaving baskets; seeing the men approach, she withdrew to the back of the shelter, leaving her awl fixed in the ground. Kabeeja stepped on it and it pierced his foot. They pulled it out, but he felt cold, and it was raining. So he asked his men to make a fire. They did so, using grass for tinder, but the fire spread and the whole house began to burn. This happened after Kabeeja had asked a Hutu in a nearby field for some beer; he had given the beer to his hunters and then the rain had started and they had gone to the house for shelter. After the house caught fire, the others ran out, but Kabeeja was caught inside it and burned to death.

After the fire went out, they collected the remains of Kabeeja and put them in the river. This is how he died in all the ways that had been predicted.

Gihanga was a descendant of Sabizeze, in the land of Kabeeja, and he became the master of skills. He learned woodworking and pottery and how to work gourds to make containers to hold milk or butter. He lived with the Ubukara, the spirit-mediums, and they performed divination for him. One day they told him he should leave that land and move to another, and he questioned them. He did not believe them. They repeated their prophecy, and promised they would leave with him; it was at this time that they made their prophecies concerning the death of Kabeeja, as evidence of the truth of their words.

After the death of Kabeeja, Gihanga and the Ubukara left. They travelled into Burundi and offered their services to the king of Burundi. Gihanga would offer him the fruits of all his skills: finished leather, pottery, bracelets, spears. The king was pleased with him and gave him a woman as a wife. After three years, however, the diviners were dissatisfied and told him he should leave that country. His wife decided to come with him. So the group travelled north, and on the way they started an animal called an *ingabe*. The Ubukara told Gihanga he should follow that animal to the land of his destiny, that it would lead him to a place where he would find a woman; she would bear sons who would found a lineage of kings. So Gihanga followed the animal through the day, resting at night when it slept, accompanied throughout by the Ubukara and by his wife.

Finally, the *ingabe* came into the land ruled by Jeni, and there it took shelter in a cattle-pen. The people of Jeni told Gihanga he could not have the animal, that the refuge of the pen was inviolable. So Gihanga and his followers settled there, and once again he engaged in his skills. He became a blacksmith and made all sorts of things for the people: spears and bracelets and rings and tools.

After he had served Jeni well for some time, he asked the king, and the king agreed to release the *ingabe*. Gihanga killed and skinned it, and made a beautiful offering for the king. Jeni had a daughter, Nyamususa, whom he had not allowed to marry; his brother had warned him that the daughter's marriage would mean the end of his kingship. So Jeni never let the maiden go free; he had her watched at all times. The maiden, however, heard of the skills and the work of Gihanga, and devised a plan to bring him to her. Her servants told the king that his daughter was sick, and they took her to a secluded house. There, Gihanga was brought to her at night. Gihanga was served some beer. After a time he decided that he would spend the night there, and Nyamususa agreed. Gihanga slept in the same bed as Nyamususa, and that night she became pregnant. He left her in the morning, having given her also a small knife and fire contained in a little box.

The Ubukara told Gihanga he should move on, and so he did; he left the land of Jeni and came to another country where the people lived in poverty. He made tools for them, and they were able to live much better. He settled there.

Five months later, the guardians of Nyamususa noticed that she was pregnant and told her father. He ordered his Twa servants to take her to the forest and kill her. Her servant-girl followed her, bringing the gifts Gihanga had left. The Twa led her far into the forest to strangle her, and they came into an area where the Ubukara had been hunting. The Ubukara had just killed a buffalo, and when they saw the Twa they enquired what they were doing. The king's servants replied that they had orders to kill the woman, who had become pregnant by an unknown man. The Ubukara offered to give them the buffalo if they would leave them the woman, and the Twa agreed. So the Twa threw Nyamususa down on the path, took the buffalo and went off.

The Ubukara went off, and the two women followed, realizing that they had been saved. On the way they had to pass the night in the forest; they opened Gihanga's gift and found the fire packed in the box. They blew on the coals and brought the fire to life, and so they were able to stay warm and safe in spite of the dangerous animals. The next day they finished walking through the forest and came into Gihanga's territory. Gihanga at first pretended not to recognize them, and continued to work at his forge. Then he laid aside his hammer and told his servants to give the women some beer, for he could see they were exhausted by their adventures. And the Ubukara told him that this was the woman they had foreseen. So he married Nyamususa that day, despite her pregnancy.

Nyamususa had a daughter, Nyira-rucyaba, and then a son, Kanyarwanda, who would found the dynasty of the kings of Rwanda, and other children. After some time, the other woman who had come with Gihanga from Burundi also became pregnant. As her time came near, Gihanga went hunting and killed a fine animal. He dressed its skin, and the two wives began arguing over it. Words proceeded to blows, and then Nyamususa, helped by her daughter, struck the other woman with a stake and pierced her body. The woman died, but her child, a son, lived. He was named Gashubi.

The daughter, Nyira-rucyaba, fled into the forest where she took shelter with a man named Kazigaba. He lived entirely from hunting; game was all his food. He took the maiden in, and she stayed with him a week. Then they married, and she bore him a number of children.

One day, Nyira-rucyaba saw cows coming out of the water, and one of them stayed behind: she had a calf, and it was stuck in the vines near their home. She prevented her husband from killing the cow, as he wished to do; instead, she tamed the animal. She was able eventually to take pots she had made and milk the cow, and when she tasted the milk she found it divine. So she and her husband lived enjoying this gift.

Time had passed. Gihanga had forgotten his daughter's part in the death of his other wife, and he wished to see her. He had fallen sick. The word was sent out and reached Nyira-rucyaba, and she determined to visit her father. She took a small pot of milk with her, and she gave it to her mother, saying it was a cure she had brought from the forest for her father Gihanga. Gihanga tasted it and found it delicious, and asked for his daughter; after she had brought him milk a few more times he

called her and she came to him and told him the milk came
from an animal that she had found with her husband. He asked
her to send him her husband, and Kazigaba came to visit him.
Gihanga demanded that Kazigaba give him the cow, and Kazigaba refused. So Gihanga had him bound in chains. On hearing
this Nyira-rucyaba tied a rope to the cow and brought her to
Gihanga; her husband meant more to her than the animal. And
so Kazigaba was freed, and the two of them went home.

Some time later, Gihanga sent men to the water where the
cattle emerged, and they began catching them as they came out
and leading them away. Gashubi, who had been born from a
dead mother, followed and watched them from a tree. Eventually a huge bull came from the waters, and Gashubi cried out
in alarm; immediately all the cattle withdrew into the waters,
and that was the end of their arrival in Rwanda.

Later, Gihanga summoned his children to tell them how he
was dividing his heritage. Kanyarwanda would be king over
Rwanda, and there were territories for the other sons as well.
Then his daughter Nyira-rucyaba asked what her share would
be, and he told her she would receive the festival milk. Every
man who became king would have to make her a great offering
of milk, and if he did not she would have the power to curse
him and refuse him prosperity. This was the division of the
heritage of Gihanga.

A POPULAR VERSION

Imana the creator made two worlds, one above and one below.
The people in the world above enjoyed a blissful life, with all
sorts of comforts and food easy to hand. They lived happily. But
one couple was childless, and eventually the mother assembled
gifts for Imana – honey and hides, milk and banana-beer – and
went before him. There she clapped three times, the greeting of
royalty, and addressed him, praising him for his creation and his
bounty. And then she explained why she had come: everything
that Imana had created produced offspring, except her. She was
sterile, and she begged Imana to grant her a child.

Imana agreed to grant her wish, but he made her promise that she would keep the secret. She promised. Imana fashioned a tiny human figure from clay moistened with his saliva, and gave it to the woman with instructions. She was to place it in a pot filled with milk, which she should freshen every day, morning and night. After nine months she should take it from the pot.

The woman took the figure away and followed Imana's instructions faithfully. Twice a day she filled the pot with milk. The child took shape, and finally when she heard it moan she withdrew it from the pot and presented it to her husband. The couple rejoiced. When the boy was old enough to be weaned, the woman went back to Imana with other gifts, praying for a second child. Imana granted her wish as before, and eventually she produced a second son. A third time she went back, and Imana gave her a third child, this time a daughter. All three children were extraordinarily good-looking, intelligent and skilful. The boys were great hunters; the girl was an incomparable artisan.

But the woman had a sister who was also childless. The sister had endured this so long as the other remained childless, but when the other had produced three children her condition became intolerable. She could guess that something unusual had happened, for her sister had shown no signs of pregnancy before the births of her offspring. The childless sister watched and wondered. And one day, the two sisters sat drinking *pombe*, the banana-beer, and the mother became tipsy and indiscreet. Her sister seized the opportunity, and asked her how she had come by her children, and the mother revealed Imana's secret.

The next morning, the childless sister assembled gifts and went to see Imana. The mother woke up, realized what she had done, and cried, fearing she had brought death to her children. She found her sister and begged her not to go, but the other insisted: the secret had been broken, the damage was done. She could go to Imana later, if she wished, and so she did. But when she came to Imana, she found him angry. He told her that he would send her children into the lower world, and that they would no longer enjoy an easy life.

So it was. The two brothers and the sister came down to earth. The elder brother was named Kigwa because he came from heaven; the younger Lututsi, and the sister Nyinabatutsi. They found on earth that they got tired and their hunting was not always successful. The plants they found to eat were bitter and tough. But they showed courage: they made themselves a shelter out of branches, to keep off the cold and to ward off the wild beasts. After some days, a bolt of lightning struck near them, setting fire to a tree, and so they acquired fire. This was because of the intercession of their mother and aunt, who had gone to Imana to pray for them. Imana had been touched, and promised that he would ease the life of the exiles. After the fire, he gave them food-plants: it rained seeds and the siblings then had beans and bananas and millet and all sorts of other crops. Later they found a bellows and a hammer, and so learned about forging iron, and after that they acquired tools as a blessing from Imana. The brothers cleared fields and the sister planted them with all the seeds; the food grew wondrously fast, and a few days later they had their first harvest.

There were already other people in Rwanda, whose ancestors had been sent down from heaven for some fault. But they had not begged pardon, and Imana had not shown pity on them; he had left them in their miserable condition, eating grasses and gnawing bark. One day, one of these people saw the smoke rising from the home of the three siblings, and came closer, thinking it was a cloud. Around the hut he saw neatly arranged fields and full of plants such as he had never seen before. Then he saw the children of Imana, and asked them who they were and where they had come from. Kigwa told him who they were, and how Imana had given them the plants. The stranger stayed to eat with them, and they showed him their tools. Afterwards, he went back to his people, taking a bit of the food with him as proof of his visit, and they all decided they should visit Kigwa.

Kigwa welcomed them, but did not have enough food stored up to feed all of them. So he offered them seeds and said he would show them how to grow their own food, and he also gave them the tools to work the fields. The people were delighted, because they were now protected from hunger and had far better meals to eat than before, and word spread of Kigwa's generosity. So the people selected him as their king.

None of the siblings had married. They had found no peers from whom to pick a mate. So they prayed to Imana, and an envoy came down from heaven. He took their plea to Imana, and Imana decided to do something more for them. He sent down the animals from heaven – cattle and sheep and goats and chickens and all sorts of other animals – and he told each pair, brother and sister, male and female, to multiply. And so they went off in couples. Then he told Kigwa and his sister to mate. Kigwa asked about his brother, and Imana's envoy said he should await Imana's orders.

So Kigwa married his sister Nyinabatutsi. They had six children, three sons and three daughters. Lututsi asked to marry the oldest girl, but Kigwa refused. So Lututsi consulted with the envoy of Imana, who led him away to a different region called Karagwe, and Lututsi settled there. After some time, Lututsi and the envoy returned in secret, and the envoy called at Kigwa's home, identifying himself as a man from Karagwe. He asked for Kigwa's daughter in marriage, and promised good gifts of foodstuff and other products. So Kigwa led his daughter to Karagwe, among the Bega people, and gave her to Lututsi, whom the envoy of Imana had disguised. Lututsi became the king of the Bega. The lineages descended from the two brothers have the custom of exchanging their women in marriage.

30

THE KINGDOM
OF BURUNDI

*Burundi lies south of its closely related neighbour, Rwanda.
The royal court of Burundi seems not to have attained the
considerable complexity of Rwanda (for instance, there were
no established historians), but in other regards the underlying
cultures and history reflect a common origin and variation
on parallel themes. This narrative is retold from the different
versions included in a collection published in 1987.*

A man named Mwezi came into the land of Burundi and found
a Hutu governing as king. The king was desperate because the
land had been without rain for some time. Mwezi sought an
audience with the king and enquired what might be his reward
if he could bring rain. The Hutu told him he could name his
price, and Mwezi suggested he might like a bride. Then Mwezi
brought down the rain, using skills he had learned elsewhere,
and the Hutu gave him his own daughter.

Mwezi and the daughter had three children: two sons, Nsoro
and Jabwe, and a girl. After a while, Mwezi arranged to have
his father-in-law, the Hutu king, poisoned, so that he remained
the sole ruler of the land. And some time later he decided to
take a second wife. But at that his wife protested loudly, and
so Mwezi ran off.

Nsoro and Jabwe grew up, and each married. Nsoro then
took a second wife. Once, when he was visiting her in his
compound, Jabwe came by. He had been hunting antelope in
the wetlands, and he stopped at his brother's home. But Nsoro
was with his other wife, and his first wife was alone. The
servants took Jabwe's clothes and dried them before the fire

and fed him, and then he set off with his companions back to his own house. But he called out that he had left the bell for one of his hunting dogs hanging in the compound, and he would go back and fetch it; the others should continue on their way. In this way he contrived to be alone with his brother's wife. She became pregnant, and after a time gave birth to a son whom they named Ntare. It is said that when Ntare was born he had seeds in one hand and milk in another.

Jabwe realized the boy was his son, and eventually invited the boy to come on a visit, so that he could get to know his nephew. But he did not return Ntare to Nsoro, although Nsoro sent messengers to demand the child. Finally, Nsoro sent messengers who found a group of children playing out in the fields. They offered the children sugar cane and other sweet things, until they learned which one was Ntare, the little visitor. Him they took away. Jabwe and his men followed them, and a fight seemed imminent until Nsoro's men challenged Jabwe and asked by what right he held on to the boy – had he married the boy's mother? Was he the one who had given him a name? Jabwe was silent and turned away from the fight, but he continued to plan how to get the boy back to him.

Nsoro sent the boy to stay with his aunt in Buha; her husband was the ruler of Buha. He sent cattle with the boy and the servants, and one of the cows gave birth to a bull-calf, which became the special pet of Ntare. Ntare's royal birth was kept secret, but Ntare and his uncle would play *kibuguzo*, a game of tokens and counting. Ntare beat his uncle all the time, so that the uncle complained to his wife that their visitor must possess some power.

In the meantime Jabwe recruited some wild men from the forest, whose leader he had healed when he was sick, and he sent them against Nsoro to seize the boy and bring him back. But when they came to Nsoro's compound, pretending to come in peace, Nsoro fed them all poisoned food and they died. But Nsoro had realized his perilous situation and fled far away. Some say he was lost in the marshes of Gitanga, others that he vanished in the forest.

The king of Buha became so jealous of Ntare's success at

kibuguzo, and so tired of losing to the boy, that he planned to murder him. But his wife consulted a diviner and learned about his plans. The diviner gave her charms with which to fool the king and protect herself and her nephew. One night, there was a great disturbance in the cattle-corral. Ntare's bull-calf was attacking the king's bull. The two bulls fought for some time, and then Ntare's bull defeated the other and knocked it through the fencing which contained the cattle. The aunt and her nephew seized the opportunity and fled, along with the cattle. They made their way out of Buha. The king sent men to chase after them when he realized they were gone. But here again the diviners helped. They found the anthill within which the *Inkoma* serpent was hidden, and they stretched an oxhide taut over the openings. When the serpent tried to leave the anthill, it ran into the hide and produced a sound like thunder. This was the invention of the royal drums, the mark of power. The men of Buha who heard the sound were terrified and turned back. The people proclaimed that a king had come among them, and they enthroned Ntare.

Jabwe heard that there was a new king and came to challenge his power. But in a fight outside the new king's home he was mortally wounded. He saw a young man come to him bearing milk to drink, and asked him his name. 'I am Ntare Rushatsi, your son.' And Jabwe blessed him for the milk, and told his servants to bury him in another place, so that he would not bring drought on the land.

So Ntare Rushatsi became king of Burundi. He had other adventures in pacifying the country, and there are many stories about him and his successors, some of whom were also named Ntare.

CENTRAL EAST AFRICA

From the area of the great lakes, which they reached some 2,000 years ago, iron-working farmers speaking Bantu languages moved south around the great equatorial forests. Those groups that passed through the eastern part of the forest (the Mongo or Nkundo groups) were apparently able to subsist on a combination of hunting and fishing with relatively small-scale farming; they also developed a close association with the Pygmy (or Twa) groups. They did not form larger political entities. Further south (in modern Congo), where the forest gave way to the savannah, a number of rich kingdoms developed: the Kuba, the Luba and the Lunda, and in the west, Kongo (see Chapter 40 below). They spread their influence among neighbouring peoples as well.

NSONG'A LIANJA, HERO OF
THE MONGO

*The Mongo are a highly fragmented group of peoples who live
south of the great bend of the Zaire or Congo river, through
the heart of the tropical rainforest of the area. Their language
belongs to the Bantu family which dominates most of southern
Africa. While individual villages would have chiefs, the Mongo
did not form states. There is relatively little political history in
their traditions: the Mongo-speaking groups migrated south
after crossing the river (one may perhaps see traces of that event
at the end of this story) and settled throughout the broad area
where they are now to be found. Their lifestyle was based more
on the natural resources in the environment than on agriculture;
they were not quite hunters and gatherers on the order of the
Khoi-San people far to the south of them, or of the various
Pygmy groups with whom they coexisted (the Batswa and
Bokele in the story), but neither did they practise large-scale
agriculture. The forest into which they moved was rich enough
that they did not need to at first – things are undoubtedly
changing. We can see the importance of hunting in the story: it
is the principal means by which people obtain food, at least at
the start. Other food-producing techniques identified in the
narrative are fish-farming in ponds which would be drained,
trapping, and the cultivation of bananas which come in a
number of varieties, some of which are used to make beer.*

*The story of Lianja exists in many variations; a full perform-
ance typically lasts two nights and includes not only the story
of Lianja, but the story of his ancestors and their accomplishments, such as Bokele and his offspring. This retelling abridges
the end, in particular the story of the 'marvellous march' of*

Lianja and his sister Nsongo, in which they gather followers with different skills and encounter various antagonists. A re-enactment of this march sometimes served Mongo groups as a ritual of purification for their village in times of trouble. This version is retold from numerous versions collected by missionaries in the 1950s and before. The complete story includes many episodes, from which a narrator may make a selection for a given performance occasion.

BOKELE STEALS THE SUN

Bokele was born from an egg. His father left for a trip, ordering that all his wives must have children on his return, and his mother showed no signs of pregnancy until she was helped by a forest spirit who drew the egg from her and hatched it. Bokele grew extremely fast, and when his father returned from the trip he was already a grown man.

Their village lived in darkness and could see only by the light of the moon. But they had heard of the sun; it was kept by the Old Man and his people across the waters. Bokele said he would go and get the sun for the village. He launched his canoe. As he was setting out, a swarm of wasps came and asked to join him.

'Why should you come?' he asked them.

'If there is fighting, we will fight for you,' answered the wasps, and he agreed. They found a place on the boat.

The turtle came and asked to join him. 'I am a magician, and I can help you find the sun,' he said. Bokele said he could find a place on the boat.

The hawk came and asked to join him. 'When you find the sun, I can help you carry it off,' he said, and Bokele said he could find a place on the boat.

The mouse came, and asked to join the expedition. 'I can creep about and learn their secrets,' said the mouse, and Bokele agreed.

They paddled for a long time over the waters until they came to the home of the Old Man. Bokele landed and was brought to the Old Man, and there he said he had come to buy the sun for his village. The Old Man sent Bokele to the guest hut while he discussed the business with his advisers. Bokele and the animals went to the guest hut, but then the mouse crept into the Old Man's hall to listen to the discussion.

'We cannot give up the sun,' said the advisers. 'He has nothing we want to pay for the sun. We should send him away or kill him.'

'We should kill him,' agreed other advisers. 'It is dangerous that he has come here. We should ask Bolumbu to boil him in her pot of magic water.' That was agreed upon. The mouse scurried back to Bokele and told him of the plan.

Bokele went for a walk around the Old Man's village and found Bolumbu's hut. She stood outside it, stirring her great pot. He talked to her and flirted with her, and she thought he was very handsome and enjoyed his company. Soon, she left her pot and they went inside her hut where they could be alone, and they became lovers. The Old Man's messenger came to find her and called her outside; she was told she was to cook the stranger in her pot of magic water.

'How can I kill him? He is my lover!' she said to herself, and she pressed her ladle so hard down into the pot that she made a hole and all the magic water ran out. She showed the damage to the Old Man's messenger, and said they must wait while she prepared a stronger potion. Then she went into the hut and told Bokele that he must run away because they wished to kill him. He insisted that she should come with him, and she agreed she would do so.

Meanwhile, the turtle had found the cave where the sun was hidden. He distracted the guards by calling to them and then hiding in his shell, so they could see no one. Meanwhile, the hawk flew into the cave and seized the sun. On the way out, the hawk picked up the turtle as well. They flew back to Bokele's boat, chased by the Old Man's guards. At the boat they found Bokele and Bolumbu waiting; they pushed the boat into the water and set off. The Old Man's guards launched their own boats and set out after them.

The wasps then said, 'We have come to fight. It is our turn

to act.' They flew out of Bokele's boat and attacked the pursuers. But the pursuers built fires that made a thick smoke and the wasps were confused and slowed down; many wasps were killed and the others returned to Bokele's boat. Further on, they found that others of the Old Man's followers had made a great fish-trap to catch their boat, but Bokele fought their leader and defeated him, and they were able to escape and return to Bokele's village with the sun.

YENDEMBE 'HEAR-NO-ORDERS'

Bokele and Bolumbu had a son, who was at first named Yendembe, which means 'Hear no orders', and later Lonkundo. If anyone gave an order to the child, rather than an invitation such as 'Come and eat', the child would die. After the child had grown old enough to travel, Bolumbu went to visit her mother and took her young son with her. Bokele sent men to accompany her, and he also gave her a little packet of *kangili-kangili* medicine with which she could revive Yendembe in case anyone gave him an order and he died.

Bolumbu's mother was delighted to see her daughter and complained that she had stayed away so long. After a day or so, Bolumbu went to join the other women at their tasks; that day they were to drain the fish-pond. She reminded her mother that she should give no orders to her grandson, and then handed over Yendembe.

The old woman waited until Bolumbu was out of sight and then turned to Yendembe. 'There, she has gone to help the women with the fish-pond. We are alone. Show me that you can be useful. Come, cut me down a bunch of bananas.'

'Grandmother, you must give me no orders,' said Yendembe. 'That is my name: Yendembe.'

'I will take that name away from you,' said the grandmother. 'I shall give you another name.'

'You may call me by another name,' answered Yendembe, 'but still you should give me no orders.'

'I have no food,' said the grandmother. 'You must help me.

It is not difficult. If you cannot cut an entire bunch, then get me a few bananas at least. Get me some bananas.'

The child took a stick and knocked some bananas from a low-hanging bunch. He gave them to his grandmother. Then he fell dead.

A little bird went singing to Bolumbu as she worked in the fish-pond. It sang a short song to tell her how her mother had given an order to Yendembe and the child lay dead. Bolumbu returned to her hut and fetched the *kangili-kangili* medicine. She put some in Yendembe's nose; the boy sneezed and rose up again. Then Bolumbu scolded her mother for disobeying her instructions and pointed out the consequences. 'I didn't believe you,' said her mother. 'I thought you were lying to me.'

But the next day, the grandmother went into Bolumbu's hut while her daughter was away with the other women working in a garden. She found the *kangili-kangili* medicine and threw it into the fire. Then she went to Yendembe and again ordered him to get her some bananas. The little boy objected, but she insisted, and so he went and fetched her some bananas. Then he died.

The little bird went singing to Bolumbu, who rushed back into the village. She looked all through her hut, but could not find the *kangili-kangili* medicine. She could not revive Yendembe. So they wrapped the boy's body in leaves and laid it in the boat and returned to Bokele's village. As they approached the village, the little boy spoke and ordered them to unwrap his body. But when they reached the village, the boy was a corpse.

The boatmen went to Bokele, and Bolumbu explained to him what had happened. Immediately, Bokele summoned the vines that grew around the village to tie up the boatmen and his wife, and the vines stretched their tendrils and twined around the people until they could not move. Then Bokele killed them all in his anger.

Bokele went to his son's body and put some more *kangili-kangili* medicine in his nose. The boy sneezed and sat up, and then flew onto the roof. There he asked his father to throw him clothes, and then he asked his father what had happened. His father told him how he had been given an order by his grandmother and died, and then again his grandmother had given him an order after burning his medicine, so that he had again died, and how his mother had brought him home to be revived.

'Where is mother?' asked Yendembe, and Bokele told him that in his anger at his son's death he had killed Bolumbu and the boatmen. 'That was wrong,' said Yendembe, and he seized a spear and killed his father. Then he left that place and went to live in Ngimokili, the 'centre of the world'.

ITONDE WHO BECAME
ILELANGONDA

Yendembe now took the name Lonkundo and he married a woman named Ilankaka. They lived together for some time, and Lonkundo learned the secrets of hunting from his father, who came to him in spirit form and taught him about traps and nets and other devices. Because he could catch so much game, Lonkundo became a chief with many servants. Eventually, Ilankaka became pregnant. During her pregnancy, her appetite became very difficult; she would not eat any food but bush-rats. So Lonkundo ordered his servants to make them a home out in the forest and to build an extended hunting-fence with snares to catch the bush-rats.

They moved out of the village into the forest. The first day, the snares brought them eight bush-rats. Ilankaka ate all of the meat; there was nothing left. The next day, the snares brought them ten rats. Ilankaka roasted and ate five almost immediately; she smoked the other five and laid them away in the smokehouse for later. The next morning she looked in the smokehouse: all the meat was gone. She cried out, and Lonkundo accused the servants and punished them with beatings for eating the bush-rats, but the servants cried out that they had done nothing, they had not touched the meat.

That day the traps had two dozen rats. They brought them to Ilankaka; she roasted and ate half of them on the spot, and smoked the others for later. She laid them away again in the

smokehouse. In the morning, as Lonkundo was going out with
the servants to tend the snares, she looked in the smokehouse
for her meat: it was all gone. She told Lonkundo when he
returned with still more bush-rats; Lonkundo threatened the
servants, but they denied that they had gone anywhere near
the smokehouse. Again, Ilankaka ate some of the meat they
brought back and put the rest in the smokehouse. But then a
clever young boy suggested to Lonkundo that they should cure
some tobacco leaves; this was really only an excuse to get into
the smokehouse. There he rigged a net over the meat that
Ilankaka had put away.

That night, while all were asleep, Lonkundo and Ilankaka
were woken up by noises coming from the smokehouse. They
were very frightened. Lonkundo touched his wife's belly; it was
flat and seemed empty. 'Ilankaka,' he asked, 'what has become
of your pregnancy?'

She asked him to make a light; he got up to revive the fire,
but then something bitter and stinging struck him in the face.
The same thing happened when Ilankaka tried to light the fire.
The two of them sat clutching each other throughout the night,
suffering from the sting of the liquid that had hit them. In the
morning, they rushed back to their village as fast as they could.
There, they told everyone about their strange experiences, and
ordered that all entrances to the village be barred and entry
refused to any strangers who might approach. Lonkundo added
that they should submit any visitor to the poison ordeal.

The night-time visitor was Itonde, the child from Ilankaka's
belly, who had been coming out at night to eat the meat and
who had got caught outside the womb by the trap set by the
clever boy. When morning came, he freed himself from the net
and left the smokehouse. He sat down in the forest and waited
by a path. A duiker came by; he threw a nut at it, killed it, and
then cooked it over a fire he made with his fire-starter. Then he
ate all of it. A larger antelope came by; again, he killed it,
cooked it and ate it. He did this with every animal that came
along the path, except for snakes.

He heard a whirring sound, and a hummingbird perched
nearby him. He picked up his nut to throw it at the humming-

bird, but the bird spoke to him: 'Why kill me? Aren't you full after all the animals you have eaten?'

'Yes, I am.'

'Then you don't need to eat me. Do you know where your family is?'

Itonde put down the nut. 'No, I don't.'

'I shall find someone to help you if you will sing me a song.'

Itonde sang a song for the hummingbird, and the hummingbird fetched the caterpillar-bird who gave Itonde a bell. 'The bell's name is the World,' explained the caterpillar-bird. 'It will give you anything you want: it contains everything. Wealth, health, fish, storms, lightning, weapons, all is in the bell.' Itonde examined the bell and saw on it the marks of all the different animals of the forest and the fish of the rivers and the birds of the trees. Gratefully, he accepted the bell and set off, singing a song about the bell. The bell put him on the path to his father's village.

He came to the village and found the gates barred. The people came out and surrounded him and asked him all sorts of questions, and especially where he came from and why he was travelling alone. He explained that he came from back there – he waved at the forest – and he was going to see the world. They brought him food. He thanked them, and invited them to join his meal. They refused, saying that since he was unmarried he would eat alone. Then he pulled the bell out of his bag and waved it over the food, and the bell sang to him that the food was poisoned and he should not eat it. So he pushed the food aside and walked on. He entered the village and settled by the great wooden gong that was used to send messages across the forest. The people came after him, nervous and frightened, and told him he should not sit by the gong, that this was a spot reserved for the chief and his servants.

Without answering them, Itonde beat on the gong and the sound carried over the village and into the forest. Confused, the people of the village rushed to Lonkundo to ask him what they should do about this stranger. Lonkundo had no idea, but decided he should go and talk to the newcomer.

When he saw Lonkundo, Itonde greeted him as father.

Indignant, Lonkundo denied that he was Itonde's father, but the young man insisted. He said he had been born in their hunting camp where they went to eat bush-rats, and that they had abandoned him there. Lonkundo denied that this boy could be their son; they had left something strange in the smokehouse. Itonde invited the people to compare him to his father: see how similar they were, even their hands were the same shape.

Lonkundo demanded that he undergo the poison ordeal. If the boy could survive the poison they would know he was telling the truth. The villagers brewed up the poison and brought it to Itonde in a cup. Itonde looked about the crowd, then took the cup. He waved his bell over the cup. He called out his name and his accomplishments and the name of his father, but Lonkundo denied that this was his son. He called for his mother Ilankaka; she seized a faggot from the fire and brandished it to hold him away. Then he drank the poison, emptying the cup.

'I am Itonde,' he cried, 'son of Lonkundo and Ilankaka, who was born in the forest and raised in the smokehouse. I am the eater of the bush-rats, the killer of the animals. I am the friend of the hummingbird, and owner of the World.'

Lonkundo brought him another potion. Itonde rang his bell over the potion and drank it down. Lonkundo embraced him. 'Now I have proof that you are my son,' he said. 'I welcome you to the village.' He sent his servants to assemble his wealth, to prepare an enormous feast with all the available goats and chickens, to empty the storehouses.

'I shall give you a new name,' said Lonkundo. 'You are now Ilelangonda.'

ILELANGONDA'S MARRIAGE

Lonkundo grew old and wanted Ilelangonda to get married. But his son refused all the women whom his father presented to him, although Lonkundo toured the neighbouring villages to select a future bride. Finally, Lonkundo told Ilele – as he was often called – that he should go and find himself a wife. Ilele left his father's village and went travelling through the forest to other clusters of villages, but nowhere could he find a woman who suited him.

One day he met a man covered with palm oil, so thickly coated with the congealed stuff that he hardly seemed a man. Ilele asked the man what had happened; the man had gone as a suitor to a woman named Mbombe, who was known as the Champion because she was such a good wrestler. She said she could only consider him as a suitor if he defeated her in a wrestling match, and they had wrestled in a great pool of oil. She had thrown him down twice and now he was on his way home, dripping.

At the next village, Ilele found four young women sitting under a tree outside the village; they were dressing each other's hair. He asked them if this was the village of the Champion Mbombe; they tittered and said that it was. He asked which of them was Mbombe, and she answered him, not at all shy. Ilele said he had come to see her because he was looking for a wife. She told him he must follow the procedures, and he should go into the village and say he had come as a suitor for Mbombe.

Ilele went into the centre of the village, where the people were collected, and announced that he had come as a suitor for Mbombe. The elders of the village chuckled and said he could have his turn in the oil like all the others. Mbombe's father sent for his servants and had them bring fifty calabashes of oil; they poured this oil out in a depression so that it stood knee-deep. Mbombe and her friends came into the village; Mbombe prepared herself to wrestle.

The two faced each other in the pool of oil. He tried holds on her; she broke them. She tried holds on him; he broke them. Neither could get the advantage on the other. Kungo-ele, the father of Mbombe, stood nearby, and he sang a song in which he told his daughter to use the grip that never failed, and Mbombe seized Ilele, and tripped him into the oil. Ilele rose, saying to himself, 'By my father Lonkundo! Shall I be beaten by a woman? I should die of shame!' He sang a small song, and Mbombe felt a strange sensation pass over her. She seized Ilele again with the grip that never failed, but this time she was unable to trip him. She tried to get her shoulder under him; she could not move him. She was the one to stagger in the oil. Her father called out, and she braced herself, but then Ilele seized her and threw her down in the oil. The people were amazed and called out. Mbombe raised herself and they faced each other for the third and last fall. Ilele grew angry and then simply swept her legs out from under her; she fell in the oil and the village cried out, 'Mbombe has found a husband!'

Ilele had won his bride. The new couple started on the trip back to his father's village. Kungo-ele gave them an ample supply of food to see them on their way, and they departed. But Mbombe found the trip difficult. At every animal track, Ilele would start in fear and cower back, until she approached and examined the spoor. Then she would say, 'Ilele, it is only the track of a duiker' or whatever animal had left the trail, and they would continue. In the afternoon they stopped at a good campsite, and Mbombe asked Ilele to cut the poles for the hut. Ilele walked right past the thicket of bembe-wood which is excellent for stakes, and instead cut some reeds by the stream bank. Mbombe had to go and cut the bembe-wood herself. Then Ilele insisted on planting the poles with the fork in the ground, rather than pointing up so the forks could support the poles for the roof. She sent Ilele into the forest to find food; he trampled down some excellent mushrooms, and with great noise brought back a mouse. She had to retrieve what was edible from the mushrooms. Naturally, she had to get the fresh water and the firewood.

The next day she sent him hunting, but he set up the net badly and the porcupine he cornered escaped. He sent her off with the equipment and the dog. She trapped a porcupine, which is considered very good food, but the porcupine changed into an antelope and tore free from the net. She headed back home, but tried setting the net one last time. An antelope got caught, but then turned into a leopard. She called for help, and Ilele heard her; he brought his spear. But he hurled it not at the leopard, but at Mbombe. She flung the net with the leopard in it at him. Ilele ran away.

Ilele ran through the forest. He knocked into a tree and a wood-dove flew out of its nest. 'I was running, I was running, from a wood-dove,' he sang, and continued on his way. He passed a pangolin. 'I was running, I was running, from a pangolin,' he sang, and continued on his way. He saw some monkeys. 'I was running, I was running, from monkeys,' he sang, and continued on his way. In this way he met and named all the creatures of the forest, the frogs and toads and snakes and the small mice and ground squirrels and the hoofed creatures and the various cats and the monkeys and the bats and all the birds.

THE VILLAGE OF WOMEN

Finally, Ilele came to a village space, marked by a single long house. In the house he found an old man sitting alone. Ilele asked him, 'Don't you welcome strangers with gifts and food here? I am new to your village.' The old man answered, 'Do not tell me your name, if you wish to avoid harm.'

As the day drew to a close, the people of the village assembled: they were all women. One or two wished to kill Ilele immediately, without further question, but the old man said that he should be allowed the usual test: they would feed him and then ask him their names. Then they would kill him, if he failed. So Ilele got food and shelter for a night. But in the morning, after the women had left with a clatter, he could find nothing to eat as he swept out the rubbish.

He took the rubbish behind the long house to throw it away, and was about to relieve himself when a voice spoke up; looking more carefully, he saw an old woman lying under the leaves, covered with ashes and grime. She asked him to wash her face; after some hesitation, he agreed, fetched some water, and cleaned her face. He asked her how she came to be in this condition, and she explained that she had been the chief woman of the village, until a younger woman took her place, and now she enjoyed no respect or consideration from the others. Then she gave him advice on passing the test. He told the old man he was going to look for some raffia for weaving, but instead he slipped away from the long house towards the pond which

the women were seining to harvest the fish. It was an artificial
pond, the waters held back by a small dyke.

Watching carefully to make sure no one saw him, he used a
long pole to break a hole in the lower end of the dyke, so the
water began to run out. Then he waited and listened. Soon a
woman noticed the damage and ran to repair it, calling to the
others to come: Byekela, Nkongaukola, Bongolobokyakonga,
Losawaila, Balafasa, Lisekela, Boswe . . . Each called the other,
and Ilele, hidden, carefully noted and remembered the names.
That evening, when all assembled for the meal, they called on
him to name them; to their astonishment, he was able to go
round the room addressing each woman by her name.

They accepted him then, and gave him lots of food; he
immediately shared it with the old man, Imentuka, and with
the old woman who had given him the advice. As they were
eating, Mbombe appeared at the edge of the village. Without
saying anything, she joined the circles around the servings of
food and prepared to eat, but the women protested: she must
first name them before she ate. She named them all, and then
sat down and in one mouthful devoured all the food before her.
In a few moments, she had eaten all the rest of the food, and
the other women withdrew in dismay. Later, Mbombe joined
Ilele where he lay under the shade-structure before the long
house. 'This is my place,' she told him. 'No one else may come
here. Were those women your wives?'

'No,' answered Ilele, 'they are just women from the village.'

MBOMBE'S PREGNANCY

Ilele and Mbombe eventually returned to his village and
Mbombe became pregnant. Her appetite vanished; try what he
might, Ilelangonda could not get her to eat. But one day a bird
flying over the village dropped something, and Mbombe picked
it up and took it to her husband. 'Tell me, Ilele, what is this?'

'It is called a safu nut; if you cook it in water it becomes soft
and good to eat.' Mbombe cooked the safu nut and ate it; she
found it delicious, and her appetite returned. But all she wanted

to eat was more safu nuts. She even began to sing love songs to the hornbill that had dropped the fruit. Ilele realized he would have to go and get her some safu nuts. He waited until the hornbill flew by again, and asked him where he had found the nut. The hornbill said that though a bird might easily get the nuts, a human would find it difficult; the tree stood in Sausau's land and was carefully guarded. Ilele assembled his household and told them what he was about to do. Rather than let his wife sing love songs to a hornbill, he would get her the fruit. If they saw the horn in the shade-house fill with blood, they would know he had run into trouble and was dead. He told them other signs as well. Then he took several baskets and left.

After some travel, he came to the safu nut tree which was guarded by a man called Fetefete who was covered with sores and boils. Ignoring him, Ilele climbed the tree and quickly filled his baskets with safu nuts.

'Throw me some nuts,' called Fetefete, but Ilele simply pelted him with unripe nuts, hitting his sores. Fetefete then gave the alarm and Sausau's village assembled with their weapons to capture the thief. Ilele sang a song of challenge, but then nimbly leaped down and ran away before they could catch him.

When he got home, Mbombe was delighted and devoured the safu nuts. As soon as they were all gone, she again began to weep and to sing her love song to the hornbill who had brought her the first safu nut. Ilele picked up his baskets and returned to the safu tree. He exchanged words with Fetefete, and climbed into the tree; Fetefete gave the alarm. The villagers assembled and spread their nets around the tree. Then they sent the bonjemba bird to fly up and knock the man out of the tree, but Ilele threw a nut at it and knocked it to the ground. Then Ilelangonda made a flying leap outside the circle of the nets and escaped.

This happened many times: Mbombe would eat the nuts as soon as Ilelangonda brought them home, and then weep; Ilele would make his way to the tree, collect more nuts, and then escape the guardians. If they came too close to him, he would pull out his little bell and call down thunder and lightning on them before leaping out of the circle of nets. Finally, the caterpillar-bird told Sausau they must change their strategy if they wished to catch Ilele. They must creep up quietly on him while he was still in the tree, and then guide his fall into their nets. Meanwhile, the turtle, who is well known as a clever trickster, had devised his own plan. He noted that the nets made of woven vines used by all the others failed to catch Ilele and so he made some nets of banana-fibre, which is weak and flimsy. The other villagers laughed at him. He also went off and dug a pit in the area where he had noticed Ilele usually escaped. Over the pit he strung his banana-net.

The next time Ilele came to steal safu nuts for his pregnant wife, they put their plan into action. Fetefete alerted them quietly; they all crept up in silence and surrounded the tree. Then Sausau gave the signal: the guinea-fowl flew up to knock Ilele out of the tree, but Ilele simply threw an overripe nut at the fowl and it spattered the bird with white marks, which it bears to this day. Other birds also flew up, but Ilele held them off with a barrage of nuts. Finally, the blue pheasant darted under his missiles and succeeded in striking the man, and both of them fell from the tree. But then Ilele vanished into the bushes; he was not in the nets they had stretched. They were looking here and there, perplexed, when they heard a cry from a distance away: it was the turtle, calling that he had captured their prey. They did not believe him. But the turtle continued to shout, and so some of Sausau's men wandered over. There they found that Ilele had fallen into the turtle's trap and was lying pierced by the stake which the turtle had planted in the pit.

They took up the body and bore it before Father Sausau. They said that they had captured and killed Ilele. When the turtle tried to break into the circle and say that it was his trap that had captured and killed the thief, they pushed him away. He could not be heard.

'If you killed him,' said Father Sausau, 'then you should cut him up.'

The four men tried to butcher the body, but they failed. Their knives had no effect on the remains of Ilele. Then the turtle came in, carrying a sharpened wooden blade. 'Let me try,' he called, and since the others obviously could not do the job, he was allowed to proceed. Almost instantly, he reduced the carcass to pieces. The people acclaimed him as the slayer of Ilelangonda.

The signs that Ilele had foretold became manifest in his village: his sister Inonge came crying that the stream had risen beyond its banks; a rope he had coiled had unrolled; the monkeys who sat in the trees over the village had begun to weep and cry, and then a woman came from the shade-house in the village to say that the horn had filled with blood. Ilelangonda's entire household went into a tumult of weeping and mourning, tearing their hair and lamenting.

Inonge went to Mbombe, who was sitting in front of their house, unmoved. 'Why are you not weeping? Your husband went off into danger, only to get you food for your special appetite, and now he has died in the venture, and you sit there while all the others are weeping. You should be mourning, you who ate the fruit. The price of that fruit was his life. Why are you not weeping?'

'I cannot weep,' said Mbombe. 'I feel the pains of labour.'

THE BIRTH OF LIANJA

Mbombe's pregnancy was huge, amazing all who saw it. She could not fit through doors; she suffered from the weight and the burden. As all around her were wailing for the death of Ilelangonda, Mbombe leaned back and began to give birth.

First came the red ants and the white ants, and then all the other insects: beetles and spiders and moths and flies and mosquitoes. Then came the birds. Finally came the various clans of men, and as they emerged Inonge asked them their names: the Balumbe and the Bolenge and the Ntomba and the Baenga, specialized fishers and other groups. Then came Entonto, younger brother of Lianja, and as he emerged he chanted, 'We shall be avenged! The insult shall be punished!'

There was a pause, and nothing came forth from Mbombe.

But her contractions continued; she was still in labour. A voice came from within her. 'My mother, I see that slaves have dirtied the path I should take. I shall not go that way; find me another passage.'

Mbombe cried out, 'There is no other passage! I have no choice! You must come that way.' But the voice within her called out, 'No, I shall not take the common path. Mark your leg with kaolin and I shall come out with my sister.'

Mbombe marked her leg with kaolin and immediately it swelled to the size of a tree-trunk. The skin split and out came a big and handsome man, fully armed and carrying a bell. With a gesture, he flew up onto the roof of the house. He called, 'Nsongo, my sister, come out!' and he was followed by a beautiful woman who shone like the sun, and she too flitted up to the roof of the house.

Looking down from the roof, Lianja Anyakanyaka greeted the people of the village by name, and then leaped down to the ground. His sister followed.

'Mbombe, my mother,' said Lianja, 'where is your husband, my father?'

'My husband has died,' said Mbombe.

'How did he die?' asked Lianja.

'He died while fishing on the river,' answered Mbombe.

'We shall see,' said Lianja. 'Turtle!' he called, and the turtle appeared. 'Take a canoe into the stream.' The turtle took a canoe into the stream; the wood split in two, leaving the turtle swimming to shore.

'How did our father die?' Lianja again asked Mbombe.

'He died while cutting down a tree.'

Lianja sent the turtle to cut a tree; it fell upon him, but he was not killed. 'That is not how our father died,' said Lianja, and Mbombe admitted the truth: Ilelangonda had been killed while fetching safu nuts for her from the land of Sausau.

THE WAR WITH SAUSAU

Lianja prepared war with Sausau. Entonto went ahead; in the forest he met Sausau's Pygmy hunters, the Batwa, numbering at least seventy. He killed them to the last one and proceeded on his way. He found Sausau sitting in an assembly, and announced himself. Sausau proclaimed that he had killed Ilelangonda while the man was stealing his safu nuts, and produced his head. Entonto said that Lianja was coming to avenge his father, and Sausau scoffed: Lianja was only a child, still trailing his umbilical cord. How could he hope to avenge his father? Entonto left the assembly and returned to Lianja, who mustered his troops.

Lianja led his army into battle. First he sent the flies and bees and wasps, but Sausau turned them away with a fire of smoke made from banana-leaves. Then he sent the clans of men: the Balumbe, who fought until their leader was killed and then ran away, the Bolenge, whose leader was also killed, then the Ntomba and the Bonsela; none of them could stand against the forces of Sausau.

Entonto marched to the front, and there he met Bongenge, son of Sausau. They fought; Bongenge pierced Entonto's shield with his spear, but Entonto pierced Bongenge's heart and he fell dead. Then Sausau leaped onto the field, fully armed, and struck Entonto down.

A bird came calling to Lianja to announce his brother's death. Lianja flew immediately to the central battlefield where Entonto had fallen and found Sausau there.

'Ah, Sausau,' called Lianja, 'summon your sister, let her join mine and watch us battle. How many spears have you?'

'I have thirty-two spears,' cried Sausau.

'Nsongo!' cried Lianja. 'Beat the bell! The battle begins!'

Sausau threw a spear which pierced Lianja; Lianja fell to the ground, but then the spear flew back through the air and his wound healed. He leaped to his feet and called to Sausau, 'Come, throw your spear! Kill me if you can!'

Sausau threw all his spears, but none of them could kill

Lianja; all flew back out of the wound and were lost in the
forest. Then the two men came to grips, and soon Lianja had
overpowered Sausau. He seized him, threw him to the ground,
and called to Nsongo for his magic knife. She came down and
handed it to him; with it, he cut off Father Sausau's head.

Nsongo spoke. 'Lianja, my brother, I love that man. Bring
him back to life.'

Lianja took out his packages of medicines; he scattered
powder over the body and then sang a spell. He brought Sausau
back to life and made him the slave of Nsongo. Then he used
his magic to revive his army, so they might join his train. But
before the marvellous march could begin, he ordered that they
cut down the safu nut tree which had caused his father's death.

They gathered around the tree-trunk with heavy steel axes;
the blades could not chip the bark. They came to Lianja and
told him the axes had been blunted by the tree. He told them
to pour a bit of water over the blades and to try again; they did
so, and this time the axes became sharp and bit into the wood.
Soon the tree fell down.

*The adventures of Lianja and Nsongo continue with their mar-
vellous march through the forest, until they reach their homeland across the river. They capture craftsmen, makers of beer
and fishers, to join their band; they capture Yampunungu the
clever hunter. Lianja struggles with Indombe the heavenly serpent, and has to capture the sun to defeat him. They fight
monsters and magicians, and finally come to a land they call
their own. There Lianja leaves his people.*

32

THE KUBA KINGDOM OF
THE BUSHOONG: MBOOM
AND WOOT

*The various peoples assembled under the Kuba kingdom in the
eastern Congo are a southward extension of the vast Mongo
grouping, extending out of the forest regions into the savannah.
This region is home to a number of kingdoms now recognized
for their cultural wealth; south of the Kuba lay the Luba states,
and to the west the kingdom of Kongo. Sheltered by the distance
from the coasts, the Kuba kingdom escaped much of the turmoil
associated with the slave-trade in central Africa and stood intact
at the time of the first extensive contacts with Europeans, at the
end of the nineteenth century. Everything about the kingdom –
the architecture, the dress, the sophisticated customs – impressed the visitors. Kuba mythology is highly variable, and
serves, as Jan Vansina has observed, as their tool for speculation
about the world; the account that follows links a number of
shorter, separate narratives published after 1950.*

At the beginning was Mboom, who was a great spirit and who
was alone. He felt pains in his belly, and then began to vomit
beings into the world, beginning with the sun, the moon and
the stars. In their light, the world took shape; the sun caused
the waters to evaporate and land appeared. After these, Mboom
vomited the crocodile, the goat, the egret, the minnow, the
leopard, the crested eagle (associated with the royal clan) and
men, along with other animals. These beings in turn vomited
other beings: the crocodile produced all the snakes and reptiles,
the goat vomited all the horned animals, the minnow all the
fish, and so on. One man vomited up the white ants and died;
the ants buried him in the earth. Another man vomited up

plants, and a third vomited up the hawk. Mboom then visited the establishments of the different beings and ordained their way of life. At that time, animals and men lived together, but this was eventually to end.

It is also said that at the beginning Mboom and Ngaan worked together, but they quarrelled in jealousy over a woman. Ngaan withdrew to the waters, and created harmful things such as crocodiles and iguanas and snakes. These creatures are now called the 'creatures of Ngaan'. It is also said that Mboom brought forth nine sons, all called Woot, each of whom was responsible for a different act of creation, from shaping the earth and making rivers flow to forging iron.

Near the village of humans was a lake of palm wine. One day, a woman soiled the lake. She was seen, and the people stopped drinking from it. The next day the lake had dried up, and there were only trees where it had been. The trees grew into a forest. Eventually, a Pygmy, hearing of the disappearance of the lake, wondered where the waters might have gone, and reasoned that the trees might have drunk them up. So he tapped various trees to see what their sap was like, and so discovered that certain palm trees gave palm wine. He collected the sap in a pot, and eventually had so much that when he drank it he became drunk and his secret was discovered. The king ordered that the seeds of the tree be collected and planted around the country. It was at this time that animals and men separated; a monkey broke the calabash of a palm-wine tapster. The tapster killed the monkey, the leopard fought the tapster, and as a result of this dispute the animals withdrew to the forest.

The king's daughter had two sons, Woot and Nyimi Longa, and two daughters. One day Woot became drunk on palm wine and lay naked; his sons laughed at him, but his daughter covered him up, and after that he decreed that only his daughter would inherit from him.

Woot contracted leprosy and retired from the village to the forest. His sister Mweel accompanied him and cared for him in his illness; they later became intimate and had a number of children. While living in the forest with Mweel, Woot discovered the items which were to become the emblems of kingship among the Kuba. When he recovered from his illness, he returned to the village with Mweel, their children, and the emblems. After his return, the incest was revealed by a Pygmy who had observed the couple in the forest, and the people of the village were outraged. The son of Mweel and Woot was forced to emigrate; he founded the Lele people. Woot and Mweel also departed the village; she went downstream, and he went upstream.

Before he left, however, Woot decided to hand over the emblems of power which he had discovered. He told his son to come to him at dawn, as Woot was leaving the village, and to ask for the 'chicken-basket'. But a Pygmy overheard the conversation and told Woot's brother Nyimi Longa what he should do. In the dim light of the early morning, Nyimi Longa accosted Woot and asked him for the 'chicken-basket', and so he, instead of Woot's son, received the emblems of kingship. Discovering the deception, Woot was furious and caused a fire which destroyed the village; his wife, Ipopa, cursed the crops and the animals so that the millet rotted on the stalk and the animals died. Then Woot and Ipopa vanished up the river.

Nyimi Longa rebuilt the village and sent messengers to Woot, and eventually they acquired new domestic animals and the fertility of the crops was restored. It is also said that on his departure Woot caused night to fall over the village, and day returned only after his brother had sent messengers to plead for the people.

Still later, there was a dispute among the clans over the kingship. The Byeeng and the Bushong clans were rivals, and they agreed to a public test of their claims: each pretender would throw a hammer into the water, and whichever hammer floated would indicate the legitimate claimant. The leader of the Byeeng clan then had his smiths make a hammer of light wood, over which they laid a thin layer of metal. But his sister was married to the leader of the Bushong, and she learned of this artifice; she switched hammers and gave her husband the wooden hammer, which naturally floated on the water when he threw it in. Therefore, the Bushong clan took the kingship. Their leader is known as Shyam Ngong, the first great king of the Bakuba and the originator of many of their distinctive practices. He gave them crops and foodstuffs, modes of dress, behaviour and customs.

THE FIRST KINGS OF
THE LUBA

The Luba kingdom formed in the area of Katanga (southern Congo) and northern Zambia, taking shape in the seventeenth and eighteenth centuries and reaching its peak in the nineteenth. Its early history was marked by warfare (for tribute and territory) and by disputes over succession. Its principal resources, exploited before the development of the kingdom, were salt and iron. This retelling is based on versions published after 1960.

The first king of the Luba was named Kongolo, who is remembered as bestial and brutal; he is said to have buried his mother alive and to have subjected his own children to the poison-ordeal because they had bothered his wives while they were cooking. But he did discover the salt-marshes which provided prosperity for the Luba people, and he is symbolically associated with the rainbow (and thus with fertility), if only because of the reddish colour of his skin. He was a conqueror, inspired by the columns of ants which he once observed at war, and he established his rule over a number of peoples. He thus became a great king, powerful if not entirely respected.

The great event of his reign was the arrival of Mbidi Kiluwe, the black-skinned hunter, who came from across the Lualaba river. He was following the pet lion of his sister, which had escaped and run away, but he had lost its trail (some say it was a large hunting-dog, nicknamed the lion, and add that Mbidi Kiluwe was himself accompanied by hunting-dogs). He met Kongolo's two sisters by the water; they had gone there to tend their fish-traps, and they were surprised to see the stranger's reflection in the water. Some say that they then ran home to announce the news, and the reactions of the crowd gave them new names: one was called Mabela, lies, and the other Bulanda, sadness. They brought the stranger into the town and welcomed him; food was laid out before him and all present began a feast. But Mbidi Kiluwe refused to eat and looked scornful. Kongolo consulted his diviner and was told that he had to make special arrangements for his guest: he must be given a specially built hut where he could eat unobserved by anyone, and there were rules for the preparation and the delivery of the food. Kongolo, who ate and drank as he wished, would never have discovered such refinements. For drinking, it appeared, the stranger required to be hidden behind a red blanket, again so that none of the common people might see him. And Mbidi Kiluwe gave Kongolo a blanket and drinking cup for his own, and taught him the rituals and decorum that are proper for a great chief. So Kongolo gave the stranger his two sisters in marriage.

After a time, either because Kongolo was showing some hostility to a rival power or, as some say, because word came that his father was ill, Mbidi Kiluwe departed for his own land. He left his two wives, both pregnant, and he gave them instructions: if their children had Kongolo's skin colour, a red-dish brown, he did not want them, but if they were black like their father they should be sent to join him. He left iron-headed arrows of a particular make for his son to bring with him when the time came. At the river which he had crossed when entering Kongolo's lands, he made a pact with the ferryman, predicting that some day his son might come fleeing Kongolo to join him. And again he said, if the son were red-skinned the ferryman should refuse him passage, but if he were black-skinned the ferryman should carry him and then refuse passage to the pursuing forces.

Bulanda gave birth to a son named Ilunga Luala, and Mabela gave birth to twins, a boy and a girl. Ilunga grew up to be a great runner and dancer and a successful warrior. He was also skilled at games, especially a game called *masoko* which involves spinning seeds in a cup-shaped hollow. It is also said that he would win at *masoko* because his seed was really made of iron in the shape of a seed. Whichever was the case, he beat his uncle Kongolo at the game and became so popular that the uncle decided it might be best to get rid of this young pretender. He tried sending the young man off to battle to conquer neighbouring peoples, hoping he would die at the front, but Ilunga returned victorious and even earned another name: Kalala Ilunga, or Ilunga the Conqueror.

So Kongolo devised a trap for Ilunga: in the centre of the dancing-ground he dug a deep pit, and at the bottom he planted spears and stakes. He covered over the top with mats and sand so the pit was invisible. But Ilunga was wary; he consulted a diviner who was well disposed to him, and the diviner told him he should pay especial attention to the drums while he was dancing. The drums were the tone drums that are used to mimic the tones of human speech, and skilful drummers would always weave messages and praises into their music during a dance. So during the dance Ilunga listened to the tones as well as the rhythms of the drums, and the drummers, who knew of the trap that lay beneath the sand, warned him when his leaps and high steps brought him too close to the pit. He carried a spear as he danced, and finally he hurled the spear to the ground over the pit, and it broke through the mats and revealed the trap that had been laid. Then Ilunga leaped over the pit, dashed through the crowds, and made his escape. He ran to the diviner, who gave him the arrow left by his father, Mbidi Kiluwe, and then he ran on out of the town and towards the land of his father. At the river, the ferryman knew him by his skin colour and gave him passage, and he came to the kingdom which his father now ruled.

Kongolo followed after, more slowly. It is said that he stranded the men who had helped Ilunga at the top of a tree, although one was able to escape. But when Kongolo came to the river he was checked: true to the promise made to Mbidi Kiluwe, the ferryman had hidden the canoes and there was no other way across the river. Kongolo's men tried to make boats of reeds, but these sank.

When Kalala Ilunga returned at the head of an army, Kongolo was forced into a retreat. He moved through the various towns of his kingdom, leaving monuments of sorts to his passage: a rock-formation which is said to be due to the axes of his soldiers trying to cut a passage, and a canal to create a moat around his campsite. Kongolo came to the Lukuvu river, and this time was able to cross – there were far fewer in his party. He rewarded this ferryman with copper-worked emblems: a red paddle with strips of copper, a copper axe, and a copper arm-ring. Then he took refuge in a cave. The only people left with him at this point were his two wives.

Kalala Ilunga followed after. He also was ferried across the river, and he also rewarded the ferryman with copper emblems matching those presented by Kongolo. The ferryman's clan has preserved almost all these emblems until the present time, at the cost of bitter and sometimes violent rivalry between different branches of the family. It is said that the paddles were kept reddened with the blood of sacrifices.

They eventually captured Kongolo. His wives were getting tired of their situation, and when one of them met a warrior scouting for Kalala Ilunga's army she quickly reached an agreement on delivering Kongolo. One day, when Kongolo came out of the cave the wives quickly blocked the entrance with the firewood they had been collecting, and Kalala Ilunga's warriors were able to capture the fugitive king. He was later beheaded, and possibly castrated as well. His parts were buried, or carried underground by termites. Kalala Ilunga became the undisputed ruler of the land, apportioning regions and positions to his followers, and his followers became kings after him, obeying the rules and procedures established by the hunter Mbidi Kaluwe.

34
THE KINGDOMS OF
THE LUNDA

The Lunda owed much of their royal political system to the Luba, as can be seen in the similarity of their stories to those of the preceding chapters. Lunda power was essentially based on conquest; they established themselves in territories lying south of the Luba kingdom, and spread both east and west so that in the eighteenth century they occupied the central portion of southern Africa, and were in contact with the Portuguese from both coasts, from Angola and from Mozambique. The older kingdom, that of Mwata Yamvu (a dynastic title), lay to the west; that of Mwata Kazembe lay to the east. They conquered many peoples, some of whose stories are told below, and the title at least of Mwata Kazembe lasted until the independence of Zambia. These narratives are retold from versions published around 1950.

THE KINGDOM OF MWATA YAMVU

A king named Nkonde ruled in the land of Kapanga. He had four children: two older sons, Kinguli and Chinyama, a daughter named Luweji, and a youngest son named Lyulu. One day, however, he burst out in anger against his two older sons. Various reasons are given for his anger: some people say that he got drunk and that his sons saw him naked. Others say that the sons found their father engaged in making grass mats. He had beside him a bundle of long grasses, and on the other side a bowl of water in which he dipped the grasses to make them supple for the weaving. The water had become cloudy from the dust on the grasses, and the two sons thought it was palm wine. They reproached their father for drinking alone and not sharing the palm wine, and he reacted angrily. Whatever the reason, Nkonde declared that they would never rule after him, and that his daughter Luweji would receive the royal bracelet and rule the kingdom.

King Nkonde fell sick soon after this episode and died. His counsellors debated, but the royal decree had been clear: the daughter must rule after her father. Otherwise, whatever the problems associated with a female ruler, they would face far more serious problems from the angry spirit of the king. So they dressed Luweji to become king and gave her the bracelet of royalty, and she ruled in the place of King Nkonde.

Luweji was not married, and she hesitated to choose a husband because of the rivalries her choice might cause among the clans of the kingdom. She ruled alone, assisted by her younger brother Lyulu. When her monthly periods came upon her, she would entrust the royal bracelet to Lyulu while she retired to the women's hut.

One day, women who had gone down to the stream to fetch water saw on the other bank a tall and handsome man, equipped as a hunter. He had entered the territory pursuing an antelope which he had wounded, and he was resting by the water, weary from the pursuit. The women reported his presence, and the strange hunter was soon invited to the royal court. There, Queen Luweji clearly found his company enjoyable, and he spent more and more time sitting on a mat beside her, even during her court sessions. After some time, she informed her counsellors that she had decided to marry the stranger. They objected strongly, but she called her lover before them and asked him to explain who he was. He told them that his name was Chibinda Ilunga, and that he was a grandson of the first king of the Luba and the brother of the present king. Where his brother preferred making war and hunting men, he preferred to spend his time in the bush and to hunt animals. It was in this way that he had come to the land of the Lunda, pursuing an animal that he had wounded. The counsellors reluctantly agreed that Chibinda Ilunga was of royal lineage, and a worthy consort for Luweji. Still, the news caused great dissension in the kingdom. The two older brothers, Kinguli and Chinyama, announced that they would depart with all their followers. They were willing to live under the rule of their sister, according to their father's wish, but they would not accept the rule of a stranger. So they left the kingdom, and many others followed them into exile. The royal town was much smaller after their departure; many huts stood empty and eventually fell into ruin.

One brother made his way west to Kambamba, where he encountered the Portuguese and allied with them for some military campaigns, which won him lands. It is said he helped the Portuguese against Queen Nzinga of Angola. Chinyama went south, across the Zambezi, and founded his own capital and ruled there.

Chibinda Ilunga then married Luweji, and they lived together. Soon after the marriage, however, her period came upon her. She handed the royal bracelet to her new husband, and ordered the people to obey him as they would her. This command caused great dissension among the people. Many who had accepted the marriage were unwilling to accept the rule by a stranger, and so more clans emigrated to new lands.

Time passed. Luweji and Chibinda Ilunga had no children. Eventually, Luweji told her husband to take a second wife, named Kamonga Lwaza. They did indeed have a son, who became known as Mwata Luseng. It was he who established the royal offices such as the Lukonkeshya, the senior queen mother. Mwata Luseng's sons engaged in warfare. On his death, his son Naweji became king and took the title of Mwata Yamvu. The meaning of the name was a threat: he promised to conquer or to kill all the chiefs who had fled the kingdom at the time of Luweji's marriage to Chibinda Ilunga. The name Mwata Yamvu became the dynastic title of the Lunda kings in that area after him.

Mwata Yamvu sent armies out from the Lunda kingdom to subdue neighbouring peoples, and over them he then placed Lunda rulers, so that in this region all the Lunda are commonly held to be chiefs. His son Mwata Yamvu Muteba continued this policy. An early conflict which ended peacefully was with

King Kinyanta, whose power rivalled that of Mwata Yamvu and who was descended from Lyulu, brother of Luweji. But the war-leader whom Mwata Yamvu had sent against Kinyanta succeeded in capturing Kinyanta's mother, and so Kinyanta submitted and swore allegiance to Mwata Yamvu. The two armies combined and launched new conquests.

In the royal capital, however, a disaster occurred. A great fire broke out and destroyed much of the town and killed a prince, Muchaili. The fire had started near the blacksmiths' quarter, and so the king held the chief blacksmith, Lubunda, responsible for the death of his son. Lubunda was ordered to build a tower that would reach the sun, so the king might have the flames of the sun as part of his ceremonial raiment. Lubunda and his workers began the task, constructing a great scaffolding of bamboo and wooden poles, bound tightly with leather thongs, and their tower rose high above the royal town. But the materials were not strong enough for the great height, and after a time, long before reaching the sun, the tower collapsed into the capital, killing many people with its fall. Lubunda survived, and immediately fled the capital. He took his tools and many of his followers, and his trail was quickly lost.

Some time later, however, a trader came to the royal capital, and among his goods were fine little iron bells and other articles of metal such as knives and copper ornaments. The king questioned him on the source of these articles, and the trader answered that the metal objects had come from a land far to the east, near the Lualaba river, where there were several rulers, among them a smith named Lubunda. Mwata Yamvu Muteba decided that this must be the Lubunda who had fled his kingdom, and so he appointed war-leaders to lead an army and capture Lubunda. He gave the principal leader, Mutanda Yembe-Yembe, a royal drum to take with him, as a sign that Mutanda enjoyed a complete delegation of royal authority. Mutanda was accompanied by Kinyanta, who was descended from Lyulu, brother of Queen Luweji.

PEOPLES OF THE LUAPULA RIVER

These stories are told by the peoples who were subdued by the Lunda and brought under the rule of Mwata Kazembe some time in the late eighteenth century. They inhabit a swampy valley south of Lake Mweru, which separates Zambia from the Congo. In recent years they have made their living from fishing in the lake; the land on which they live is not really suitable for agriculture. The peoples of the valley settled there in different times, before the conquest by the Lunda.

There were two brothers of the Clay clan. One was named Kaponto, the other Matanda. They lived beside the river. One day the children were playing by the river. Kaponto's daughter was playing with a doll which belonged to Matanda's daughter, and she accidentally threw it into the water farther than she could reach to get it back. The doll drifted with the current and was lost. Matanda's daughter complained to her father, and her father complained to his brother, demanding that Kaponto's daughter become his slave to make up the loss. Kaponto refused, although he offered some restitution for the doll. But Matanda was stubborn, and so Kaponto decided to take his family away.

They travelled down the river, and came eventually to a great grassy plain; beyond them they saw a rise with seven distinct hills. They decided to move to the hills and settle there. But the group moved slowly, and so they had to camp before they reached the hills. In the morning, they failed to stamp out their cooking-fire as thoroughly as they should have done; it smouldered and set fire to the grass. The fire spread swiftly over the plain, and brought death to the odd people who lived there: tiny people with huge heads who fell over and were then unable to rise again. All the tiny people died in the fire except for one old couple. The old couple instructed Kaponto on the rituals to follow when burying the dead, and what he should do when he wished to bring rain, and on other practices which they told him to continue. He and his followers were preparing to bury the small people when the rains began to fall. The rains brought a great flood. The humans took refuge on the hills, but even there they were threatened. It was Kaponto's sister who saved them: she showed them how to make themselves canoes from the trees, so that they could ride the waters. She modelled the boat upon her body, and even now the footrests for the paddlers are known as the 'breasts of Kaponto's sister'. The name Kaponto then became the title of the ritual land-master of the territory, although chieftainship was then unknown in the area. The rains eventually stopped, but the waters did not vanish: they became Lake Mweru. The place of the seven hills is known as Kilwa island.

Some time later, in the hills to the east of the valley, there was a dispute among the Bemba of the Crocodile clan. The cause of the dispute was also a doll lost in the water; Nkuba refused to offer a human life to make up for the loss of the doll, and chose rather to go into exile. He sent scouts ahead to find a place to live. The scouts came to the land where the descendants of Kaponto and his people lived, and found them living very simply. They had no chiefs, and they had little idea of the value that other humans placed upon goods: they used ivory as if it were stone. The scouts went hunting and killed an elephant; as was their custom, they then presented the tusks of the elephant to the ritual land-master, treating him as the chief of the land. But he complained he had no use for the ivory, and suggested they should give him meat instead. The scouts returned to Nkuba and told him they had found a land where people had no unity or power. So Nkuba moved into the valley and took power, through a combination of battles and marriage alliances with the various clans. The older inhabitants of the land became known as the Bwilile, while the Bemba newcomers took the name of Shila.

THE KINGDOM OF MWATA KAZEMBE

Mutanda Yembe-Yembe led his troops east, conquering lands in the name of Mwata Yamvu. In the meantime, Mwata Yamvu Muteba died, and was succeeded by Mwata Yamvu Mukanzu. Mutanda returned to the royal court to swear allegiance to Mukanzu, and he was confirmed in his rule of the lands he had conquered. These lands included an area which provided salt of good quality, far better than the poor stuff made from burned reeds which was available at the Lunda court. The salt would cause problems. At a later time, Mutanda was again summoned to the royal court; a wound on his leg prevented him from travelling, and so he sent Kinyanta as his emissary, warning him not to mention the salt plain which was part of their domain. But Kinyanta hid two lumps of salt and at a suitable moment brought them out to season the food of Mwata Yamvu Mukanzu. Mukanzu then appointed Kinyanta to be Kazembe (governor) of the province of the Lualaba, because Mutanda had shown himself untrustworthy in the matter of the salt. Kinyanta returned to his domain, but Mutanda Yembe-Yembe had been warned of the royal order. He immediately imprisoned Kinyanta. But Kinyanta escaped, thanks to his wife: she pleaded to be allowed to bring him food, and Mutanda agreed. In the food-bowl she hid a knife, and with it Kinyanta cut his bonds and escaped. But he was quickly recaptured: Mutanda threatened to torture his son, and the child's mother revealed where her husband was hiding, waiting for her to bring him more food.

However, they were unable to kill Kinyanta. Despite all their attempts and the torments to which they put him, he did not die. At last his wife told them how he might be killed: he should be wrapped in a fishing-net with a mortar and pestle, weighted down with grindstones, and submerged in the river. When they did this, Kinyanta perished. Mutanda also killed Kinyanta's brother Kisombola, and the two became tutelary spirits of the waters, honoured by paired shrines throughout the lands of the eastern Lunda.

News of Kinyanta's death was brought to the Lunda court, and Mwata Yamvu Mukanzu appointed Kinyanta's son Nganga a Bilonda to be the first Kazembe of the lands of the Lualaba. He sent him back accompanied by a large army, and at this news, Mutanda Yembe-Yembe took his followers and fled to the south. Kazembe Nganga found only smouldering ruins when he turned to his town.

Kazembe Nganga followed Mwata Yamvu Mukanzu's instructions, and undertook conquests to the east, spreading Lunda power. But he died soon after; people say that it was because of contact with the head of a king whom he had conquered. Following a divination practice, he had spent a night using the dead king's head as a pillow, and a vision came to him that he would soon die, and that the Lunda would never win a passage to the north.

There was a dispute over the succession: two groups arrived at the court of Mwata Yamvu Mukanzu to claim the power. But messengers had already reached the king to inform him that the people's preference was for the claimant who would place a freshly cut head at his feet. One claimant produced the head of the king that had caused the death of Nganga a Bilonda; another the still bloody head of a slave, slain that morning. Mwata Yamvu Mukanzu appointed a contest which favoured the second contender: each should shoot an arrow at a hollow in a great tree near the royal compound. In this way Kanyembo Mpemba was appointed the second Mwata Kazembe, and the dividing line between the two royal domains was the Lualaba river.

Mwata Kazembe Kanyembo returned to his side of the Lualaba river and prepared to launch new conquests. He was blocked for a time by the Luapula river; his army could not find a safe ford. The army captured a man named Kapwasa, who promised to show them the ford, but after they let him go to find other guides, he vanished. Some time later, they captured a chief named Kisamamba, who pleaded to be allowed to fish for them; when they let him go in his dugout canoe, he too vanished. They captured Kisamamba's brother, who told them he would show them how to make oil from *mufutu* nuts. He pounded the nuts in a great mortar, and placed the pulp into a pot of boiling water. Soon he was sweating profusely, such was the heat of his work and of the day, and so the guards allowed him down to the river to draw some water. He dived in and vanished, for the fishermen of the Luapula were all capable of swimming underwater from one side of the river to the other.

At last, Mwata Kazembe Kanyembo succeeded in crossing the river: his scouts found three women digging up roots, and the women showed them the ford. The army crossed the river and arrived in the lands of the chief Kipepa. The women were in fact the wife and daughters of Kipepa. Kanyembo drove a spear into a great tree near the ford, to mark the place where the Lunda had crossed the river, and swore a pact of friendship with Kipepa.

Kanyembo then overcame Makumba, the divinity of the Baushi. His soldiers captured Makumba, and then they tried to burn the great block of wood (some say it was amber), covered with oils and feathers and cowrie-shells from past offerings. But the statue would not burn; instead, the men tending the fire suffered burns from sparks flying out of the fire, and they developed blisters and boils. Kanyembo then ordered them to put out the fire. He came forth and placed cowrie-shells and crane-feathers on the block of wood, and they stuck immediately. He told Makumba that they were henceforth united. Makumba showed agreement by healing the king's men of their burns and blisters.

Mwata Kazembe Kanyembo died an old man, after continuing his conquests throughout his lifetime. He was buried in the river: his servants diverted the flow of the water, dug a great pit, and there they placed the body of the king and the offerings to accompany him, including slaves and servants. Then they released the waters, and the river flowed over the tomb.

It was the third Kazembe, Ilunga, who completed the conquest of the Luapula valley and the lands ruled by Nkuba. Nkuba had successfully resisted the Lunda up to that point, because they were unable to penetrate the swamps in which he dwelt. But a family quarrel brought him down. One day, he became very angry with his nephew, and threw a piece of wood

at him which struck him on the head and killed him. Nkuba
then had the body skinned and made a seat from the tanned
hide. He told the boy's mother, his sister, that her son had
died hunting. But Nachituti soon learned the truth and swore
vengeance. She left Nkuba's court and went to find Mwata
Kazembe Ilunga. As she was talking, she undid the cloth around
her waist and threw it into the Kazembe's face, saying that if
he did not avenge her, he was nothing but a woman.

The king sent out a strong force. They quickly captured
Kisenga, Nkuba's town, but the ruler had escaped. They pursued him through several villages, and finally Nachituti had
the satisfaction of beholding her brother's severed head on
the ground before her. The army returned to Kalandala, the
Kazembe's seat, and they displayed their trophies. Last in line
came Nachituti, carrying a small basket of earth and a small
gourd filled with water. She hailed the Kazembe as her avenger,
and then, kneeling, proffered the basket and the gourd. Thus
the Kazembe became the master of the land and the waters of
the Luapula.

THE BEMBA OF ZAMBIA

The Bemba are politically an offshoot of the Luba kingdom, representing a wave of colonization that moved south-east to the headwaters of the Lualaba river. They brought with them the Luba practice of expansive warfare, and in the nineteenth century were assisted by superior weapons from the Arabs trading for slaves from the east coast of Africa. This version is principally based upon an account published by a missionary in 1933.

There was a woman with ears as large as those of an elephant, and she ruled in her territory because her uncle had come down from the sky. She married a man named Mukulumpe, and they had four children: three sons and a daughter.

The three sons decided to build a great tower with which to return to the sky, and they compelled people all over the country to come and help them, cutting trees and branches and building the tower out of wood. But after a time the tower grew too high and collapsed upon itself, and as it did so many people were killed either from falling or from the wood that fell on them. Mukulumpe was furious with his sons for this disaster and ordered that they all be killed. But two of them escaped his guards and fled into the forest. He blinded the one son he had caught, named Katongo, and then planned how he might lure the other two back to be executed. He ordered his servants to go out and dig pits along the paths, and to plant spears at the bottom of the pits. Then he sent messengers out across the country to proclaim that his sons would be forgiven if they came to their father in the dead of night. He hoped, of course, that in the dark they would fall into the pits and die on the spears. But the blind brother, Katongo, learned of the plan and he too sent messengers out to his brothers, telling them to avoid the great paths and the traps that their father had set for them.

The two brothers, Nkole and Chiti, heard both messages, and decided to return home. They took small sidepaths and avoided the places where their father had set the traps, and so came in the dead of night to his hut. There they called loudly on him and identified themselves, and since he had given his word that if they came to him in the dead of night, he was bound to forgive them and he did so. But he did punish them: he ordered them to sweep out the entire space of the royal compound, as though they were servants. Despite the humiliation, they obeyed.

But they got into trouble again, and legend suggests that it was because of one of their father's younger wives. Mukulumpe wanted to punish them by making them sweep the royal cemetery, but they resisted this humiliation and killed some of the messengers. Then they fled, taking with them some of their half-brothers. Mukulumpe, seeing the collapse of his kingdom, sent his first wife, the woman of the elephant ears, back to her village, where she died of sorrow, and he assigned lands to the rest of his sons. But he kept his daughter, Chilufya Mulenga, with him, for power ran through the female line. As she was nubile, he enclosed her in a hut without entrances and had her guarded.

The princes, Nkole, Chiti, Katongo and their half-brothers, set out guided by an *nganga* (a diviner; some say the diviner was white, and perhaps Portuguese). They crossed a river, marking the spot with spears and arrows shot into the trunk of a tree and on the far bank they built a first village. At that point, Chiti began to miss his sister, and he sent a group of men, led by his half-brother Kapasa, back to their father's compound to fetch her. The group travelled stealthily back into the kingdom of Mukulumpe; they slipped past the guards and the bells that had been set to sound the alarm, and raised the roof of the doorless hut. Whispering, they told Chilufya Mulenga who they were and why they had come. She agreed to depart with them, and the party slipped out of the town and started on their way back. They came to an island in the middle of the Lualaba river, and Kapasa told his men that they would rest there for a day or so. He sent two messengers to inform Chiti that they had been successful; the first began to run at dawn, in the cold, and when he arrived Chiti rejoiced and placed him in the royal seat and gave him his own pipe. The second messenger did not leave so quickly, and was embarrassed when he arrived and found his companion being honoured. This event remains the basis of a royal ritual. On the island, Kapasa seduced his half-sister Chilufya Mulenga during the night and she became pregnant. They kept the secret for some time after her reunion with her full brothers, but eventually it could not be hidden any more. Kapasa was expelled from the royal clan and withdrew in shame to another country.

The brothers consulted their diviner to learn what they should do next; he replied that they should see whether the spirits would provide food for them in another country, and then put a fishing-line with a hook into a mortar. After a time, he drew out a fish, and they interpreted this omen to mean that they would have food if they continued on their way, and so they moved on. But Kasemba, one of the half-brothers, stayed in that place and became ruler. Other clans also split off from the group in their travels. One became known as the Mushroom clan (the Bena Ngona) because a woman had refused some tasty mushrooms to the mother of a hungry child, saying she had no more; it was later discovered that she did have more mushrooms when her servant became mired in mud and the load he was carrying was spread out in front of everyone. They came to the land of a chief named Mwase, whose wife was Chilumbulu. Chilumbulu was very beautiful, and her body was adorned with a complex pattern of scars. Chilumbulu and Chiti felt a strong attraction for each other, but Chiti dared do nothing with the wife of his host. But Chilumbulu made a ball of gum and dyed it red; she rolled the ball over the pattern of scars on her breast and then sent it to Chiti. The invitation was clear, and the two of them arranged a rendezvous at a little camp by a river. They spent three nights together, until Mwase became suspicious and went looking to see what was happening. He brought his hunting equipment, a bow and poisoned arrows, and he caught the pair in the act. In the struggle that followed, he managed to scratch Chiti with a poisoned arrow. Then he escaped with his wife.

Chiti died some days later of the poison, and Nkole swore vengeance for his brother. He executed the companions who had not protected Chiti, and then led an army against Mwase. The town was overrun; Mwase and Chilumbulu died. They made a charm to ensure fertility for the millet from the ornamented skin of Chilumbulu's body. Then Nkole ordered a sumptuous royal funeral for his brother. He himself died soon after and was buried next to Chiti. His heir was the son of his sister Chilufya Mulenga, although he was then too young to take power.

Guided by their *nganga*, the people eventually established the Bemba royal town, Ngwena, because of two omens: one adviser caught a warthog, and the presence of game was interpreted as a good sign. Another adviser came upon the carcass of a crocodile, which was the royal emblem, and they interpreted this sign to mean that they should build the royal town at that site. They did so, and the son of Chilufya Mulenga became king under the name of Chilufya.

THE PEOPLES OF
SOUTHERN AFRICA

The history of southern Africa, from Zimbabwe south to the Cape of Good Hope, is complex and well documented. It is in part a history of immigrations: of Bantu-speakers from the north, who brought with them cattle and formed the Nguni peoples (Xhosa, Zulu, Swazi) which now compose the majority of black South Africans, and of European immigrants from the south: first came Portuguese traders, who left names (the province of Natal in South Africa takes its name from the Portuguese word for Christmas, the date on which a Portuguese explorer sighted the land) and also established colonies on the east and west coasts (Mozambique and Angola). Then in the early eighteenth century came the Dutch settlers who became known as Boers (farmers, in Dutch), later as Afrikaners. Last came the English, ensuring the sea-routes to their empire in India. All of these peoples displaced the original inhabitants: the San hunting peoples (see Chapter 1) and the Khoi-Khoi (Chapter 38). Colonization, followed by the struggles for liberation and against apartheid, have coloured the political history of the region with intense hues. But other events have also shaped the human landscape, and perhaps none quite as much as the mfaqane, *the upheavals of peoples caused by the foundation and expansion of the Zulu empire under Shaka at the start of the nineteenth century. His wars of conquest sent peoples fleeing to the north in a pattern of displacements which reached the Ndebele peoples of Zimbabwe. This movement of peoples was continued by the great Boer trek across the Vaal river in 1834, and subsequent struggles over land (and mineral resources: the diamonds and gold of South Africa are legend-*

ary). *The Shona of Zimbabwe, invaded by the Ndebele under Mzilikazi, seem to form the northern limit of this turbulence. To the south, the Nguni-language peoples separated into a number of related groups; the division of Zulu and Xhosa, for instance, is relatively recent, although the separation has been accentuated by the close contacts between the Xhosa and the Khoi peoples.*

In terms of the traditions of origin, there is a great deal of similarity and homogeneity to the stories reported from the various peoples. Creation and the origin of death are linked; perhaps not surprisingly, there are also many stories explaining the origins of the different peoples of the region, accounting not so much for skin colour as for the uneven distribution of wealth. But we do not find the extensive multi-generation accounts which are so common further north, around the great lakes. Throughout this region, royalty is associated with rain-making, and cattle also are a mark of wealth and nobility.

THE SHONA OF ZIMBABWE

*The Shona are spread through southern Zimbabwe and north-
ern Mozambique; unified by language, they are divided by clan
and lineage divisions and are really an amalgam of peoples
pushed together in relatively recent times (since 1750?) by the
warlike movements of their neighbours. Shona traditions are
not unified, although some practices are relatively widespread,
particularly spirit-mediumship and its accompanying musical
instrument, the mbira or thumb piano. The nation of Zimbabwe (in colonial times, Southern Rhodesia) takes its name
from the celebrated ruins, dating from the Middle Ages, but the
dynasty that built those structures has long since vanished.
These narratives are retold from accounts collected in the first
half of the twentieth century.*

CREATION: THE CULT OF MWARI
AND CHAMINUKA

In the beginning, a god known by many names – Musikavanhu,
the maker of people, or Dzivaguru, the great pool, or Mutan-
gakuvara, the one who existed at the beginning, or more simply
Mwari – created the world. He filled it with beings – humans,
animals, plants – and his power is still visible in the procreation
of creatures, for it is he who brings new life into being. But
Mwari has very little to do with the world directly. He is great
and remote. Far more immediate are the various spirits whose
actions can be seen in the world, and who communicate with

humans through mediums. There are many kinds of spirits, and the greatest is called Chaminuka.

People learned about Chaminuka a long time ago. A great tree had fallen over, and Chaminuka dwelt in the tree-trunk. People passing by heard a voice coming from the trunk, and they stopped to listen. It called them over, and then told them to shut their eyes. They did so. When they opened their eyes, there were all sorts of foodstuffs lying before them. They ate their fill. Then they closed their eyes again, and all the remains of the food and the vessels vanished.

Later, Chaminuka taught people to grow their own food, and he taught them the art of the blacksmith. He would communicate with people through dreams. He chose a young girl to teach the arts of cooking and brewing beer, and a boy to tell about the stones that contained metal which people could use to make hoes.

Eventually, Chaminuka settled on a specific human as a medium, and he would communicate with people when the medium went into a trance. Over time, many mediums have served Chaminuka. One of the greatest was Pasipamire, who lived over a hundred years ago. He was killed by the Ndebele, who were moving north into Shona territory at that time. It is said that Pasipamire and some companions were travelling when they were trapped by the Ndebele. But none of their weapons had any effect on Pasipamire. He sat calmly, smoking a pipe, while they tried every means they could think of to kill him. Finally he told them to let a young boy stab him with a spear, and that killed him. But his heart kept on beating after they cut it out, and when they put his body on a fire to burn it, they heard a voice saying that Chaminuka would return in another part of Mashonaland, and this is what happened.

Chaminuka continues to help the people by bringing rain, and this is one of the ways by which people can identify the true medium of Chaminuka.

HOW MUSKWERE BECAME CHIEF OF THE WAHUNGWE

Muskwere was a great hunter; at one time he came into the territory of Madziwa. Since Madziwa was the chief, Muskwere offered him the chief's portion of meat, the breast of the animal; Madziwa asked rather for a haunch. Muskwere interpreted Madziwa's request as the refusal of the chief's portion, and thus a denial that he was the chief, and therefore took the chief's place.

THE SOURCE OF THE SABI RIVER

The king of the Barozvi, the earlier rulers of Zimbabwe, entrusted his rain-making magic to a man named Nyakuvimba, and Nyakuvimba stole it. The king sent men with dogs to capture Nyakuvimba; they were ordered not to kill him. Nyakuvimba heard the dogs coming and knew he could not escape. He gave the bundle containing the rain-making magic to his wife, who was pregnant, and told her to escape, while he awaited his fate. The hunters caught up with him, surrounded him, and then, in the excitement of the chase, one of them killed him. They cut off his head and mounted it on a pole and began the return journey. But on the way, the head began to swell up, larger and larger, until they dropped it to the ground, and still it swelled up to an enormous size before, at last, it burst open. Out poured the waters, and they continued to pour, forming the Sabi river.

His wife continued safely on her way and eventually gave birth. The river ran past her home, and she recognized it as the sign of her husband's death. She kept the rain-making magic for her son, and he became a chief because of his powers.

THE POWER OF THE MBIRA

A man and his wife once had two sons. But they were poor, and he had very few cattle with which to pay the *lobolo*, or bride-price, for his sons. He had only enough for one wife, and after some discussion, the younger son was allowed to marry. The elder left home to find his own way to a wife. He took with him his *mbira*, for he was an accomplished player and the music was his consolation and delight. He played as he walked.

His path led him past the den of some hares, and when he tried to walk through their land they buffeted him with their paws and pushed him back, so that he could not pass. He wondered how he could pass, and then began to play his *mbira*. The hares began to dance, and as they danced he was able to pass through. He continued on his way.

His path then led him into the grazing land of large herds of wildebeest and zebra and antelope. He looked at them and considered trying to pass through, but he knew they could crush him with the weight of their bodies and their horns. He wondered how to pass through, and began to play his *mbira*. As he did so, all the grazing animals began to dance. He was able to pass through their land as they danced.

Further on, he came upon a large pride of lions. As usual, most of them were asleep, but one or two were awake and looking about, and when they yawned he could see how long and sharp their teeth were. Again, he wondered how to pass them by, and he played his *mbira*. The lions slowly rose up from their lazy slumbering and began to dance, and as they danced he passed through them and continued on his way.

He came finally to the shores of a lake, and sat by the waters playing his *mbira*. A water-spirit came up and heard him playing; the water-spirit fetched another to listen to the music, and then the two of them fetched yet more of their people. Finally, they decided that their king must hear this music. They summoned the young man and gave him a special medicine which allowed him to live under the water, and then led him down to the king's hall, where the young man played his *mbira*. The king was delighted and rewarded the young man with a village of water-spirits and a wife. Eventually, the young man returned to the dry land to tell his brother what had become of him, but the younger brother refused the invitation to visit the water-world. The older brother went back under the waters and remains there still.

37

THE NGUNI PEOPLES OF SOUTHERN AFRICA: ZULU, XHOSA, SWAZI

The differentiation of the Nguni-language peoples into their now distinctive ethnic groups is relatively recent, the consequence of different factors: separation through migration, contact with the earlier inhabitants such as the Khoi-Khoi (Xhosa), isolation in the mountains (Swazi), and, for the Zulu, the political determination of Shaka, who created the Ama-Zulu (the people of heaven) out of the union of groups under his military leadership. Issues of ethnic identity have been complicated by the colonial and later racial policies of the governments in South Africa and the notion of homelands. Swaziland and Lesotho are independent states entirely surrounded by the Republic of South Africa, so politics may exaggerate some of the differences between their peoples and their neighbours. The following versions of the stories are retold from various sources, the earliest from the late nineteenth century.

CREATION

The creation story is simple, and varies according to region and language. Among the Zulu, it is said that the creator made men from reeds (*uthlanga*) of different colours, each reed giving rise to a different lineage of humans. Among the Xhosa, the word *umhlanga* may designate a cave, and the story then is that humans and all the animals came into this world from a cave, and then took their places. Among the Swazi, reeds (*umlanga*) were the means used by the founders of the royal clan to make

boats with which they crossed a river and came into the present
territory of Swaziland.

DEATH

The creator watched the humans and decided that they should
live for ever. He summoned the chameleon and told him to
carry the message to the humans that they would not die. Then
he watched as the humans multiplied, and decided that perhaps
it would be better for them to die after all. So he summoned a
lizard, and told him to carry the message to the humans that
they would die.

The chameleon moves very slowly and deliberately. The
lizard skitters along at great speed. The lizard arrived long
before the chameleon and told the humans what the creator
had decided for them. When the chameleon arrived with his
more pleasant message, it was too late.

THE DIFFERENT PEOPLES

*There are numerous stories in this region describing the differ-
ences among peoples and the disparities of their wealth. The
following is offered as a sample, retold from a modern academic
account (see also Chapters 8 and 17 for other examples).*

At the beginning, the three kinds of men lived in the homestead
of the creator: the Khoi, the Bantu and the white. The Khoi was
given to wandering about the land, following the wild animals
and hunting them, and he particularly loved the honey-bird
who would lead him to the hives and share their sweetness. He
spent more and more time away from the homestead, and
eventually stopped coming back altogether.

The Bantu fell in love with the cattle, and would spend all his
time leading the cattle to pasture and water and salt and watching
them to ensure that no lions preyed on them or that they caught
no diseases. This became his share of the inheritance.

The white remained at the homestead, watching the creator and trying to help in his works. Because he was dutiful and diligent, he was rewarded with many of the creator's secrets, and that is why now the whites have so much more wealth than the Bantu and the Khoi.

A SWAZI STORY OF A KING

A king had many wives and many children. The principal wife's son was Madlisa; a junior wife, with her hut far out of the line of huts, had a son named Madlebe. Madlebe was unlike other children; he wept tears of blood, and he was born with a magic bracelet on his arm which cried when he did.

After many of the boys were growing up, the king decided that he should select his heir. He determined a test for the heir: the children would spit, and the one who was able to spit past the king would become the prince. The first to try was Madlisa; he spat towards his father and his spittle landed on his father's chest. Others tried; some barely cleared their own toes, while others spat four or five feet and one or two spat even further. Eventually, it was Madlebe's turn; his spittle shot out past the king and was lost in the grasses. Thunder rolled overhead and Madlebe's bracelet cried out.

The king was not sure the test had given him the right heir; Madlebe's mother was powerless and unimportant. He determined to test the boy further. He gave him a gourd for milk, a clay pot and a wooden spoon and told him to keep these items intact, on pain of his life. Madlebe's mother placed them on a shelf in her hut where they would be out of harm's way. One day Madlisa and Madlebe were playing together, and Madlisa told Madlebe he was hungry. They could not find any food in the hut. Madlisa pointed out the pot that the king had given Madlebe, but Madlebe refused to try to get it. Madlisa insisted, and eventually Madlebe agreed that they could share the food in the pot. When he reached up to bring the pot down, his hand slipped and the pot fell to the ground and broke.

Madlisa went and told the king that Madlebe had broken

the pot that had been entrusted to him. The king looked very hard at Madlisa, wondering if he had had some part in this, and then sadly turned to his guards and told them they should take Madlebe out over the savannah and kill him, since he had failed to keep the pot intact. The guards fetched Madlebe and led him out over the savannah, but when they pointed their spears at him to kill him, thunder rolled overhead and a bolt of lightning struck nearby. Madlebe was weeping tears of blood, and his bracelet also was crying. The guards recognized the signs of royal power and spared Madlebe's life. Later, he became king instead of Madlisa.

THE KHOI-KHOI: STORIES
OF HEITSI-EIBIB

*The Khoi-Khoi, concentrated in modern Namibia, are related
by language to the San hunting peoples of southern Africa, but
they have modified their lifestyle, adopting cattle-herding as a
supplement to their other food-gathering activities (see Chapter
8 for Khoi-Khoi stories about cattle). They were formerly
known as the Hottentots but that term is no longer used. They
inhabit the south-western quarter of the Kalahari desert, in a
territory which became a German colony before the First World
War (and in 1904 was the scene of a brutal campaign of
repression following a rebellion of the Khoi-Khoi against the
German colonizers), and then a protectorate at the end of the
war. Their years under the protectorate of South Africa, before
Namibia became independent in 1990, were not a period of
great prosperity.*

*This account of the adventures of Heitsi-Eibib is taken from
sources collected at the end of the nineteenth century, and the
doings of this figure might be compared with the San stories of
Khaggen/Mantis (Chapter 1) or the Maasai stories of the origin
of cattle (Chapter 10).*

THE BIRTH OF HEITSI-EIBIB

There are different stories about the birth of Heitsi-Eibib. One
says that he was born of a cow which ate from a luxuriant
clump of grass and then became pregnant. She gave birth to a
bull-calf which grew into an extraordinarily large animal. One
day the people decided it was time to slaughter the bull, but

when they came with their knives it ran away down a hill until they lost sight of it. They followed in its direction, and when they came to the place where the bull had disappeared they found a man carving milk-containers from gourds. They asked the man which way the bull had gone, and he asked them, 'Which bull?' But in fact the man was Heitsi-Eibib himself.

Another story says that Heitsi-Eibib was born to a young woman. She and the others had gone out to fetch firewood, and she pulled a stalk of grass from a rich clump and chewed on it and swallowed the juice. And so she became pregnant. When she gave birth she had a son who was very clever.

HEITSI-EIBIB'S MISCHIEF

Once, a cow was slaughtered and Heitsi-Eibib made himself into a large pot. The people put the meat and the fat in the pot to cook. But the pot absorbed all the fat, so when they took out the meat it was dry and flavourless.

Another time, when he was a young child, Heitsi-Eibib accompanied his mother and some other women as they were travelling. He was very difficult and fretful, requiring his mother's attention, so she had to carry him. Then he soiled himself, and she had to stop and clean him while her friends went on ahead. This happened again, and the friends went out of sight. Then the child suddenly grew into a big man and forced his mother to have intercourse with him. Then he resumed his former childlike size. So when they reached his mother's mother's home, his mother, distressed, put the child on the ground and refused to have anything to do with him. Finally, the grandmother asked, 'Don't you hear your child crying?' The daughter answered, 'If he will behave as an adult he should help himself as adults do.'

ADVENTURES AND EXPLOITS
OF HEITSI-EIBIB

The people of Heitsi-Eibib lived surrounded by dangers: on one side was Gama-Gorib, and people who went into his lands did not return. On other sides were Han-Gai-Gaib and the lion who at that time lived in a tree.

When he saw that his people did not return from their excursions, Heitsi-Eibib went to search for them. He passed by the kraal of Gama-Gorib, but did not stop to greet the owner, as is usually done. So Gama-Gorib sent Hare to call Heitsi-Eibib, but at first Heitsi-Eibib did not answer Hare. After Hare had called to him many times, Heitsi-Eibib answered, 'I have come to look for my people.' Heitsi-Eibib then wished to continue on his way, but Hare insisted on leading him to the kraal of Gama-Gorib. Heitsi-Eibib agreed, and followed Hare. Near the kraal was a pit, and this was where Gama-Gorib would throw everyone who came by.

Gama-Gorib challenged Heitsi-Eibib to play a game of knock-down, and at first Gama-Gorib knocked Heitsi-Eibib into the hole, but Heitsi-Eibib then spoke to the hole. He said, 'Hole of my ancestors, lift up the bottom a bit and boost me, so I can jump out,' and the hole did so. So the two of them resumed their game, and again Gama-Gorib knocked Heitsi-Eibib into the hole. Again, Heitsi-Eibib called on the hole to help him, and again the hole pushed him up so he could resume the game. Then Heitsi-Eibib knocked Gama-Gorib into the hole by hitting him hard behind the ear, and when Gama-Gorib fell into the hole he perished. Then Heitsi-Eibib cursed Hare and told him he would carry no more messages, and he would not feed during the day; he could only feed at night.

Then Heitsi-Eibib continued on to the kraal of Han-Gai-Gaib and passed by without stopping to greet the owner. So Han-Gai-Gaib sent out a messenger to invite Heitsi-Eibib to the kraal, and when eventually Heitsi-Eibib came, Han-Gai-Gaib challenged him to a game. Han-Gai-Gaib had a stone in the centre of his forehead, and he would challenge visitors to throw this stone at him, but it always bounced back and killed the person who threw it, and their body would fall into a great hole. But Heitsi-Eibib realized this, and so when Han-Gai-Gaib challenged him to a game, Heitsi-Eibib said, 'First you must close your eyes, and then I shall throw the stone.' So Han-Gai-Gaib closed his eyes, and then instead of throwing the stone at Han-Gai-Gaib's forehead, Heitsi-Eibib hit him behind the ear with the stone so that he fell dead into the pit. Then Heitsi-Eibib cursed Han-Gai-Gaib's messenger.

Heitsi-Eibib went on his way and came to the place of the lion who lived up a tree. He passed by the tree without a word, and then came by a second time and stopped and asked a vulture in the tree where the lion had gone. The vulture said he did not know, and perhaps the lion was out hunting. But in fact the lion was hidden in a nest. So Heitsi-Eibib took out his fire-drill and made a fire at the foot of the tree, so that the entire tree burned down. Then he told the lion that he could no longer live in trees, and he cursed the vulture.

THE DEATH OF HEITSI-EIBIB

Heitsi-Eibib and his family were travelling, and they passed a grove where the berries were ripe. Heitsi-Eibib fell ill almost immediately. His second wife observed that he had fallen ill because of the berries, and said death must be in that place. Heitsi-Eibib told his son Urisib that he expected to die, that they should bury him in the grove and that they should not return, or he would infect them so that they all died in the same way. Then he died, and the young wife blamed it on the berries. So they buried him as he had instructed, laying soft stones over him, and then they went away from that place. They made their camp, and they heard noises from the place behind them: it was the sound of people feasting on berries and singing, and the song was:

I, the father of Urisib,
I, the father of the unclean one,
I, who ate these berries and then died,
And having died, I live again.

The young wife sent her son Urisib to look at his father's grave. The son went and saw footprints leading away from the grave to the berry-bushes. So he came and told the wife, and she gave him instructions: he should stalk his father from the lee-side, moving upwind and placing himself between Heitsi-Eibib and his grave so he could not escape. The son did so, and when Heitsi-Eibib saw him coming he ran from the berry-bushes where he had been feasting and singing, and tried to return to his grave, but the son caught him and held him fast.

'Let me go,' cried Heitsi-Eibib, 'for I have been dead and I do not wish to infect you.' But the young wife refused, and they held him fast and brought him to their camp. From that time forth he was again healthy and well.

OTHER STORIES

The story of Heitsi-Eibib and his fight with Gama-Gorib echoes that of another hero, Tsui-Goab, and his struggles with Gaunab. It is said that at the beginning, Gaunab would kill people by throwing rocks at them, or by throwing them into a pit in which he had planted a spear with its point up. But Tsui-Goab came and fought him, and either threw him into the pit or killed him with a rock. His victory came at a cost, however, for when Tsui-Goab struck Gaunab behind the ear with a rock, Gaunab struck Tsui-Goab in the knee, and this gave Tsui-Goab his name, which means 'sore knee' or 'wounded knee'. Tsui-Goab and Gaunab rule different heavens: it is said that Tsui-Goab lives in a red heaven that is beautiful, while Gaunab rules a black and unpleasant world.

THE CENTRAL ATLANTIC

The Atlantic coast of Africa was sparsely populated south of the grasslands of Angola. Moving around the Cape and then north, one first finds the Namib desert, then the brush and grasslands of Angola, then, north of the Congo river and the Democratic Republic of Congo (formerly Zaire), the dense equatorial forests in the present nations of Congo-Brazzaville, Gabon and Cameroon. The kingdom of Kongo developed along the lower reaches of the Congo river, and its prosperity and trade relations with the Portuguese spread among neighbouring peoples; Kongo had some relations with the kingdoms of the Kuba and the Luba, further inland. The Yaka kingdom, lying to the south of Kongo, was influenced by it to some extent, as were the kingdoms in Angola (they also owe something to Portuguese stimulus for trade). Further north, the populations were far more fragmented, isolated within the forest and in the highlands of Cameroon. The Fang are representative of such peoples, although they actually moved into their current territory within relatively recent times. The story of Jeki, from the Duala of coastal Cameroon, portrays the world of fishermen and hunters who lived along the lagoons, and has been preserved even after most of the Duala turned to trade for their livelihood. In western Cameroon, many of the peoples were organized into kingdoms and small states, possibly responding to pressure from the north as the Muslim Fulani of northern Nigeria moved into the Adamawa area south of Lake Chad and then pressed south, or possibly on their own; the traditions of Bamun are representative of this group.

THE YAKA OF THE KWANGO RIVER

The southern Atlantic coast of Africa was heavily influenced by the early Portuguese trade with the kingdom of Kongo, and in the area around the kingdom peoples moved and conquered each other, competing for access to the trade goods. In Angola, the Portuguese actually controlled some of the territory; elsewhere, they were largely participant observers and traders. The kingdom of the Yaka developed as a result of the movement of peoples in a middle ground between Portuguese-controlled Angola to the south and the Congo to the north, but appears more indebted to Congo culture and institutions. While the original Yaka were apparently wandering hunters, the population of the kingdom was composed of numerous distinct clans, each with their own traditions of origin and an account of their incorporation into the state. This account is based upon historical studies published in the last few decades.

The first ruler to take the title of Kyambvu (king) along the Kwango river was Sangwa Mwaku Kambamba. He led a band of warriors, and they devastated the lands they crossed, taking the heads of all the men they encountered. He followed the river towards its source and then crossed to the eastern bank. There he met the local ruler, Buka Phangu, and they reached an agreement on the division of lands. Kambamba settled in Ipeshi, but after some time his followers ceased to show him the admiration and deference which had been their wont, and he left them and continued on by himself into the Portuguese territory.

Buka Phangu would later cede political authority to Muni

Putu, who is considered the first true Kyambvu of the Yaka, but Buka Phangu and his descendants retained ritual power and were considered the 'masters of the land' whose participation was essential to ensure the fertility of the soil and the regularity of the seasons. The story of Nzadi Membo illustrates the abilities of these first inhabitants. Nzadi Membo was a famous magician in his time. He once caused his village to disappear as he walked through it with his magical objects under his arms: men and women going about their business were astounded when all at once the houses around them vanished: sleeping chambers, storerooms, granaries, bath-houses. All were gone, leaving their contents exposed to view, and the people stared out at Nzadi Membo as he walked on. Fortunately, when he reached the end of the village he restored it.

When Nzadi Membo died, he gave his sons very precise instructions about his burial rites: he was to be enclosed in a basket, but not interred. They obeyed him. They wrapped the corpse and fitted it into a large basket, which they left at the place he had specified. Then they made their farewells and final offerings and withdrew. Only his wife remained, kneeling by the basket in her grief. As soon as the sons were out of sight of the basket, a rainstorm broke out, and it poured for days until the area was flooded and a huge lake was formed. This lake remains a significant stop in the series of rituals performed at the enthronement of a new Kyambvu.

Muni Putu, also known as Muni Kongo and by innumerable praise-names, was the grandson of a king named N'teeba. When N'teeba died, his children divided: the men returned to the clans of their mothers, while his two daughters remained in his town. Power passed to the eldest daughter, and after a time she married a hunter named Ilunga who came from beyond her borders. They had a son whom they named N'teeba, after his grandfather; later he became known as Muni Putu.

There are various stories about Muni Putu: how he gained his name, and why he left his mother's lands to found his own kingdom. One popular but inaccurate story says that his name comes from a phrase uttered in a dispute with his maternal kin:

they questioned his father's ancestry, saying a hunter could have come from anywhere and had no claim to precedence. He challenged them to make good their claims by proving their courage, and suggesting to his main accuser that each of them should cut off a finger. The other man refused, but Muni Putu made good his boast and cried out 'Mono puto' (I have the wound). Later, though, he found their opposition to his claims so strong that he departed the kingdom.

He came to the Kwango river and there he met Buka Phangu, who ceded lands to him. There is some suggestion that he may have engaged in a deception, going first as a single hunter to ask permission of the ruler to establish himself, and then bringing in his large crowd of followers. At any rate, he was able to establish himself as Kyambvu in the area, and he is considered the first true Kyambvu.

40

THE KINGDOM OF KONGO

The BaKongo live inland from the Atlantic coast around the mouth of the Congo river; most of the territory lies south of the river in the modern Democratic Republic of the Congo and in northern Angola. They were organized into a kingdom when the Portuguese navigators encountered them in the fifteenth century. The kings of Kongo became Christian and entered into diplomatic relations with Portugal, although traditional beliefs remained strong outside the court. In the seventeenth century a civil war split the kingdom, weakening it greatly. In the nineteenth century the territory was colonized by the Belgians and so became the Belgian Congo. It was at first the private colony of King Leopold, until his oppression of the people led the Belgian government to take it over. At the time of the first encounters with Europeans, the BaKongo claimed their kingdom had been founded four or five generations before (in the mid-1300s); the story changed somewhat over time, as did the king-lists, and for that reason several versions of the foundation story are given. Such early written documentation for the kingdom is exceptional for sub-Saharan African states. Stories of the BaKongo trickster, Moni-Mambu, are given in Chapter 15.

LUQUENI: A VERSION FROM 1687

A man named Eminia N'Zima married a woman, Luqueni Luasanzi, who was the daughter of Nsaku-Klau. They had a son, Luqueni. Eminia N'Zima settled in a high rocky place where he could control the trade routes and exact tribute from those passing through, and where he controlled the ferry crossing of the river. One day his son was managing the ferry when a woman came and refused to pay the toll, claiming that she was the sister of Eminia N'Zima. The son refused to let her pass without payment, and the argument became so violent that he stabbed her, even though she was pregnant. His father proposed to punish his son, but the people rose up and acclaimed the son as their king. Luqueni led them on a path of conquest, and then settled the kingdom, dividing and allocating the provinces, laying down the laws. His uncle, Nsaku-Klau, established a separate but subordinate lineage in the province of Batta.

MUTTINU: A VERSION FROM 1710

A woman named Ne Lucheni wanted to cross the river, but the ferryman was taking too long, waiting for the boat to fill up before he started his passage. She reproached him, complaining that he was taking so long, and he mocked her, asking if she was a queen or the mother of the king, to require and deserve immediate service. She went home and complained to her son, Muttinu a Lucheni, and he consoled her with the promise that she would become the mother of a king. So he assembled his people, crossed the river, and launched a career of conquest. This was the origin of the kingdom of the Congo.

NTINU WENE: A VERSION FROM THE EARLY TWENTIETH CENTURY

Wene was the youngest son of the ruler of Vungu, a small state, and he regretted that his father's domains were so small, and he so far down the line of succession. He had little scope for his ambitions. But nevertheless he gathered about himself a group of friends and supporters, men who were willing to follow him into new lands to establish a new kingdom.

In the meantime, he fulfilled the function his father had assigned to him: he managed the boats and pirogues which provided a ferry service across the river, and collected the fees which were demanded of all the passengers. One day a woman came who said she was his aunt and refused to pay the toll; the dispute escalated, and Wene killed the woman. His father was furious and was prepared to punish Wene severely, but Wene's supporters rallied to his defence and began acclaiming him with the title Ntinu, or king. Each night they held demonstrations marked by drinking and frenetic dancing, and enthusiasm for the prince and his cause built up. Eventually, he led his followers across the river, as he had planned, and conquered a new territory in which he would be king. This became the province of Nsundi, and it retained a certain pre-eminence over the other territories that were later incorporated in the great kingdom of Kongo. The former ruler was not completely dispossessed, and was given a ritual function in the new court.

Ntinu Wene's followers continued their expansion and military adventures, and brought other provinces under the king's rule. The king eventually divided them among the various lineages following a series of feasts and dances, during which the participants danced in pairs with the regalia of kingship, the sword and the fly-whisk, before coming to kneel before the king and pledge their loyalty, and in which the claimants sang their own praises and boasted of their skills and qualities. These boasts have entered into the clan and lineage praises and are remembered today.

While Ntinu Wene ruled the people in his new lands, he could not yet claim to rule the land itself; he was a conqueror who ruled through power and not because he had been properly consecrated or hallowed. The spiritual authority in the region was held by Nsaku ne Vunda, a medium who communicated with the spirit world and the ancestors, who regulated the seasons for planting and harvesting, and who held cures for all sorts of ailments. One day, Ntinu Wene was seized with convulsions, and his servants, recognizing the probable cause, went to Nsaku ne Vunda, knelt before him, and begged him to come and help to cure their master. Reluctantly, Nsaku ne

Vunda agreed and he came to Ntinu Wene's court. There, the king greeted him as an elder, to whom respect was due, and requested that Nsaku strike him, the king, with the buffalo-tail fly-whisk to drive out the convulsions. This action became part of the ritual of enthronement of the Kongo kings. Thereafter, Ntinu Wene ruled the land without any rival claimant to his power.

THE FANG OF GABON
AND CAMEROON

*The Fang now live in the dense equatorial forests of Gabon
and Cameroon, having migrated into the region during the
nineteenth century, apparently moving south towards the
source of trade goods. Although they practised some forms of
agriculture, much of their lifestyle was based on foraging the
resources of the forests in which they lived, and it is only in the
last century that they have become sedentary. Their language
links them with a number of other groups in Cameroon (the
Bulu, the Beti), as part of the wider Bantu-language family, and
in fact their original homeland probably lay around the centre
from which the Bantu languages spread, thousands of years
ago. Little of their traditional lifestyle now remains; they are
settled, the forest in which they lived is vanishing, and on
reaching the coast they converted to imported faiths, although
their religious practice remains syncretic. The stories are retold
from accounts collected by anthropologists and missionaries in
the colonial period.*

CREATION

The first being was Mebege, although it is also said that the earth
was created by a spider which descended from the heavens on a
long thread and then released an egg sac which became the earth.
Mebege created humans: he fashioned a lizard of clay and after
five days placed it in some water (fresh or salt? We do not know).
After eight days he came and called to it, and it came out of the
water and became Nzame, the first man. Some say that he later

created a woman from Nzame's big toe, but it is more likely that
the first woman was created at the same time as Nzame. Her
name was Oyeme-Mam and she was Nzame's sister.

Nzame and Oyeme had sexual relations. This was the first
act of incest, which continues to be considered the greatest
defilement among the Fang. As a consequence, Mebege removed himself from the earth, leaving Nzame and his sister to
continue the work of creation. Oyeme gave birth to eight pairs
of offspring who became the ancestors of the various Fang
groups, the Pygmies, the coastal peoples, the whites and chimpanzees.

Nzame went to Mebege, perhaps in spirit form, and returned
with knowledge of various skills such as agriculture. Although
he did not die – the Fang say he has no tomb to be found above
or below – he did depart the world, after leaving instructions
for the organization of society. But there were quarrels over the
inheritance, and the younger sons practised trickery to get what
was not theirs, and so the knowledge was not distributed as he
had intended. Some say that this is why the whites have so
much more wealth than the Africans.

MIGRATIONS I: THE SEPARATION
OF THE PEOPLES

The kinship of the Fang, the Bulu and the Beti peoples is recognized. The difference is explained through their history. At one
time, they all lived together, far to the north of their present
territory. But they were persecuted there, attacked by red giants,
and so eventually they fled south. The giants pursued them.
The people came to a river, and there were blocked; at that
time they did not have the skill of boat-building. But they
encountered a great crocodile, and it offered to help them: it
lay across the river, so they were able to use its body as a bridge
and cross the waters. The crocodile then waited for the pursuing
giants, but after they had advanced onto its body, the reptile
sank into the waters and drowned the giants.

Having crossed the river, the people then encountered a forest and their path was blocked by an enormous tree. As they stood debating which way to proceed and how to get past the great *azap* tree, some Pygmies came to them. After consultation, the Pygmies showed the people the way through the tree: there was a narrow passage through which they could go. At that time, however, they quarrelled over the order in which they were to proceed: older and younger disputed the right to lead. So once they had passed through the tree, they divided into different groups and each group went their own way.

MIGRATIONS II: NGURANGURANE,
SON OF THE CROCODILE

In the beginning, the Fang lived by the shores of a great water, a water so wide that one could not see across it. They fished the shores, but did not travel over the water, because they did not yet know about boats. One day an enormous crocodile, a beast so great that its head was as large as a hut, its eye as large as a goat, armoured in scales, swam up. It called the chief of the village and gave him orders: each day, they should deliver to the crocodile a captive: the first day a man, the next a woman, and at each new moon they should add a beautiful young girl adorned with sandal-wood markings and glistening with oil. Otherwise, the village would be destroyed. So spoke Ombure, the greatest of crocodiles.

The village lamented, but the people had no choice. They used up all their wealth in purchasing captives taken from other lands until the chief had nothing left in his storehouse: no skins, no horns, no tusks, no stones. So they consulted and decided that they had no choice but to flee. They would leave the land by the river and travel over the mountains and through the forests, and then Ombure would lose them and they would be free of his exactions. But the chief took some precautions first. He made offerings to the spirits of the water and the winds, of the forest, of day and of night, begging them not to reveal their route to Ombure the crocodile. Then, at the start of the dry season, the people packed what goods were left and slipped away from their village at night. They marched as long and as far as they could until they had to halt from exhaustion. Then they waited, huddled together, fearing at any moment to feel the earth tremble beneath the weight of Ombure's mass. At dawn they looked about, hardly believing they were safe, and then continued on their journey. The chief consulted his talisman of power to determine their route; he did not know that the talisman obeyed Ombure.

The people crossed mountains; the talisman told them to move on. They passed through a forest; they were told to continue. Finally, they came to the shores of another great lake. There the talisman told them to settle.

In the meantime, Ombure had long since discovered their absence. At his accustomed time he came to the village on the first day of their absence, and was surprised not to find his dinner tied up by the shores of the lake. He left the water and crossed the village, sweeping his tail from side to side in rage and smashing the houses, the shelters, the empty granaries. He came to the fields on the far side of the village: they had not been hoed or planted. They lay fallow. He realized then that the people were trying to flee. He returned to the water and made his magic. He summoned the spirits of the water and the winds and asked them where the people had gone. But the spirits of the water and the winds had made a bargain, and they replied that they did not know, they had not seen them. Ombure summoned the spirits of the forest and asked them which path the people had taken. But the spirits of the forest had made a bargain, and they replied that they had not seen Ombure's people pass through their domain. Ombure summoned the spirits of day and night and asked them when and where his people had gone. But the spirits of day and night replied that they had no knowledge of his people.

Finally, Ombure summoned the spirits of the storm, of thunder and lightning, and asked them if they had seen his people. The spirits of the storm had made no bargain, and they replied that they had seen Ombure's people on the path, and that they had settled by a great lake far away. So Ombure knew where they had gone and he set off himself.

The people settled by the lake and built themselves a new village which they named Akurengan (freedom from the crocodile). But that night, as the full moon shone down on the village, they heard a great noise and a wave washed up from the lake. The people left their homes to see what had happened. There, in the centre of the village, was Ombure the crocodile. He stopped right in front of the chief's house, and when the chief came out of the door, the crocodile caught him in his jaws and swallowed him. 'Here is your freedom from the crocodile,' he said, and slipped back into the waters. The next day he returned and imposed his terms on the village: they must give him two men each day, one in the morning, one at night, and the next day they must give him two women, one in the morning, one at night. At every new moon, he was to receive two young maidens, stained with sandal-wood juice and glistening with oil.

The people obeyed. They became raiders to feed Ombure's appetite, and they were successful because Ombure's power protected them. Years passed. People forgot how they had once tried to flee and how Ombure had caught them, and they once again decided to run away. The young men and women went first, followed by the children, and lastly the warriors. But they took no precautions. The next day Ombure came to the shore and found no sacrifice. 'Aha!' he said, and he summoned the spirits who served him and gave them orders. The people found that the forest closed before them, the trails vanished, and the winds beat in their faces. They were forced back, until they found themselves once again in the village they had left, and there lay Ombure waiting for them.

'Now,' he said, 'you shall give me maidens. I want two young women each day.' And so they were forced to offer him maidens, and soon there were very few in the village. Finally, the former chief's daughter was one of the two presented to Ombure, her skin marked with sandal-wood and her skin gleaming with oil, as Fang brides are today. That evening, both maidens had vanished. But to the people's surprise, the chief's daughter returned the next day: she had been spared. Nine

months later, she gave birth to a boy and they named him
Ngurangurane, son of the crocodile.

Ngurangurane grew prodigiously fast: one day a toddler,
the next a child, the third an adolescent, and then a man. He
was quickly named chief of the people, and his mother, Alena
Kiri, gave him the talisman which had belonged to her father.
Ngurangurane was able to make sure it obeyed him and no
other, and from the talisman he learned of arts which might
serve his people and which also would fulfil his own two goals:
to avenge his mother's father, and to free his people from the
tribute they paid the crocodile.

Ngurangurane discovered palm wine, made from the fermented sap of certain palm trees. He ordered the village to
assemble every pot they possessed, and when he had examined
the stock he ordered the potters to produce more. Then he led
the villagers into the forest, and he scored the bark of selected
trees. They left the pots to collect the sap which ran out, and
on their return they collected the pots, covered them and set
them in Ngurangurane's hut to ferment.

Meanwhile, Ngurangurane ordered the people to build two
large basins of clay at the lake-shore. When the wine had
fermented and become heady, he ordered the pots brought from
the storeroom and had them emptied into the basins until both
were full of fresh palm wine.

The next day Ngurangurane waited in hiding when the crocodile came for his daily meal of maidens. As the monster left the
water he saw the basins and smelt the contents. He tasted the
liquid and found it good; he emptied the first basin and went
to the second. He drank deeply. He emptied the second basin.
Then he was drunk, and he forgot the two maidens waiting,
trembling, just beyond the basins. His head slipped down and
he slept on the lake-shore.

Ngurangurane slipped out of his hiding place and brought
ropes; he tied Ombure's feet, he tethered the great tail, he bound
the jaws. Then he fetched his sharpest spear and thrust it as
hard as he could into Ombure's neck, which seemed the softest
part. The spear bent and Ombure muttered and twitched, as
might a man who had been bitten by a mosquito in his sleep.

Ngurangurane got his heaviest axe and climbed on top of the crocodile. With all his might he swung the blade down against the crocodile's skull between its eyes. The blade bounced off; the skin was not marked. The crocodile blinked and grunted, but did not wake up.

Alena Kiri came to her son and gave him the talisman. 'You must use this,' she said. Ngurangurane took up the talisman and summoned the lightning. He ordered the lightning to strike Ombure, and by the power of the talisman the lightning was forced to obey. The bolt fell from heaven and struck the crocodile between the eyes. The crocodile grunted and died.

Ngurangurane then used the skin of the crocodile to make the first boat known to the Fang. But because he was also the son of the crocodile whom he had slain, he instituted a cult of the crocodile. All the people ate the flesh of the great beast, and then they mourned him as a kinsman. In this way, the spirit of Ombure was checked, for although it wandered the village seeking a human on whom to take revenge, all the humans were now flesh of his flesh and immune to him.

42

JEKI LA NJAMBE OF
THE DUALA

The Duala are a coastal people of Cameroon, and for centuries now they have gained their living mainly as trading middle-men between the Europeans and the peoples of the interior. The story of Jeki has been preserved as a performance tradition, and may well reflect the survival of cultural elements dating back to a period before the development of trade. The world of Jeki is a world of hunters and fishers living among the lagoons and waterways of coastal Cameroon, and his story is kin to the tales of other forest-dwelling foraging groups (as, for instance, the story of Lianja of the Mongo, Chapter 31, or the stories about the BaNyanga child-hero Mwindo). The Duala admit that they do not really understand the story of Jeki nowadays, but they continue to perform it. This version is retold from editions made by Cameroonian scholars around 1990.

There was a man named Inono Njambe. He had many wives and children, but he gave himself up to the practice of sorcery and began to sacrifice his children and then his wives to gain power. Finally, he only had one child left, known as Njambe Inono, and the people who lived around him felt he had gone too far. They assembled and broke in on Inono Njambe; they tied him up and buried him to the waist in the ground and then they beat him with palm fronds and hurled palm nuts at him until he swore that he would give up his sorceries and let his one son live. Then the people released him. He did not live long after that, but he passed on his knowledge to his son.

His son, Njambe Inono, married. But after a while he was

tempted by his father's secrets and occult power, and people began to disappear from his compound. When his neighbours realized this they came to him and reproached him for following the evil path laid out by his father. Rather than kill him, they placed Njambe Inono and his wife in a huge canoe and sent them over the waters.

At last they came to land, and Njambe established his settlement. He planted a palm tree that grew quickly to an enormous height, and on the tree he placed a great bird. Into the waters he released a crocodile, and in the centre of his compound he placed a chest in which he kept a powerful leopard. These creatures provided magical protection to the compound.

He and his wife Ngrijo had a child, a daughter. Ngrijo would take the child with her when she went to work in the fields, and one day as the baby was crawling in the shade near the edge of the forest a chimpanzee came down from the trees and began to play with it. At first the mother was alarmed, but the chimpanzee talked to her and reassured her, and after that the play became a daily occurrence. When Njambe heard of this arrangement he disapproved and at first prepared to hunt the chimpanzee. But he and the chimpanzee also talked. The chimpanzee showed him where to find shrimp in the nearby ponds, and so Njambe agreed not to hunt him.

Years passed. Ngrijo went to work in her fields; she took her daughter and the chimpanzee watched over the child as the mother worked. The girl became nubile, and one day the chimpanzee took her away. The mother finished her work in the fields and came looking for her daughter; she found no sign of her. She called and walked a little way into the forest, thinking the pair had hidden themselves in some game, but no answer came to her cries. She ran back and forth, and finally made her way home to give the news of their daughter's disappearance to her husband. Njambe went immediately into the forest and summoned the chimpanzee, and it swung through the branches into a tall tree above him.

'Where is my daughter?' demanded Njambe.

'I have taken her,' said the chimpanzee. 'I have shown you and your wife where to find food. For years I have helped your wife at her work, minding the child while she was in the fields. Have you ever returned my kindnesses? Have you left me fruit or food? Have you offered me anything? No. And so I have taken your daughter. She will live with us, among the spirits of the forest.' With those words the chimpanzee vanished into the foliage of the high tree, and Njambe was left alone to return to his home.

Njambe and Ngrijo did not get on after that, and Njambe took many other wives. After some time, all his wives became pregnant. A year later, there were eight baby sons crawling around in the compound yard; Ngrijo alone had not given birth, although her belly showed signs of swelling. More time passed, and another group of sons were born. Still Ngrijo did not give birth, although her belly was now quite round and she had trouble moving about. Njambe told her she must leave the compound, since she alone had no child, and she moved into a shabby hut near the water's edge.

More years passed, and Njambe's compound was filled with sons of all ages crawling, toddling, walking, running and playing around their mothers' cooking pots and household items. Still Ngrijo did not give birth; she made her painful way through the bushes, her vastly protruding belly parting the branches well ahead of her arms, and she stumbled about her tasks.

Finally, one day when she went out to cut some firewood, a voice spoke to her.

'Mother, let me out!' called the voice. 'Let me out, and I shall help you.'

After the voice had repeated the call several times, Ngrijo lay back against a tree-trunk and spread her legs. Somewhere beyond her belly a child appeared and grew immediately to the size of a great adult.

'Wait there, mother,' said the child, and set about chopping and stacking the wood. Then it vanished back into her belly, and she painfully rose and made her way back to her hut. When she got there, she found she had a huge supply of firewood, neatly cut and stacked by the side of the hut. After that, as she went about her work the child would emerge and help her. But it refused to admit it had been born, and she was not allowed to see him or to cut his umbilical cord.

One day, the child showed itself to all the family. Ngrijo and her co-wives had gone out over the tidal flats to catch the shrimp that swarmed in the remaining pools, and they were returning to the shore with their baskets full of the shrimp, but looking anxiously back at the returning waters.

'Stop, Mother,' called the child. 'Let me out here over the waters.'

'No,' objected Ngrijo. 'The tide is coming in, we shall be trapped and drowned.'

'Mother, I shall help you. But you must let me out on the waters!' insisted the child, and so Ngrijo lay back and parted her legs. The child emerged and quickly grew up.

The co-wives were watching from the sands closer to the shore. Seeing the child appear beyond Ngrijo, they dropped their baskets of shrimp and fled in amazement and terror.

The child transported his mother and her baskets to the shore, over the waters which had now flooded the sand-flats. Ngrijo found herself at her hut, surrounded by bulging baskets of shrimp to clean and dry. And to their surprise, her co-wives also found that the baskets which they had dropped on the sand-flats as they fled were standing before the doors of their individual huts in the compound, each as full of shrimp as it had been when they started on their way back.

Soon after that, Jeki announced to his mother that the time had come for him to be born. With a sigh of relief his mother spread a cloth over the ground and then lay back and went into labour. Out of her vast swollen belly poured an avalanche of goods: trade-goods such as cloths of all kinds, bottles and containers, chests and ingots of metal. Then came musical instruments, and tools, and magical implements such as bells and charms. Principal among these was *Ngalo*, the amulet which would serve Jeki in his adventures. Out came the huge canoe which Jeki would use to travel over the waters, and with it a nine-pointed paddle. Then there was a pause.

'Mother, mother!' called Jeki. 'You must move. I cannot be born over the cloth. You must move to the dumping ground for broken bottles and potsherds!' Ngrijo stood and moved herself so that she squatted over the broken pieces of glass and pots. There Jeki was born, he came out. Ngrijo cut the umbilical cord, and Jeki transported the enormous pile of goods to her hut.

Njambe's hostility towards Ngrijo carried over to his new son, and was aggravated by the reports of the oddities involved in Jeki's birth and his care for Njambe's estranged wife. This hostility was the cause of Jeki's earliest adventures.

One day, Njambe's two oldest sons by other wives came to summon Jeki. Their father wished to test the abilities of the latest addition to the family. Jeki should come immediately to his father's compound. When he arrived, Jeki found all the other children sitting in a great circle in the courtyard. At the centre was a wooden chest, such as was used for trade-goods. Near it sat Njambe.

'Come, Jeki,' said Njambe. 'You must show us your abilities. Tell me what is contained within this wooden chest. If you fail, the children shall beat you.'

'Ah,' said Jeki. 'I see. This is an opportunity for my brothers, who hate me, to do me harm. But you are my father and I must obey you. Let me see.' Jeki walked around the chest, looking at it from all sides. 'I think it must contain cloth,' he said, and Njambe snorted.

'Ha!' exclaimed Njambe. 'Children, beat him!' Immediately, all Jeki's siblings fell on him and beat Jeki with their hands and with palm-frond whisks and bits of vine until his skin glowed lividly.

'It is not cloth,' said Jeki. 'Might it be copper ingots?'

'Ha!' exclaimed Njambe, and again the children fell on Jeki and beat him until he lay apparently unconscious, gasping on the ground.

'It is not copper,' said Jeki, and he looked around at the children and then at his father, and saw that all of them were ready to beat him to death if he gave them the slightest cause. The time had come to end this game, for Jeki had learned what he wished to know: how badly they disliked him.

'I will tell you, as I might have done at first,' said Jeki. 'I wished to learn the truth of your feelings towards me, and you have shown them. The chest contains a single louse which you plucked from your head this morning. You may not know it, but the louse is female.'

At that Njambe sat silent, for Jeki had correctly identified the contents of the chest. His trap had failed, and Jeki had won this round.

A first failure did not stop Njambe. It increased the threat represented by this preternatural son, and so he decided he must use more serious measures. One day, the two oldest sons came to Ngrijo's hut by the waters and announced that Njambe required Jeki for a task.

'Ah!' cried Ngrijo. 'He will try to kill you. You must flee!'

'No,' answered Jeki. 'He cannot harm me. I shall obey him.'

Jeki accompanied his brothers to Njambe's compound, and there his father sat waiting.

'Come, Jeki,' said Njambe. 'I have a small job for you, for we cannot abide idle hands here. There is an old chest in my hut, and I wish to sell it. You must clean it for me, you must scour it inside and out and polish the wood and metal so that it gleams. Go and fetch it.'

This was of course the chest in which Njambe had enclosed a leopard when he first arrived at his homestead. Jeki entered the hut, and then he raised *Ngalo*, the amulet which he kept hanging on his neck. 'What shall I do?' he asked, and *Ngalo* replied, 'Carry the chest down to the waters and wash it there.'

'I see,' replied Jeki, and immediately he lifted the chest onto his shoulders and made his way down to the edge of the waters, followed secretly by his brothers who wished to see the end of this horrible child.

Jeki did not stop at the water's edge. He waded out until the water came to his hips and then he plunged the chest into the water and climbed on top of it. He scrubbed the top, then he turned it and scrubbed the sides, and finally he scrubbed the bottom.

'I think I can open it now,' he said, and *Ngalo* agreed. He opened the chest, and there within it was one large leopard which had drowned, and several small ones which also had drowned in the waters. 'Hmm,' said Jeki. 'My father is careless

with his animals.' And he took the chest and its contents back
to the shore so he could scrub the interior more easily. Then he
carried the chest back to his father, still sitting in his compound
and now looking older and weaker. The two sons who had
followed Jeki had told him what happened at the waterside.

Njambe tried again. Two boys went and summoned Jeki. His
father wished him to run an errand. Jeki listened to his half-
brothers and then followed them. In the compound his father
sat waiting.

'Jeki,' he said, 'out in the waters there' – and Njambe gestured
towards the ocean – 'lives a great crocodile. You must bring it
here.'

Jeki returned to his mother's hut by the waters and brought
out his great canoe and the nine-pointed paddle. He launched
the boat all by himself, pushing it through the sands into the
water and then leaping into the stern. As soon as his paddle
touched the water, the canoe sped out over the waves.

'*Ngalo*, what does this task mean?' asked Jeki, and from his
neck the amulet replied, 'It is another trap that your father has
set. He wishes to see you killed. But you can succeed. Just be
polite.'

Jeki thought over the amulet's words, and dipped the paddle
into the waters so that the canoe ran even faster. Soon he saw
something at the horizon; he drew nearer and found himself
facing a great green scaly cliff. 'What is this?' he asked himself,
and immediately continued, 'It is the side of the crocodile. I
must find its head.' So he turned the canoe and proceeded until
he made out the brow and the eyes of the crocodile. It seemed
large enough to eat a village in one gulp.

'Uncle!' called Jeki, and the crocodile opened its eyes and
slowly turned its snout towards the canoe, creating whirlpools
and waves as it did so.

'Who calls me?' asked the crocodile.

'It is I, Jeki, son of Njambe,' answered Jeki, 'and my father
has sent me to you. They wish to hold a council in the village,
and they require the great wisdom which you have gained over
the years, living so long in the great waters.'

'Indeed,' said the crocodile, pleased. 'It would hardly be a council without me. They do need me. It is good to know that Njambe has not forgotten my powers. I shall come. You shall lead the way.'

Jeki turned his canoe towards the shore where his father's compound lay and advanced slowly. He paddled with long slow strokes, sending the waters behind him back against the crocodile's great snout, and as he paddled he and *Ngalo* sang songs of power, so that the water washing against the crocodile delivered the magic and brought the enormous beast under Jeki's control. By the time they reached the shore, Jeki had mastered the crocodile.

'Do not stop at the shore,' advised *Ngalo*. 'Bring the crocodile into the village.' So Jeki created a great wave that bore the crocodile over the beach and in among the houses. Then the waters receded and the crocodile lay, almost helpless with its great weight, among all the houses. But it was not quite helpless; it could move and bite, and it did so readily. Snap! and a house vanished. Snap! and goats that had come too close disappeared. The crocodile writhed, and its tail knocked down several houses.

'Father!' called Jeki, 'I have brought your crocodile. What shall we do with it?'

'Send it back! Send it back!' cried Njambe. 'See! It is eating our goats, it is eating my wives and children and my people! It is breaking our houses! Send it to the waters!'

So Jeki summoned another great wave which lifted the crocodile out of the village and turned it about so that it faced the waters, and then Jeki sent the crocodile on its way into the great waters. This was the second of the creatures that his father had placed about his compound when he first settled in that land.

Some time later, the two older brothers again came to Ngrijo's hut. 'Father wants Jeki for another task,' they announced, and knowing what the previous tasks had been, Ngrijo began to lament at the dangers facing her son.

'Do not worry, Mother,' said Jeki. 'I can face any challenge my father puts. I shall return to you.' Then he followed his brothers to his father's compound.

'Jeki,' said Njambe, 'do you see that tall palm tree?' He
pointed to the tree he had planted so many years before, and
on which he had placed a great bird. 'Notice how thick the
clusters of palm nuts are beneath the fronds. I wish you to
climb the tree and harvest them. This task is long overdue.'

'Ah!' said Jeki, for he knew that above the fronds was the
great Kambo bird which his father had placed there, and that
the reason the palm nuts grew so thick was that no one could
harvest them: the Kambo bird would skewer them with its long
beak or fly down and rip them off the tree with its talons. But
he would not allow Njambe to defeat him, and he was sure he
could master the bird. 'Very well, Father,' he answered. 'I shall
harvest the palm nuts.'

'Do so,' said Njambe. 'I am going into the village, to the
men's hut.'

As soon as he was out of the compound, Jeki rounded up his
brothers. 'Come,' he called them. 'Father has told us to harvest
palm nuts, and so let us get to work.' The brothers assembled
at the foot of the great palm tree, staring up at the fronds which
hid the huge bird.

'Father said you alone should do this!' protested the older
brothers.

'And I say you shall help me!' answered Jeki. 'If you do not,
you shall die.' He waved Ngalo over his brothers and they were
cowed. They did not dare to disobey. The eldest shuffled up to
the tree and tied the climbing-strap around the trunk. He
stepped into the loop and pulled it round his waist. He shifted
the cord higher on the trunk, and then stepped up, planting his
feet firmly against the bark. Again he shifted the cord, again he
moved his feet up. But when he was halfway up the tree, the
Kambo bird leaned out over the fronds and saw him. Like a
flash, the beak darted down and pierced the boy. With a twist
of its beak, the bird gutted the boy and the empty carcass fell
to the ground by the tree.

'He did not know how to climb,' said Jeki, and threw the
body behind the nearest hut. 'Now you shall try!' he ordered,
pointing to the next oldest. Trembling with fear, not daring to
disobey, the second boy began the ascent. Soon he too lay

behind the hut. So it went for all of Njambe's children, all those who had beaten Jeki and whose mothers were preferred to Ngrijo.

'I must do it,' said Jeki, when he had laid the last on the great heap behind the huts. He dripped a bit of a magic potion he had at the trunk of the tree, and then slipped the loop around his waist and began the climb. As he went, he tapped *Ngalo* against the trunk each time he lifted the strap.

The Kambo bird looked down over the fronds and saw yet another child climbing the trunk. It stretched out its neck and beak, and then thought. The tapping against the tree-trunk bothered it. This child was not like the others. It stirred uneasily on its nest.

Jeki reached the top, just below the canopy of fronds. The bunches of palm nuts hung thick and spiky about him. He unsheathed his little axe, a tool that had been born with him, and swung it at the first bunch. *Shhk!* The stem was cut cleanly through and the bunch fell all the way down to the ground where it burst, scattering palm nuts across the courtyard and over the village. With only a few more such blows, Jeki harvested the abundant crop, and below him the palm nuts filled the courtyard and almost covered some of the houses.

'I must get the bird as well,' Jeki said to himself, and he scrambled up through the fronds until he was perched on top of the tree. But the Kambo bird had taken flight as soon as he laid his hands on the fronds. It soared above him in the sky. But it was not safe there. Jeki pulled from his pouch a piece of vine, one of the magical implements that had appeared at his birth. He stretched it and whirled it about, then threw it high into the sky. It whistled through the air, following the Kambo bird as it soared on the winds, and then it caught the bird and pinioned its wings so that the bird plummeted through the air. The vine caught the beak and bound it tightly against the bird's breast. It twisted itself around the talons and pressed them into the bird's feathers. The bird fell, trussed up, onto the fronds at the peak of the tree, in front of Jeki. With his foot, Jeki pushed it off the tree and it fell to the ground far below, landing on a pile of palm nuts. Then Jeki let himself down through the fronds, slipped into the climbing-rope, and made his way down the trunk.

At the bottom, he took the bird, covered with palm oil from the nuts it had crushed in its fall, and set fire to it. It burned quickly to cinders, and Jeki ate some of the ashes and put the rest in his pouch with his other magical instruments. Then he turned to the compound entrance. Njambe had come from the village as soon as the palm nuts began to fly about, scattered by the fall of the bunches. He found his home awash with palm nuts. He had seen the corpses of his children piled behind a hut. He found the last token of his power being consumed by his strange offspring. He fell down, weakened and faint.

Jeki put his father into his hut, on a bed, and then went into the forest. There he gathered certain herbs and leaves and roots and prepared them as he knew how. He returned to the compound and laid the bodies of his brothers out in a row. One by one he dosed the bodies with the compound he had prepared, and one by one they were restored: the parts that the Kambo bird had swallowed reappeared, the hearts began to beat, the eyes opened, and the children rose up.

With the failure of this last attempt, Njambe ceased trying to kill his son, and the brothers, although they still disliked a child they considered a monster, also abandoned their attempts to destroy him. But a current of malice and envy still ran through all their conversations with him, and they always sought ways to belittle him despite his manifest powers. Njambe gave them fuel one day, when he revealed that Jeki was actually Ngrijo's second-born child, and that the first, a daughter, had been lost to a spirit that took the form of a chimpanzee.

'Ah, the second-born!' said the oldest son when he next greeted Jeki by the waterfront. Jeki was puzzled but said nothing until each of the other children in turn greeted him with the same words. Then he went to his mother.

'Mother, the children have been calling me the second-born. What do they mean by this? I am the only child in your hut, I am the only child to care for you.'

'I cannot tell you what they mean. It is surely some trick. Disregard them.'

Jeki was not satisfied with this answer. He went to his father, who now spent his days sitting in his compound watching the activities of his wives and many sons.

'My father,' Jeki greeted him. 'The other sons have been calling me the second-born, yet I am the only child in my mother's house. What is the reason for this?'

'You do not know everything,' replied Njambe, and his eyes gleamed. 'You do not know why your mother's hut stands at the water's edge, away from the compound. You do not know what happened before I married my other wives. You are indeed still a child.'

'But you know what happened,' said Jeki, correctly guessing that his father wished to be prompted.

'Indeed. Ngrijo bore a child, a daughter, and she would take her to the fields. There, a chimpanzee came down from the trees and cared for her daughter. One day, the chimpanzee took her daughter away. We searched for her, but we could not find her. The chimpanzee was a *bedimo*, a spirit, and it took your sister to the land of the spirits. Perhaps she is still alive there.'

Jeki understood the hint. 'Then I must go and look for her,' he declared. 'If she lives, she must be restored to her family.'

'This task may be beyond even your powers,' muttered Njambe, and turned away.

Jeki returned to his mother's hut and sorted through his amulets and charms and powders and implements. His mother asked what he was doing, and he explained. For once she did not protest at this adventure but sat watching him make his preparations. Finally, *Ngalo* said that he was ready.

Jeki walked away from the waters into the heart of the forest, where the trees grew huge and all was silent about him in the sunless dark. He followed a path out of the village, and then, guided by *Ngalo*, followed other paths into the woods. At last he came to a clearing: nine paths led out of it.

'Which is the right one?' he asked, and *Ngalo* answered, 'You must sort them.'

Jeki waved a vine, and it twined around four paths to the left. He waved another vine and it twined around four paths to the right. One path lay before him. He stepped forward, and *Ngalo* spoke. 'Do you enter the world of the *bedimo* as you would visit another village? Turn around.'

Jeki turned around, and there before him was a great shining metal gate. He pushed, and it opened. Beyond, all was dark.

'Before you enter, you must protect yourself,' said *Ngalo*. 'Living humans do not see spirits, but they may smell them. You must make yourself invisible and give yourself the smell of the spirits.'

Jeki chose the right powder and swallowed a little bit. He became invisible. He rubbed himself with a special gum and his body took on the smell of the spirits. Then he stepped through the gate and onto the path that led before him.

He entered a strange dark land in which paths led over ground on which no grass or trees grew. *Ngalo* pointed him onto the right paths and he followed them until he began to see spirit dwellings on either side of the path. Several times he encountered spirits walking along the paths in the other direction, and each time they nodded to him in greeting and he wondered why they should greet him. He was not like them, he was not a spirit. He was a living human. How could they mistake him for a spirit? But when he voiced these thoughts *Ngalo* reminded him that he had taken the smell of a spirit.

He came to a cluster of huts. *Ngalo* pointed him to one of them, indicating that his sister was inside. He entered. He saw not one girl alone, but a dozen, all virtually the same: young, attractive, cheerful, well dressed.

'Which of them is my sister Engome?' he wondered, and *Ngalo* helped him with a strategy.

'I have come to claim my sister,' announced Jeki, and the girls lined up in front of him.

'Choose me,' said each of them, their voices musical and tinkling.

'Only one of you is my sister,' answered Jeki. 'I do not know where the others have come from.' He waved an antelope's horn at them, and a bee flew from the horn and buzzed about the room. Eventually it settled on the elaborate coiffure of the girl fourth from the left, and Jeki stepped forward.

'You are my sister Engome,' he said. 'You are the daughter of Njambe Inono and Ngrijo, and you were taken from them by a *bedimo* in the form of a chimpanzee. Do you wish to return to the land of humans with me?'

'I am your sister,' agreed Engome, 'and I wish to return. Take me with you.'

Jeki gave his sister the gum with which to rub her body, and some of the powder which made her invisible. Then they left the hut and followed the paths back to the great metal gate that shut off the spirit world. As they passed the gate, it rattled shut. Then they skipped down the forest paths back to the village.

There is no end to the stories about Jeki la Njambe and his deeds. He had countless other adventures, which can be heard and read in other places.

THE BAMUN KINGDOM OF CAMEROON

The kingdom of Bamun (or Bamum), in south-central Cameroon, can perhaps be seen as typical of a number of the small polities established in the grassland areas. In these kingdoms, the ruling dynasty often claims a northern origin and an implicit connection to the nineteenth-century conquest of much of northern Cameroon (especially the province of Adamawa) by Muslim Fulani expanding their territory from Sokoto in northern Nigeria. Bamun is noteworthy in one regard: the invention of a local writing system by Sultan Njoya, the seventeenth ruler, at the beginning of the twentieth century. This retelling is principally based upon the history of the kingdom prepared by Njoya and translated into French in the 1950s.

A trader came from Egypt to Bornu and married a local woman named Nejibu. She gave him three daughters, of whom the third had three sons. Mbuon, the eldest of the sons, led his brothers in migrations to the south and then in successful wars of conquest, and so Mbuon became king of the Mbuenkim.

After a time, their northern kinsmen, descended from the first two daughters of Nejibu, sent messengers to find the travellers and to bring news back. To show how far away they had gone, the messengers tried to bring back a fish which they caught fresh on the day of their departure. But the fish had decayed so much it had to be abandoned before they got back. This gave rise to two names for this group: the Tikar, or distant ones, or the Baful, which means rotten.

The *Fon* Rifum, king of the Mbuenkim, had three sons. Each of them went some distance from their father's palace and established a fortified community, surrounded by a moat. When the father heard of this, he sent messengers to summon the sons to return. Instead, the three brothers collected all their followers and departed. When they came to a river, Nshare, the first brother, persuaded his siblings to let him cross first. But after his own people had crossed to the far bank, he destroyed the boat so his brothers could not follow; instead, one brother went upstream and the other downstream.

Nshare continued on his way, conquering the peoples he found on his path and settling at last at Djimon. From Djimon, his line later conquered Foumban, and made that town their capital, and it was there that his descendant Njoya ruled. While in Djimon, Nshare decided that he must get one of the war-dance costumes of his father, and so he returned in secret to Bankim, his father's capital. There he tried to steal a costume from the storehouse where they were kept, but a guard surprised him and killed him. Since his companions had no means to carry his body back to Djimon, they cut off Nshare's head and brought it back with them. It was preserved in the palace, and the hair taken to the site of the royal graveyard.

FROM THE FOREST TO
THE NIGER

The Atlantic coast along the Bight of Benin (from Cameroon west to Ghana) used to be called the Slave Coast, in contrast to the Gold and Ivory Coasts further west because the dense populations near the Niger river as it reaches the sea provided a rich source for the Atlantic slave-trade. East of the river lived the many disunited Igbo-speaking peoples; on the west were the Yoruba whose city-states rose at times through conquest to the status of empire (the best known is Oyo, which flourished in the sixteenth to eighteenth centuries). North of the Igbo, along the Benue river, were numerous other peoples. This region is generally considered the cradle of the Niger–Congo language family, from which peoples emigrated east and west towards other lands. This area is also the home of yam-culture, and archaeology shows that a pattern of semi-urban settlement is of considerable antiquity. Until the arrival of the Europeans along the Atlantic coast, the trade routes lay to the north, through the territories of the Hausa and the Kanuri to the Sahara.

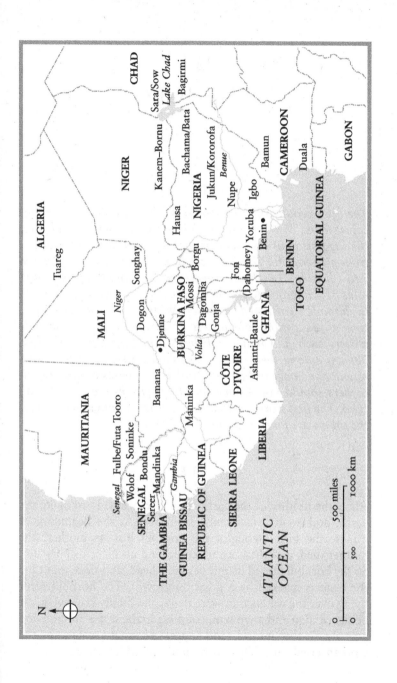

44
THE IGBO

The Igbo peoples offer tremendous variety in social and politi-
cal systems. They were never unified by conquest and alliance;
the suggestion of historians is that their cultural unity derived
from a respect for shared institutions such as oracles (Eri and
Aro-Chukwu). Inhabiting areas from the foothills of the moun-
tains of Cameroon to the delta of the Niger, their practices and
livelihoods varied tremendously. With colonization, the Igbo
took to education as a means of advancement, and include
writers such as Chinua Achebe, Buchi Emecheta and Flora
Nwapa among their stars. The following stories offer a rep-
resentative image of Igbo political and religious traditions, but
readers should not assume that these stories are valid for all
Igbo. The first story is retold from a version published in 1932;
the others are taken from more recent sources.

ALE

Ale is the mother of the earth. She gave her body to make the
earth, and good things come from her. At the beginning of
things, the bird Ogbughu the hornbill lost its mother; the
mother died, and the hornbill could find no place to bury her.
So the hornbill buried its mother in its head, and since that time
the head is marked by a great outgrowth. The hornbill went
flying over the waters that were there, and finally saw two great
beings, a man and a woman, coupling in the water and moving
actively. As they moved, land appeared from the water, and the
woman cried out, 'This is the land, in which those who die

should be buried.' And when she and the man had finished their business, Ale spread herself over the land and became one with it. This is why crops come from the land, and why humans return to earth when they die.

ERI AND THE CITY OF NRI

Chukwu, who is also known as Chi, created all. At the start of things, he let the man Eri down from heaven on a rope, and Eri alighted on an anthill which rose above the soggy ground of the plain. Eri complained to Chukwu, and they summoned a blacksmith and with his bellows and forge the blacksmith dried out the land so that Eri could walk upon it.

Eri married and had children. Food was scarce, and he asked Chukwu to provide for them. Chukwu told him he should sacrifice his son and daughter and bury them. Chukwu said that he would send down a person to perform the *ichi* scarification upon them, so they would be recognized.

Very unhappily, Eri buried his son and his daughter. Then he watered their graves, as Chukwu had instructed. After three weeks, the yam grew from his son's grave and the cocoyam from his daughter's grave. It was after eating the cocoyam that Eri fell asleep for the first time. Chukwu told Eri that he should share this food with other peoples, but Eri was reluctant, for the yams had cost him two children. But in exchange, Chukwu created the *eze* title and appointed Eri's people to grant and confirm it, and also gave the people of Eri the function of purification of the land from various defilements.

Eri later sacrificed a slave man and woman, and buried their bodies; from these came the palm oil and the coconut. Some say that he sacrificed the slaves first, before he sacrificed his children, hoping thus to deceive Chukwu, and that is the reason Chukwu determined the *ichi* scar-marking to identify the children of Eri.

Some time later, four guests came to visit Eri, each bearing a basket. They did not tell him their names. According to custom, he fed them and gave them a place to sleep. But in the night, he let a rat loose by the baskets and then listened. The rat went to the first basket and began to gnaw. One of the visitors woke, listened, and then called out, 'Èke! Èke! A rat has entered your basket.' Èke awoke and chased the rat away. The rat then went to the second basket, and Èke, hearing, called out, 'Oyè! Oyè! A rat is at your basket.' So Oyè awoke and moved his basket. Then the rat went to a third basket, and Oyè called out a warning, 'Afo! Afo! A rat is gnawing your basket.' Afo awoke and chased the rat away. Then the rat went to the fourth basket, and when it began to gnaw Afo called, 'Nkwo! Nkwo! A rat is trying to get into your basket.' So Nkwo awoke and chased the rat away.

In the morning Eri was able to greet his guests by their names, and so they agreed to stay with him. They were four divinities, and they have given their names to the four days of the Igbo week.

Eri's children moved away from the town of Nri and founded other communities, but Nri remained a religious centre for the Igbo, and the people of Nri retained the ritual functions which Chukwo had granted to Eri.

ONOJO OBONI OF IDDAH

Iddah lies close to the Niger, where peoples were influenced by the city of Benin and its practices of warfare. As a consequence – in defence or in imitation – central authority and military power had more importance there than in some of the communities lying further east.

Abatama of Ogurugu was a hunter who travelled in the bush. He spent some time with a woman named Ebuli before leaving her. Onojo Oboni was born of that union, but in his childhood people mocked him because he had no father. His surname, Oboni, refers to his illegitimacy. He was a giant of a man, and had besides six fingers on each hand and six toes on each foot. He eventually left his home and went to find his father, who immediately bowed down before him. He settled at Ati-Idah, perhaps because of a dispute with his half-brothers, and became a raider. He peopled the area of Ogurugu with his captives.

It is said that at one time he heard a strange noise from within the river, and so he had his servants pour a thousand pots of palm oil over the waters, to quieten them and allow him to look below. He was then able to fetch from the waters a seat made from a log of wood. The seat had covers, and after Onojo looked under them, it is said he could no longer recognize people properly. But this is said favourably, to indicate that his judgements were just and not swayed by acquaintance. It is also said that after hearing unfavourable divinations from one source, he sacrificed his own son in divination, because he did not believe the son would lie to his father. After his time, the Atah, or king, of Iddah would on his accession send a sacrifice to the shrine of Onoja-Aboli (Onojo, son of Ebuli) to ensure a just and successful reign.

Onojo's wars were so successful that there was no one to oppose him, and so he determined to make war on the people of the heavens. He had his servants build a great tower of packed earth, to allow him to rise to the sky. But the tower collapsed, and many people died. So then Onojo decided to make war on the deities of the earth. He ordered his servants to dig a great tunnel into the earth, and then he rode down into it, ordering the army to follow him. But they refused; instead, they filled up the pit and Onojo was buried there.

45

THE KINGDOM OF THE
NUPE: TSOEDE

*The Nupe kingdom formed around the confluence of the Niger
and Kaduna rivers, controlling a route between trading partners
to the south and the Hausa states in the north; the main impetus
may have been the trade from the south (the founder, Tsoede,
came from there). The area is good for agriculture (millet and
sorghum as well as yams). The people also practised crafts, and
were particularly known for trade beads. This version is retold
from different accounts collected in the first half of the twentieth
century.*

The son of the *Atta* (king) of Idah was hunting north in the
territory of the Nupe, who at that time paid tribute to Idah. He
encountered an attractive woman, the daughter of a chief, and
lived with her for some time, until he heard that his father was
dying and that if he wished to ensure his succession he should
return home. As the woman was pregnant, he left her tokens to
give to the child when it was born: an amulet and a ring. The
woman gave birth to a son, and named him Tsoede (although
among the Hausa he is more often known as Edegi).

When Tsoede was thirty years old, he was sent to Idah as a
slave by the new chief, his uncle. His father had become *Atta*
of Idah and was still living; he recognized his son by the amulet
and the ring and so brought him into his household. Their
relationship became particularly close after the king fell ill, and
the diviners pronounced that he could only be cured by the
fruit from a very tall oil-palm. The sons born to the *Atta* by his
royal wives tried to climb the tree but failed. Tsoede then tried,
and succeeded by his determination, pushing through the fronds

at the top even when they cut his lip, until he seized the fruit and was able to bring it down. Thereafter he had the appearance of a harelipped man.

Despite the father's fondness for the son, the *Atta* knew that Tsoede could never become king of Idah, and that after his death this love child would be in peril. So when he felt that his last days had come he summoned Tsoede and gave him rich gifts, and advised him to flee. These gifts included emblems of kingship: a great canoe, plated with bronze; the bronze trumpets known as *kakati*, drums, iron chains and fetters of great magical power.

Tsoede then fled from Idah in the canoe, and as soon as his father the *Atta* died, his stepbrothers pursued him. But he eluded them in the creeks along the Niger, and then made his way north and returned to Nku, his mother's town. He sank his bronze canoe into the waters, and began to make war. First, he seized power in Nku, and then proceeded to conquer the neighbouring towns. Two men who had helped him in his flight he made ministers; the servants who paddled the canoe became chiefs of towns around his capital and were given the right to show and bear iron chains like those that had been given to Tsoede.

Tsoede also brought to this land the arts and crafts which he had learned during his long stay in Idah. He introduced blacksmithing and canoe-building, as well as other forms of power. It is also said that he brought the custom of human sacrifice, and that his first victim was the uncle who had sent him to Idah as a slave. Most of all, however, Tsoede brought the art of war to his people, and in later years his capital was known as the city of horses, because there were so many mounted warriors at his call. He died after many years of reign while on an expedition of pillage.

46

THE JUKUN KINGDOM OF THE KOROROFA

The Kororofa peoples live along the upper Benue river, midway between the Niger and the kingdoms near Lake Chad; their traditions show an interaction with the Kanuri of Bornu to the north. The Jukun were the royal clan; the kingdom itself seems to have shifted capitals over time, and Wukari was the last royal city. These accounts are retold from the works of a colonial administrator.

THE SON OF AMA

The Jukun believe in a creative divinity with two aspects: one celestial and male, known as Chido, and the other earthly and female, known as Ama. They may be a couple; they may be a twofold entity; identification depends upon the context. It is Chido who sends rain; it is Ama who causes the crops to grow. It was Ama who created people. She brought them, along with certain animals, from the spirit world. But at first they were not fashioned as they are today: the woman's vagina was placed under her arm. Ama rearranged the organs of the man and the woman so they would fit together. Ama also brought forth the animals and spirits that now populate the world.

Among these spirits is Aki, death, who in the earliest times travelled on foot across the earth, wrestling those he met. If anyone could overthrow Aki, that person would live. But he once had a conversation with an ant who told him that he would do better if he avoided direct confrontation; ants do their work unseen, beneath the ground, and their presence is

known only when their tunnels cause walls and houses to collapse. Aki took the ant's advice and now does not attack a
person openly. He kills from within.

There is a story of Adi-bu-ma, a son of Ama, which perhaps
shows a different side of her character and explains why evil
and witchcraft exist in the world. There was a woman in the
earliest times, and she ate all her young. She swallowed everything she encountered. But one child she swallowed caused her
problems. After she had swallowed him, a lump appeared on
her thigh, and a voice came from within her body, asking her
to cut the skin and make an opening. She did so, and a boy
leaped out, fully armed with bow and arrows and hunting
equipment. She named him 'Adi-bu-ma' which means 'child of
Ama', and tried immediately to devour him. But he avoided her
and told her to wait, that he would provide her with something
better, since after all he was very small just then.

He went out hunting and brought tremendous quantities of
game to his mother, and she devoured all of it and asked for
more. He was the dish she particularly wanted; she would eat
whatever game he brought – duiker, gazelle, bush-pig, hartebeest, buffalo – and then ask him to come and be eaten, and
each time he would put her off. But he quickly grew into an
adult, and his mother then told him that he had grown up and
it was time for him to be eaten. Then he brought her an especially large quantity of game, enough to keep her eating for days,
and slipped away from their hut.

He travelled for several days, until he thought he had gone
far enough, and then he made use of the hunter's magic which
he had brought with him into the world. He took an egg from
the hunter's bag and broke it, and the egg immediately became
a walled town with inhabitants and their domestic animals. The
people of the town made him their king, and he settled in the
royal palace with many wives and servants to help him. He told
the people to clear fields around the town and he gave them
crops to plant from his bag.

One day, when Adi-bu-ma had asked the people to come
with him to work in the fields, his senior wife, who ruled the
women in the palace, told him that she could not come, that she

was sick. He excused her, but asked a small girl to watch over her and tell him what the wife did while the others were away. Eventually, he learned how his wife had left the village and gone off into the bush, where she met a woman. She bargained with this woman for spices and the ingredients of a special soup, and they agreed on the price. But when the woman from the bush produced the spices and began to measure out the quantities, the king's wife was surprised how little she was getting for her price. As is the Jukun custom, she used her husband's name as an exclamation, 'Adi-bu-ma, indeed, those are small piles of spices! With what do you measure them?' At that, the woman added more spice to each of the piles, saying, 'We should not be in conflict. Perhaps I do not know the measures used in your city. Tell me where it is, and I will bring my wares to your market.'

The king's wife led the stranger to the town, and as soon as they passed through the gate in the walls the woman from the bush seized the king's wife and swallowed her up. Then she seized the little girl who was following them (although the king's wife had not seen her) and swallowed her. She seized the guards at the gate and swallowed them up, and then she roamed through the town swallowing up every living thing that she encountered until the town was empty and lifeless. Only a chicken escaped her, and it scuttled around the huts and flapped up to the wall and then out onto the road. Down the road it went towards the fields where Adi-bu-ma and his people were working, and every now and then it fluttered up into a tree or a bush and clucked loudly, crying out 'Adi-bu-ma, your mother has come! She has eaten your town!'

Adi-bu-ma heard the chicken and understood its message, and immediately sent his people off to gather roots and plants to be used in a special medicine. Meanwhile, the king and his warriors gathered their weapons and hastened to the city. The king had sixty spears, and he knew that his mother had sixty teeth that she could use as weapons. When they met, just inside the walls of the city, he called to her and reproached her for her voracity that left nothing alive around her. But she simply opened her mouth and gestured for him to come and be swallowed up like the others.

He hurled a spear at her; it missed. She plucked out one of her teeth and threw it at him. It too missed. So they traded missiles, teeth and spears, until almost all were gone: the king had one spear, the mother only one tooth remaining. Then the chicken, which had followed the king back into the town, clucked at him, and the king understood its message: he should not throw the spear, but only brandish it, and when his mother threw her last tooth he alone would have a weapon. So he brandished his spear and went through the motions of throwing it, but at the last moment he made the spear spin in his hand and then he held it behind his body. His mother threw her last tooth: it missed. Then he rushed against her and pierced her belly with the spear, and as though he had burst a dam everything she had devoured came pouring out of her belly: people, animals, everything.

But they were dead. They lay limp in piles on the ground. The king then called to his people and they brought the roots and plants that he had ordered. With these he made a magical water into which he placed the dead bodies that had burst from his mother's belly. The bodies came back to life. The bodies that had been longest in the belly had their skins bleached to a pale white; those that had not spent so long had reddish skins, like the Fulani, and the latest arrivals had dark brown and black skins.

The little girl who had accompanied the wife told the king what had happened (but he had guessed most of it already: only his wife could have brought his mother to his town) and so he did not revive his senior wife. Instead, her body was burned, and the ashes from the fire were taken down to the river. But the wind carried some of the ashes away from the river, and where the ashes touched the ground calabashes grew up, along the path to the stream where the people got their drinking water. There was an enormous calabash at the centre of the patch, and it soon grew large enough to swallow up the women as they came to fetch water at the stream.

The king fed a goat with medicines and sent it against the calabash: although the goat butted it and pierced the shell with its horns, it could not destroy the calabash. So the king fed it more medicines, until the goat was able to break the calabash when it charged. And then again the king revived the people who had been swallowed up in the calabash and they burned the pieces. But some of the ashes escaped and touched people, and this is how witchcraft and sorcery came into the world.

KINGSHIP OF THE KOROROFA

It is said that the first capital of the Jukun kings was the town of Kundi. But kingship passed from the rulers of Kundi because of a disobedient son. The king had grown old and felt himself near death, and so summoned his son to learn the secrets of his kingship. But the son disregarded the call and went off, hunting or seeking pleasures. When the king was told his son had left without attending to him, he was angry and decided that this son would not be a worthy king. So instead, he called his grandson and revealed to him the secrets of kingship. He then told the young man to go to his father's town, which was Kororofa, and establish his court there. When the disobedient son returned, his father scolded him and told him he would never be a king. But in consolation, the father appointed him the ritual master of the earth, responsible for ensuring the fertility of the soil and the growth of the crops.

A very similar story is also told to explain how kingship ended in Kororofa, and again how kingship passed from Kororofa to Wukari. An added detail is that the dying king enters a great tree, and that the brothers pursue each other.

The history of the Jukun kingdom is marked by warfare with the Kanuri of Bornu. But at one time, at least, their relations were peaceable. It is said that a Jukun king went out to war against Bornu, and the two armies met in battle. The king of Bornu, a Muslim, called on Allah for help against his enemy, and brought down a fire to earth which set the grasses blazing and surrounded the Jukun army. The soldiers were terrified by the flames and began to throw down their weapons in panic, seeking some path through the circle of fire. But their king reassured them, reminding them of his ritual authority, and used his powers to call down a heavy rain which extinguished the flames. His soldiers were heartened by this proof of his power and renewed their attack. The battle was inconclusive, and the kings realized they were too evenly matched. The Jukun king withdrew to his capital.

The king of Bornu later sent the Jukun king a reminder of the way in which he had called down the fire from heaven: a burning coal was laid on a bed of cotton and enclosed in a basket and delivered to the Jukun king. In return, the Jukun king sent to Bornu a sealed basket filled with water, reminding his peer that he possessed the power to call down the rains. As a result of this exchange, the two kingdoms made peace and exchanged ambassadors.

47

THE BACHAMA AND BATA
OF THE UPPER BENUE

*The Bachama and Bata were groups closely related by language
and culture living on either bank of the upper Benue river, close
to the border between Nigeria and northern Cameroon. They
were part of a large cluster of peoples living just south of the
area conquered by the Fulani during the nineteenth century,
and may in some ways have been influenced by them; however,
they also preserved their own traditional beliefs and practices.
The groups were patrilineal, although with strong evidence of
relatively recent matrilineal practices (that is, the importance
of the uterine link and the mother's brother); they were not
united in larger political units. Subsistence was derived from
a combination of agriculture (millet and sorghum), some
livestock and hunting. The cult of Nzeanzo, common to the
Bachama and the Bata, was essentially a rain cult associated
with agricultural fertility. These accounts are retold from the
work of a British colonial administrator published in 1931.*

NZEANZO

Venin was the mother of the gods. She came from heaven,
although it is not said when or how, and on earth she gave
birth to five sons. Her brother was Wun, the god of death, and
he also came down from the heavens and settled on earth.

Venin's fifth child, Nzeanzo, gave her the most trouble in
childbirth. He spoke to her repeatedly from the womb, giving
her instructions and finally asking her if he could be born,
although the full term of months had not yet been completed.

'I cannot help you,' his mother told him, 'but if you can find some way for yourself you may try it.'

After she spoke, a huge lump formed on her thigh, swelling until it was the size of a small child; then the skin split and Nzeanzo emerged. From birth he could walk and talk, and he performed wonderful tasks.

For instance, he noticed how the flies bothered his mother and the other members of the household, and so he collected all the flies of all sorts: the little fruit flies, the middle-sized houseflies, the large biting flies, and enclosed them in a calabash which he stopped up securely. He left the calabash before his chamber, telling his older brothers that they should not open it while he went to bathe in the river. But they were scornful of their younger brother, and suspected that he had prepared something to eat or drink, so they opened the calabash. Out swarmed the flies, free to afflict people once more, and Nzeanzo never again tried to do away with them.

Venin at one point decided she should visit her brother Wun, to buy some cattle from him. She took her four older sons, but decided to leave the youngest, Nzeanzo, at home. He thought this was a bad idea, and feared that they might get into trouble. So he secretly followed his mother and his brothers.

Venin and the four boys reached Wun's home after a short trip, and Wun greeted them warmly. He had four daughters, close in age to the boys, and he told the children to play together while he and his sister discussed the selection and price of the cattle. Later in the day, as dinner was being prepared and served, he built a large fire at one end of his compound, and over it he hung a large metal pot which he filled with water.

After dinner, he sent the children to sleep in the children's hut, while his sister was given her own place, and Wun retired to his own chamber.

It was in the dark of the night that Nzeanzo arrived at Wun's settlement, and he looked carefully around the area, noting the large fire and the big pot. He made his way to the children's hut, and found his brothers lying in a row, and nearby Wun's daughters slept covered by a loose sheet. 'Let us take some precautions,' said Nzeanzo to himself, and he removed the loincloths from his sleeping brothers and draped them over the hips of Wun's four daughters, and he took the sheet from the daughters and spread it over his brothers. Then he waited. In the middle of the night, Wun came into the dark hut. He felt the first bodies he encountered: they were Venin's sons, but covered by his daughters' sheet. 'I told the girls to sleep at the back of the hut,' muttered Wun, and he carefully made his way past the sleeping boys to the second group of children. He reached down and touched: there were the loincloths. These, he thought, were the four sons of Venin. One by one, he picked them up and took them to the iron pot where the water was now boiling. He tossed them in. When he finished, he returned to his chamber and went to sleep.

When all four of Wun's daughters were boiling away, Nzeanzo woke up his brothers and showed them how they had narrowly escaped becoming a meal for their uncle. Then he woke up his mother and told her what had happened. Secretly, they all slipped away from the settlement and began the journey to their home.

In the morning, Wun woke up and looked around. He could not find his daughters, and his sister was not in her hut. He looked more carefully into the pot and understood what had happened: he had been tricked. He quickly located the tracks left by Venin and her sons and followed them. When he saw Nzeanzo, he hurled a river to block the path, but with a few words Nzeanzo made the river shrink down to the size of a stream so that he and his brothers could leap over it. Then Wun hurled a charm that became a great swamp before them, but again Nzeanzo spoke a spell and the swamp became a puddle of water. So they escaped Wun, although he now roams free in the world to kill people. From that time on, Nzeanzo's brothers acknowledged that, though he was the youngest, he was the most powerful of them.

Nzeanzo is also responsible for the development of canoes, although this came at some cost. He was sent out to herd the cattle, and his grandmother came with him. As the heat of the day increased, she asked him to let her rest, and so he found her a place in a tree where she could rest, and he gave her a gourd with some fresh milk. Then he drove the cattle on. While she was waiting through the noontime, a hippopotamus came by and saw the gourd. The hippopotamus demanded some milk, but the gourd was empty; the old woman had drunk it all. She could not offer any to the great animal, and showed him how the gourd was empty. But this simply made the impatient hippopotamus more angry, and so it pushed against the tree with all its might until the tree toppled over, and then it trampled the old woman to death.

On his way back to the camp, Nzeanzo returned to find his grandmother. It was clear what had happened. She lay dead among the shattered limbs of the tree, and the tracks of the hippopotamus led towards the river. Nzeanzo followed quickly after the killer, and soon found him. Immediately he hurled his spear and pierced the animal through the heart. As the hippopotamus was dying it uttered a curse, promising that any humans who tried to cross the Benue river by swimming would be attacked by hippos. This is why Nzeanzo devised canoes for the people.

Venin eventually died, although it is not said how, and she became the object of a ritual cult. Her four older sons also became divinities: they are Hamabulki, Hamagenin, Ngbirrim and Gbeso. But none of their cults is so important as that of Nzeanzo, which is based at Fare. Nzeanzo settled there after living for a time in Kwolle. In Kwolle he was kept awake at night by the harsh and constant croaking of the frogs, so he built a great iron canoe, and travelled to Fare.

THE SEPARATION OF THE BATA
AND BACHAMA

The Bata and Bachama were originally one people, and they moved south out of the desert areas to the north. They were forced to move after their chief's daughter refused to give water from a well to the daughter of the king of Gobir, despite their kinship; this act of hostility aroused the Gobir against them.

*

The people reached Demsa, and there a dispute between the twin sons of the king caused them to break into two groups. The older son was worried about the succession and jealous of his brother, and decided he would kill him while they were hunting, so it would seem an accident. He made his preparations and instructed his followers, but his plans became known to his father's sister, and she warned Jaro Dungi, the younger son. He stole the pot that contained the rain magic of the people and fled away. He was pursued by the older brother. But when the older brother caught up, Jaro Dungi was already on the other side of the Benue river. The older brother threw a long roll of cloth across the river, holding one end, and when he saw that his younger brother had caught it, the older brother cut the cloth in two with a knife and pronounced an oath: Jaro Dungi would be the 'slave of the cults', responsible for rain-making and healing and other such duties, while the older brother would hunt and make war against the Fulani in the north, and neither of them would be allowed to set eyes on the river which separated them. So the Bachama became responsible for the rites, and the Bata for war.

THE PEOPLES OF
THE COAST

*The lands immediately west of the Niger delta were dominated
by the Yoruba peoples, who formed many city-states and kingdoms and now constitute one of the largest language groups in
Africa, with numbers now over twenty million. Yoruba influence can be seen in the traditions of the city of Benin (in Nigeria;
see Chapter 48). In the late eighteenth century, the Yoruba
kingdom of Oyo conquered the kingdom of Dahomey (in the
modern Republic of Benin; see Chapter 51), and their influence
is particularly visible in the shared practice of Ifa divination.
This densely populated part of the Atlantic coast was known
to eighteenth-century travellers as the Slave Coast, and so many
Yoruba and Fon slaves were sent to the New World that some
of their culture survived the crossing. The Fon belief in vodun
(deities) became the basis of the Caribbean practice of voodoo,
as it is popularly known.*

*North of the Yoruba kingdoms, Borgu (see Chapter 50)
managed to remain independent of its southern neighbours and
of the Muslim states of the Hausas. West of the kingdom of
Dahomey, in the modern states of Ghana and Côte d'Ivoire,
Akan-speaking peoples formed the Ashanti kingdom in the
seventeenth and eighteenth centuries, and a fraction of them
moved west to become the Baule. Vegetation probably affected
the expansion of the kingdoms. The dense tropical forests that
used to mark the coast of West Africa become more open in
western Nigeria, around the Niger, and so allow easier traffic
of people, goods and on occasion armies.*

THE CITY OF BENIN

The city of Benin, situated in the Niger delta and inhabited by the Bini, was long involved in trade up the river, as well as with the Europeans coming from the coast. The city deserves special mention for the importance of its artworks: the many brass and bronze castings which were dispersed after the British captured and destroyed the city in 1897, but which have become icons of African art. Like the city of Djenne (along the middle Niger; see Chapter 62), it remained relatively independent, although clearly influenced by the Yoruba states to the west; the city also deserves special note in recognition of the Oba (the king) who banned the slave-trade, at least for a time, because of the harm it did to his people. These narratives tell of the foundation of the city and of a major king; they are retold from the works of a Benin historian published in the 1950s.

THE FOUNDATION OF BENIN

It is said that the people who founded the city of Benin first came from Egypt. After passing Ife, the holy city of the Yoruba, they sent a hunter to scout ahead, and the hunter told them they were coming to a proper site. There they built their city. The first king, or *Ogiso*, was named Igodo; he ruled long and made the people prosperous. He was succeeded by his son Ere, who devoted much effort to stopping the quarrels of the people, so that his name has become something of a byword. He also promoted agriculture and established the groups of craftsmen of Benin.

It was during the rule of this first series of kings that a monster used to come from the sky to attack people as they went to market in a certain quarter. But a hero named Evian defeated the monster. He went to the marketplace ahead of time, and took with him an iron hammer which he heated in coals so that it glowed. Then he waited until the people began to assemble, and as they came, so too did the monster, flying down from the sky. But as it opened its maw to swallow the people, Evian hurled his iron hammer into the beast's mouth, so that it roared in pain and flew off, never to return. To honour his deed, the Bini perform an acrobatic masked dance.

The last *Ogiso*, Owodo, was not a good king, and in his reign barrenness struck the women of the kingdom. The king sent Esagho, his first wife, to an oracle to learn what the remedy might be; the oracle replied that if the king sacrificed his first wife, the people would be cured. But on her return, Esagho told the king that the oracle had demanded that he sacrifice his son Ekaladerhan. The king banished the son, but did not kill him. However, after three years, when the barrenness of women had continued, the king sent other messengers to the oracle. Again, the oracle told the messengers that the king should sacrifice Esagho, his first wife. When he received this message, the king immediately had Esagho executed, and sent messengers to his son (who had founded a village some distance away) asking him to return. But the son refused, and succeeded by stratagems in defeating the troops sent to bring him back by force. The *Ogiso* was eventually deposed for killing a pregnant woman.

Following the deposition of the last *Ogiso* the people of Benin sent messengers to Odudua, the Yoruba king in Ife, to ask that one of his sons come to rule over them. Odudua sent his son Oranyan. Oranyan came to Benin, married, and fathered a son. But after a few years, Oranyan said he would leave Benin; the people were too quarrelsome, and only some-one born among them would be able to govern them properly. It is from these words of Oranyan – 'Ile Bini' or people of vexation – that the city of Benin takes its present name. But Oranyan did not depart abruptly; he moved instead to a nearby community for some years, while his son grew older, and then still further away. His residences are still known.

His son, at first, did not speak. But his father sent him some charmed seeds, which the son used for the game of *wari*. And when he won the game, he exclaimed in delight 'Owomika!' (I have succeeded!) which later, shortened, became his name: Eweka.

EWUARE

King Ohen became crippled, and had to be carried about. He disguised this fact, but his *iyase* (minister) discovered it, and so the king, to preserve his secret, had the *iyase* killed. But the man was very popular, and learning of his death the people rose up against the king and stoned him to death. He left four sons. On his death, the eldest became king, but was not popular, and his rule was marked by civil unrest. He exiled Ogun, the third son of Ohen, and died. The second son then came to the throne and ruled well, but he died young. The fourth son, who had accompanied Ogun into exile, came back to learn the intentions of the city elders; he then took the throne in place of his brother. But Ogun came and killed him in the market, and took the throne. He became a great king, known by the name Ewuare.

Some stories are told about his adventures during his exile. He returned to the city at one point, but was spotted and had to run. He took refuge in the compound of the *Ogiefa*, the chief loremaster of the city, and hid in a well. A slave named Edo put a ladder down the well so that he was able to escape before dawn, when people would come looking for him. In gratitude for Edo's help, when Ewuare came to the throne he gave the name Edo to the city, and that remains a second name of the city of Benin. A market woman also sheltered him in the city, and in gratitude to her a tree was planted where her stall had been, and after that tree another and another, until in the modern era a statue was erected.

Having escaped from the well, Ogun (who would be Ewuare)

spent the night in the bush under a tree. In the morning, he woke to find drops falling on him; when he opened his eyes he saw the drops were blood, coming from the kill of a leopard in the tree above him. And he saw further that he lay next to a poisonous snake. He quickly drew his weapon and killed both beasts, and later established a shrine at this place.

He lost his son, however. He had sent the son to be fostered with the remaining son of a famous general, who had died in a rearguard action, and at first the two boys got on very well. But then the general's son insulted the prince, calling him a peasant and giving him a hoe in exchange for a gift of yams the prince had made. After that, they began to hate each other, and finally each poisoned the other on the same day.

After the death of his son, Ewuare became inconsolable. He decreed three years of mourning, during which no one in the land could wash or take pleasure or have intercourse. The people responded by leaving Benin in great numbers and taking refuge with neighbouring kings. It was to prevent this that Ewuare instituted tribal markings on the faces. He was eventually induced to relax his decree by the advice of an old man known as 'Old Man Chameleon'. The reign of Ewuare is remembered for the walls he built and for the number of heroes and magicians who lived at that time.

49

THE YORUBA OF
SOUTH-WESTERN NIGERIA

The Yoruba compose one of the largest ethnolinguistic groups of Africa in terms of the number of speakers, and Yoruba has also spread outside Africa, as a liturgical language, through the slave-trade and the practice of Ifa divination which involves memorization of a corpus of verses. Yoruba history is rich and complex. At different times, different cities have risen to power and controlled their neighbours. All, however, acknowledge the city of Ile-Ife (old Ife) as their point of origin, and rulers claim some dynastic connection to Ife for legitimacy. Oral tradition and written sources (from European traders and travellers) document the history back to approximately 1500; archaeology indicates cities in the region at least 2,000 years ago. Some people now claim an Egyptian (or other Middle Eastern) origin for the Yoruba (see below, 'The Migration from the East') but the claims are improbable.

Yoruba culture was never unitary; while united to some extent by language and customs, people were divided by geography, political systems and religious practice. One of the principal factors of unity, however, is the Ifa divination system in which the babalaawo *(the Ifa diviner) reads the future (or the state of the world) by throwing cowrie-shells or palm nuts; the arrangement of the items yields patterns which are associated with verses and interpretations, not unlike the Chinese I Ching. In other respects, the region was fragmented into specific territories, each with its own history and set of religious practices. In the past century, however, the Yoruba view of their past has largely been homogenized through the influence of the Revd Samuel Johnson's* History of the Yorubas; *this book, written*

*by a converted Yoruba and published in 1921, has become the
accepted version of history. Johnson views the gods as deified
kings. This selection of stories tries to offer a sense of the variety
among traditions: in one (older) story, Odudua is a goddess,
the consort of Olorun, and much the same name (Oduduwa)
is later applied to a male deity who creates the earth. The
sources for the stories include European works published in the
late nineteenth century, colonial era and modern accounts.*

THE ORISHA

The Yoruba have numerous deities, or *orisha*, of whom Olorun
is now considered the principal. Olorun is the sky-god, and
he is known by a number of names and attributes: *Eleda* the
creator, *Alaye* the owner of life, *Olodumare* the almighty.

In the past, it was believed that Olorun had a consort named
Odudua, also called *Iya Agbe* or 'Mother of the Calabash'.
This name referred to the way in which the pair enclosed the
world as the two parts of a calabash, the bowl and the lid, fit
together tightly. But Odudua objected to this state of affairs;
she was shut in the dark, being the bottom half of the calabash.
She complained and upbraided her spouse. Her complaints
made him so angry that he blinded her by ripping out her eyes.
She responded by cursing him, saying he would only eat snails
from then on, and snails are now the proper offering to Olorun.

They had a pair of children, male and female, who married
and produced a son named Orungan. Orungan forced himself
upon his mother, and so she fled from him. He chased after her
and was about to catch her when she tripped and fell. She then
transformed herself. From her breasts came rivers, from the
parts of her body came many of the other *orisha* who are
worshipped by the Yoruba: Shango, the *orisha* of lightning, and
his wives Oya, Oshun and Oba who are rivers, Olokun, the
orisha of the ocean, Ogun, the *orisha* of blacksmiths, hunters
and warriors, and many others. This is said to have happened
in Ife.

Another story of the origin of the *orisha* says that they are the fragments of the great Orisha, who was killed and whose body was broken into tiny bits by a slave whom he kept to do his cooking. Many of the fragments were gathered by Orunmila, the *orisha* of Ifa, and kept in the city of Ife. But he could not assemble them all, and so there are small *orisha* throughout the world where the fragments fell.

THE CREATION OF THE WORLD

This story may be told with different protagonists. In some versions it is Obatala who descends from the heavens and creates the earth and humans, in some that task is undertaken by Oduduwa (here a male, in contrast to the previous story).

After Olorun had brought forth the many *orisha*, they lived together in heaven. Below them was only the sea, which was the province of the deity Olokun and her spouse. After some time, Obatala grew weary of looking down over the grey waters; he found them monotonous and depressing. He asked Olorun if he might find some way to add variety and difference to what lay below, and Olorun said that if Obatala was willing to do the work, he should proceed.

Obatala went first to Orunmila, the *orisha* of Ifa divination. He asked Orunmila to read the signs and tell him what would be required for the task, if it could be accomplished. Orunmila threw the palm nuts, he read the signs, he chanted the verses, and he told Obatala that he could indeed accomplish his purpose, but that he would need certain items. He would need a gold chain of great length. He would need a snail's shell filled with sand. He should take a chicken. He should also take a palm nut and a cat.

Obatala had to spend some time collecting gold from the different *orisha* who lived with him in heaven, and then he took the gold to the smith, and the smith forged a chain with all the gold Obatala had collected. Eventually the chain was complete, and Obatala hung it from the edge of heaven and began climbing down as far as he could until he hung over the waters. Then he took the snail's shell of sand and upturned it, so the sand fell down onto the surface of the water. There it stayed, and it increased in quantity and spread to cover the waters. Obatala then released the chicken, which fluttered down to the new land and immediately began scraping at the sand and casting it up this way and that to form hills and valleys. Obatala watched until the chicken had passed out of sight, still shaping the new earth, and then he came down off the chain onto the land. He planted the palm nut, which immediately grew to full size. Obatala lived beneath the palm tree with the cat. The place is now known as Ife, or Ile-Ife (old Ife).

Obatala began to make figures of clay. Olorun breathed life into them. They became people whom Obatala placed in his new land. Other *orisha* came down from heaven to join him in the new land. Olorun created the sun and moon to give them light.

The sun made Obatala thirsty, and he drank the fermented sap of the palm tree. The palm wine made him drunk, and some of the human figures he made at that time were deformed or incomplete. He fell asleep after a while; when he woke he saw what he had done, and regretted having brought misshapen people into the world. He swore never to drink palm wine again, and he became the protector of the children of his drunkenness.

ODUDUWA, IFE AND OYO

This version of the story makes Oduduwa the creator of the world, and is associated particularly with the city of Ife.

At the beginning, the various *orisha* who had come into being lived in heaven, in the realm of Olorun. Beneath them lay the sea, with nothing in between. The *orisha* wished to create something; with Olorun's permission, they consulted Orunmila who instructed them to prepare a snail's shell full of sand and to find a five-toed chicken; with these tools they would be able to create a world beneath them. Obatala and Oduduwa were selected for the task, and they set off to find the way down from heaven. But on the way they found a palm tree and tapped its sap; Obatala drank heavily and became intoxicated. He fell asleep.

Oduduwa had envied Obatala for his primary role in this process of creation. While Obatala was asleep, Oduduwa took the snail's shell of sand and the chicken and proceeded on his way. When he had come to a place just above the waters, he cast the sand over the waters and then released the five-toed fowl. The sand spread over the water, covering it; the fowl fluttered down onto the sand and immediately began scratching away, kicking the sand up behind it into hills. The central place, where Oduduwa and the chicken first came to earth, is Ife, and Oduduwa made himself king of that town. It is because Oduduwa usurped the place intended for Obatala that the world now knows wars and other catastrophes; under Obatala, the world would have been a far more hospitable place.

Eventually, Oduduwa passed on, leaving his possessions to his six sons, of whom the youngest was Oranmiyan. He left his possessions divided into bundles of wealth: cowrie-shells, beads, cloth, foodstuffs. He also left one bundle of earth with some pieces of iron. The older sons immediately took the bundles of wealth, leaving the last (the earth and iron) to Oranmiyan. Thus Oranmiyan became the master of the earth. When the older brothers wished to exploit the land, they had to pay him tribute. When they tried to overcome him, the pieces of iron became weapons in his hands and he easily defeated them. So he became king in Ife and his elders became his subjects. Each of them became a king in his own town, but all were subordinate to Oranmiyan in Ife.

It is said that Oranmiyan was called to the city of Benin for some time, to be their king. But he returned from Benin. After some time, he left Ife. He led his armies north-east, towards the Niger, because he wished to attack the Nupe people who lived across the river. But when he came to the great water, he could find no way for his army to cross in safety: the Nupe people were ready on the other side, shooting arrows at any Yoruba warrior they saw. He realized he would have to abandon his project, but that meant that he would return to Ife in defeat. This outcome was unacceptable, and so he led his army west for a time, unsure what to do. He came to Borgu, and the king of Borgu gave him assistance: he charmed a python and released it. He told Oranmiyan to follow the python, and any place it settled for seven days would be his new home. So Oranmiyan led his army after the python until they came to the site of Oyo, and there he built his new kingdom.

There are different stories told about the succession in Ife. In Oyo, they say that when Oranmiyan was about to depart, he appointed a household slave to rule in his place; this slave was the son of a woman who had been offered as a sacrifice to Obatala but spared when it was found she was pregnant. He had grown up in the palace and had gradually taken over the responsibility for the shrines and rites. In Ife, they deny this story; they say that they have never been subject to Oyo.

Oranmiyan returned to Ife to die. A pillar of stone, the staff of Oranmiyan, still stands there. It is believed that Oranmiyan promised to return from the underworld if Ife needed his help. But once, during a festival, some drunken people called him up, and Oranmiyan emerged from the earth fully armed. In the dark, he could not recognize his people, but hearing the noise and commotion of the festival he thought the city was being attacked and began to slay all around him. When dawn came he could see the corpses lying scattered about the streets; he saw that they were unarmed, and he recognized them as the people of Ife, without scars on their cheeks. He realized that he had made war upon his own people, and so he swore he would never return from the underworld.

MOREMI

After the departure of Oranmiyan, the city of Ife was troubled by raids from the east by the Igbo. The people of Ife did not understand that the Igbo were humans, for in warfare the Igbo would dress themselves in raffia and cloth and they would cover their heads with elaborate wooden masks. The people of Ife thought they were being attacked by spirits of the wild or by *orisha* whom they had angered in some way. They offered prayers and sacrifices, but no response came.

A woman, Moremi, determined to help her people. She was married and had a son, but she grieved at the suffering of the people of Ife. She made a vow in the name of the river-goddess Esinmirin that she would free her people from the oppression of the attackers, and if she succeeded she would offer the river the dearest sacrifice she could make. The river *orisha* heard her prayer and accepted it. Then she sought a way, and she consulted Eshu. She sacrificed six goats and six bags of cowrie-shells to Eshu, and he showed her the plan and gave her protection.

Moremi's plan was simple: she allowed herself to be captured by the Igbo during the next raid. The Igbo took their captives back to their own country and then divided the spoils. Moremi was extremely beautiful; many men desired her, and since it was a time of war, they had their way with her. When they returned to their town, Moremi became a harlot at the edge of town. From the men who came to her she learned the language of the place, and then she learned their customs and their secrets – for men will let their tongues run free when boasting to a beautiful woman. She learned that the supernatural beings who accompanied their armies were only men, dressed in costumes of raffia and wood; she learned how much these maskers feared fire.

Eventually, she decided she had learned enough. She slipped away from the town one night and made her way carefully and secretly back to Ife. There she told the people what sort of attacker they faced, and she taught them the strategy of using fire against the demon-warriors. The next time the Igbo attacked, they were met with fierce opposition, for the warriors of Ife did not fear simple humans, however dressed up. The warriors of Ife also used fire, so many of the Igbo died in agony when their costumes caught fire.

Moremi then went to the river to fulfil her vow to the *orisha*. But none of the sacrifices she offered proved acceptable: she offered goats, sheep, oxen, but to each of these the *orisha* made a negative response. Moremi consulted a diviner: the dearest sacrifice she could make was her son. And so she offered up her son. To make up her loss, the people of Ife declared themselves to be her sons and daughters, and on her death she was venerated as an *orisha* herself, a protector of the city.

(Some people say that when Moremi came among the Igbo, she was given to the king because of her beauty, and that it was in the palace, living as the king's concubine, that she learned the secrets of the Igbo.)

THE MIGRATION FROM THE EAST

As well as the stories which describe the creation centred at Ife, there are traditions that the Yoruba migrated from the east, the lands of the Bible and of Islam. The following story is the version of the Revd Johnson, which he interpreted to mean that the Yoruba were descended from Coptic Christians.

The Yoruba are descended from Lamurudu, who was a king of Mecca. His sons were Oduduwa, who became the founder of the Yoruba, and at least two others whose descendants moved to Gogobiri and Kukawa in Hausaland; their kinship with the Yoruba is shown by the common scarifications.

Although Islam had been revealed, Oduduwa abandoned Islam and relapsed into paganism. He and his priest Asara transformed the great mosque into a cult shrine and filled it with idols. Asara was a maker of these statues, and his son Braima was sent out to sell them on the streets. But Braima remained true in his belief in Islam, and when selling the statues he would call out 'Who wishes to buy falsehood?'

At that time, all the men of the city went out to hunt just before the annual festival of these gods. While they were gone, Braima took an axe and destroyed the statues in the temple that had been a mosque. He left the axe hanging by its thong round the neck of the largest statue. When the men returned from their hunt with the offerings for their gods, they found that the statues had been destroyed and their shrine desecrated.

They enquired and quickly learned who had done it. They brought Braima up before a tribunal of judges. 'Did you destroy the statues in the shrine?' they asked him.

'Ask that great statue who performed the act,' answered Braima.

'Can it speak?' asked the judges.

'If it cannot speak, why do you worship it?' retorted Braima. The judges easily found him guilty and he was condemned to be burned alive. A great stack of firewood was assembled, and Braima was led to the pyre. But at this point, that part of the city which had remained true to Islam revolted and rose up to preserve the life of Braima and to overthrow the idolators. There was a bloody struggle; the Muslims were victorious. In the fighting, Lamurudu was killed. Oduduwa escaped with his followers, as did the other two sons of Lamurudu who settled in Hausaland.

Oduduwa came to Ife, and there encountered the founder of the Ifa divination system. After defeating an army that had pursued them, they established their cities in that land and lived there.

THE ORIGIN OF IFA DIVINATION I

This is a story recorded before the writings of the Revd Johnson, and it refers to a version of the creation story somewhat different from the story of the descent to Ife by either Obatala or Oduduwa.

It is said that at the start of creation there were very few humans making sacrifices to the *orisha* and so they often felt hungry. Ifa was trying unsuccessfully to find some food when he encountered Eshu Elegba and they discussed their plight. Eshu told Ifa that if he had sixteen palm nuts he could show Ifa how to read the future, and this activity would become a reliable source of abundant offerings.

At that time, the only palm trees were owned by Orungan, the first human. Ifa went to Orungan and asked for the nuts;

Orungan tried to get the fruits of the palm down, but could not reach so high. He was forced to pick up the nuts, the oily kernels, which had been thrown down by monkeys eating the fruit. Orungan's wife Orishabi brought the nuts, tied in her waist-cloth. This is why the *babalaawo* invoke Orungan and Orishabi when about to begin divination, because they are the pair who first provided the nuts for divination.

THE ORIGIN OF IFA DIVINATION II

This is the story which the Revd Johnson recorded.

The man who discovered Ifa divination was Setilu. He was born blind in the land of the Nupe, and at first his parents were uncertain whether to raise him or to expose him. They decided to keep the child, and he amazed them. By the age of five, he was able to tell them who would come to visit them that day; later he began to predict greater events. In his practice, he used sixteen pebbles.

The Muslims took over the land, and expelled Setilu. He crossed the river, and after staying for a time in the city of Benin, he eventually settled at Ife. There he attracted followers and began to teach his practices. In time, palm nuts were substituted for the pebbles.

BORGU AND THE LEGEND
OF KISRA

North of the Yoruba states, south of the Songhay and west of
Sokoto and the Muslim emirates of the north lay the kingdom
of Borgu, now split between modern Nigeria and the Republic
of Benin. The people of Borgu, speakers of Busa and Ba'tonu,
preserved their independence despite challenges from all their
larger neighbours, although they took something from them
as well: from the Songhay certain institutions (festivals and
praise-singers) associated with kingship; from the Muslims a
legend of origin which defines them as opponents of Islam from
the very beginning. Elements of this legend are found among
other peoples as well (for instance, among the Bachama), but
it is particularly associated with Borgu. The name 'Kisra' is the
Arabic form of the Persian title Khusrow, and is particularly
associated with Khusrow Anushirwan, the Sassanian ruler of
Persia in the period before the life of the Prophet Muhammad.

Kisra was a king of the Persians who made war against the sons
of Nuhu. Among the Hausa, it was said that he obtained the
help of a jinn who lived in a stone; after Kisra had made
offerings of red cloth and red animals, including a man, the
jinn provided him with a great spear which enabled Kisra to
take the victory. But later Kisra neglected the jinn, and the jinn
passed over to the side of Nuhu's brother Annabi, and so Kisra
was defeated.

Others say that Kisra lived in Mecca at the time of the advent
of the Prophet Muhammad, but that he refused the teachings
of the Prophet and so fled to the west. And others say that Kisra
was a Persian king who lived at the time of the Prophet and

conquered Palestine and Egypt, taking the provinces from the Byzantines (or Romans) who held them. He settled in Egypt for a time, until the Byzantines rallied their forces and conquered it. Then, not wishing to take refuge in Arabia because the teachings of Muhammad were spreading there, Kisra moved to the west, taking with him the king of Napate (who may have settled in Nupeland). He passed first through Bornu and then lived for a time in towns which he founded east of the Niger river. He had three sons, Woru, Sabi and Bio.

Kisra vanished from the earth while living at Koko, in Gwandu. His three sons then had to move west, for reasons that are not recalled. Most probably, they migrated to escape the Muslims, who had pursued Kisra because he was such a staunch refuser of the faith, and threatened his entire family. The sons came to Illo and crossed the river just ahead of their pursuers; the river was at that time a small stream, but once they had crossed it the stream immediately grew into the great watercourse that we know in modern times. The sons then founded kingdoms of their own in Nikki (in modern Benin), Bussa and Illo (in Nigeria).

THE FON AND THE
KINGDOM OF DAHOMEY

*The kingdom of Dahomey developed inland from the coastal
lagoons in the Bight of Benin, and its capital was Abomey. The
Fon people practised agriculture and fishing; they were also a
military power and supplied the Atlantic slave-trade with so
many people that certain elements of their religious practices
survived in the Caribbean in the form of vodun or voodoo. In
the eighteenth century, Dahomey was conquered by the Yoruba
of Oyo, who took from them some practices such as Ifa divination, which among the Fon is called Fa. Despite the British
attempt to stop the slave-trade after 1807, it continued in
Dahomey (particularly through the port of Ouidah or Whydah)
towards Brazil until the end of the nineteenth century when the
French conquered the territory. For nineteenth-century Europeans, Dahomey was marked by two striking images: the
annual 'customs' in which criminals were put to death, and the
king's bodyguard of 'Amazons', women warriors devoted to
him. These stories are retold from versions collected by American anthropologists during the 1930s.*

THE CREATION

It is said that at the beginning of things, Mawu the creator
travelled with Aido-Hwedo, the great serpent, and that the
serpent's movements shaped the land: as it twisted its body
it moved hills and laid river-beds, and its droppings formed
mountains. Mawu made the world like a calabash, one of the
large gourds used to make serving bowls. First she shaped the

lower bowl and then she shaped the sky as the lid. When she had finished, she found the world was sinking from the weight of the hills and the trees and other growth upon the surface, so she asked Aido-Hwedo to serve as a support, to coil himself at the base of the world and to hold it up. Aido-Hwedo coiled himself up – in the same way that women now coil a cloth to put on their heads when they are going to carry a burden – and so stabilized the world. Because Aido-Hwedo is a creature of the cold, Mawu created the sea around the world to keep the serpent cool.

Mawu and her consort Lisa form a dual deity, and the *vodun* are considered their children. Mawu and Lisa live in the sky; Mawu is associated with the moon, and Lisa with the sun. Most of their offspring live on earth. Their children take many forms. Gu, the god of iron, came as a headless body; where the head should be was a great blade. The last-born was Legba, who became Mawu's pet. Legba acquired other responsibilities as well. Mawu posed a test for her children, to see which of them, if any, could play several musical instruments at the same time: a flute and a drum, a bell and a gong. While playing, they should dance and sing as well. Only Legba could accomplish this feat, and so Mawu made Legba the go-between and messenger of the gods.

Mawu apportioned the earth among her children. To Sagbata, who had come into being as a couple, male and female, she gave rule over the earth. To Sogbo, who was born a hermaphrodite, she gave control of the sky. And she cautioned them not to quarrel, but to work as closely together as the lid of a calabash fits onto the bottom bowl. To Agbe and his consort she assigned the rule of the sea. To each she gave a different language, and Legba is the only one who can speak all languages.

EARTH AND SKY

Sogbo had wished to go down to the earth and rule there, but Mawu denied him. Mawu said that the earth was further from her, and so the elder Sagbata should be sent down. Sogbo grumbled at this show of preference, and so was receptive when Legba came to him with a suggestion that perhaps this would be the occasion for a test of their respective powers.

When Sagbata had departed Mawu's residence in the skies for his new realm on earth, he took all sorts of wealth: the seeds of useful plants and crops, the tools and skills by which humans shape their world. But he did not have room for two items which therefore remained in the skies: water and fire (fire was eventually stolen and brought down to men). Legba's suggestion was that Sogbo should withhold the rains which water the earth and see what occurred. Sogbo readily agreed. At the same time, Legba went to Mawu and expressed concern that there might not be enough water in the heavens for the needs of its residents, and Mawu gave him a message for Sogbo, ordering her second child to stop the rains for a time.

When Sagbata descended to earth with all his seeds, he was welcomed by the humans who had been placed there, for his gifts promised to make their lives much easier. But the crops he had brought required rain, and the rain did not fall. Soon the humans began to curse Sagbata for the false hopes he had raised and the change in weather that had come about after his arrival.

After a time, Mawu sent Legba down to earth to see how the eldest was doing. Legba came down and found Sagbata in a miserable state, for the earth was parched and barren and the people were very hostile to him. Legba promised to intercede on his behalf with Mawu, and told Sagbata to watch for a messenger who would soon bring him instructions. Then he returned to Mawu's house and found the *wututu* bird. He sent the bird down to Sagbata with the message that all the people on earth should unite and light a great fire, so that the smoke would rise to heaven and signal their distress. The bird flew down to Sagbata and gave him Legba's instructions. Ever since that time it is honoured as the messenger of Mawu.

Sagbata assembled the people and they built a great fire. All the vegetation on earth was so dry that it quickly ignited, and soon the flames were leaping high into the sky and the smoke of the burning rose out of sight into the heavens.

When he saw this, Legba went rushing to Mawu and told her that the earth was on fire, burning so strongly that it might even set off a fire in heaven. Mawu looked down and saw the flames and the smoke, and she ordered Legba to tell Sogbo to release the rains. Legba went to Sogbo, and Sogbo in turn released the rains which put out the flames and restored fertility to the earth.

After that, Mawu decided that while Sogbo controlled the rains in heaven, the people of earth should have the power to call down rains as well, for the perils of the earth might eventually have an effect above. The *wututu* bird was sent to live below, among people, to serve as a messenger who would inform the powers of the skies when rain was needed.

THE ALLADA DYNASTY OF ABOMEY

People came down to earth from the sky at Adja, and Dada Segbo, the king of Adja at that time, appears in many stories about the early days. The rules of nature were not fixed then. Births, for instance, were entirely random. A woman might give birth to a goat; a goat might give birth to a human child. It was a woman from Adja named Hwandjele who changed this by bringing the *vodun* to humans and creating the medicines and magics which ensured that humans would give birth to humans and goats to goats. Other people brought humans the knowledge of Fa divination, which is called the writing of Mawu.

At this time, or perhaps under different circumstances, a female leopard took the shape of a human and became a wife of the king of Adja. She made him promise not to reveal the truth of her origin to anyone, but he did tell some of his other wives. The leopard-woman, named Agasu, bore him a son whom they named Adjahuto, and then some time later she died. But she promised her children that if ever they got into trouble and had to leave Adja, they should take her remains with them, and she would serve as their personal *vodun* to protect them.

The king of Adja died, and the people wished Adjahuto to rule over them. But the other wives, now widows, spoke against this and protested that they did not wish to be ruled by the son of a leopard. There was a fight, and Adjahuto killed some people of Adja. It is said that one of those he killed was a friend of his, named Kozoe, who had been induced to betray Adjahuto's whereabouts. Adjahuto took his mother's remains and fled from Adja into the bush. There he met a man named Tedo who helped him find a path.

The people from Adja pursued him, but Adjahuto put down his cloth upon the ground and prayed for a river to start flowing and cut off his pursuers; his prayer was fulfilled. Then he activated some of his magic and said a prayer over his spear, wishing that the spear would fall in a place where he would be safe. Then he threw it in the air. He followed its course, asking people if they had seen his spear, and finally he found its landing spot. There he established his town, and there also three *vodun* cults were established: that of Agasu, that of Tedo, and that of Adjahuto himself, the founder of the line. His wives were known as 'wives of the leopard', and his descendants were the *kpovi*, the children of the leopard.

HWEGBADJA, THE FIRST KING

Among the descendants of Adjahuto were two brothers, Te Agbanli and Dako who later became known as Hwegbadja. Dako was a tremendous troublemaker, and eventually Te Agbanli arranged to have his brother thrown into the river during the night, in the hopes that he would drown or disappear. But a boatman found the child and pulled him out of the water, and raised him for a time as his own.

After six years Dako returned to his father's house. He revealed himself to his father and told how Te Agbanli had thrown him into the water to be rid of him. It was at this time that he took his new name, Hwegbadja. The father reproached Te Agbanli for having tried to murder his brother, and at Hwegbadja's request Te Agbanli went into exile, riding backwards on a horse. Eventually he settled in the town now known as Porto Novo.

Hwegbadja moved around, and he is remembered for bringing cloth to people who till then had no woven clothing, but only used skins and leaves. It was Hwegbadja who encountered the great serpent Da and asked him for land on which to build a house; he came back a second time and asked for more land. The third time he came, Da asked if he wanted to build in his belly. At that, Hwegbadja seized Da and cut him in half so that he would indeed build on Da's belly. This is the origin of the name of the kingdom, Dahomey: the land of Da's belly.

Hwegbadja did not easily or quickly become king in the area of his new settlement, for Agwa-Gede, the local chief, had power over the earth. His ancestors had come from the sea. When Hwegbadja wished to assert his rule of the earth, Agwa-Gede prayed by his ancestry for the rains to stop falling, and they stopped. When the people acknowledged Agwa-Gede's authority, the rains fell again. He proved his powers with other tokens as well: he pulled up weeds and found peanuts among the roots, and he found cowrie-shells (used as money) under the earth.

Eventually, Agwa-Gede died and Hwegbadja began to rule. He then laid down laws concerning justice and punishment which remained in force until the time of King Behanzin, the last king to rule Dahomey from the royal palace in Abomey, who was sent into exile by the French to the West Indies.

52

THE AKAN-ASHANTI AND THE BAULE OF THE FOREST

West of Togo, the coast of Africa was marked by thick equa-torial forest which slowed trade and traffic. There is no record or tradition of states before the period of European contacts through the sea (from the fifteenth century on). The region was certainly inhabited by small groups of hunters and gatherers, speaking languages of the Akan family, but it is after trade in different commodities became established that kingdoms and states begin to appear in the records of the Hausa or of the Portuguese and other European traders and travellers along the coast. The principal locally used commodity was the kola nut; in Mande languages of the empire of Mali, this region is known as worodugu (kola-nut-land), but ivory was also a major export to the north over the centuries. From as early as the fifteenth century, gold was discovered in northern Ghana and became a major trade item; the coast became known to traders as the Gold Coast. The Ashanti kingdom developed to regulate this trade. The Akan-language peoples include the Ashanti, the Fante, the Baule and the Anyi. Ashanti traditions include the stories of Ananse the Spider (see Chapter 19).

ORIGINS

There are many different but related peoples living in the forests that used to cover the countries that are now Ghana and Côte d'Ivoire, and they claim different but local origins. Many say that their first ancestors came from beneath the earth at some nearby place which they can point to. Others say they are descended from a spider, Ananse. Others say they came from some other land within the forest zone.

Along the coast, some people say that they came from the sea, led by two giants named Amamfi and Kwegia. After a journey of many days, the people had come to the shore and were emerging when they were seen by a hunter coming out of the forest. He exclaimed in wonder at the sight, and at the sound of his voice all the people who had not yet reached the shore were transformed into rocks, which can still be seen.

Kwegia and his people remained near the shore; they were fishermen. Amamfi and his people moved further inland, and Amamfi invented agriculture for them. He used a huge iron billhook, large enough to require six bars of iron. He also once brought some cannon to Assibu, where Kwegia lived, because he was in the custom of visiting his kinsman and bringing a gift, and that day he happened to have nothing else to bring. It is also said that he invented palm wine, although others say also that the discovery was made by a hunter who saw an elephant punch a hole into a tree-trunk with its tusk. When the hunter brought his new discovery to the king, the king drank so much that he fell down drunk and his followers thought he had been poisoned, and so they killed the hunter.

OSEI TUTU AND THE RISE
OF ASHANTI

Many kingdoms succeeded each other in the forest lands. The Denkyira established one of the earlier kingdoms, at the southern end of the trade routes, but the most famous was that of the Ashanti. The Ashanti look back to the lost city of Asantemanso as their origin.

In the town of Akwamu, there was conflict over the succession at the death of a king. His sister, the queen-mother Nkansa, had twin sons. The elder was chosen king. To avoid future conflict, Nkansa left the country with the younger son, Obiri Yeboa, and many followers, and they travelled amid

difficulties and hostilities, until the king of Bono granted them
some land on which to establish themselves. This became the
town of Asantemanso, and soon after Obiri Yeboa had been
named king, a Denkyira princess came from the north to take
up residence. She had also lost an election, and her sister had
been named queen-mother. The town prospered for a time, but
then some fifty or sixty years later a bitter dispute arose between
the various groups of people involved, and a civil war broke out.
Asantemanso was destroyed and its inhabitants were scattered,
save for one prince of the family of Obiri Yeboa who remained
to watch over the royal graves. The Denkyira soon exerted their
power and made the entire region tributary.

Obiri Yeboa's sister was married to the king of the Ashanti,
and for a long time they were childless, until they consulted a
celebrated diviner and he found the means to ensure them a
son. They named the son Osei Tutu, in honour of the diviner,
and he was a fine young man with all the marks of royalty. As
a prince, though, he was soon called away from home: he was
summoned to the court of the king of Denkyira, in part to serve
as a hostage for his parents' good behaviour. He immersed
himself in the Denkyira court, despite his captive status, learning as much as he could about their manner of administration
and maintenance of power, and he proved his worth so effec-
tively that he was made a royal sword-bearer.

This function brought him often into the inner circle of the
royal court. There he met and loved Princess Abena, the king's
sister. This was imprudent, of course, since she was of the ruling
family and because she was already married to an elder. Their
love affair became known. It became dangerous when she fell
pregnant, and people knew clearly who was responsible. Osei
Tutu realized he would have to leave the court and flee. He did
not stay at home with his parents. To do so would bring death
upon them; he knew the king of Denkyira would send soldiers
to punish him. He fled beyond their lands, and there he continued to study the ways and knowledge of the different peoples.
In particular, he went to Akwammu, which was the town of
the diviner who had assisted his parents in the matter of his
own birth.

In Akwammu he met a new diviner, a master of occult powers, named Anokye, to whom he was distantly related. The two young men took a liking to each other, and on one occasion Osei Tutu interceded with the king of Akwammu to release Anokye from a punishment. So, when word came to Osei Tutu that his uncle, Obiri Yeboa, had been killed in a war with the Domaa and that he was summoned to assume the throne, it was natural for him to ask Anokye to accompany him. Osei Tutu was made king of the Ashanti, and Anokye became his chief diviner.

Their first challenge was to settle the war that had brought the death of Obiri Yeboa, and with Anokye's help and some skilful organization, Osei Tutu quickly and victoriously accomplished this. He unified his own kingdom, which had been splitting apart, and then rode the crest of that victory to subdue the neighbouring peoples and to found the great Ashanti state that would rule the forest zone for three hundred years. He established the golden stool of the Ashanti as a symbol of their unity.

Princess Abena gave birth to a son, and the son became the king of Denkyira by the rules of matrilineal succession. He was named Ntim Gyakari, and he was the king who had to face the challenge to Denkyira rule represented by the growing power of the Ashanti under Osei Tutu. Matters came to a head when he sent messengers to demand the annual tribute in gold, and the assembly of the Ashanti unanimously declared that they would give no gold; one Ashanti went so far as to slash a messenger with his sword and cut off an ear. They sent the messengers back, filling the great brass pan of the king of Denkyira not with gold, but with stones. Then, realizing what they had done, they turned to Anokye. He told them to delay the war for a time, while he prepared magical defences for the kingdom. He also asked for volunteers, men who would rush to death, to ensure victory for their people. A number of volunteers came forward, and as a reward for their devotion it was decreed that their descendants could never be executed.

The king of Denkyira also had a diviner, of course, by name Kyenekye, and Kyenekye informed his master of the steps that

Anokye was taking. Ntim Gyakari ordered him to do what was necessary to counter Anokye's magic. The two continued working against each other. At one point, Anokye challenged Kyenekye to undo a knot that he had tied in an elephant's tusk; Kyenekye's counter was to challenge Anokye to undo the knot he had tied in the water. In the meantime, the Denkyira armies advanced and the Ashanti armies retreated, acting on the instructions of the diviners, and the war dragged on.

The turning point came as the Denkyira approached Kumasi. Anokye predicted that Kyenekye would never reach Kumasi, and he was proved correct: the Adansi, a people against whom Ntim Gyakari had waged war in the recent past, plotted and arranged for the murder of Kyenekye. News of his death so emboldened the Ashanti army that they attacked the Denkyira and put them to flight; a nobleman found Ntim Gyakari playing *warri* (also known as *mankala*) with a concubine and killed him. They brought to Osei Tutu the golden bracelet which Ntim Gyakari had worn, and the brass pan in which he collected the tribute, and which they had filled with stones.

Osei Tutu died in battle some time later, but he had established the Ashanti kingdom. He was the first Asantehene, the supreme chief of the Ashanti people.

QUEEN POKOU AND THE BAULE

Following the death of Osei Tutu, there was a power struggle to determine the succession. The principal rival claimants were nephews of Osei Tutu: Opoku Ware, who eventually became the ruler, and one Daken, whose sister was Pokou. After Opoku Ware was chosen, Queen Pokou of Assabu decided that she should lead her people out of the Ashanti lands, because she feared the reprisals of the new Asantehene.

The Assabu people travelled west, into what is now Côte d'Ivoire, until they came to the Comoe river. There they halted, because they had no boats with which to cross the river. But they could not wait long, for they knew the king's men were following them closely and would punish most severely their queen's failed bid for power and the people's attempt to escape Ashanti dominion. Queen Pokou had a diviner with her, named Nansi. She asked him what they should do, and after performing his rites he came to her and said he had the answer. She must make a sacrifice. She must sacrifice to the river that which she held most dear.

She pondered the riddle for some time: what was most dear to her? Her people? The signs of her power? But the answer seemed obvious. She had one son, a baby. Surely, this was the sacrifice the river demanded. Sorrowfully, she gave the baby to Nansi, and solemnly he took the child to the river and cast it out into the deep waters. The baby sank beneath the surface. Then the face of the river changed. Waters receded, trees bent down, and a clear path was marked for the people. They crossed the river, and the last ones, looking back, saw the trees rising again and the river resuming its former face.

The people took the name Baule from this sacrifice of their queen. She died soon after, and it was her niece, Akwa Boni, who established the Baule state on a firm footing.

THE MOSSI PLATEAU

North of Ghana, Togo and Benin, and south of the course of the Niger river, rises the Mossi plateau, from which the Black and White Volta rivers flow to the Atlantic. The plateau takes its name from the most populous group living there, the Mossi, who over the centuries have formed various kingdoms and at times expanded (in war at least) far enough north to attack Timbuktu, but other groups also live around them, and have moved freely across the savannah lands.

THE FOUNDING OF GONJA

Gonja is an example of a state founded within the context of the Mande trading networks from the Niger to the south. The foundation probably occurred in the sixteenth century; the story is based on Arabic accounts written locally in the eighteenth century. It seems likely that the Mande names (Jara, Sheghu) in the story represent a confusion of the kingdom of Mali and the Bamana state of Segou which was in power at the time the chronicles were written: Jara was the name of the dynasty in Segou (see Chapter 63). Although the dynasty claimed a Mande origin, the state itself was largely Dagomba (see Chapter 54).

The king of Mande Kaba, Jigi Jara, heard of the wealth in gold of Sheghu and sent messengers to demand a share in this gold. But the lord of Sheghu refused him. So the king of Mande assembled his army. They cut down a great tree and laid the trunk across the road; his cavalry then rode over the tree-trunk until the hoofs of the horses had worn completely through the wood. He sent his two sons in command of this army to conquer Sheghu, and they were quickly victorious. The elder son, Umar Jara, settled to rule over Sheghu, and sent much of the gold they had captured back to his father. The brothers heard of more gold in a town called Ghuna, and so the younger brother, Naba, led his army to that town and captured it. But then he recalled a prophecy made to him in his youth. He had been told that he would never be king in his own land. So he led his army further on, and they settled in a place called Yagbum, and there he founded his kingdom.

A DAGOMBA HERO

The Dagomba belong to a cluster of peoples, sometimes called the Lobi, living north of Ashanti, south of the Mossi, and east of the Mande trading routes into Côte d'Ivoire. They live at the forest edge, and while they may at one time have been hunters they have long since been incorporated into the agricultural economy of the region. Linguistically, they are related to the Mossi, the Dogon, the Gurunsi, and other peoples connected to the Mossi plateau. This account is retold from a version published by a Ghanaian in 1931.

The Dagomba claim as ancestor Ad, a descendant of Noah. Ad's people lived in the Hadramaut until they offended God and most of them were exterminated by a hot dry wind which blew for seven days and nights. After that, the tribe migrated to the west until they came to Dagbon. It is said they were enormous in size, ranging from twenty-five to well over thirty metres tall. They were blacksmiths, and they wandered over the country collecting the ore to smelt and leaving the remains of their activity. Eventually, their descendants were reduced in size to that of normal humans.

There came a drought. A hunter named Tohajiye left his cave in the hills and came down into the village looking for water. At the edge of the town he found an old woman named Malle, and he asked her for water. She answered that she had none. A wild bull was keeping the people from drinking at the lake that lay nearby. Tohajiye the hunter asked the path to the lake, and she pointed it out to him; along the way he saw people lying exhausted and parched, dying of thirst.

As soon as he began to fill his containers, the bull attacked him. He shot it with arrows and killed it; then he cut off its tail, filled his containers and returned to the old woman. She was amazed that he had brought water, and at first could hardly believe that he had killed the bull.

The king of the town was delighted that the hunter had accomplished something none of his warriors had been able to do, and offered him a reward: he might choose any of the king's daughters. Tohajiye asked only for a lame girl who could not walk. Her name was Wobega, and she is also called Pagawobga. The king agreed. The hunter picked her up in his arms and carried her away, stopping to greet Malle, the old woman, on the way. As soon as he was gone, she called two young men and told them to follow Tohajiye to his home, and when they got there to plant some calabash seeds so they would know the spot in the future. Quietly and stealthily the young men followed the hunter, who was making no effort to hide his trail, until he reached his cave in the hills. They saw him enter the cave, and then they planted their seeds and returned to the village.

Some time later, war came to the land. The town was attacked and the ruler was desperate for help. He asked his attendants where the heroic hunter was who had killed the bull and taken his daughter Wobega; none could answer him. He called for Malle, the old woman who had been Tohajiye's host when he came; she said she could point out the trail, for the calabash seeds that her scouts had planted had grown into vines and reached all the way back into the village.

The king's men went to the hunter's cave. They found only a young man there, named Kpogonumbo. His parents had died and he had grown up by himself. He was huge, many times the size of a normal man, and his eyes oozed blood and mucus. The king's men were terrified of him, but they explained their mission and Kpogonumbo said that he would come to help the man who was, after all, his grandfather. He returned to the town with them, joined the army, and attacked the enemy.

The enemy, too, were terrified at the sight of this giant, and they fled. Kpogonumbo chased them far into the forest, until he was sure they would not return, and then informed his grandfather of his victory. Then he continued his travels.

He came to Biung, an old village ruled by a priest called the Tindana. He did not enter the village immediately; he concealed himself at a spot by the stream where he could see when people came to draw water. The Tindana sent his daughter, called Sisagba, to get water for the people working in the fields; when she approached, Kpogonumbo revealed himself. She was terrified, but he reassured her and sent her to fetch her father.

The Tindana came with some other men, and they talked with Kpogonumbo. To prove his knowledge and powers, Kpogonumbo gave him a calabash seed and told him to plant it, and gave him some millet and told him to plant it. The Tindana bent down and planted the seeds in the soil by the stream. Immediately, the calabash plant sprouted, grew, flowered and produced ripe gourds. The millet immediately grew up, formed heads, ripened and hung heavy in the air.

'Take the millet,' said Kpogonumbo. 'Give it to your daughter, have her grind it and mix it into millet beer, and bring me the drink in this gourd.'

The Tindana took the small harvest, and Sisagba made millet beer from it, which she poured into a gourd from the seeds Kpogonumbo had planted. She brought the beer to him. He drank it thirstily.

'My daughter,' said the Tindana to Sisagba, 'this is a fearsome stranger who has come among us. But I think he has come on your account, and so you must marry him.' So Sisagba married Kpogonumbo, and they eventually had a son.

The son was ill-treated by his relatives. He would go hunting with his mother's brother, but if he killed anything – a bird, a small animal, a guinea-fowl – his uncle would take the animal, cook it, and give him only a small part of a leg and the head. At first the son complained, but the uncle answered him with a blow and harsh words. 'You are the son of an unknown man, a monster. We do not know where he came from. Be content that we give you anything!'

The son complained to his father, but his father told him to suffer in patience and to bide his time. A festival came some time later, the great annual festival at which the Tindana presided. In the days leading up to the festival there was great rejoicing among the people, and vast quantities of millet beer were drunk. Sisagba joined her family members in drinking, and returned somewhat tipsy to her husband's home.

Kpogonumbo greeted her with praises and song when she entered, and so she herself began to boast of her knowledge: she was the daughter of the Tindana and she knew his secrets. Kpogonumbo offered her more beer and flattery, and she continued to talk, revealing what she knew to her husband.

This was the occasion Kpogonumbo had awaited. He went out that night to the Tindana's house; when the priest came into the dark to relieve himself, Kpogonumbo speared him and then cut off his head. He threw the head into the washing area of the compound of his wife's brother. Then he went in to the Tindana's house and dressed himself in the Tindana's ritual robes.

The next morning, when the people came to bring the Tindana to the shrine to celebrate the festival, they found the body of the old Tindana lying headless before the door. As they approached, the door burst open and Kpogonumbo appeared.

'I have killed him! I have taken his place!' he announced, and no one dared to challenge him. So he became ruler of the country. The kingdom later became known as Yendi.

55
THE MOSSI OF
BURKINA FASO

The Mossi are the dominant group of modern Burkina Faso, and the most widespread on the Mossi plateau. While they have not always been politically unified, the central authority is that of the Mogho Naba whose palace is in Ouagadougou and who traces his descent (and legitimacy) from the line of Princess Yennenga. The Mossi are known principally as farmers (millet and sorghum), although their kings also engaged in warfare and on occasion raided as far north as Timbuktu, and there was trade with their neighbours to the north and east. This retelling is based upon a number of accounts collected in the early twentieth century.

Perhaps nine hundred years ago, there was a king in the lands to the south, among the Dagomba who lived along the forest's edge. He had a daughter named Yennenga the Slender who was old enough to be married, but her father did not find her a husband because he wished to keep her by him. She planted a field of okra before the king's house, and when it was ripe she left it past its time on the ground without harvesting it. When the king commented on the waste, she retorted: 'You say the harvest is past its time? But what about a woman who has not been married?' Her father still did nothing about her marriage.

Yennenga took care of the matter herself, but we do not know who her chosen partner was. She became pregnant, and when the king learned of this state of affairs he swore to put her to death. Friends warned Yennenga, and so she took horses from the royal stables and fled to the north. However, she raced her horse so fast and hard that she suffered a miscarriage.

She continued her flight to the north and came to a land that seemed empty. There she stopped with her followers. In fact, the land was part of the territory of the elephant-hunter Rialle, and he discovered the party when he returned from a hunt. He greeted them warmly, and bowed to Yennenga, whom he took to be the lord of the group, since she was dressed in men's clothes and gave orders as would a king. After a time, Yennenga came to Rialle in secret and told him of her true origin, daughter of a king among the Dagomba, and after that the two of them married in public.

A son was born of this union, whom Yennenga named Ouedraogo (Stallion) in memory of the horse which had carried her from her father's house, and thanks to which she had found the husband she wanted. When Ouedraogo was fifteen, Yennenga sent him to visit his grandfather in the south. His grandfather was delighted, and gave him rich gifts of horses and cattle.

He returned accompanied by many people, because the land of the Dagomba was overpopulated, and with them he founded the town now known as Tenkodogo. He married a number of women, and placed the sons they bore in charge of various areas that are now part of the Mossi kingdoms. He died while travelling.

Ouedraogo's third son, Zoumbrana, remained in Tenkodogo and inherited his father's rule. He married Pougtoenga (the bearded woman), a woman from the Ninissi; her people had sent her to Ouedraogo, asking for the king's help, and Ouedraogo married her to his son. They had a number of children.

The people of Ninissi returned to Zoumbrana to ask for a ruler, and he assembled his sons. They chose Oubry, the son of Pougtoenga, who was thus of their people. But Oubry was too young to leave immediately, and it is said the Ninissi cast a spell on him to make him a cripple, so they would recognize him later and so Zoumbrana would not be tempted to substitute another.

Oubry grew up, and eventually Zoumbrana sent him into his mother's country. He founded a village, now thirty-five kilometres from Ouagadougou, which bears his name, and he succeeded in conquering the territory. He was the first to bear the title of Mogho-Naba, the Naba (king) of the Mossi people. Under his rule the Dogon were pushed up to the cliffs of Bandiagara and Mossi authority spread to the north.

THE DOGON OF THE
BANDIAGARA ESCARPMENT

The Dogon live in central Mali, along the Bandiagara escarp-
ment that runs east from the town of Bandiagara and on the
plateau that lies within the great northern bend of the Niger
river. They are cultivators of millet who moved into their rocky
homes, pushed by Mossi expansion, to escape the troubles of
war, and because the cliff offers a good supply of waterholes
in an otherwise arid area. While somewhat influenced by Islam
(increasingly so in the modern era, when Islam is almost univer-
sal in Mali), they have preserved a traditional animist culture
(the word by which the French knew the Dogon at the start of
the twentieth century – habbe, sing. kado – is a Fulani word
meaning a pagan, like the Arabic kafir*) that is remarkable for*
the aesthetics of its masked dances. They have become one of
the best-known and most studied traditional peoples in west
Africa, thanks in large part to the work of the French anthropol-
ogist Marcel Griaule and his school, who have been working
with the Dogon since 1931. But there is some question about
Griaule's most famous work, Dieu d'eau *(in English,* Conver-
sations with Ogotemmeli), because later anthropologists have
had difficulty replicating his findings. Griaule also started
another controversy with his report that the Dogon believed
the star Sirius to have a twin; in fact, Sirius is a binary star, but
the second one is invisible to the naked eye. This report has led
to the firm belief in some circles that the Dogon possess arcane
knowledge derived from extraterrestrial sources.

The Dogon are in fact far more diverse than Griaule's team
had reported; the villages, stretched over several hundred
kilometres of the escarpment, offer linguistic and cultural

diversity. It has been suggested that Dogon should be divided into four languages. While under French rule, the Dogon began to claim the empire of Mali as their point of origin, and said that they had reached their present territory crossing the river on a bridge of crocodiles. But by language they are more closely related to the Mossi–Gur and Dagomba groups lying to the south.

CREATION: A POPULAR VERSION

Amma created the world in layers separated by a metal post. He created the earth and the sky and the Nommo spirits, whom he sent down from the sky to the earth on the rainbow. The Nommo spirits are associated with water. Amma also populated the earth with beings, beginning with spirits such as the *andumbulu*, the little red spirits who inhabited the cliffs before the Dogon and whose 'cities' can still be seen high up in the cliffs, and the *gyinnu*, spirits placed in trees, and animals such as the chameleon and the turtle. Then he created people.

There was a quarrel for supremacy between earth and sky. Amma knocked down the metal post that separated the earth and sky, so that the layers collapsed together and the sky crushed all the living things on the earth except for the spirits, who were not material, and the old people, who at that time took the form of snakes as they aged and so were not harmed by their burial in the earth. After that, the earth recognized the supremacy of the sky and the metal posts were restored. But the sky hung much lower than now; it was close enough for the moon to be marked by the hyena's paws, and so low that humans could not grow to their full height.

The separation of earth and sky occurred because of women's work. As they raised their pestles to pound the food in the mortars, they would bump into the sky, and one day an old woman, irritated, pushed the sky so that it moved off.

Amma sent down a blacksmith from heaven – one of the workers whose activity can be seen during storms when lightning flashes from their anvils – with a packet of seeds; he lowered the smith on a long chain from the sky to the earth and then drew the chain back up again.

There are two stories about the discovery of fire. In the first, a goatherd was drawn by strange noises whose source he could not identify. He did not know it, but the sound came from invisible spirits working by an invisible fire. On his father's instructions, he collected a pocketful of pebbles, and the next time he heard the sounds he tossed the pebbles in that direction; every spirit who was touched by a stone became visible and powerless, and the goatherd was able to bring the spirits and their tools to his family. In the second, an old woman was attracted by the fire that resulted after a stroke of lightning; having burned her hands at first, she used a stick and was able to bring fire back to the cave. In this way, humans who until then had eaten their meat raw could cook it.

The blacksmith who came down from heaven with the seeds also taught humans the art of kindling a fire, so they did not need to keep the flame burning all the time.

The blacksmith also played a part some time later, when earth and sky again quarrelled and Amma withheld the rain from the earth. In the drought, a leather-worker made a drum which he played, singing praises of Amma while the blacksmith beat on his anvil, to signify the power of heaven. Appeased, Amma released the rains.

DEATH AND THE DANCING COSTUME

This story also occurs as a folk tale, and provides the plot of the Malian movie Taafe Fanga *(Skirt-Power).*

Amma had two earthly wives: an ant and a termite. He gave to each of them a grass skirt, dyed red, as a test. After a time, he called on each of them to come out wearing the skirt. The termite could not, because she had eaten the grass. It was not only greed, though. She did so in part because she was aware that death would come into being through these costumes.

One day the ant laid out her costume to dry in the sun. The

jackal came by and called out to her in amazement: what was this bright red thing he saw? Could it be fire? Had the sun come to earth? And after a bit of pleading, he borrowed the costume from the ant so he could wear it to his father's funeral. Although the jackal is untrustworthy and given to lies, in this case he had told the truth. He was going to the funeral. When he appeared, wearing the red costume, everyone ran away in fright. The jackal was delighted with the result of his new costume and put it away. But a bird found it and carried it off, thinking from the colour that it was raw meat. After one bite, the bird dropped it and it fell onto a tree. A female *andumbulu* spirit, one of the little red people, came across it and learned what it was from questioning the jackal. She then took the costume and wore it into the village. Terrified, all the men ran away.

This gave the woman power over the men, and she exercised it. The strange red spirit forced the men to do the work of preparing food, and they began to groan, for they had not realized how much toil was involved.

One day, however, an old woman came to the *andumbulu* woman's husband. 'Give me some food,' she begged, and he asked why he should. 'I shall tell you something,' she answered. Curious, he offered her some food. She then told him that the spirit was only a costume worn by his wife, and she also told him where it was kept when it was not in use.

The man went and put on the costume. He leaped out at his wife as she was coming back from the waterhole with a pot of water; she dropped it, breaking the pot and spilling the water, and ran. He chased her into a neighbour's house. He chased her into her own house. Finally, she fled to the edge of town, to the house for menstruating women. He did not pursue her there. She remained safe. Men then kept the costumes out of the sight of women.

Death came later to humans, after they had acquired the secret of masked dancing from the spirits, and with the masks the sacred language of the spirits that was used. An old man used the wrong language after he got drunk, and so lost the ability, which old humans had till then, of becoming a snake instead of dying.

CREATION: THE ESOTERIC VERSION

This is a shortened version of the story which Ogotemmeli revealed to Marcel Griaule.

Having created the earth, Amma wished to have intercourse with his consort. But the earth had not been purified by excision, and the termite hill, her clitoris, rose up against Amma. He cut it out and possessed the earth; she was still bloody from the wound and the act of intercourse was a violation. The offspring was not a pure being, but the pale fox, Ogo Yurugu, which would become a spirit of mischief and disorder in the world, but which also, having been born first, possessed knowledge that is used in divination.

After a second union, the earth produced the Nommo spirits: twin serpentine and aqueous beings who brought fertility and order to the world. They were disturbed by the sight of their mother the earth lying naked, and so they created a cloth of vegetable fibre with which to cover her. But Ogo Yurugu saw the cloth and envied it, and also lusted after the earth. He stole the cloth and raped the earth; from this union were born various spirits which now inhabit the world. The act also gave the fox a power of knowledge, for the woven fibre was a first expression of the language of the world which is involved in divination. After the earth had been raped by the pale fox, Amma decided to attempt new methods of creation, and he made the first eight human ancestors using clay shaped in the form of human genitalia which then engendered the humans. In the meantime, the Nommo spirits penetrated the earth to purify her with their moisture.

The ancestors lived for a time on the earth, until they became old, and then – beginning with the first and on to the eighth – they sank into the earth and were received into a womb created by the Nommo. With the seventh ancestor, a new revelation occurred, for the seventh ancestor represented the sum of the male figure (three) and the female figure (four) and so attained a form of perfection which endowed him or her with a new form of speech. From this speech came the weaving of cloth and other cultural techniques that were taught to men by the ant, which also lived in the earth. All eight ancestors were transported from the Nommo's underground space to the sky, where they lived for a time with Amma until they were cast out.

The offence for which they were cast out is not clear, but it involved food and the breach of one of Amma's commandments. As a consequence, one ancestor, the smith, created a granary into which he placed seeds and the elements of all the forms of life, inside and out; the ancestors rode the granary down the rainbow to the earth. It is said that the jarring impact of the granary on the earth caused the limbs of the ancestors, which until then had been serpentine and fluid, like the limbs of the watery Nommo, to break and develop joints such as humans have today; the joints would serve the humans in their new world and under the new conditions.

This is how the Dogon came to be on the earth.

LAKE CHAD AND THE CENTRAL SUDAN

The basin of Lake Chad, in the centre of Africa, now seems a remote hinterland. But for fifteen hundred years, before the growth of the ocean-borne trade, this region was almost the first line of contact between sub-Saharan Africa and the rest of the world. Trade routes north through the Hoggar and its line of mountainous oases to Tripoli (in modern Libya), or east through the Sudan to the Nile, linked this region with the wider world. The misfortune of the region, in contrast with Mali for example, was the lack of a luxury commodity such as gold. The principal export from the central Sudan was slaves, captured in raids on less warlike, non-Muslim peoples to the south. Kanem, the dominant kingdom in the early Middle Ages, eventually fell to the pressure of the Tuareg from the desert, and the dynasty moved their centre of power west of Lake Chad to found the new state of Bornu which maintained hegemony and power until the nineteenth century, and joined with the Hausa states (especially after they were taken over by Muslim Fulani leaders) in forming a Muslim belt across the Sahel.

THE SARA AND THE SOW
OF LAKE CHAD

The Sara live south-east of Lake Chad, in the territory of the legendary Sow (or Sô) hunters (see also the traditions of Kanem and Bornu in Chapter 59), although the creator figures Loa and Sou, who appear in the stories below, do not seem to be of giant size, as the Sow were reputed to be. The Sow practised agriculture, growing millet, but also made extensive use of the natural resources, engaging in fishing and hunting. They did not form a major state, but were rather the victims of slave-raiding by the Muslim kingdoms and emirates around them. The stories about creation come from a collection of tales published in 1967, and the stories about the towns from an anthropological study published in 1943.

CREATION BY LOA AND SOU

Loa and Sou were there at the start of things. Neither Loa nor Sou had parents as we understand the concept. Later, a bird laid an egg on a mound of millet lying in the bush. Loa watched over it and cared for it; a woman was hatched out. Sou found her fascinating, but her behind was red and seemed inflamed: she seemed to be wounded. Sou poured water over it, and then rubbed his hand against it, but it simply became redder. Eventually Sou found something else to do with her, and she became pregnant. Loa then went to Sou and told him that Sou should pay him brideprice for the woman.

When the time came for the child to be born, she had great difficulties. She went into the bush, where a monkey approached her and served as midwife: the monkey poured water over the belly and supported the child as it came out. Then the monkey cut the umbilical cord and buried it. Since that time, monkeys have been entitled to raid people's millet crops, because of this primordial service. After the first child, other children were born, singly or as couples, and so the earth was populated.

There are some stories about animals from this time. It is said that at first the entire earth was covered with millet fields, but the dog approached Loa and asked to have some fallow ground in which to defecate. Loa then divided the world, so that part is arable and part is bush. It is also said that the bustard, a great hunting bird, decided that humans were becoming too prosperous and should be killed off. The bustard brewed a great pot of a virulent poison, planning to use it on the humans. Its actions drew all sorts of small crawling things: spiders and scorpions and ants and bees and wasps and snakes and other reptiles, and they sat about watching the pot brewing. But the warthog and the monkey, who benefited illicitly from the humans' crops, did not want to see the humans vanish, and so they schemed together to break the pot. The monkey came up to ask the bustard what he was doing; the warthog followed, complaining about the monkey's behaviour at some time in the past. The monkey turned and answered rudely. The warthog pushed the monkey, the monkey pushed back, and the warthog stumbled against the pot and knocked it to the ground. The pot broke, the poison spilled out, and the crawling and creeping things waiting in the circle were all drenched in the poison. This is why their bites now sting.

SOU AND THE ARTS

Loa and Sou worked in very different ways. Loa made things very carefully: the pirogue he carved from the trunk of a tree was graceful and smoothly polished, and along the sides he carved geometric figures. He made tightly woven fish-traps, and the webbing he wove to guide fish into the mouths of the traps

was even and smooth. Sou was a clumsy workman. Imitating
Loa, he carved a pirogue: the sides were notched, the bow
dipped into the water and caught oncoming waves, and the hull
was so thin in places that a person might put their foot through
it. Sou's fish-traps were a mass of reeds bound together; fish
could hardly get in, and if they did they easily found their
way out. Loa, watching Sou's work, never said anything. They
exchanged no words, and perhaps Sou found this, rather than
Loa's evident superior craftsmanship, most galling.

Eventually, Sou decided to force Loa to speak. He went
before dawn to Loa's fish-traps and broke them open. He
released the fish, piled the traps on the ground, and jumped
repeatedly on them, so they were crushed. Then he hid in the
bushes nearby to see what would happen.

Loa came in the morning to check his traps. He saw the mess
that Sou had made and exclaimed, 'Oh, Sou! Must you be a
destroyer?'

Sou came out. 'Why is it that the first thing you say about
me is an insult?' he asked.

Loa did not answer, but simply turned about and left. He
left Sou, he left the earth; he withdrew into the sky and there
he made his home.

Sou decided to follow Loa. He wandered far over the earth
until he found the path into the sky. He made his way to Loa's
compound. At that time, Loa was in the fields watching workers
clear an area for millet. He had brought large amounts of food
and drink to reward the workers, while he lay back on a couch
of rich wood and gold.

Sou came to Loa's home and entered the first hut. There he
found Loa's rain-making stone, carefully placed on a shelf
behind Loa's sleeping couch.

'What is this stone doing here?' asked Sou, and he threw it
out of the door. Immediately the rain began to fall on the
workers clearing the fields for Loa, and Loa said to himself,
'Sou has come.' Loa returned to his compound and found his
brother there playing with other possessions of his.

'What has brought you here?' asked Loa, and Sou explained
that he wished to see how his brother lived, and that he thought

they should not be estranged. But Loa said that Sou could not live in the skies with him, that he must return to the earth. Sou complained that the way was too long; Loa told him he could take a vine straight down and come to his home immediately. Sou complained that life on earth was too hard, whereas Loa clearly lived in comfort in the skies. So Loa promised Sou all sorts of wealth, if only he would leave. He gave Sou foodstuffs and clothing and tools and musical instruments. But he warned Sou that on the way down birds would attack him, and try to cut the vine above his head. He should menace them with his weapons, but he should not throw the weapons. Sou listened and promised to obey.

Eventually, Sou loaded all his gifts into a pack and slung it over his back, and then he began to climb down the vine, keeping his weapons ready to hand against the birds Loa had told him about. Sure enough, they appeared: they flew around him crying loudly, and then they began to dart closer, threatening him with their sharp beaks and talons. Sou pulled out a stone axe and waved it at them; they retreated for a time, and then flew back. Sou threw the axe at them and they flew far away. But soon they returned. Sou took out his flint-headed darts and threatened the birds; they retreated, but then returned. Sou threw one dart after another at the birds. He did not strike any, but he used up all his weapons, and it was still quite a distance to the ground.

The birds returned and circled closer, and then seemed to realize that Sou could not harm them. They flew against the vine and nipped at it with their sharp beaks, and soon the vine frayed and wore through and Sou came tumbling through the air with all his wealth. He landed on the ground so hard that he sank into it. That is why the Sara say that Loa is in the heavens and Sou in the earth.

SOU AND THE STAR WOMEN

There are other stories told about Sou in the region. One story says that at the beginning, Sou was alone in the world. He hunted by himself. His only companion was an old woman. He found her ugly and he knew she could bear no children, so he did not sleep with her. One day, while he was hunting, he saw some young women dancing in a ring near a great rock. He pursued them, but they vanished. Cursing and mumbling to himself, Sou headed towards his camp. On the way, thinking about the women, he did not watch the path and he tripped over a stump.

'Why did you hurt my foot?' demanded Sou, and the stump answered, 'What were you thinking of, that you did not watch the trail?'

'I saw some young women,' said Sou. 'They were beautiful. I approached them, but they ran away.'

'I can help you,' said the stump. 'These young women are stars who come to earth to dance. If you wish to catch them, you should plant some white eggplants near your home. When you have done so, return to me.'

'Bless you, my sweetheart!' cried Sou, and he raced home. Immediately, he planted black eggplants. After the plants had sprouted and were bearing fruit, he returned to the stump.

'I have planted the eggplants,' he announced. 'What should I do next?'

'Go and fetch some of the *yanre* vine, and squeeze its juice over the eggplants,' instructed the stump. Sou went off and cut some of the first vine he found – a green fruitless vine – and squeezed its juice over the black eggplants. Nothing happened. A moon went by, and no women from the stars came down to dance at his eggplants.

Sou took his axe and returned to the stump. He kicked aside the grass, and raised the axe for a first blow.

'Stop! What are you doing?' protested the stump. 'Didn't I help you? Why should you cut me?'

'You tricked me!' cried Sou. 'I planted the eggplants and I squeezed the juice over them, and no women have come.'

'Did you plant the white eggplant?' asked the stump.

'No, I planted the black variety,' answered Sou.

'Did you use the juice of the *yanre* vine?'

'No, I just took some vine I found.'

'You must use the white eggplant,' explained the stump. 'The women from the stars use it in their cooking. And you must make sure to use the juice of the *yanre* vine; no other vine will catch their feet and stick them to the earth so that you can catch them.'

'Ah,' said Sou, and this time he followed the stump's instructions precisely. In the middle of a moonless night, the women from the stars came down with baskets to gather the ripe white eggplants; Sou emerged from a hiding place. The women tried to flee, but the juice of the vine stuck to them and they had difficulty breaking free. Sou was able to catch several of them before the rest escaped. Sou took the women he had captured as his wives, and that is how people came onto the earth.

THE FOUNDATION OF GOULFEIL

The Sow lived in the north, near a sea of dark and salty water – the water was so salty that no boat could be made to float on it. They were so large that their bows were made of entire palm trees. To fish, they dammed a river with their hands, and then gathered up handfuls of fish. They plucked hippos from the water and munched on them like snacks. They drank from earthenware goblets six feet high. Birds of prey would nest in their locks. They simply shouted from city to city, to communicate. At that time, gold was a living liquid that flowed out of the earth and floated into the air. The Sow would pinch off a bit and put it in their houses to serve as light. The walls of their city were made of blocks of stone and gold, randomly mixed, as the builders happened on the material. They left this city because of the exactions of their ruler, who demanded a heavy tribute of woven rugs and fine woods. They marched south, and by chance passed into the lands between Lake Chad to the

west and the Bahr el-Ghazal to the east. They came to the banks
of the Chari river.

The first Sow to arrive were three brothers, Mamba, Teri and
Abrapimon. They were joined later by their wives. Mamba had
three daughters. One day, while Mamba was out hunting, his
two brothers decided the time had come to establish their city.
They started by building walls, and they took Mamba's daughters and buried them in the foundations of the walls: the eldest
under the south-west wall, the middle one to the east, and the
youngest in the north-west. Mamba returned from his hunting
and looked for his daughters; his brothers did not dare confess
what they had done. But some days after the daughters had
been buried, great lizards emerged from holes in the walls at
the places of sacrifices; the lizards made their way to the house
of Mamba and found Mamba and his wife sitting and weeping
with grief. Laying their heads in the laps of the mourning
parents, the lizards somehow conveyed to the humans that they,
the lizards, were their daughters, transformed.

After some time, other Sow arrived from the north and settled
in the city. They learned how the walls of the town had been
consecrated, and inevitably Mamba learned the true fate of his
daughters. His rage against his brothers was great, and he
gathered followers to attack and slay them. But the elders of
the other groups intervened and a compromise was reached.
To the lizards was given the power of choosing the new king
of the town. When the old king died, the new candidate would
make offerings of honey, milk and meal. If the lizards emerged
from their lairs and accepted the offering, the candidate would
be confirmed. If they refused, another candidate would be presented.

It is said that Goulfeil eventually fell to the Muslims because
of a break in the rituals. The town was protected by a magical
book, a copy of the Koran, and this book was kept in a magical
case that was remade with the accession of each new king. At
the accession of a new king, they would bring forth an ox and
the king's mother. Both would be killed and skinned; their skins
were tanned and sewn to make a new cover for the magical
book.

But at last one king, Memachi, refused to order the death of his mother. He asserted that he held his kingship through his father's line and that his power did not need such a sacrifice. There was division in the city at that time, and many people who held to the old ways fled into the bush and there they died of starvation. Others remained and supported the king. But it was because the magical book no longer had its powerful case that soon after the Muslims of Abecher were able to capture the city of Goulfeil.

THE CITY OF MAKARI

A Sow named Abdullah came from the east. He was guided by a great lizard, which went into the earth at the future site of Makari, and so Abdullah settled there. Later, his descendant Moussa Kalla built the wall which surrounded the town. After he died, he was succeeded by his grandson, Ahe. But Ahe did not have human form; he was a great black serpent. He communicated with his subjects by moving his tail; he would raise it to signify assent, or twitch it to deny their request. He lived in the centre of the town, under a grove, and was fed one sheep each day.

The people eventually began to tire of being ruled by a non-human being. There were mutters of discontent, but no one dared to do anything against the being that had ruled them for so long, until a prince came from a nearby kingdom: Hussein, son of the ruler of Ngazargamu in Bornu. He found the people gathered and complaining and learned why they were unhappy, and so he simply marched into the centre of the city, to the serpent's place, and pierced it with a spear. It died quickly. Its offspring scattered throughout the town, and some fled to other towns.

Hussein laid out the serpent's carcass and it was butchered. The head was buried under the shrine to the lizard which had led the founder Abdullah to the site; the entrails were buried in a place of power, and the other parts of the body were buried in the different neighbourhoods of the town; even today (at the time of telling) the town of Makari has something of the shape of a serpent. Hussein then declared himself king. He and his descendants ruled over the town.

In typical human fashion, the people of Makari mourned the serpent and resented their new rulers.

THE KINGDOM OF BAGIRMI

The kingdom of Bagirmi was established in the sixteenth cen-
tury among the Barma, living to the south-east of Lake Chad
along rivers that feed into the lake. The story is clearly Islamic
in origin, but includes local elements as well; it is a dynastic
legend rather than a regional creation myth. It also indicates
the degree of ethnic fluidity in the region; the presence of the
Fulani woman may be technically an anachronism but does
reflect the current mix of peoples in the region. This story is
retold from an ethnographic study published in 1977.

The kings of Bagirmi traced their ancestry to Yemen. They said
that the wife of Abd el Tukruru (of the line of the Prophet
Muhammad) gave birth to a black child. The father interpreted
this oddity to infidelity on his wife's part, accused her of adultery and fornication, and ordered that mother and child be
burned alive in a structure made of *mbese* wood. But mother
and child survived the fire, and Abd el Tukruru's sister was the
first to reach them. Amazed at finding them alive, she took the
child and threw it up in the air, exclaiming, '*Baggar mia!*'
(colloquial Arabic: a hundred cows), referring to the compensation the father owed after this visible proof of his wife's
guiltlessness.

Nevertheless, the father eventually ordered his son, named
Muhammad, to leave Yemen and travel west. His son departed
in the company of his eleven brothers and ten other companions, and they took also three pack-oxen carrying an anvil,
musical instruments and hunting weapons. Along the way,
some brothers died and others chose to settle down. One

brother stayed in a town called Erla, and there Muhammad also left the anvil. At that time a Muslim holy man sacrificed the pack-ox that had carried the anvil, sprinkling its blood over the metal. The anvil vanished into the ground.

Finally, Muhammad came to a place where an old Fulani woman named Nyo-nyo was making salt from the ashes of the *jan* tree; she was sitting under an *mbese* tree. She was near a watercourse, and a rhinoceros was drinking from the water. Using his hunting weapons, Muhammad killed the rhinoceros, and from that deed received his regal name, Dala Birni (rhinoceros king).

59
THE KINGDOMS OF KANEM AND BORNU

The history of Kanem and Bornu is lengthy and complex. The kingdom of Kanem arose first in the savannahs east and north of Lake Chad; its capital was Njimi, and the Maighumi dynasty which ruled traced its ancestry to Yemen. In the fifteenth century the nomadic Bulala displaced the Maighumi rulers (the king was called Mai) from Njimi. The kings wandered for some time, but then settled in what is now called Bornu, west of Lake Chad, and established a second capital, Ngazargamu. The king at this time was Mai Ali Ghaji Dunamami, and the date around 1470. Over the next few hundred years, Bornu reconquered their old territory of Kanem to the east, and held off first the Songhay and then the Hausa and Fulani Muslim states to the west. Finally, in the eighteenth century Muslim Fulani rulers displaced the Mais and a thousand-year dynasty ended.

The people of Bornu are the Kanuri, tracing their origins to the Tubu and the Kuwar (equated with the Sow), with a strong Arabic influence. Their documented history goes back to the conversion to Islam of Mai Umme, c. 1080. While the economy depended in some part on slave-raiding to the south, among the unconverted peoples, trade, agriculture and various forms of industry were also central. Their traditions of origin are heavily influenced by Islam, and echo the traditions found in other Muslim kingdoms of the savannah. These stories are retold from undated local Arabic writings translated into English.

THE FIVE TRIBES OF KANEM

The Ngalawiyu, the Kuburi, the Magumi, the Kangu and the Kajidi all trace their origin to Ayesha, who was the daughter of the Sultan of Baghdad. The Sultan married her first to his brother, Maina Ahmed, and to this husband she gave a son named Ngal. But Maina Ahmed died. The Sultan of Baghdad then married Ayesha to Abraha, the Sultan of Yemen. She gave him a son named Sayf. But then Abraha died.

The Sultan of Baghdad then married Ayesha to the ruler of the city of Medina. She gave him a son named Mani. Then the ruler of Medina died. Then the Sultan of Baghdad married Ayesha to the Sultan of Misra (Egypt). She went to Egypt and there she gave the Sultan of Egypt a son, named Abdurrahman. Then the Sultan of Egypt died and Ayesha returned to the home of her father.

After some months she married Kaigama Barka; to him she gave a son named Jidi Gaji. After some time, she died, leaving her five sons. Each of them became the ancestor of a fraction of the people of Kanem:

From Ngal came the Ngalawiyu.

From Sayf came the Magumi of Yemen.

From Mani came the Kangu.

From Abdurrahman came the Kuburi.

From Jidi Gaji came the Kajidi.

After the death of their mother, these five sons travelled to the land of Kanem, and then took counsel to choose a king among them. They chose Sayf, who became the founder of the Sayfawa dynasty of the Magumi. His elder brother Ngal then came to him in secret and warned him that the people might challenge his rule, because he was not the eldest, and told Sayf that he should execute him, Ngal, in public so that there should be no question about his power and his authority. Sayf was reluctant to kill his elder brother, but Ngal reassured him that a blow from a sword would not be enough: he would seem dead, but would actually be alive. If Sayf came to him after the crowd had dispersed and called him by name, Ngal would rise again. So Sayf assented.

He announced to the people that because some were challenging his authority on the grounds that Ngal should be king, he would execute Ngal. Then he struck Ngal with a sword upon the neck, cutting his throat so that blood flowed and his brother fell dead. Then he waited until the crowd had left and returned to revive his brother, but no life returned to the body. This was Ngal's trick to assure the authority of his younger brother. Now there was no rival claimant, nor was there any doubt that the new Mai would protect his throne. This was far-sighted, for in later years the kingdom of Kanem was destroyed by wars of succession among rival brothers.

THE SAIFAWA AND THE SOW

The land of Bornu into which the new people wandered was then inhabited by the Sow, hunters who were great in stature. A Sow hunter would return from the bush with an elephant slung over his shoulder, and they used hills for pillows when they slept. Their leader at this time was Dala Ngumani. He was astounded one day to see a new people coming out of the dry lands to the north with a new animal: it had no horns or hoofs, and its feet were great pads, split in two. Its neck was long, like that of the giraffe, and its body was topped by a great hump.

He talked with the leader of this people – and one legend says it was Mai Ali Ghaji, leading the Kanuri who had been expelled from Kanem – and agreed to give them land and shelter. In one story, he traced out a circle of land for them using a stick, and so encompassed a great expanse of land; in another, he offered them a bullock's hide of land, and the king told his people to cut the hide into a very long continuous thong with which he was able to measure a far greater space than Dala Ngumani had intended. It is also said that Dala Ngumani helped them build their new town, bringing great bundles of wood and planting them in the ground to form the stockade around the town. There were six gates, and the name of the new city was Ngazargamu.

For a time the Saifawa and the Sow lived quietly together, but inevitably there was friction and then conflict. One cause was the children's play: when Sow and Saifawa children played together, the newcomers invariably got the worst of it, and sometimes they were even killed in the rough and tumble. So the Saifawa considered how they might defeat the mighty hunters. They could not compete in strength: people who tossed elephants about like balls were clearly beyond them. So they settled on a stratagem.

Like many desert peoples, they practised the art of dyeing their skin with henna to form intricate patterns on their hands and feet. One week, all the people of the town dyed their hands with ornate designs. Naturally, the Sow whom they met noticed their hands and admired the beauty of the work; eventually, the Sow asked their neighbours to do the same for them. The Saifawa agreed, and all settled upon a particular day to invite the Sow to have their hands and feet coloured with the henna. They then proceeded to prepare many strong leather thongs, which they wet.

The operation of henna-dyeing requires the person to sit still for some time after the henna paste has been spread over the masking pattern, so that the colour will set and take hold. The longer the person waits, the darker and more durable the pattern that results. The Saifawa told the Sow what was required, and said that to ensure that the paste was not disturbed while colouring the skin, they would have to tie the Sow with the leather thongs. Innocently, the Sow agreed.

Then the Saifawa waited a day or so, until the thongs had dried out and tightened, immobilizing the Sow. They attacked the helpless hunters and killed almost all of them, although some managed to put up a good resistance despite having their hands and feet bound, and killed a number of the Saifawa. They spared the life of Dala Ngumani, because he had been so helpful to them.

THE WARS WITH THE BULALA

There was conflict between the new rulers of Bornu and the occupiers of Kanem, the Bulala. In an attempt to end the conflict, the Emir of the Bulala gave his daughter, Ya Juma, to Mai Dunama of Bornu. But the hostilities broke out again some months later, and in the fighting, Mai Dunama was killed.

Ali Ghaji Zeinam was chosen as the new Mai, because Dunama had left no sons, although he had seventy wives and all were with child at the time of his death, including Ya Juma, daughter of the Emir of the Bulala. Mai Ali decreed that any male child born to one of these wives would be put to death, although any girls would be allowed to live, and so it went for sixty-nine deliveries. Ya Juma was the last to give birth, and her child was a son. But she found an opportunity to preserve her son's life, since one of her servants had also given birth at the same time to a girl. She exchanged the babies, and when the messenger came from Mai Ali Ghaji to ask about the birth of the child he was told a girl had been born.

All went well for a few years, until Mai Ali Ghaji called diviners together to augur the future of his reign. They performed their operations and then informed the king that there was living in the city a king's son who would succeed him. Mai Ali Ghaji was disturbed by this, but they could not tell him how to identify the child. Hearing of the results of the divination, Ya Juma became worried and sent her son, whom she had named Idris and passed as the son of the servant, into the Fezzan, and from there he was taken to live with the Emir of the Bulala.

Mai Ali Ghaji Zeinami died, leaving no heir, and a daughter of Mai Dunama, Aissa Kili, was chosen to rule as Mai, although the people were not told she was a woman. She ruled for seven years, until Idris, the son of Ya Juma, sent a message to her asking if she did not know she had a brother living. She sent for Ya Juma and asked about her son, and at first Ya Juma denied that she had given birth to a boy, but finally she admitted that she had switched her son with the servant-girl and later sent him to live with the Bulala, after Mai Ali's divination.

Aissa Kili followed the messenger into the desert, seeking her lost brother. When she came among the Bulala, she was told she should identify him among a crowd of horsemen, and they organized a *fantasia*, a riding spectacle in which all the participants would demonstrate their skills.

Idris distinguished himself among the crowd: he was the foremost rider, and when the horsemen charged the crowd he alone did not stop short, but charged in among the people. So Aissa Kili identified him and abdicated the throne to him. But Idris had listened incognito to the talk of the Bornu people who accompanied Aissa Kili, and he realized they were discontented at the thought of having been ruled by a woman (for Aissa Kili had passed as a man) and might cause trouble. So Idris went to his grandfather, the Emir of the Bulala, and asked for a force of soldiers to accompany him back to Ngazargamu to quell any opposition to his rule. The Emir agreed and sent a force of horsemen with Idris.

After some months, the Bulala horsemen wished to return home, for they had seen no signs of opposition to the rule of the new Mai Idris. Idris arranged to have them killed. Later, he made war on the Bulala, and finally captured his grandfather, the Emir of the Bulala.

'Where is Mai Dunama, my father?' asked Idris.

'He died from wounds received in our battles,' answered the Emir.

'Then go and join him and continue your battle,' ordered Idris, and the Emir was put to death.

60

THE HAUSA

The Hausa are the people who settled in the territory between the Niger, as it flows south out of the desert, and the Benue flowing west from the Mandara and Cameroon mountains. The cities of the Hausa became renowned trading centres, acting as middlemen between the trans-Saharan caravan trade that led north to Tripoli (in Libya) and to Egypt and the southward trade in ivory, slaves, kola nuts and other commodities. Islam was adopted by the rulers in many cities around the sixteenth century, but they made accommodations with the traditional practices of their subjects. In the late eighteenth century, Muslim Fulani took power in most of the cities, beginning with Uthman dan Fodio in Sokoto and continuing with others; this period of the 'Fulani Jihad' involved a wave of conquests towards the south and east that ended with the arrival of the British a century later.

The Hausa divide their cities into the 'Hausa Bakwai' (the seven true sons) and the 'Banza Bakwai' (the seven bastards), looking to the descendants of Bayajida, founder of the ruling lineage. Among the seven 'true' Hausa cities, the principal ones were Daura (the first), Kano, Zazzau (now Zaria) and Katsina.

BAYAJIDA AND DAURA

Bayajida was a son of the king of Baghdad. He settled in the land of Egypt, but was forced to leave because of his passion for horses. The king of Egypt had a stallion that was considered supreme in the land; when it whinnied, all other horses remained silent. Even the people would stop what they were doing until the horse had ceased its call. Bayajida had a wonderful mare, and he longed to have her breed by the stallion.

He approached the king's grooms, but they refused outright. They told him it would cost them their lives if they let the king's stallion mount another man's horse. But Bayajida cultivated their acquaintance and finally bribed one of them to help him. When the stallion was put out to stud, the groom would collect any semen that dribbled on the ground and deliver the ball of dirt that formed to Bayajida. The occasion arrived; the man delivered the wet sand to Bayajida, and Bayajida carefully introduced it into the womb of his mare. Soon he knew his efforts had been rewarded: the mare was heavy with foal. Some time later, she gave birth, but died in the process. Bayajida carefully raised the colt, until it was old enough to be saddled and ridden.

One day, the king of Egypt's stallion whinnied, as it was accustomed to do. But the silence that followed was broken by an answering call: Bayajida's young horse was answering the challenge. There was consternation in the palace; the king was outraged and demanded that they find the horse which dared disobey his commands. The groom who had assisted Bayajida went to him and warned him that he should flee; they would undoubtedly find his horse in their search of the town. Bayajida immediately gathered his belongings, mounted the horse and departed. At the city gates he told the guards that he was on an errand for the cadi of the town, and as he had previously performed such services they let him pass without question. From Egypt he rode west.

The pursuers turned back when they encountered a sign which Bayajida had left for them. Coming from Baghdad, he brought with him a marvellous sword on which were engraved verses of the Koran, and if the wielder of the sword recited the verses while swinging the blade he might cut even through stone. Bayajida had cut through the trunk of a tree with one blow, and then carved a saying on the standing trunk: the rash should beware, for the consequences would be on their heads. The king of Egypt's riders, racing after the fugitive, came upon the tree-trunk, read the signs and decided to turn back.

Bayajida came to the town of Daura, which at that time was ruled by a queen. The city obeyed a great serpent called Dodo which lived in the well and controlled their water supply. Bayajida stopped at the edge of the town and found a lodging with an old woman in a hut. But when he asked her for water to refresh the horse which had carried him so far and so well, she had none to give him: her supply was out, and she was not allowed to draw more.

'Give me the bucket and a basin for the horse,' said Bayajida, and he led his horse to the well. There, he shouted down into the darkness, 'Oh, dweller in the well, let me draw water for my horse. And then if you wish we can introduce ourselves.' He lowered the bucket until he heard it splash in the water, and then he twisted the rope quickly to make the bucket dip into the water; when he felt it was full he hauled it up and poured it out into the basin. The horse drank thirstily; their path had led them through the desert. Bayajida poured out more water, and then called down into the well, 'My horse has drunk; now is the time for us to meet.' And he drew his sword and recited the verses.

The serpent emerged from the well, and with one stroke Bayajida parted the head from the great sinuous body. The head fell to the ground; the body continued to emerge until it was wrapped around the well's retaining wall. Bayajida cut off the tip of the tail, placed it in his shoulder bag, and returned to the old woman's house.

'Are you well?' asked the old woman.

'I was able to water my horse,' said Bayajida. 'The guardian of the well and I reached an agreement.'

The next morning, the people were amazed and frightened at the mass of the serpent's body lying around the well. The women approached cautiously, carrying their basins and pots, and then fled when they saw the serpent's mouth. But after a time they approached again, closer, and soon everyone in town knew that the serpent had been killed. Queen Magira made enquiries to learn who had killed the serpent, and several men claimed credit for the deed. But they were quickly exposed as frauds and punished. Finally, someone told the queen that the old woman who lived at the edge of town had a lodger who might know something of the affair. She summoned Bayajida, and he admitted he had killed the serpent, and produced the piece of tail as proof.

'This is a great deed, and worthy to make you my consort,' said Queen Magira. 'But I feel I am now too old for marriage.'

'Do you still have the monthly flow?' asked Bayajida, and she answered yes. 'Then it is permissible for you to marry, and as I find you beautiful I would be honoured.'

The queen agreed to the marriage, but nevertheless she hesitated to share her bed with the stranger. She sent a concubine to him, and then, after the concubine had become pregnant, she herself went to Bayajida's bed. They had a son, known as Bawo; Bawo in turn had six sons who became kings of the other cities of the Hausa.

BAGAUDA AND THE FOUNDING
OF KANO

Before Bagauda came from Daura, the land of Kano was occupied by a people of hunters whose leader was named Barbushe. Barbushe was descended from Dala, a great man who was the first inhabitant of the country. Dala was an elephant hunter; he would club the animals and then carry them back to the village on his head. Dala had children, and Barbushe was his great-grandson. They worshipped at a shrine dedicated to a deity named Chunburburai, who was believed to be housed in a tree, and the tree was surrounded by an enclosure which none might enter save Barbushe. Barbushe presided over the sacrifices. He foretold that a man would come who would take power from the descendants of Dala, and that the tree would be uprooted, the shrine destroyed, and a mosque built at that spot.

Bagauda came a generation later. The men of the time went to Janbere, the heir to Barbushe and officiant at the shrine, to ask if this was the stranger whom Barbushe had foreseen, and Janbere confirmed that he was, and that he would take their lands and rule over them. But they did not believe him. They were wrong. Bagauda settled in the land, having brought men from Daura, and then other people came from Bornu and such places, having heard of the land, and soon they were very numerous. The newcomers looked to Bagauda as their leader, and so he and his people displaced the old descendants of Dala.

THE KINGDOMS OF THE WESTERN SUDAN

The Niger river rises in the highlands of Guinea, flows east and then north into the desert, before turning south again to the Atlantic. The lands around its middle course were the home to a series of states, beginning in the ninth century or earlier, which succeeded each other with some recognition of continuity. The states were based to some extent on control of the trans-Saharan flow of gold from minefields near the headwaters of the Senegal river (Bambuk and Bure), and later from Ghana. The first state of record was the Soninke empire of Ghana, the capital of which lay somewhat north of the modern city of Nioro du Sahel (the legendary Wagadu, identified with Kumbi Saleh). This was followed by the empire of Mali (c. 1250–1600). As Mali declined, Songhay grew in power further down the river, centred on the cities of Timbuktu and Gao. After Songhay fell to the Moroccans in 1591, the Bamana states of Segou and Kaarta arose in the eighteenth century on either side of the Niger.

THE SONGHAY PEOPLES OF THE MIDDLE NIGER

The Songhay peoples look back to a period of unity under the Songhay empire, which flourished from the mid-fifteenth century to the end of the sixteenth. It was a successor state to the empire of Mali, and counts as one of the great Islamic states of medieval sub-Saharan Africa. Under the Askias, who took power from the Sonni dynasty around 1500, Islam was promoted across the area, and learned men were attracted to Timbuktu from the other parts of the Muslim world. The empire fell after 1590–91, when an expeditionary force from Morocco, equipped with firearms, defeated their army at the battle of Tondibi. Although the Moroccans attempted to maintain the empire, they failed; it fragmented into separate states and communities, and many of the Songhay fled south and east along the Niger as far as Busa in Borgu (see Chapter 50). A new, smaller Songhay kingdom was established in Dendi.

The Songhay were principally a river people (see the Sorko stories in Chapter 3), and the principal activity of the empire was trade between Timbuktu, lying where the Niger bends furthest north into the Sahara, and Djenne, lying on the Bani (a confluent of the Niger); Timbuktu was the terminus of a trans-Saharan trade route, and Djenne the northern endpoint of a trade network reaching south into the lands of gold (Ghana), ivory, kola nuts, cloth and slaves. Millet was grown on the floodplains, fishermen worked the river, and cattle-herders such as the Fulani exploited the drier pasture lands.

ES-SADI'S ACCOUNT OF THE ORIGINS
OF THE SONGHAY KINGDOM

The historian Abdurrahman es-Sadi wrote the Tarikh es-Sudan, *a history of the Sudan, in the early seventeenth century, and gives an account of Songhay origins current at the time.*

Two brothers from Yemen were forced to flee their land. They travelled west through Africa, until they came to the land of the Songhay, exhausted and parched. When they reached the river, they found a people who welcomed them; the people asked who they were, and the younger brother answered, for the older, 'Ja min al-Yemen' (Arabic: He has come from Yemen). The people understood this to be their name, and so henceforth the elder brother was known as Za Alyaman.

The people at the time worshipped a great fish that would come to the surface of the water to receive its offerings. Za Alyaman determined that he would kill this fish, and so he obtained a great harpoon. On the day of the offerings, he made his way close to the banks of the river, and then hurled his weapon at the fish. The harpoon struck home, and the fish expired. The people, seeing that Za Alyaman was mightier than their previous protector, made him their king. This is the origin of the Za dynasty, which ruled Songhay for many generations.

The Sonni dynasty took power after Songhay had been subject to the power of Mali for some time. Za Yasiboi, the prince of the Songhay, had married a woman named Fati, but they were childless. Fati suggested that he marry her sister Omma, and he did so. Both women became pregnant at the same time, and both gave birth on the same day. The two babies were placed in a dark room and left there overnight; only the next morning were they washed and given to their mothers. The first to be washed was named Ali Kolon, and he was declared the elder; the second was Selman Nar. When they grew old enough, the emperor of Mali took them to his court to serve him and to ensure their father's continued obedience.

While living in the court of Mali, Ali Kolon often went on riding expeditions, and during these expeditions he carefully explored the territory lying between the court and his home-land. He prepared stocks of food and weapons and left them in secret places along the paths. When he felt his preparations were finished, he gave the signal to his brother and the two of them fled the court of Mali. They were pursued, but whenever the pursuers got too close they would turn and fight them off. Sustained and speeded by the stores of food which Ali Kolon had placed along their way, they reached Songhay in safety. There Ali Kolon declared Songhay to be independent of Mali, and named himself king.

MALI BERO AND THE ESCAPE
FROM MALI

The modern oral accounts of the origins of the Zarma, a Songhay-speaking group living south-east of Gao who moved there after the fall of the empire in 1590, reflect more recent conditions (nineteenth-century oppression by Fulani and Tua-reg raiders) and offer somewhat more symbolic elements, recalling regional creation myths. The story is retold from several versions collected by a Nigerien scholar before 1980.

Zabarkane was a warrior who came to Mecca to serve the Prophet Muhammad in his wars, for a leader without men cannot make war and the Prophet had put out a call for men to come to him. Zabarkane fought on behalf of the Prophet for many years. He had a daughter; the daughter was taken captive by the enemies of the Prophet and carried off. Zabarkane went to the Prophet Muhammad and demanded his assistance in the return of his daughter; the Prophet summoned his Companions and told them they must rescue the daughter of Zabarkane. They did so, and she was restored to her father.

The daughter was young and beautiful, but after her captivity no man asked to marry her. Zabarkane went to the Prophet

Muhammad and complained that his daughter remained unwed. The Prophet told him to wait, that the young woman must be considered as a widow and that the stipulated period of mourning should pass. Zabarkane exercised his patience and waited for a time, but still no man asked to marry his daughter. He went again to the Prophet and requested his assistance but the Prophet had no more advice. So Zabarkane left the land of Mecca and travelled until he came to Mali. There he settled. A son was born to him there, and they named him Sombo. He was the first Zarma-Koy, or leader of the Zarmas.

At that time, the Fulani and the Tuareg ruled the land. They tormented Zabarkane's people in many ways. The one which Sombo found most offensive involved clothing. The young men would go down to the river to bathe and leave their clothes on the banks; the Fulani and Tuareg youths would come and steal the clothes, forcing the Zarma men to walk naked through the village. Often the Tuareg and Fulani would use the clothes of the Zarma youths to clean themselves of filth. Sombo determined to end these outrages and insults, and he took counsel with other young men of his age. One night, they hid their spears in the reeds by the riverbank. The next day they went to bathe as usual; the young Tuareg and Fulani came as usual and seized the clothes. Then Sombo and his companions dashed from the water, seized the weapons they had concealed, and slew the Tuareg and Fulani youths. They spared none; they killed them all and left the bodies lying by the riverbank. Among the slain were the sons of the prince of the Tuareg and the prince of the Fulani.

At that time the Zarma had seven drums of different sizes which they used to send signals. Sombo and his companions returned to their village and sounded the largest of the seven drums, known as Sombonkana. At the sound of Sombonkana, the most urgent of the drum calls, everyone would drop what they were doing and come running. Men would seize their weapons and their horses and come ready for war; women would seize food.

The Zarma assembled, and Sombo informed them that he and his companions had killed the bully-boys of the Fulani and the Tuareg, and that among them were the sons of the princes. The Zarma decided to leave the country. One of them was a slave named Almine, a wise man; he alone in the country possessed a bull. He told them what to do. They gathered reeds and grasses and wove them into a great mat, such as are used at the bottom of granaries to keep the grain dry. Then they assembled all the Zarma on top of the mat. They placed all the people and the sheep and the goats and the horses on the mat; they did not have cattle. They used Almine's bull as their guide: they left the bull on the ground to indicate their course.

In the meantime, a blacksmith, a *garassa*, went to an old Fulani woman and asked her for tobacco. She refused him: why should she give him tobacco? For news, he answered, and he told her how the Fulani boys had been killed on the riverbank. Then he came back to the Zarma village, to find all the people on the mat and the mat rising into the air. He cried for help, calling on Sombo; he said he was like a blind hyena that could not survive in the wild and could not live in the town. Sombo took pity and stretched down his whip; the *garassa* seized it and so was carried into the air.

Following the bull, the flying granary travelled along the river, landing at night for the people to sleep. They made many stops.

Along the way, Sombo's brother Tilomboti planned treachery, envying his brother's new authority. He went to the Tuareg and told them how Sombo had killed their young men, and how he and the Zarma were travelling on a granary down the river. The Tuareg came and attacked the Zarma, but Sombo had foreknowledge of the attack; he prepared his warriors and they defeated the Tuareg. They were driven off, and Tilomboti went with them. He became the ancestor of the Daussahane.

The Zarma finally settled near Sargane, and that is where Sombo, who took the name Mali Bero, is buried.

KOUKAMONZON AND THE KINGDOM
OF DENDI

*Dendi was founded beside the Niger river, well downstream
from Gao, by Songhay peoples displaced by the turmoil following the Moroccan conquest. This account is based on a retelling
of the legend by a Malian scholar around 1970.*

Koukamonzon and his younger brother, Farimonzon, came
from Zanfara in Nigeria. They wandered through the lands, for
Koukamonzon had seen visions in his mind, although they had
yet to be fulfilled. Farimonzon would grumble as they travelled,
but he was a devoted brother and he followed his elder when
Koukamonzon settled on a direction and began to stride
towards the unknown. They came to the Niger river and travelled along its banks; at that time it was a much smaller stream
than it is now. When they came to the area in which they were
to settle, they heard a great groaning coming from the earth,
and then they saw a long thing, very much like a log but much
lighter – soft to the touch and mottled – lying straight across
the flow of the river. Farimonzon hid his head at the sounds
that came from the earth; Koukamonzon looked about and saw
the log. He called his brother, for he saw the log as a miraculous
bridge intended to lead them across the river. Farimonzon was
more sceptical, but let his brother lead him. As they crossed the
river, they heard the call of a dove.

'We must follow the call,' said Koukamonzon, and as soon
as he set foot on the ground he hastened in the direction of the
call. They found the dove in the branches of a tamarind tree,
whose thick foliage gave them a cool shade and whose boughs
were bent with the weight of their fruit. As they approached,
the dove called again.

'This is a very propitious sign,' said Koukamonzon. 'I feel
that this land will be good to us. But we must consult the earth
oracle, to be sure of accomplishing her will.'

The first day, the earth oracle gave them no sign. The second day, the sign was mildly unfavourable. The third day, Almahaw the wind spirit came down in the form of a whirlwind. He came to earth near them in a tumult of dead leaves, dried grasses and husks raised from the ground by his passage, and then proceeded on his way towards the hills that lay some distance from the river. Koukamonzon and Farimonzon hastened after him, Koukamonzon delighted with the explicit signs sent by the earth oracle and confident that no harm would come to them.

At the mouth of a cave, the signs of the whirlwind – the heaps of dust, the trail of dead leaves – ceased. Instead, they found a white ram and a white cock. These were the shapes that Almahaw and his steed had taken. As the two men arrived, the cock crowed loudly and woke the earth spirit, the owner of the Dendi hills. The spirit spoke from the cave to the two men, greeting them and asking them how they had come.

Koukamonzon explained that they had come from the tamarind tree, following the signs of Almahaw who had been sent in response to their question to the earth oracle.

'And how did you cross the river to the tree?' asked the spirit.

'We crossed upon a strange log, soft to the touch, that appeared and lay across the flow of the stream.'

'I was that log,' said the spirit, and emerged from the cave: it was a great python, whose coils covered the ground. 'I have brought you here to occupy the land. In exchange, you shall make me an offering of a ram or a cock and neither you nor your descendants will eat my flesh or that of my kind.'

In this way, Koukamonzon and his brother reached an agreement with Kombolati, the spirit of the hills. Kombolati gave to Koukamonzon and his lineage the power to communicate directly with him, so that they were the guardians of the cult.

When Koukamonzon and Farimonzon consulted the earth oracle to learn the place where they should settle, the earth oracle first disapproved of the spot they had proposed. The dove called to them again and led them further from the river to a dead baobab tree. There the dove halted, and there Koukamonzon again consulted the earth oracle. In answer, the baobab tree burst into leaf, the grass turned green, the plants flowered, and suddenly all the insects that had died around the tree returned to life and rose in a great humming of wings.

The sign was clear. They settled there. The town was known as Gayna, and it became the capital of Dendi.

ZWA THE HUNTER

Like the story of Koukamonzon, and in partial contrast to the first two stories with their connections to Mali, the story of Zwa highlights the cultural continuities along the southern part of the Niger from the Songhay to the Hausa and even to the Yoruba. The story of Zwa is a fairly typical foundation story (one might compare him with the figure of the hunter in the Mossi traditions), associated in this case with the Anzuru region of Niger. This version is retold from one collected by a Nigerien scholar in the 1960s.

When Zwa entered the land of Anzuru, he found nothing there but God, the bush and lions. He had come from Mali, forced to flee after his older brother had killed some griots (praise-singers) because of a song they sang. He came into the land of the Zarma, who at that time were ruled by Zabarkane. He encountered a hunter and offered to trade him his clothes, his belongings and his horse in exchange for his hunting equipment and the knowledge which allowed him to remain safe in the bush. The hunter agreed, and prepared for him the protective charms he would need and also made him a bow and arrows. Zwa handed over to the hunter all the belongings he had been able to bring from Mali and headed into the bush. He passed through it, avoiding all human dwellings, until he came into Anzuru.

A lioness had gone hunting, but just as she sprang out to seize her game she stumbled, for her paw had been pierced by a great thorn. She tried to gnaw it free but failed, and wandered moaning in pain through the wilderness. She found Zwa sleeping in the shade of a bush and woke him with her paw. Zwa roused himself, saw the lioness, and then saw her paw, bloody from the thorn. Gently he worked the thorn free, and then he poured some of his water over the paw to clean the wound. He left the lioness under the bush, where her two cubs soon joined her, and went off to kill some game. Soon he returned with food for the lioness, her cubs and himself.

After that, the lioness and Zwa hunted together, as though the lioness and her cubs were his dogs. Zwa lived for a time in the company of the lions until one day he met a man named Amara at a waterhole; Amara would become the ancestor of the people of Ceygooru. Although at first they were prepared to kill each other, they decided it would be better to talk. Zwa learned that Amara came from a village, and enquired about the possibility of getting a wife from among the women of the village.

Amara answered that he would ask his sister, for she was a diviner. The next day they met again at the waterhole. Amara had the response from his sister.

'If you wish to have children, there is only one woman you can marry. She is the daughter of the ruler of Gobir [a Hausa state].' Amara told Zwa the tokens which would allow him to recognize this woman. Her name was Alzuma.

Then Zwa used the magic the hunter had taught him. He cast a spell and wings grew on his back, so that he could fly over the bush. He flew south into the land of Gobir until he saw a group of maidens in a sand quarry, and among them he recognized the daughter of the chief: she wore a great silver bracelet on one arm, and an anklet on one leg. He swooped down and carried her off, flying back into Anzuru. He put her down in the middle of his lions. Alzuma was terrified, but he reassured her and offered her food. She calmed down when she saw how the lions played around him and obeyed his slightest sign.

The chief of Gobir got no peace after the abduction of his daughter. He sent all his people to seek her, but they had little to go by: there were the footprints in the sand quarry, so they knew a man had appeared and seized her, but there the track disappeared. A Fulani came to him one day and admired one of the cattle in the chief's herd. He heard of the chief's loss, and went into the bush. Herdsmen, like hunters, wander far from the houses of men.

He came to Zwa's camp in Anzuru, while Zwa was away hunting. He found the chief of Gobir's daughter and greeted her; immediately the lions pounced on him and prepared to kill him. Then Alzuma spoke up. 'Come, find something better to do than kill a Fulani.' The lions got up and left him alone. Alzuma gave the Fulani her bracelet and he left. When Zwa returned from his hunting, he was suspicious; he sensed that a human being had come and gone, but Alzuma denied that anything had happened.

The Fulani returned to the ruler of Gobir and asked for the cow he had admired as a reward. When he had heard the Fulani's news, the chief of Gobir gladly gave it to him, and then he assembled his army and marched out. Soon, from a height, he recognized the signs the Fulani had indicated: a great tree stood out in the flat plains below. By the tree was Zwa's camp.

Zwa quickly became aware of the strangers in his valley. He and one of the lions prepared for battle. He shot his arrows, and wherever they fell they slew the men around them. The lion raced here and there knocking men to the ground. But the men of Gobir speared it at last, and suffering from the iron it took cover under a bush. Immediately the men of Gobir brought torches and wood and prepared to burn the lion out of its cover.

Zwa uttered a prayer: 'Do not let me see my lion burned before my eyes.' Immediately clouds formed over the place of the struggle and rain poured down on the men of Gobir, extinguishing their torches. Stunned by this wonder, the people of Gobir paused.

'You in the bush,' called the chief of Gobir, 'I am looking for my daughter who is lost. I was told you held her captive, and that is why I have come after you.'

'I did not take your daughter to make a slave of her,' answered Zwa. 'I was told that if I wished to have children there was only one woman I could marry, and it was your daughter.'

'You have killed many of your in-laws,' answered the chief of Gobir. 'This is a strange way to greet your kin.'

'You came with an army,' answered Zwa. 'I would not let you kill me first.'

So the chief of Gobir and Zwa came to an agreement, and Alzuma stayed with Zwa to become his wife and the mother of his heirs. Other people came later, bringing skills and knowledge which Zwa and his people needed to appease the local spirits of the earth and to protect the land against the raids of the Tuareg and others. This is how Anzuru was populated.

62

THE CITY OF DJENNE

Djenne is an almost legendary city lying on the Bani river, upstream from its confluence with the Niger. Although Muslim sources such as the Tarikh es-Sudan *say the city was founded in the ninth century, archaeology shows that the settlement is much older, although the city has moved from its former site (Djenne-Jeno) to its current location. The town lies in a floodplain and becomes an island during the rainy season. Its importance came from trade: Djenne was the southern end of the Songhay river trade routes paired with Timbuktu to the north. From Djenne rock salt from the Sahara and luxury goods from the Mediterranean travelled south, while in return gold, ivory, kola, slaves and other commodities travelled north. Although subject to the various empires, and occasionally sacked by the Mossi raiding to the north, Djenne enjoyed a certain autonomy. The stories are retold from versions collected early in the colonial era.*

A MUSLIM VERSION

At the battle of Badr, against the people of Mecca, the Prophet Muhammad noted one man fighting with unmatched valour. After the battle he summoned the warrior and asked who he was. The warrior said he had come from a land in the west.

'Return to your country,' said the Prophet. 'There you shall found a great town lying underneath Paradise [*al-Jana* in Arabic] which shall become a centre of the faith.'

The warrior returned to the land near Djenne. There he found the Bozo fishermen and the Nono living. They agreed to cede him land for his new town, and so he and his followers began to set up the town and to surround it with earthen walls. But the walls collapsed regularly, and so the warrior went to the Bozo and Nono for their assistance in learning the cause. They helped him to reach a bargain with Shamawruchi, chief of the spirits of the place. They were told they must bury a maiden alive in the walls to obtain the jinn's favour. The chief of the Bozo fishermen gave his daughter; as she stood in the pit and the earth mounted around her body she called on the spirits to bless the Bozo and Nono people of the town. After that, the walls stood, and the tomb of the Bozo maiden can still be seen on the south side of the town.

A VARIANT

A man named Sunta Mori was travelling to bury his sister, who lived in a town on the eastern border of the empire of Mali, when he encountered a spirit in the region where Djenne is now situated. The spirit told him that after he had buried his sister he should return to this place and found a city. He followed the spirit's instructions; he returned to the place with followers who were interested in the new and well-watered lands, and they began the construction of the city. His followers were largely composed of Bozo fishermen. They laid out the sites of the gates and began to build the walls. But the walls would not stand; each morning they found the previous day's work destroyed.

The cause was the hostility of the local spirit, a female named Pama. She was married and had a young daughter. Another female spirit named Wono came to visit her, and at the end of the visit warned Pama that her husband was paying too much attention to the pretty Bozo girls who were gathered at the place where the men were building their new city, and she advised Pama to find a way to drive them off. Pama summoned her spirit slave, Musa, and told him that he was to go and destroy the walls of the city each day.

'If you do so,' she promised, 'you shall have my daughter in marriage without paying any bride-price. Your work on the walls will be payment enough.'

So each day Musa destroyed the walls of the city. Eventually Sunta Mori consulted a diviner and learned why the walls were collapsing. Through the diviner, he reached an agreement with Musa: Musa would be given a maiden in marriage, and he would let the walls stand.

Sunta Mori gave his own beautiful daughter as a bride to the spirit Musa. She was buried standing in the foundation of the walls; her last words were 'Now I am become bride to a slave.' And after that the walls stood. When the spirit Pama asked Musa why he had ceased destroying the walls he answered that he had found a bride and no longer needed her daughter. Pama was furious, but she had no one else to send on this task.

63

THE SONINKE

The Soninke are generally accorded precedence among the sedentary agricultural peoples of the upper Niger valley; they first established a kingdom recalled in modern oral tradition (Wagadu, known to the Arabs as the kingdom of Ghana), and although it fell in due course – the Arabs claim that it fell to the Almoravids in the eleventh century, but Soninke tradition speaks rather of drought and a migration towards the river – its precedence was recognized by subsequent states. Soninke praise-singers influenced court practice in Mali and Songhay (among the Songhay, the word for a griot is the Soninke term gesere*). Today the Soninke are spread in groups from the upper Senegal river, in the Guidimakha region of Mauritania and eastern Gambia, through Mali to the Niger, and they clearly moved east into Songhay territory as well. While agriculture is part of their lifestyle, they have also been traders and warriors, working in relatively close relationship with the peoples of the desert. A pattern of migrant labour, in which men travel afar and send money and food back to their home villages, seems to have marked Soninke communities for several centuries, and continues today. There are many versions of each of these two stories, recorded over the past century by locals and foreigners.*

THE LEGEND OF WAGADU

Mama Dinga came from the east with a retinue of magicians and other people. He came to a well at a place called Kumbi, and found a young woman there drawing water. He asked her for some water, and she refused to give him any. Angered, he struck her and she called out. Immediately, a female spirit came out of the well and demanded who had struck her daughter. Dinga said he had done so, because she had refused him water. The spirit cast a spell on Dinga, and he was paralysed; he cast a spell on her, and she was paralysed. She cast another spell, and he was blinded. He called on all his magic, and freed himself of her spells, and in turn was able to subdue her.

They reached an agreement. The spirit had three daughters. Dinga married the three of them, and each bore many children, who now count as ancestors of the Soninke clans. But three of them are particularly important, each born to a different mother. The eldest was not human: it was the Bida-serpent, a great snake with a mane which immediately took refuge in the well. Of the others, Khine was the eldest human and the young Djabe is central in the story.

After some time Dinga left Kumbi and returned to the east taking with him most of his family. In the east he grew old, and his sons grew up. Khine and Djabe were of very different characters. Khine was arrogant and selfish; Djabe was more considerate. Their behaviour towards the old slave Siture can illustrate their behaviour. Siture would sit at the doorway while they ate. Rising, Khine would wipe his hands on Siture's hair as he left. Djabe would save a handful of good food and give it to Siture as he left.

Dinga felt his death near, and decided that he should pass on his secrets to his son. One evening he told Khine, who was a great hunter, to come to him in the morning with whatever game he had, and he would prepare him for the succession. Siture heard this, and went secretly to Djabe and told him to prepare to take his brother's place in the morning. Djabe went to his brother and found a pretext for borrowing a bracelet which Khine always wore. He used a lambskin to simulate his brother's hairy chest, and he relied on Dinga's fading eyesight for the face.

In the morning, Khine went hunting. Djabe took an animal he had already killed and went to his father, disguising his voice to mimic that of Khine. Dinga took his hand and felt the bracelet; he reached out and felt the hair on the chest, and was sure this was Khine. He then led his son into his secret chamber, where he stored the magical items that gave him his powers. He made Djabe wash himself in the water from each of seven pots, and then roll on the sand: this anointed him with royal power, and promised that his subjects would be as numerous as the grains of sand that clung to his body. Then Djabe went away.

Khine returned some time later and went to his father. After some hesitation, Dinga realized that he had been tricked and that he had given the secret intended for the elder son to the younger. But there was no way to take it back. Instead, he gave Khine the secret of calling the rain.

Fearing his brother, Djabe ran away. He spent a long time herding animals in the wilderness. One day, he came across a very old hyena, and the hyena spoke to him. 'Who is the friend of God whom I hear?'

'I am Djabe Cisse, son of Dinga,' answered Djabe.

'I knew Dinga,' said the hyena, 'and he entrusted a secret to me, for me to pass on. A debt is a thing to remember.' And the hyena told Djabe Cisse about the land of Kumbi, and how that was to be his predestined kingdom.

'But where is Kumbi?' asked Djabe.

'I cannot show you,' said the hyena. 'But I can lead you to someone who will know the way.' The hyena led Djabe to a tree, and at the top of the tree was an ancient vulture, even older than the hyena.

'This is Djabe Cisse, son of Dinga,' said the hyena. 'He wishes to know the path to Kumbi, of which his father spoke to us. Can you show him the way?'

'I greet you, Djabe Cisse,' said the vulture. 'I remember Dinga, and I remember the path to Kumbi. But I have grown old, and I no longer have the strength to lead you there. But if for forty days you feed me each day the liver of a colt, and give the heart to the hyena, we shall regain the strength to show you the way to your kingdom.'

So Djabe Cisse fed the two ancient animals the heart and liver of a young colt each day for forty days, and they became visibly younger as the time passed. At the end of the forty days they had regained their youth, and they were able to lead Djabe Cisse and his followers to the land of Kumbi.

When he came there, he found the well and in the well was the Bida-serpent. It rose from the well to greet him as a half-brother, and asked why he had come. Djabe Cisse told him that it had been foretold that he would establish a kingdom at Kumbi. The Bida-serpent said that first they would have to come to an agreement, for he was presently the ruler of the land of Kumbi. So they bargained, and eventually agreed that each year the serpent would receive the sacrifice of one maiden and one horse. In exchange, the Bida-serpent promised an annual rain of gold which would make the kingdom rich.

The Bida-serpent gave Djabe four drums, one of copper, one of iron, one of silver and one of gold. He said that whoever could lift the gold drum should be king in the land of Kumbi. Djabe Cisse was the only one who could do so, and so he became king. He established the kingdom with its four quarters (in Soninke, *wage*) and it became known as Wagadu, the land of the *wage*.

For many years the kingdom prospered. Every year the serpent caused a rain of gold to fall and enrich the land; every year the humans selected a young woman and a horse and offered them to the serpent. But this age came to an end.

Several people were involved in this event. There was Siata Bere, the maiden who was the chosen sacrifice. There was Mamadi Sefa Dekhote (Mamadi the Taciturn), who loved her. And his uncle Wagane Sakho played a part as well. Wagane Sakho had the best horse in Wagadu, a stallion. Mamadi secretly bred a mare by the stallion, so that he had a horse the equal of his uncle's.

When the lots chose Siata Bere as the sacrifice, Mamadi decided he would not allow it. On the appointed day, the king's ministers dressed the maiden in her finest and set her astride a noble horse and led her to the well. There they left her for the Bida-serpent to take. Nearby, Mamadi waited on his horse.

The serpent stuck its head out of the well, and swung it low towards the maiden. She did not flinch; the sacrifice was her fate, and she was honoured to give her life for her people's prosperity. But Mamadi Sefa Dekhote rode up and with a great sword cut through the serpent's neck. Then he seized the maiden, swung her over his saddle, and raced out of town, heading to the south where his mother lived near the river.

The serpent's head flew into the air, and as it did so it called out a curse on Wagadu: there would be a seven-year drought, and the rains of gold would end.

The people of Wagadu rallied, and quickly a pursuit party was formed. Wagane Sakho led it, and his horse outstripped the others very quickly. He was the only one who had a chance of catching up. But each time he was within range, he cast his spear wide so that it missed his nephew, and then he was delayed as he picked it up again. Mamadi Sefa Dekhote reached his mother's home by the river.

The pursuing party arrived, and the mother asked them what they wanted. They told her that her son had committed a sacrilege and broken the pact which linked the people and the land of Wagadu, and that the people would now be without food for seven years.

'I shall feed them,' said the mother. 'In my storehouses is enough grain for Wagadu for seven years.' And so she did. But the prosperity of Wagadu was ended, and the Soninke people dispersed to other lands.

DAMAN GILLE AND THE KINGDOM
OF JARA

The kingdom of Jara grew up in the seventeenth and eighteenth centuries, based in the region around Nioro du Sahel, and fell to Muslim conquest in the nineteenth century.

Daman Gille was a hunter of elephants who lived in the Manden, the land of Sunjata. He spent a good deal of time in the bush, far from other people. One day, he encountered a marabout, a Muslim holy man, who was travelling to Mecca on pilgrimage. He entertained the marabout, giving him food and shelter for the night. In the morning he found that the marabout had walked off leaving a purse of gold where he had slept, and he ran after him to return it. Grateful, the marabout asked him what return he might make, and after some thought Daman Gille asked for a great knife or a sword that he might use to cut up the elephants he killed.

The marabout went on to Mecca and accomplished his pilgrimage, and then went on various commissions. He forgot about Daman Gille. But as he was preparing to depart, he paid a call on a great holy man in Mecca, and the holy man asked him if there weren't some promise he had forgotten. The marabout remembered Daman Gille, and told the great man about the hunter's request for a sword. The great man gave the marabout a sword. It was a sword of kingship, and when it was removed from its scabbard it shone with a great light.

The marabout returned to the Manden. At that time Daman Gille was out in the bush hunting elephants, and no one knew where he might be found. So the marabout entrusted the sword to Sunjata, the king of the Manden, to be held for Daman Gille, and he continued on his way.

After some time Daman Gille came to the king's town and stayed with his usual host there, a leatherworker. From the leatherworker, he learned that the king was holding a sword for him, brought from Mecca, and so he went to retrieve it. Now, Sunjata was well aware of the magical properties of the sword, and reluctant to let anyone else have a token of kingship within his own lands. So when the servant he had dispatched to the storehouse brought back the sword from Mecca, he said it was not the right one. He sent the servant to fetch a different blade, and the servant, understanding the king's mind, did so. But when the servant reappeared, the blade in his hands was again the sword from Mecca. This happened yet again, and Sunjata realized that he could not keep this sword from Daman Gille. So he gave it to the hunter, but he laid down a condition: that the hunter must leave his kingdom and settle in another land.

Daman Gille left the Manden and travelled north into Jara.

At that time, Jara was ruled by the Nyakhate clan. Daman Gille lived there for a time, and had a son. When the son grew up, the ruler of Jara was Bemba Nyakhate, and he was widely known as a cruel and evil man. The people of Jara performed a divination to learn how they might overthrow him: it required someone to rub an ointment on Bemba's hands which would drive him mad. The son of Daman Gille performed this deed, and Bemba vanished. Daman Gille's son was named king in his place, establishing the Diawara dynasty of Jara. The sword of kingship remained with the family until the nineteenth century; it is said to have vanished when al-Hajj Umar Tal conquered Jara.

THE MANINKA AND THE EMPIRE OF MALI

The empire of Mali was formed in the fertile lands around the headwaters of the Niger, in eastern Guinea and western Mali, and it counts as a successor state to the Soninke empire of Ghana, which lay somewhat to the north. The era of empire (c. 1250–1500) seems to have been something of a golden age in the region. Many peoples around this territory look to Mali for their origins or political legitimacy. The empire stretched from close to the Atlantic (the Gambia river) east to Timbuktu. The founder of the empire, Sunjata Keita, is also a culture hero to the Maninka, and his story is still retold in a vibrant oral tradition. In recorded history, the empire's most celebrated ruler was perhaps Mansa Musa, who made a pilgrimage to Mecca around 1325, and left enough gold along the way to place Mali firmly on the map of the medieval world. The empire declined in the fifteenth and sixteenth centuries, and eventually fragmented under blows from Songhay and Segou. In the nineteenth century, the warlord Samory Toure reconstituted a great state, and opposed French penetration of the territory, but was eventually defeated.

A RITUAL STORY OF CREATION

The following narrative was reported in the 1950s, associated with the reroofing ceremony of the Kama Bloñ, a sacred hut in the town of Kangaba. This ceremony takes place every seven years, and is performed by the Keita nobles, who claim descent from Sunjata, and by the Diabate (or Jebate) jeliw (griots), who

are traditionally linked to them. In the course of the ceremony,
the singers recite the history of the world, down to the establish-
ment of the shrine. The narrative has not been reproduced
elsewhere, although elements of it are attested in other contexts.
Since the 1950s the stories told at the reroofing ceremony have
changed and now include much Muslim material (see the next
story).

In the beginning, Mangala created an egg which contained
seeds and two pairs of beings. One of the beings within the egg
came to consciousness earlier than the others, and desired to
take over the work of creation. The being, later known as
Pemba (*fen-ba*, 'great thing'), tore loose from the womb and
descended to earth with that portion of the enveloping matrix
which held his umbilical cord. From the matrix he created the
earth, but it was sterile, and although he later succeeded in
planting seeds in this earth, they polluted the earth by using the
residual blood for moisture.

To purify the earth, the male portion of the other paired
being was sacrificed and came to earth in the form of water,
which washes all things. This being, named Faro, spirit of the
waters, is represented by twin catfish, perhaps because after
the rainy season catfish will follow the seasonal floods out of
river-beds and into fields. Faro came to earth in a great ark,
and landed in the mountains of Kri, in the heartland of the
Manden. His ark contained plants and animals and four pairs
of humans, male and female. The names of the men were
Kanisimbo, Kaniyogosimbo, Simbumba Tangnagati and Nunu.
The place where the ark came to earth became a shrine, near
Nyagasola in Guinea; a second shrine was later built in Kangaba, near Bamako in Mali.

Three other beings also came down from heaven: first Surakata, the ancestor of the *jeliw* or griots (the praise-singers and
musicians of the Mande) and then the ancestor of the blacksmiths. Each of them in turn appealed to the heavens for rain,
Surakata by beating a drum made from the skull of the heavenly
Faro, and the blacksmith by beating a rock with his hammer.
The rains came in answer to the blacksmith's prayer. Later an

old woman came down, Muso Koroni. She was the female twin of Pemba and had remained within the world egg, but she shared something of Pemba's rebellious nature and she soon fled east to join him where he had settled, far to the east of Kri.

Kanisimbo was the first ancestor to die, and on his death Simbumba Tangnagati created the first *balafon*, a xylophone, and with its music he restored Kanisimbo to life. But the resurrected ancestor did not return to human form. He became instead a great serpent and withdrew into the caves of the mountain. The fourth ancestor, Nunu, travelled east along the course taken by Muso Koroni, and he eventually found her and settled in an area near present-day Segou. There, he too died, having been led by Muso Koroni to capture and kill one of the catfish of Faro. On his death, Faro sent the antelope, *dage*, to restore fertility to the land; the antelope travelled from Segou west to the land of Kri and in its path the earth became green and covered with plants. To commemorate this event, the blacksmith carved the antelope mask which is now well known as a *chi-wara*; the *chi-wara*'s dance is associated with agricultural rites.

Faro travelled east to oppose and overcome Pemba, whose actions continued to be a source of pollution and impurity in the world. The course of Faro's travels can be seen in the course of the Niger river, running from the mountains of Kri down to the inner delta. They met and struggled, and Faro was victorious.

MIGRATION FROM MECCA

This narrative was given at the start of a performance of the epic of Sunjata, and may serve to illustrate a conflation of traditional west African motifs with a Muslim context.

Jon Bilal served the Prophet Muhammad in Mecca, and became the first muezzin (caller-to-prayers) of Islam. Jon Bilal's oldest son, Mamadu Kanu, had three sons: Kanu Simbon, Kanu Nyogon Simbon and Lawali Simbon. Because of his love for

Jon Bilal, the Prophet Muhammad on his death bequeathed to each of the grandsons a chest, with the instructions that they should take the chests to a distant land and there they should found their own kingdom. They should not open the chests until they had been three years in that land.

The three young men took their chests and travelled far to the west from Mecca, until they came into the Manden. There they settled and founded the village of Kri-koroni (old Kri). They laboured there for three years, and at last determined to open their chests. That of the eldest, Kanu Simbon, was full of gold. Kanu Nyogon Simbon's share was the bark of trees. Lawali Simbon's chest contained nothing but earth. The division of wealth seemed to them a great injustice, but they could not believe that the Prophet Muhammad, who had so loved their grandfather Bilal, would be unfair and so they decided it was a mystery they must clarify. So they set out for the land of Kabaku (Mystery) to ask him to solve this riddle.

On the way, they came to a row of three wells. The two outermost wells were full of water, and it flowed through the air from one well to another. The central well was dry.

'This is a mystery,' said one of the brothers. 'We are coming close to the land of Kabaku.'

They met a man carrying a gourd of water, and crying out in thirst. 'This must be Mystery,' said the brothers.

'No,' said the man. 'I am only his water-bearer. You must go further to find Kabaku.'

They found a child sitting on an anthill. His hair was black on one side of his head and white on the other. 'This must be Kabaku,' said the brothers.

'No,' said the child. 'I am his son. You must go further to find him.'

They found an old man lying on a mat, his eyes misty with age.

'This man is Mystery,' said the brothers.

'No,' said the old man. 'I am Kabaku's younger brother. You must continue on your way a bit further to find him.'

They met a grown man and greeted him.

'People of the Manden!' he exclaimed. 'Welcome! I am

Kabaku. You have come to me with a problem. Explain it to me.'

They told him of their three chests, filled with such strange substances.

'You do not understand', said Kabaku, 'that gold is worth no more than the bark of trees or earth. The chests are of equal value, if used in the right way. But more important than any of these is work. If you work you will prosper in the Manden.'

The brothers accepted Kabaku's interpretation. 'But tell us,' they asked, 'of the curious things we saw as we came. There were three wells . . .'

'The wells', said Kabaku, 'show that the rich, those who have, will overlook the poor, even their neighbours.'

'There was a man with a gourd . . .'

'A miser gains nothing from what he hoards.'

'There was a child whose head was . . .'

'Knowledge does not belong only to the old. The young who enquire will learn.'

'And an old man on a mat . . .'

'Work is much older than him, and after a lifetime spent in honest work you will have the right to rest.'

The brothers returned to the Manden, pondering the advice of Kabaku. After they arrived, they set about planting fields. But as soon as Kanu Simbon began to cut the trees to clear his fields, Kanu Nyogon Simbon came running.

'My brother,' he said, 'you are touching my heritage. You must compensate me for the trees.' Kanu Simbon agreed, and gave his brother a share of the gold from the chest he had brought from Mecca.

When the two older brothers began to turn the earth to prepare the soil for planting, Lawali Simbon came to them. 'My brothers,' he said, 'the earth was the share given to me, and if you wish to use it you must compensate me, as owner of the earth.'

The brothers agreed, and so they each shared the portions that had been allotted to them. For a time they prospered, and men came from other lands to live with them. Then came a period without rains, and the inhabitants of the Manden began to suffer. Lawali Simbon helped them, because he had stored food in his granaries and he shared it with the people.

After a time, they determined they should choose a king. Kanu Simbon objected that he was the eldest and should by right become king, but the people answered that they wished the powers of earth and sky to approve their choice. It is said that they dug a pit and hid a man with a great drum in the pit, then covered it over.

On the day they had named, the three brothers and their people came out and invoked the heavens: which of them should be king?

Kanu Simbon stepped forward, but there was no sign. Kanu Nyogon Simbon stepped forward, but again there was no sign. Lawali Simbon stepped forward. The heavens were silent.

'Let us call upon the earth,' cried the people.

'Shall Kanu Simbon be our king?' cried a spokesman. The earth was silent.

'Shall Kanu Nyogon Simbon be our king?' Again, the earth was silent.

'Shall Lawali Simbon be our king?' This time, the earth (or the man in the pit) answered with a rumble, and so Lawali Simbon became the ruler in Kri-koroni.

SUNJATA AND THE EMPIRE OF MALI

What follows is a short retelling of the epic of Sunjata, a great narrative corpus with many variants and versions recorded over the past century.

In the earliest days, the Manden was divided into three kingdoms: Do, Kri and Tabon. Dumogo-nya-mogo was the ruler of the land of Do. One day he slaughtered an ox and invited all his relatives to join in the feast. But he excluded Du Kamisa, his father's sister, although she had witnessed his birth and it was she who buried his umbilical cord. She was outraged and swore revenge. She took the shape of a great wild buffalo with horns of gold and tail of silver, and she began to kill people in the land of Do. No one working in the fields was safe: the buffalo would charge out of the bushes at the edge of the field and gore or trample the farmers and their helpers. People walking on paths between villages would be slaughtered. Dumogo-nya-mogo sent hunters out to kill the buffalo, but they died. The buffalo killed them all. The land went into decline: fields were not cleared, the earth was not turned, crops were not harvested. No one dared to leave the village space.

The ruler sent out word of the trouble facing his land, and men came to hunt the buffalo. They were killed. The buffalo with the horns of gold and the tail of silver overcame all the hunters and warriors and adventurers.

Two poor brothers in the Manden decided to try their fate against the buffalo. They consulted a diviner before they left, and they were told they must befriend the first person they met when they came to Do. They were called Dan Mansa Wulanden and Dan Mansa Wulanba. They assembled what supplies they could find and set out on the paths that led to Do. As they approached the town, they came across a decrepit hut, whose mud walls were crumbling and whose thatch was thin and sparse. In front of the hut, an old woman sat staring at an empty fireplace.

'Greetings, grandmother,' said the two young men. She did not answer them. 'We hope you are in good health.' Still she said nothing, which was unusual. The elder brother was about to say something sharp when the younger nudged him. 'Remember the oracle.'

'Have you no fire, grandmother?' asked the elder. The answer was clear. The two young men put down their packs and went into the bush looking for firewood. Soon they found enough to make two bundles, which they brought back and laid beside the hut.

'You have no water, grandmother,' observed the younger brother. The two young men found vessels beside the house and walked down to the stream. They filled the pots and returned to the hut.

'Let us prepare you a meal,' they said, and they took some rice from their provisions and set it to boil over the fire. Then they prepared a sauce with the meat from an animal they had killed along the way and some herbs they had found. When the two parts of the meal were ready, they spread the rice in a dish and poured the sauce over it. They placed the dish in front of the old woman. She leaned her head forward to smell the food, then she looked down at the dish and up at the young men. Hesitantly, her hand went out and made a small ball of rice which she dipped in the sauce. She brought it to her mouth.

'You must eat some meat, grandmother,' said the brothers, and they each picked out chunks of the meat and fed them to her. Bite by bite, the old woman ate the entire dish of food. Then she leaned back against the wall of the hut and her eyes closed again. The young men washed the dishes and sat beside her. Night fell. The old woman rose from her seat and withdrew into the hut. The two brothers spread mats near the fire and slept there.

In the morning they built up the fire again and set some meal to boil. When the old woman came out of the hut, she found her breakfast already prepared. She sat down, and again the young men fed her. When she had finished the dish she belched loudly in appreciation.

'Ha! children!' she said. 'You have been very kind to me. You have shown me kindness that I did not receive even from my kinsmen. I must make some return to you. Tell me why you have come to the land of Do.'

'Ah, grandmother,' they said. 'You need make no return. You are our elder, we owe you our help. But we cannot refuse your help, if you wish to give it. We have come to hunt the buffalo of Do, for in our homes we are poor.'

'Many men have hunted the buffalo, and they are dead,' said the old woman. 'If you wish to escape their fate you will need my help. I shall give it to you. In the hut you shall find three eggs and a spindle. You must use these items when hunting the buffalo. Do not shoot an arrow at the buffalo; the arrow will not harm it. Shoot the spindle at the buffalo. Then you must flee, using the eggs to delay the buffalo as it pursues you.'

The brothers found the items she spoke of. They placed the eggs and the spindle in their hunting bags and took up their bows.

'There is one more thing,' said the old woman. 'If you kill the buffalo, the king will offer you a reward. You are young men; he will offer you a wife and give you your choice of the maidens in the village. You must not choose the beautiful maidens he will show you. There is a hunchbacked girl covered with warts. You must choose her. She will be the mother of an empire.'

They thanked the old woman again and proceeded towards the village. When they came to the edge of the fields they circled around until they found a trail, and there they entered the bush. They walked very carefully, listening attentively for any sound of the buffalo. They heard nothing, but soon they saw a flash of light among the shrubs and grass, and then they saw the buffalo with its horns of gold and tail of silver.

The elder brother, Dan Mansa Wulanba, was paralysed at the sight. He could not move. But the younger brother pulled the spindle from the quiver and set it to his bow. He drew the string and released the shaft. It struck the buffalo in the shoulder. The beast bellowed so loudly that the two men fell down, and then it leaped into the air. As it came down it tossed its head and sniffed, to find its enemy. The two brothers backed away, and then, when it had spotted them, they turned and ran. As they ran, the younger brother took an egg from his bag and threw it behind him. They glanced back and saw that where the egg fell a pond had appeared and was spreading. The buffalo charged into the water, but it could not continue its gallop; it had to swim across the pond, and by the time it reached the further bank the brothers had pulled far ahead. But the buffalo ran more quickly than they. It soon caught up with them. Again, the younger brother threw an egg. This time a thick hedge of spiny bushes appeared, and the buffalo was caught among the tough stems. But it trampled its way through. Soon it was close behind, and the third egg was thrown. A small mountain appeared, and the buffalo was forced to climb up and over the hill.

By the time the buffalo reappeared, the two brothers had reached the edge of the fields. They turned there, to await the buffalo, and soon saw that they were out of danger: the beast was staggering, half-blind. When it reached the fields, it fell dead.

'My brother!' exclaimed Dan Mansa Wulanba, the elder. 'You have done a great deed! Your courage is surpassing! You have slain the buffalo!' In this way he became his younger brother's praise-singer, or *jeli*. He became the ancestor of the Jabate clan of singers, who are bound by hereditary links to the Traore clan, descendants of the younger brother.

They discussed what to do next, and decided it would be best to bring tokens to the village. They cut off the silver tail from the buffalo, and broke off the golden horns. One brother left his sandal, the other the leather sheath to his knife. Then they went into the village and sat down at the edge of the market square.

At the end of the day, a villager who had ventured out to look at his fields found the dead buffalo. He came running back and the word spread. Soon the ruler, Dumogo-nya-mogo, came out with his advisers, and made his way across the fields to inspect the carcass of the buffalo. When he returned, his advisers announced that the buffalo was dead and a reward would be given to the person who had killed it. Soon, men were jostling each other to claim the reward. But they all failed the test the king set them: he asked them to put on the sandal he had found by the buffalo, or to produce the knife to fit the leather sheath. No one had such a knife; no one's foot fitted the sandal exactly. Soon all the claimants had been dismissed and the advisers were left wondering who might have killed the buffalo.

'There are two young men in the market square,' said one. 'They are not from Do. Perhaps they know something of this affair.' They called the two brothers. The sandal fitted one of the brothers perfectly, and he had its mate. The other brother could show the knife that fitted the sheath. Then the brothers opened their hunting bags and brought out the silver tail and the golden horns.

'Ah! These are the killers of the buffalo!' cried all the people, and the ruler told them he would give them a reward: their choice of the most beautiful maidens of the village. The maidens

were assembled and brought before the brothers, and both
young men were tempted. But they remembered the last words
of the old woman who had helped them so greatly, and so they
refused the beautiful maidens. They asked instead about an
ugly maiden with a crooked back, and she was brought out:
Sogolon Conde, known as Sogolon Kuduma, Sogolon of the
warts. The people of the village were astounded and muttered
in amazement, and some in disgust, as the two young men took
the maiden and led her from the village.

The elder brother tried to lie with the maiden that night, but
she repelled him. Neither young man could approach her, and
so when they returned to their home in the Manden, in Narena,
they were puzzled what they were to do with her. But the ruler
of Narena, Nare Famagan Cenyi the Handsome, had consulted
a diviner who told him that two young men would bring a
strange woman to Narena and he must marry this woman, for
her son would found an empire. When he heard that two
brothers had come with a strange woman, he sent for them. He
offered them a different woman in exchange; it is said that she
was Nana Triban, sister of Famagan Cenyi and a powerful
sorceress. They agreed, and left Sogolon Kuduma with Nare
Famagan.

Different stories are told of the wedding night of those two.
Some say that the man was able to sleep with her only after he
held a knife to her throat, or that her pubic hair stretched into
great porcupine quills that held him off. Some also say that his
knife had magic powers, and that when he laid it on her skin
the warts fell away and her back straightened, so that she
became beautiful. They also say that after the marriage was
consummated, Sogolon wished to observe the dancing in the
square, and so she stretched her neck so that her head went out
of the chamber, across the courtyard, and over the wall so she
could see what was being done.

Whatever the truth, Sogolon Conde became pregnant. By
coincidence, another wife of Nare Famagan also became pregnant at that time: Sasuma Berete. The two women came to term
at the same time. It is not certain who gave birth first. It is said
that Sogolon gave birth and an old woman went to bring the

news to Nare Famagan. But along the way she met some people seated around a bowl of food, and they invited her to join them. She did so, and did not rise until all the food was eaten. By that time, Sasuma Berete had also given birth, and the messenger had reached Nare Famagan, who declared the son of Sasuma Berete, named Dankaran Tuman, to be the first born. The old woman protested that Sogolon's son had been born first, but Nare Famagan would not listen to her. He declared the news that had reached his ears first was the news that counted. In this way Sogolon's son became the second-born. He was named Sunjata.

Sasuma Berete was uneasy about her son's claim to primacy, and determined to remove Sunjata from the succession. She consulted diviners and magic-workers, and they cast a spell on Sunjata so that he was crippled in his legs. He could not walk; he crawled everywhere like an animal. His condition was a humiliation to his mother that not even the birth of several other children could erase. Everywhere, she heard people talking about the worthless son of Sogolon, how he could do nothing like other children and was little better than a beast. Years passed, and still Sunjata crawled around the compound.

It was the time of year when women prepared a special meal, seasoned with the leaves of the baobab tree. The children went swarming over the trees to pluck the leaves and bring them to their mothers. Sogolon had no children to bring her the baobab leaves: Sunjata could not climb, and the others were too young. She swallowed her pride and went to Sasuma Berete, her co-wife, to ask her for some baobab leaves. Sasuma Berete said she could not spare any, and asked Sogolon, 'Surely your son can bring you the leaves?'

Sogolon returned quickly to her hut, walking almost blindly because of the tears of rage in her eyes. She almost tripped over Sunjata as she came to her fireplace. 'Oh, will you not rise up?' she exclaimed. Sunjata saw her pain and sorrow, and resolve filled his heart. 'I shall rise,' he said to his mother. 'Tell the blacksmiths to forge me iron bars, and with them I shall stand up.'

Sogolon went to the blacksmiths, and for the wife of Nare

Famagan they forged two strong iron bars. She brought them to Sunjata, who seized one in each hand and heaved against them. They snapped in two, like twigs. Sadly, Sogolon brought the fragments back to the smiths who marvelled at the breaks and then set about forging iron bars that were three times as strong. The smiths themselves brought the bars to Sunjata, but again the bars broke when he put his weight upon them.

'Iron bars will not serve,' he said. 'Mother, fetch me a staff of *jonba* wood.'

Sogolon went into the bush and found a *jonba* tree. Before she laid her small axe to the tree, she swore an oath. 'If I have been faithful to my husband, if I have been a dutiful wife, if I have borne the troubles put upon me as one should, then let this staff help my son to rise.' Then she cut a staff and brought it to Sunjata. He set both hands upon it and pulled. Then, hand over hand, he drew himself up against the staff, so that his body and then his legs straightened beneath him. Finally he was standing erect, with only one hand upon the wood. He took a step, and then another step. Watching, Sogolon was overcome with joy. She sang, for her heart was full, and some of the songs are still remembered. 'Today is a great day,' she sang. 'There has never been a day like today.' As she sang, Sunjata walked out of the compound and down the path to the baobab tree. She followed, still singing out her joy, and as she did so the other women in the neighbourhood came, saw and joined her in wonder.

Sunjata came to the baobab tree. He stretched his arms round its trunk, and somehow seized the entire tree (a baobab tree can be five metres in diameter). He shook it and uprooted it. The children up in the branches fell to the ground, and from this incident comes a praise-name for Sunjata: 'bone-breaking Jata'. Then he carried the tree back into his mother's compound.

'Mother,' he said, 'now the other women will have to ask you for their baobab leaves.'

Sunjata took to hunting, and became a great hunter who kept the entire town supplied with meat. But he did nothing to challenge the standing of Dankaran Tuman, whom he considered his older brother. Dankaran would receive the second share of meat, after that of his father, and his mother the third. But Sasuma Berete was not reassured, and Dankaran Tuman shared her uneasiness. Nare Famagan the handsome died after some time, and Dankaran Tuman was named ruler in his place. Sunjata did not change his behaviour: Dankaran Tuman received the part of the hunter's kill that went to the ruler, and others were served later.

Dankaran Tuman resolved to be rid of his brother. He sent an ox to the nine witches of the Manden, asking that they do away with Sunjata. But Sunjata heard about this; his distribution of meat throughout the town had made him many friends. He went to the nine witches, whose leader is said to have been Nana Triban, his father's sister, given to the hunter brothers who killed the buffalo of Do. He gave them nine buffaloes, one for each witch, and they agreed that they would refuse the gift from Dankaran Tuman and accept Sunjata's offering.

But the signs were clear, and on the advice of all around him Sunjata decided to go into exile. His mother and her other children accompanied them, and before them went the old woman singer Tumu Maniya, singing the song of the bow: 'Pick up your bow, Jata, pick up your bow and go.' (Some people say the song was composed when Sunjata bent the iron bars while trying to rise.)

He went through the lands of the Manden, but wherever he stopped, a messenger from Dankaran Tuman soon followed and bribed the ruler or gave orders, so that Sunjata was told he was unwelcome. He travelled further and further until he left the Manden entirely and came to Mema, which was ruled by Farin Tunkara. There he and his family settled, and there he took service with the king as a warrior and a hunter.

In the Manden, affairs were not calmed by Sunjata's departure. Soon, the kingdom was threatened by a powerful neighbour: Sumanguru (sometimes called Sumaworo), the ruler of the Sossos, was exerting his might. Sumanguru was a man of extraordinary powers. It was said he was the child of two, or even three mothers: the pregnancy would move from one mother to another, one day at a time, and it lasted far longer than the usual period. The baby was born only after one mother, Sunsun or Dabi, realized that at night her child was leaving the womb to play in the dark. On the advice of a diviner, she left a mortar lying on the ground; the fetus mistook it for the womb and curled up in it and so was discovered at daybreak. Sumanguru was the man who had brought musical instruments into the world. One of them cost him his sister: the *balafon*. He heard the spirits of the wild playing it and asked them to sell it to him, but he could not pay their price at the time: they wanted the life of a family member, and his parents were dead and his sister had been given away in marriage. But his sister learned of his situation, and once her child Fakoli had been weaned she went of her own accord to the spirits, and they gave Sumanguru the *balafon*. He kept it in a secret chamber along with other items of magical power.

Hoping to appease Sumanguru, Dankaran Tuman sent him one of his sisters as a bride, and with her he sent Jankuma Doka, the singer. When they came to Sosso, Jankuma Doka somehow sensed the presence of the secret chamber and was drawn to it. Sumanguru at that time was off hunting. Jankuma Doka came in, sat before the *balafon*, and began to play it. From afar, Sumanguru sensed the intrusion into his secret chamber and returned immediately, prepared to kill whoever it was who had entered. As he approached, Jankuma Doka began a song:

> 'Sumanguru, the first and native king,
> Sumanguru with the hat of human skin
> Sumanguru with the shirt of human skin
> Sumanguru with the trousers of human skin
> Sumanguru with the shoes of human skin.'

Hearing the song of praise, Sumanguru was appeased. 'It is sweet', he said, 'to be praised by another,' and so he spared Jankuma Doka's life. But to keep him in his service, he cut the singer's ankle tendons, and he renamed him: Bala Faseke Kuyate. The descendants of Bala Faseke Kuyate preserve the *balafon* of Sumanguru in Niagassola, in Guinea.

But in other regards, Sumanguru was not satisfied with the offering made by Dankaran Tuman. He invaded and easily conquered the Manden; Dankaran Tuman fled into the forests of Guinea, where he and the people who accompanied him became known as the Kissi because they called their new home Kissidugu (place of safety).

Sumanguru established his rule over the Manden, and the people were very unhappy. Every aspect of their lives was controlled, they could not speak freely, and Sumanguru imposed heavy taxes. The people of the Manden wondered what to do: who could save them? And some remembered Sunjata, the hunter, who had gone into exile. But where had he gone? They did not know.

A group went to seek him, among them the singer, Tumu Maniya. They took with them typical plants of the Manden: leaves from the shea tree, spices. In each town they came to they laid out their wares, and because the people outside the Manden did not know what they were, they passed them by. So it went until they came to Mema.

They laid out their Manden spices in the market and sat waiting. Sunjata's sister came to the market, for since their mother was old she no longer went out to supply the household. Sogolon Kulunkan, the daughter, looked over the wares on display, and was amazed to see plants that she recognized, plants from her home. 'Ah!' she exclaimed. 'These are from the Manden!' She quickly bought the supplies and invited the travellers to come and eat with them at home. When they reached the compound, however, she realized they had no meat to cook for the meal. But Sogolon Kulunkan was the true daughter of Sogolon Conde, and she had inherited powers from her mother. She knew her brothers were hunting in the bush, and she knew through her magic sight that they had each killed a large antelope. She drew the livers and hearts from the two kills and brought them to her fireside, so she could cook them as a meal for the guests.

In the bush, Sunjata and his brother Manding Bori began to butcher their kills. They were amazed to find that the two large antelopes had no hearts or livers. Then Sunjata laughed. 'This must be the doing of our sister,' he said. 'Surely she has guests she wishes to feed, and there was no meat in the house.'

'How dare she take the parts of our kills!' protested Manding Bori, and he fumed about his sister's arrogance all the way back to the town. When they reached the compound he shouted aloud in anger, and Sogolon Kulunkan's wrap-around cloth fell from her hips, baring her legs and groin. She cried, and the cloth rose up again around her. Again Manding Bori shouted and the cloth fell, again Sogolon covered herself.

'Control yourself, brother,' ordered Sunjata. 'You have already shown that your children will never be kings.' He moved forward to greet his sister and then to meet the guests. After all had eaten, the guests explained their mission. They told how Sumanguru had come upon the Manden, driving out Dankaran Tuman, and how the people felt oppressed and wished for a saviour to free them.

'You are the son of the king,' they concluded. 'The people call you. You must return to the Manden.'

'It is not that simple,' answered Sunjata. 'I am also the son of my mother, and she is old. She cannot travel to return to the Manden, and I will not leave her here alone. So long as my mother lives, I cannot return to the Manden.'

That night Sunjata went out into the dark, and he offered a vow. 'If it is my fate to rule the Manden, if I am truly destined to lead the three and thirty clans of the Manden: the clans of quiver bearers, the Manding *mori* clans (the Muslim leaders), the clans of the blacksmiths and the *jeliw* and the leatherworkers, if I am to become king, then let my mother die tonight in peace.'

That night, Sogolon Conde, Sunjata's mother, died. They wrapped her in a cloth, and then Sunjata went to Mema Farin Tunkara to tell him that his mother had died and he wished to bury her. He asked the king for land.

The king had advisers, three old men known as See-all, Hear-all and Know-all. They reminded the king that this man was a stranger who had come among them, and that he should ask for good payment for the land he was to give as a resting place for Sunjata's mother. The king asked Sunjata for nine mithqals of gold.

'It is a high price,' answered Sunjata. 'I shall bring it to you later in the day.' But when he returned, he gave the advisers a battered old calabash bowl filled with dust, ashes, arrowheads and partridge feathers.

'What does this mean?' the king asked his advisers. 'This payment is not gold.'

'It is a warning,' answered the advisers. 'If we do not give him the land, he will return with war. That is the message of the arrowheads. Our houses will be burned and broken down. That is the message of the dust and the ashes. Partridges shall play where we lived. That is the message of the feathers. It is best to give him the land.'

They gave Sunjata the land, and he buried Sogolon Conde. Then he and his remaining family, and the envoys who had come to seek him, took the path of return to the Manden.

They came to the river, to the passage which was served by the boats of the Somono boatmen. On their way out, Sogolon Conde had given the leader of the boatmen two silver bracelets. He asked why she made him this gift, and she answered, '*Sinin ku* [a thing for tomorrow].' After Sumanguru took power, he gave orders to the boatmen that they were to transport no one across the river without permission from the court. The boats lay idle on the far bank.

Sunjata came to the river and shouted across. He summoned the chief of the boatmen and asked for passage. The chief of the boatmen answered he could not let them pass without permission from Sumanguru.

'Ah, chief!' cried Sunjata, 'raise your arms!' Intrigued, the boatman chief raised his arms in the air.

'Cross your wrists!' cried Sunjata, and the chief did so. As his wrists met, the two silver bracelets rattled against each other.

'What was that sound?' asked Sunjata. 'Was it not a gift that my mother called "a thing for tomorrow"?' The chief of the boatmen did not answer, but turned and ordered the boats to fetch Sunjata's party across the river.

People rallied to Sunjata from across the Manding. Village chiefs and rulers of lands assembled their soldiers, the bowmen and the swordsmen and the riders, and came to join Sunjata. Sumanguru in turn assembled his soldiers and came to meet the challenger. There are many stories about the battles they fought, and where they took place. Some say they met four times, others that they met nine times, others that they met twenty times. But in all these battles Sumanguru's forces had the upper hand; as they say, the laughter went to the Sossos, and the tears to the Manden. While Sunjata's men fought bravely, somehow they could not defeat Sumanguru. Even when they thought they had him pinned down or cornered he would somehow escape them and turn defeat into victory.

Spirits were getting low. They were raised slightly by a defection from Sumanguru's army: his nephew Fakoli who came to the side of Sunjata. Fakoli was the son of the sister who had given herself to the jinns to obtain the *balafon* for Sunjata. He had an extraordinary wife: when she cooked, her one pot would feed as many people as the three hundred pots prepared by his uncle Sumanguru's three hundred wives. Sumanguru had taken Fakoli's wife, jealous of her powers. Fakoli renounced his kinship and came to Sunjata. He confirmed to them what they had already guessed: that Sumanguru was protected by more than weapons, and that to defeat him they would have to learn the secret of his occult powers.

Sogolon Kulunkan went to Sumanguru's capital. Her hair was done in intricate braids, her body was rubbed with aromatic oil, the cloths that covered her body shimmered and somehow highlighted the sway of her hips. She came by Sumanguru's palace, and soon she was invited in. It was not long before she and the king were seated at a dinner, and his eyes followed the movement of the cloth around her shoulders, and the grace of her arms as she reached out for food. He quickly decided that he must have this woman, that very night.

But when he asked her into his bedchamber, she demurred. Up to that point she had seemed more than willing. She matched smile for smile, she offered him meaty morsels, she shrugged in ways that almost made the cloth slip from her shoulders, revealing hints of a bosom. But she stopped at the door.

'I do not know enough about you,' she said. 'When a man

and a woman share a bed, there should be no secrets. I must be assured of your trust.'

He argued with her, but she held firm. In the course of the argument, Sumanguru's mother intervened. She had heard of the strange woman who had appeared, and she was worried for her son. She came to him and listened for a time to the discussion. To her, it seemed clear what was going on.

'Oh, my son!' she called. 'Do not give your secrets to a one-night woman!'

Sumanguru was enraged at the intrusion and the interruption. He turned and seized the old woman violently, dragged her across the room where he had been eating with his guest, and threw her out of the door. Then he shut the door. When he turned back, Sogolon Kulunkan was standing before the small fire, and somehow the shadows limned her body and her bright smile.

'I am a man of power,' said Sumanguru. 'Surely you must know that. I am the king.'

'It is clear you are powerful,' said Sogolon. 'You are well protected. But how can you be sure no one will somehow violate the secrets? Can you be sure of your protection?'

'No ordinary matter can harm me,' said Sumanguru, coming close to her.

'That must be true,' she answered, looking up at him. 'So you are safe from everything?'

'Not everything,' he admitted. 'An arrow . . . Not an ordinary arrow, but one tipped with the spur of a white cock. That could harm me.'

'No one makes arrows from the pieces of a fowl,' answered Sogolon Kulunkan, and she moved closer to him. 'Come, let us go within.'

Sumanguru's desire was not immediately satisfied. Although she entered the bedchamber with him, Sogolon Kulunkan broke off before any serious lovemaking had occurred and said that she must go to wash herself. Sumanguru waited a while. He called. Her voice answered from the neighbouring privy. He called again, and again she answered. The third time he went to see what was keeping her: she had fled. She had left two small tokens which she had enchanted to answer for her.

At the next battle, the tide changed. Sunjata's forces had the secret of Sumanguru's power. Sunjata carried his bow, and kept ready a new arrow, one tipped with the spur of a white cock. Sumanguru avoided him, and this time the forces under Sunjata were able to overcome the Sosso army. Sumanguru fled on horseback, closely pursued by Sunjata, Fakoli and several other leaders of the army. Sumanguru caught up his wife and charged away. They reached the Niger river, just as Sunjata caught up with him. Sumanguru's horse gave a great leap and landed on the far side of the river, just as Sunjata's arrow struck the rider. Sumanguru, his wife and his horse all turned to stone; it is said you can still see them there today, at the falls of Koulikoro.

Sunjata and his generals turned back into the Manden. In Sumanguru's palace they found Bala Faseke Kuyate, crippled by Sumanguru. They made Sumanguru's son his steed, to carry him everywhere he wished to go.

Soon after the last battle, Sunjata and all the leaders of the Manden held a great assembly at a place called Kurukan Fugan. There they established the rules that would govern their new state. They apportioned territories and defined principles. Thus was the empire of Mali born.

There are very few stories about the death of Sunjata. The most common says that he drowned while crossing the river, although the context varies. Instead, most performances of the epic end with the growth of the empire, and in particular the conquest of the Jolof by Tira Magan Traore, which is told below in the section on the Mandinka (Chapter 66).

THE BAMANA OF THE
MIDDLE NIGER

The Bamana or Bambara (the older French name) are the people occupying the lands along the middle Niger, between the cities of Bamako and Djenne. The population of this region is ethnically diverse, originally composed of Soninke, Fulani, Bozo/ Sorko (hunters) and many other groups who have fused together in the course of a long and tumultuous history, under the sway of the empires of Mali and Songhai and then the Tukolor Islamic conquests of the mid-nineteenth century. The Bamana states were the kingdoms of Kaarta, on the north side of the Niger, and Segou, on the south; of the two, Segou was by far the more powerful. Their period of eminence lasted from the early eighteenth century to the middle of the nineteenth, when both were conquered by the forces of al-Hajj Umar Tal. The Bamana language, very close to Maninka, its western neighbour and parent, has now become the dominant African language of the region. During the period of the kingdoms, warfare and slave-taking were the principal economic activities; slaves were sold for guns, or set to work on farms. The river and the rains make millet-farming possible; fishing and trade are also major activities. The Bamana also have strong artistic traditions, and while most are now Muslim, one popular etymology for their name is 'they who refused [Islam]', stressing that in the period of the kingdoms they held closely to their traditional beliefs.

THE CREATION

The original source of this narrative was not identified by the scholar who first reported it in 1951, but it appears to have been a branch of the Komo initiatory association. It is also possible that a number of separate accounts were combined to create this master-narrative, which has strong parallels with the Maninka myth given in Chapter 64.

The sky-god sent Pemba ('great thing') down to create the earth. Pemba used the knowledge and the materials with which he had been equipped, and in the form of a whirlwind he travelled to the four corners of the earth and so shaped the land into hills and plains and valleys. At the same time, the sky-god sent another spirit, Faro, into the upper air, and there Faro performed a similar movement, establishing the limits of heavens by his movement. Faro was called to assist Pemba, who proved unable to complete the fashioning of the earth, and Faro fell to earth in the form of rain, which filled all the empty spaces left by Pemba as he had moved the clods of earth about. It was Faro's presence that made possible life on earth.

Pemba remained a whirlwind (and this is still a preferred form for spirits) for seven years, and then settled and took the shape of a great acacia tree. But the tree died for lack of water; the trunk decomposed down to a great log under which a pile of dust built up. He eventually moistened this dust with his saliva and blew life into it. A creature came into being that was part fox and part human, a female who is known as Muso Koroni of the white head. She was the female double of Pemba, endowed with his powers and knowledge, and she was also his wife. She brought forth all sorts of animals and creatures which began to populate the earth in riotous disorder. Pemba wished to establish his authority over these creatures, and so he took the form of a *balanza* tree, the acacia albida which unlike other trees remains green throughout the dry season.

The humans (whom Faro had created) took refuge beneath this tree, and eventually came to worship it since it was not subject to the rule of the seasons. The tree instructed them, and they acquired arts. At that time, humans were immortal, but they had no language. They were fed by fruits sent down from heaven by a spirit of the air whom Faro had set in place. The fruits were the nuts of the shea tree, also known as the *karite*, from which oil is made. One day, after a woman had eaten some nuts and made her hands oily, she wiped them on the trunk of the tree. Pemba was pleased by the savoury moisture, and asked for more; soon, all the women and later the men were making offerings of *karite* oil to the tree.

From offerings of oil, the demands of the tree soon increased. He asked the women to become his brides, coupling with a wooden member which was shaped for the purpose, and from the lovemaking he drew renewed strength. But this behaviour created problems, for Muso Koroni became jealous of the women with whom she shared Pemba's love, and developed ill-will and malice. These emotions became so strong that she was estranged from Pemba and fled far away; in the course of these throes, she mutilated her genitals and so brought about menstruation among women. Her malice also infected everything she touched, so that the earth lost its purity. At the same time, her actions eventually benefited humankind, for it was she who discovered the skills of farming and gardening.

The *balanza* tree that was Pemba grew ever hungrier for power, for the world was growing and he needed more energy to rule it. He soon discovered another source, when a human accidentally bled upon his bark and brought him a burst of heat, which is the materialization of occult strength. He began to require blood-offerings from the humans: the men would go to the tree and offer their blood several times a year. In exchange for this gift, the tree would rejuvenate them when they became old.

Eventually, however, the tree's demands became too great for the humans to fulfil. They were too exhausted even to find themselves food. One day, a woman fainted near a patch of *ngoyo* fruit (a form of wild tomato); Faro came to her in a dream and told her to eat the fruit. She did so, and was strengthened so that she went swimming in the waters of the river. There Faro took her as an offering to himself. He then challenged Pemba: while Pemba had some power over the earth, life required water which was the domain of Faro. Pemba uprooted himself and lumbered forth to struggle with Faro, but he was eventually defeated. After his defeat, humans lost much of their respect for him, although they still continued to make offerings to him. But after one disrespectful man climbed to the top of the tree and cut off the fruit that was the quintessence of the blood-offerings the people made, the tree ceased to protect them from death. The man who performed the outrage fled to the west, but could not escape his fate: he fell dead. The people among whom he died did not realize he had committed a sacrilege, and so they buried the body; in this way, his taint spread into the earth and all people who came in contact with it eventually died.

THE KULIBALI DYNASTIES

Both Segou and Kaarta were ruled at first by different branches of the Kulibali lineage. The lineage that ruled Segou died out practically with the founder, however, while that in the Kaarta remained in power until the second dynasty to rule Segou, the Diarras, conquered them at the end of the eighteenth century. The legend is retold from various accounts collected in the past century.

Two brothers, Nchi and Nchian, came from the east, pursued by enemies. When they reached the river, they thought they were trapped, but a *poyon*, a great fish, emerged from the water and offered to carry them across. The brothers quickly accepted the fish's offer. This is how the Kulibalis got their name: they crossed the river without a canoe (*kulun bali*). But when they reached the other side, one of the brothers then turned back and killed the fish that had helped them. Some say he did so because his wife complained that their children would have nothing to eat. The two brothers then separated: one remained on the near shore of the river, in the area that would become

Segou, while the other moved on into the area that would be the Kaarta.

THE DIARRAS

The kingdom of Segou was founded by Biton Kulibali, as told in the next story, but after his death his sons failed to hold power, and after a period of anarchy a second dynasty, that of the Diarras (or Jaras), came to power. This is their story of origin, retold from the account of a Bamana performer recorded around 1980.

A man in the Manden named Madiba Kone had many wives, of whom one was the most unfortunate example of the 'despised wife' that might be imagined. Nevertheless, she became pregnant. Her husband was reluctant to admit the paternity of her offspring, because of her low status in the household and the hostility of the other wives. When she had almost come to term, he threw her out of the household, ordering her to disappear.

Weeping and staggering, she made her way into the bush until labour was upon her and she could not go any further. But the birth was easy, and she brought forth two fine male twins. She did not know it, but she had come to a lair of spirits, and they assisted her. When she had finished giving birth and looked about her, she saw she was lying close to a lioness who had just given birth to three lion cubs, and at the sight she almost fainted with fear. She was sure that she had breathed her last, and that she and her new children would be food for the lioness and her cubs. But the spirits then spoke, calming her, and they told her to leave her sons with them and to return to the world of humans. They would care for the boys, who would eventually be returned to her.

Hardly believing in her escape, the mother returned to Sankaran, where Madiba Kone lived, and as she came without her children she was allowed to resume her miserable place in the household. Time went by: the seasons succeeded each other, and in the lair of the spirits the two boys grew into fine young men. Eventually, they were sent off to take their place in the world. But they wished to find their mother. Everywhere, they announced they were seeking their mother, and many were the claimants who wished to be connected with such paragons. But of each woman who said she was their mother, the young men asked simply: 'Where did you give birth to us?' and the answers invariably proved the woman wrong: in the bedchamber, by the fireside, in front of the chamber, in the fields, and sometimes in the bathing areas or by the well.

They came at last to Sankaran, where again women crowded around calling them their sons. But none could answer their question, until an old woman came and told them she had lost two boys who might be their age.

'And where did you give birth to these boys?' asked the men.

'In the bush, by the lioness's lair,' answered the woman, and the two young men knelt before her to acknowledge that she was their mother. Then they took her away from her husband's home, and they travelled east from the Manden to Sekoro, the region that would become Segou. And because they did not wish to keep the name Kone (although it is honourable in the Manden) they gave themselves a new name that recalled their origin: Diarra ('lion').

BITON KULIBALI AND THE FOUNDING
OF SEGOU

Mamari Kulibali, later to be called 'Biton', and his mother, Sunu Sako, came to the land around Sekoro. He was a hunter, and had once wounded a spirit in the form of an antelope. He tracked it as far as he could, and then became the apprentice of a kinsman who taught him a great deal about healing and about hunting. Eventually, he went back on the trail of the wounded antelope that had vanished, and this time he followed it to the home of the spirits. He came among them, and there he found one who was wounded, whose wound would not heal. He bargained with the spirits, and they promised him good fortune if he would heal the wounded spirit. Then, using the knowledge he had acquired, he healed the spirit. In exchange, the others told him to move to the land of Sekoro, and there he would be able to found a kingdom.

He and his mother moved to Sekoro, and she planted a garden. In it she grew the *ngoyo* fruit. But when the fruit ripened, she was unable to harvest it for sale in the local market: every night some creature came and plucked the ripe fruit. Her son Mamari said he would see to the matter. He concealed himself near his mother's fields, with his loaded gun aimed and ready to fire, and then he waited throughout the night to learn what thief was taking the fruit. Soon he saw a young water spirit come out of the dark shadows and approach the *ngoyo* fruit. The spirit moved from plant to plant, plucking the ripest fruit and leaving the rest, until Mamari coughed. Then the spirit froze and looked around.

'Spirit,' called Mamari, 'are those your fruit? Did you prepare the earth? Did you plant the seeds? Did you bring the plants the water they need?' The spirit did not move. It had seen Mamari, and saw also the gun barrel aimed straight at its heart.

'No,' said the spirit. 'I will admit that I am stealing these fruits. But you should spare my life.'

'I should not spare your life,' said Mamari. 'I have caught you, and I know that you are the thief who has been taking my mother's fruits.'

'You should spare my life because I can offer you something,' said the spirit. 'Come into the water with me to my father, and he will make you prosper.'

'How will he do that?' asked Mamari, and the little spirit told him what her father would offer him and what he must say. So Mamari agreed, and he and the spirit together went down to the riverbank and then into the waters. They came before Faro, the spirit ruler of the waters.

Faro at first wished to punish the human who had intruded on his domain, but the little spirit interceded and explained how she had been stealing the *ngoyo* fruit from Mamari's mother's garden, and how he had caught her.

'He has spared my life,' she said, 'and I have promised him a reward.'

'I shall offer him a reward,' said Faro. 'Human, let me give you one hundred cattle.'

'Faro,' answered Mamari, 'I do not want one hundred cattle.'

'Then let me offer you one hundred sheep and one hundred goats.'

'Faro, I do not want sheep or goats.'

'I offer you one hundred mithqals of gold.'

'Faro, I do not want your gold.'

'You do not want gold or cattle or sheep. What shall I offer you?' asked Faro.

'Faro, give me a handful of millet to sow in a field.' Faro gave him the millet.

'I shall add something,' said Faro's wife, the mother of the little spirit. 'Come, and suckle at my left breast.' So Mamari approached and took milk from the breast of the spirit woman. Then he returned to the land.

After the next rainy season he sowed the millet he had received from Faro, and his fields grew full and luxuriant. But somehow he was called away just before harvest time – a commercial venture, he told the neighbours – and while he was travelling the flocks of birds which feed on grasses and seeds (it is usually the task of little boys to scare them away from the fields) descended upon his fields. When he returned his fields were bare and the neighbours were muttering about his wastefulness and foolishness. But he was content, for he had been told that wherever the birds carried the millet seeds from his fields, those lands would eventually come under his power.

Mamari's mother would make a honey beer which proved very popular among the young men of the area of Sekoro. They gathered weekly to drink her beer with Mamari, and after a while they began to take up a collection to pay for her expenses. Later, they began to raid neighbouring villages, and with the plunder they got yet more beer to drink together. They became an association, a *ton*, and then came the question who should lead the association.

They drew lots. Mamari's lot was chosen. But there was

opposition, because he was a stranger who had come recently among them, and was not a native to the area. Again they drew the lots, but again Mamari's lot was chosen. There was yet more discussion. Some were still strongly opposed to making an outsider their leader, while others felt that they must stand by their promise: they had said they would draw lots to determine their leader, they had drawn the lots, and they must accept the result. Otherwise, they would be breaking their word.

Mamari was chosen leader of the association. In this way he gained the name by which he is best known, 'Biton' (leader of the *ton*). It grew in strength and activities, becoming a strong army that dominated the region. His capital, near Sekoro, was named Segou.

THE PEOPLES OF
SENEGAMBIA

The coastal region between the Rio Muni of Guinea-Bissau and the Senegal river is rich in history and the interactions of peoples. The empire of Mali extended west to the upper parts of the Gambia river. North of the Mandinka kingdoms of Kaabu (or Gabou), Badibu, Niumi and others lay an ethnically hybrid state, Bondu, ruled by the Sisibe dynasty, while the Sine and Salum rivers along the coast were the territory of the Serer kingdoms which practised matrilineal descent through the Guelowar lineages for their rulers. The central coastal area, south of the Senegal river, was the home of Wolof kingdoms, rarely unified: Cayor, Baol, Waalo, but linked by a common origin and culture. The area along the Senegal river, known in Arab sources of the Middle Ages as the Tekrour, is now generally called the Futa Tooro, inhabited by the Tukolor or Haal-Pulaaren (speakers of Pulaar), a branch of the far-flung family of Fulbe. They were ruled until the eighteenth century by the Denyankobe dynasty, and then installed a form of Muslim government (the Imamate) in which rulers were elected for a year.

THE MANDINKA OF SENEGAMBIA

The Mandinka of the Gambia are speakers of a language very close to Maninka/Bamana, but with strong dialectal differences. They trace their origins to the time of Sunjata. Their kingdoms were spread about the upper reaches of the Gambia river, and trade was an important economic activity. The major kingdom was Kaabu, which fell to Muslim forces from the Futa Jallon (a Muslim Fulbe territory to the south, in Guinea) in 1857 when the capital of Kansala was taken.

THE CONQUEST OF THE JOLOF

This story, often given as part of the epic of Sunjata, describes the westward expansion of the empire of Mali. Tira Magan Traore, the general who conquered the Jolof, is considered the founder of the Mandinka kingdoms. This retelling is based on the many versions of the epic of Sunjata published in the last fifty years.

After Sunjata had defeated Sumanguru, and he and his generals and subordinate kings had held their great assembly and established the principles of their new empire, he decided that he needed horses for his army. So he sent men with gold into the land of the Jolof to buy the horses that were traded down from the Arab regions in the north. But when the men came into the Jolof they were seized and taken to the king. He took away their gold and gave them some leather scraps, as well as a message for Sunjata: Sunjata, he said, was only a hunter king, and so he needed shoes, not horses. The leather would serve to make him shoes.

When the messengers returned to Mali, there was some discussion how to break the news to Sunjata. No one wanted to tell him the message of the king of the Jolof. The princes refused, the diviners refused. They asked the chief blacksmith; he refused. But the *jeli*, Bala Faseke Kuyate, said that he could take the message, and so he did: he sang to the king and spoke of the limits of his power, and then he explained how he had been insulted by the king of the Jolof. In this way, the *jeli* showed the worth of his art.

The natural response to the insult from the king of Jolof was war. Different war-leaders made their claims to be sent on a punitive expedition. Having heard them out, Sunjata looked around the assembly.

'One of your number is absent,' he observed. 'Where is Tira Magan Traore? I expected him to be first among you.'

'He is outside,' answered someone, and Sunjata went out to see what had kept Tira Magan from the gathering. They found a freshly dug grave nearby, and in it lay Tira Magan.

'I see,' said Sunjata. 'If I do not send you to the Jolof, we should bury you? Tira Magan, you are the slave of the tomb.' Those words have become a praise-name of the Traore lineage: *Su Saare Jon*.

So Tira Magan was sent with his army into the land of the Jolof. He told everyone that as he served a hunter, he was only walking the dogs. The army came to the ford near Salakan and defeated an army. Tira Magan said he was only walking the dogs. They came to the king of Nyani and defeated him. Tira Magan said he was walking the dogs. They met the king of Sanumu and defeated him. Tira Magan said he was walking the dogs. Finally, Tira Magan defeated the army of Jolof-fin Mansa. They captured the king trying to hide in a burrow. They brought him out and removed his head. Tira Magan said he had finished walking the dogs. Tira Magan's descendants established the Mandinka kingdoms of the Gambia.

NIUMI AND JARRA

Other kingdoms were formed further down the river, in areas where the Mandinka came in contact with the Sereer, and there was some fusion of customs. Niumi was the principal kingdom, lying on the north bank closest to the mouth of the Gambia river, not too far from the Serer regions north-west of them. This account is based on information collected by an American historian around 1975.

The first rulers of the region of Niumi were women. There were twelve women rulers, until one lost an election to her brother and moved away to Bakindiki. After that time, women rulers began to give way to men, especially as the men turned to the empire of Mali – *tilebo*, they called Mali: the land of the sun, for it was in the east – to receive *mansaya*, the authority of kingship.

The women who ruled in Bakindiki, Fogny, Kiang and Jarra all exiled their brothers, to prevent them taking power. Jasey was the half-brother of the woman ruler of Jarra. He assembled these princes and built a great fire. Then he tossed his cloth into the fire and invited them all to do the same. After he did so, he announced, 'I wish to go into Mali, to seek *mansaya*. Anyone who wishes to accompany me, let him take his cloth from the fire.' With that, he stretched his hand into the fire and withdrew his cloth. His hand was unburnt.

One by one, the other princes announced, 'I shall go into Mali,' and they too withdrew their cloths. Only the prince from Fogny was unable to pull out his cloth, and Jasey told him he could not accompany them. The princes travelled east until they came to Mali, where they found Mansa Jali Kasa ruling. They told him the purpose of their visit. He heard them out, and then explained that the land was troubled by a monstrous bird, and if they could defeat the bird he would certainly endow them with *mansaya* to take back to Niumi. Since he had led the group into Mali, Jasey said that he would fight the bird first.

Jasey's full sister had great magical powers. She had warned her brother that he would face an ordeal in Mali, and that if he ate any of their food he would fail the ordeal. She would cook a pot of food for him and place it on a great rock near Jarra, between two villages named Sutung and Bureng. From that rock, Jasey was able to reach the food, even though he was far to the east in Mali. Thus he was sustained during his struggle with the bird.

For several days the struggle was even-handed and inconclusive. The bird would sweep down and swallow Jasey whole; the bird then defecated and expelled Jasey. Jasey would then swallow the bird, and the bird would pass through him and be expelled by defecation. This went on for several days.

Then the sister changed the song she used when charming the food for delivery to Jasey. Where before she sang how the princes were in Manding but Jasey's food was in Jarra, now she sang that the food was in Jarra and Jasey did nothing but eat. Jasey took this as a rebuke and stopped eating for two days. When the pot which she sent from Jarra to Mali returned full, the sister grew concerned, for she did not think her brother could defeat the bird if he was weak with hunger, and so she sent him a word of advice on a means to defeat the great bird.

Jasey built a fire and placed a great pot in it, so that it was heated until it glowed. The next time he had swallowed the bird, he came and squatted over the pot. When the bird emerged from Jasey's anus, it was killed by the heat. In this way, Jasey satisfied the demands of the king of Mali.

When the princes from the Gambia were assembled, it was found that one of them, Samake Demba, had seduced a daughter of the king of Mali. Mansa Jali Kasa insisted that the punishment for this deed was death. Samake Demba pleaded that he should be allowed to make his farewells before he died, and begged a week's grace in which to return home. The king refused until Jasey spoke up and announced that he would stand in Samake Demba's place for the week, and that if Samake Demba did not return they could kill him instead. Struck by this instance of nobility, the king then agreed.

Samake Demba then rushed home, made his farewells, and returned to Mali. Because of the distance, even though he had hurried he only reached Mali on the eighth day, the day on which they had said they would execute Jasey if he had not returned. So for the last stretch of his journey he carried a banner, a tall stick on which he had tied a cloth, so that they would see him coming from far away and spare Jasey's life. It was well that he did so, for they were preparing to execute Jasey when someone saw the banner in the distance and announced that Samake Demba was near at hand. When Samake Demba arrived, Mansa Jali Kasa asked him why he had come back.

'I could do nothing else,' answered Samake Demba. 'My friend Jasey has taken my place for me. I could not let him die. It is better to die than to live in shame in Niumi or Jarra.'

'You are truly a noble man, and worthy of *mansaya*,' said Mansa Jali Kasa, and so he spared Samake Demba's life. He gave the princes animals to guide them back to Mali, with instructions to follow where the animals led them. The animals were monkeys, and even today the people of Niumi can be praised by reciting the names of the monkeys: Sema and Tako, Jakali and Bubu. To Samake Demba he added that when the monkeys had led him to his home, he should find a dog and go hunting with it, and the dog would lead him to fortune.

They returned home. Jasey became the king of Jarra, and is remembered as Jarra Mansa Jasey Banna. Samake Demba returned with him, and then he went hunting with a dog. The dog led him to Berending, and there he found a female ruler who fell in love with him. After some time, she made him king and renounced her own authority in his favour. Samake Demba was thus the first male ruler in Niumi.

THE SEREER OF SENEGAL

The Sereer occupy their present location, along the coast of Senegal between Dakar and the river Gambia, as a result of their migration south at some point in the past from a region closer to the Senegal river. It is suggested that they share a common origin with their neighbours, the Wolof and the Pulaar (or Fulbe), and that all three groups separated some thousands of years ago. Having reached their new territory, perhaps seven hundred years ago, the Sereer there came into contact with the Mande peoples who had expanded west from their heartland on the upper Niger and Sankaran rivers; the expansion is generally associated with Sunjata's general Tira Magan Traore (see Chapter 66). The society that resulted was marked by matrilineal descent of the ruling class, a warrior aristocracy and the practice of agriculture. Over the next few hundred years, the Sereer kingdoms would at times be incorporated into the larger Wolof states and at times remain independent. The Guelowar aristocracy of the Sereer, perhaps because of the matrilineal element, continues to inspire the imagination, although the original misalliance of a princess and a griot remains a delicate issue, usually left tacit. These stories are retold from the work of a French scholar, published in 1983.

THE GUELOWAR LINEAGES

The founder of the Guelowar lineages was a Mande princess. She left her home because she had become pregnant out of wedlock and wished to avoid unpleasant consequences. Her story varies. One account makes her a daughter of the emperor Sunjata who became pregnant after her husband had been absent for several years; she then went into exile, accompanied by a *jeli*. They lived in the forest west of Kaabu for nine years, until they encountered the inhabitants of the region.

The better known story says that the Mande princess was Amina Coulibaly, a woman renowned for her beauty. A king claimed her for his heir, but before the marriage Amina's beloved came to her disguised as a *jeli*. Amina became pregnant, and so she collected her belongings and some followers and fled into the west. They came at last to the shores of the sea, and there Amina took shelter in a great cave. There she lived for a time; her followers did what they could to supply her with food. Eventually, a wandering hunter came across the cave and discovered the princess. He reported this sight to the king, who rode out immediately to find the wondrous woman and confirm the report of her beauty.

At first, she refused to come with him. She had not yet given birth. But he insisted. She told him (and it is unclear if this was a prophecy or a condition) that if she joined him, her yet-unborn child would rule the land. The king accepted this statement: he said that her child would rule after him. At that, Amina Coulibaly went with him. She won over his followers, who might have muttered about a queen taken from a cave, by her lavish distribution of gold bracelets and rings. When her child was born, it was a girl. Her husband proclaimed that her male descendants would be the rulers of his land, and so the principle of matrilineage was established for the Sereer aristocracy.

LINEAGE STORIES I: THE CAXER

In earlier times, the Tewan and the Caxer lived together. The Tewan had acquired occult powers, and could transform himself into any sort of creature. The Caxer was eager to acquire this knowledge, for he was not rich. So he learned what he could until at last he was able to summon one of the spirits of the forest. He did so, standing before one of the great trees in the area (they were considered the home of the spirits), and indeed, a spirit appeared and asked him what he wanted. The Caxer asked him for wealth; the spirit named his price: a human life. The Caxer had two sisters; he offered the spirit one of them. That night, the sister died.

The next night, the Caxer went out to the tree and the spirit gave him his reward: a cowrie-shell, a millet seed, and one hair from a cow, a goat and a sheep. The Caxer began to return home. But the Tewan was dreaming at the time, and saw what was happening. He changed himself into a hyena and went to meet the Caxer; the hyena so frightened the man that he dropped the little packet the spirit had given him and lost his sight as well.

The Caxer groped his way back to the village, and to the home of a Sowan. The Sowan was a healer, and with a powder he was able to restore the Caxer's sight. The Caxer then became suspicious, believing that only one who had caused the affliction could cure it so easily, and so the two men went before the village judge, the Katy. The Katy had second sight; he was able to explain his mistake to the Caxer and to suggest a means by which to regain his lost wealth. The Caxer burned a rope in his home, and then took the ashes to the home of the Tewan. He spread the ashes on the floor. The Tewan lost his sight. The Caxer was able to retrieve his packet and to release its contents in his house: immediately, he had a wealth of cattle, goats, sheep and cowrie-shells, and his granary filled with a store of millet seed.

His clan thus became rich, but they were never numerous, for they had given up one of their child-bearers in exchange for their wealth.

LINEAGE STORIES II: SIRA BADIANE

Sira Badiane was a Guelowar princess who had borne five sons to the king of Salum. Despite this, her life was miserable and so she ran away with her sons and daughters, and taking the royal drums, the junjun. They fled through the bush, through the wilderness, until finally they collapsed, exhausted, near a stream. There they established a village named Petj. It grew, and Sira Badiane became a respected and powerful ruler, and the junjun drums sounded her praises.

The king of Salum learned how she had set herself up and determined to destroy her, for he felt power should be reserved in the hands of men. He resorted first to sorcery: he had a powerful and noxious amulet sewn into a fine leather saddle which he had delivered to Sira Badiane as a peace-offering. Sira Badiane's eldest son was the first to try the new saddle. He placed it on a fine horse, rode off, and died when the animal went wild and charged headlong into a great tree-trunk. Two other sons died, before a hunter named Samba Sarr identified the cause. Samba Sarr was Tukolor, from the Futa Tooro, and he had great skills. He detected the amulet in the saddle, and so they threw the saddle into the stream. But the saddle would not stay there. Any fisherman who cast his net into the stream after the saddle had been thrown into it would find himself hauling the saddle back to land.

The king of Salum then tried trickery. He came to Petj and camped nearby. He sent a messenger to tell the queen of his grief at the death of their children, and of his desire to share in the mourning. He asked that the surviving sons should come to lead him into the village. But he prepared a trap for the innocents who came to greet their father: his servants dug a pit and covered it with a great straw mat, and then they all sat around it as the boys arrived. The boys fell in; the servants immediately filled the hole with earth, and he released his soldiers to raid the area.

The surviving sisters threatened to kill themselves, and so they were tied to trees near the river for a time, and at that spot they received food and beatings, and their lamentations disturbed the spirits of the place.

However, Samba Sarr had received a blessing: he had killed an enormous elephant. An ear of the elephant is said to be preserved in his lineage. It endows the wearer with occult power, and marks the legitimacy of the *Saltigi*, the Fulbe or Tukolor leader of the community. Anyone who ate the flesh of the elephant, or drank from his well, then felt a compulsion: they moved to the area of Djilof where he lived. So even Sira Badiane moved, leaving the village of Petj an empty and forlorn spot, the home of angry spirits who must be appeased each year. Sira Badiane ruled over the new community, and it enjoyed great prosperity.

NJAAJAAN NJAAY AND
THE WOLOF

The Wolof are the major linguistic and ethnic group of Senegal, and occupy the lands between the Senegal river in the north and the Gambia river to the south. In the last thousand years they have formed numerous kingdoms, sometimes unified and often independent, and have come to terms with their powerful neighbours: the Maninka (and Mandinka of Gambia) in the east and south, the Fulbe (or Tukolors) of the Futa Tooro to the north-east, the Moors to the north, and eventually also the traders who came along the Atlantic coast. Wolof origins lie on the south side of the Senegal, and that region was the core of their kingdom. The story of Njaajaan Njaay was first recorded in the late eighteenth century, by a French traveller, and many modern versions are now available.

It is said that Abu-Bekri bin Amer came from Arabia bringing Islam, although others say the man's name was Abu Derday. He came to the lands by the Senegal river accompanied by a servant, and took a wife there. They had a son. Abu-Bekri then determined to return to Arabia. He told his wife that if he did not return, she should take another husband. He recommended that she choose her husband carefully: a man of self-control and discretion, and suggested that she could tell something of men's character by how far they went from the village for their morning excretion.

He left, and died on the road. After a time, his wife decided she would marry again, and she began watching the men as they left the village in the morning. She quickly noticed that Abu-Bekri's servant, who had not gone with his master, went

the furthest and was the most discreet about his morning ablu-
tions, and so she determined to make him her husband.

Her son by Abu-Bekri was most distressed by the thought
that his mother would remarry, and worst of all that she would
marry a servant. When the time came for the wedding, he threw
himself into the river. He did not drown. He lived in the river
for seven years, travelling far downstream from his mother's
home.

He eventually came out of the water. This is how it happened.
The children of a village used to go fishing, and they would pile
their catch together. There were always disputes and quarrels
when the time came to divide up the catch: each claimed to
have caught the largest fish, none was happy with his share.
Their quarrels bothered the village, and they bothered Njaajaan
down in the waters. One day he came out of the river and
showed the children a way to avoid such quarrelling: he gave
each child a loop of vine to run through the gills of the fish he
caught, so each would know exactly which were his fish, and
there would be no disputes about ownership. The children were
delighted with this arrangement. The adults were amazed that
the quarrels and fights over the fish seemed to have stopped,
and eventually they asked the children how this had come
about. The children told them how a man had come out of the
waters and showed them how each could keep his own fish.

The adults decided they wished to find this man who could
settle affairs so well for children; he would be a good ruler for
them as well. So they set to work, and eventually they trapped
Njaajaan in their nets and brought him to the village. But he
refused to say anything. He sat there silent. For two days he sat
where they had him tied and said nothing. Finally, a woman
said she could make him talk, if they would just let him go one
more day without eating. They agreed.

The next day the woman came to Njaajaan and built a small
fire. Then she filled a pot with water and spices and pieces of
fish, and prepared to set it on the fire. But she only put two
stones by the fire, and she could not quite balance the pot on
the two stones. It kept tipping to one side or another, and
sometimes the water spilled out. Njaajaan was watching her

eagerly, it seemed. Finally, after she had kept up these attempts for some time, he spoke. 'Use three stones!' he cried, and then realized he had spoken.

After that, he agreed to talk to the people, and they made him their king: the first king of the Jolof, the land of the Wolof. He later learned he had a stepbrother, from his mother's remarriage, and the stepbrother became the first Brak (king) of Waalo, which is another part of the land of the Wolof and one of their four kingdoms.

THE FUTA TOORO

The Futa Tooro was known in medieval times as Tekrur, and that name offers the best etymology for one of the names of the current inhabitants of the region, the Tukolor. The Tukolor, also called the Haal-Pulaaren ('speakers of Pulaar'), are a sedentary group of the Fulbe (or Fulani) whose language is a form of Fulfulde. The region lies along the middle course of the Senegal river, and is probably the original home of the Fulbe (see also Chapter 9), from which they dispersed east and south through the territory of Mali to northern Nigeria, the Adamawa region of Cameroon, and elsewhere. The Fulbe are widely associated with cattle-herding, and this practice may also explain their wide dispersal over the savannah regions of west Africa. Some scholars have claimed a connection between the Fulbe and the makers of the stone-age rock art in the Sahara that depicts cattle-herders.

The Futa Tooro was also one of several areas in which Fulbe who had converted to Islam established theocratic states, beginning in the early eighteenth century. These include the Futa Jallon in Guinea, from which Muslims marched in 1857 to overthrow the Mandinka kingdom of Kaabu in the Gambia (see Chapter 66) and Maasina in Mali; the most influential was the emirate of Sokoto in northern Nigeria, which extended its control over most of the Hausa city-states and triggered a wave of conquests by Muslim Fula leaders throughout the central savannah region. In the nineteenth century, al-Hajj Umar Tal led a movement of conquest from Senegal east into Mali, conquering the Bamana states of Kaarta and Segou before he died in an explosion.

THE ORIGIN OF THE FULBE

The importance of this story is the way in which it justifies a new religious vocation for the Fulbe, distinct from their former association with cattle and nomadism. It is a claim by Fulfulde speakers of divine sanction for their rise to religious and political eminence, and goes back at least to the eighteenth century. This retelling is based on an oral tradition collected in Mali and published in 1974.

It is said that the Prophet Muhammad foresaw that in a future time, a people and language would arise in west Africa to continue his work. The people would be the last of the created peoples, and the language would be something new. So he told his followers to pay attention to that land, and in the years following his death, as the armies spread across north Africa carrying his new faith, the leaders of the armies were mindful of his words and sent an Arab named Oqba south across the desert. He came to the green lands south of the sands, travelling with his slave, and there he took a wife, named Bintu Doucoure. She gave him four sons.

A few years after the birth of the fourth son, Oqba departed, leaving his slave behind. He told his wife that if he did not return from his trip to the north she should take his slave as her husband. With the consent of her family, she did so. In the north, Oqba married an Arab woman, and they also had four sons; these sons became the ancestors of the Jatara, also known as the Tuareg.

The sons of Oqba and Bintu Doucoure were most unusual: they did not speak as others do. They remained silent, it seemed, until the eldest was almost nine years old. Then their mother happened to give them a branch of a jujube tree, with many ripe berries. The boys began happily plucking and eating them, until very few were left. The youngest wanted to take the rest of the berries, but the other brothers felt they should get them. They began to argue over the berries, using a language that had never been heard before: this is the origin of Fulfulde. After that they began to talk normally, but with each other they continued to use their strange and rich new language.

When they grew up they heard how the Prophet had indicated that their land would deserve special attention, and they decided to return to their father's land to see what they might gain from the visit. They crossed the desert and came to Mecca, where their simple piety won them attention. Curious about these strangers, the people of Mecca determined to test their faith. They placed four sheep in a house, and then a leader of the faith came into an assembly where the four young men were sitting, and asked if there were any present ready to meet their maker, through love of God and his Prophet.

No one in the crowd said a word. After a space, the eldest of the four sons of Oqba rose and said he would offer himself. They took him into the house, and there they slaughtered one of the sheep so that it cried as they cut its throat, and the blood ran under the door into the street. Holding the bloody knife, the leader of faith came out and asked if anyone else would meet his fate, for love of God and his Prophet. In turn, each of the other three sons presented himself.

This demonstration convinced the people of Mecca of the truth of the prophecy concerning the people of west Africa. A further confirmation came when they consulted their papers. They found a list of words that the Prophet had made in the new language that he had foreseen, and the words corresponded to the language spoken by the four brothers. So they sent the four men back to their own country with blessings. The brothers settled in the Futa Tooro, and gave rise to the four clans of Fulbe: Diallo and Diakite, Sidibe and Sangare. And from the Futa Tooro their descendants eventually also populated other regions: the Futa Jallon of Guinea, Wasulu in the Manden, and Massina along the middle Niger.

KOLI TENGELA AND THE
DENIYANKE DYNASTY

*The Deniyanke were the dominant dynasty in the Futa Tooro
from the sixteenth to the eighteenth century; they were replaced
eventually by a system of Islamic government known as the
Imamate, in which a different leader was elected each year.
Koli Tengela is said to have established the dynasty, but numerous stories about a leader and founder named Koli are told
from Senegal south into Guinea, particularly in the region of
the Gambia. This retelling is based upon an account prepared
by local scholars and translated into French in the last century.*

Tengela was a Fula leader who served Sunjata well, and the
king of Mali rewarded him with the gift of a wife. But he
warned Tengela that he had already slept with the woman, and
that if she gave birth to a child within the space of nine months
the child would be his. This proved to be the case; the woman
gave birth to a son whom they named Koli and whom Tengela
raised as his own son.

When he grew older, Koli became a war-leader and led his
men against the Soninke kingdom of Jara, then ruled by the
son of Dama Ngille. It is said that one of Koli's followers may
have killed a prince of Jara; whatever the case, the war went
against Koli and he was forced into the wilderness lying west
of Jara. He determined to pass through the wilderness and see
what he might find. But provisions ran very low, and water was
hard to find. His army of three thousand men began to despair
of escaping the wild lands.

Koli gave them hope when he saw a bird high on a tree branch
holding an ear of millet in its beak. He noted the direction from
which the bird had come and sent men to scout out the land;
they soon returned to announce that there was rich territory
ahead of them. The army pushed through and came into the
Futa Tooro, the lands along the Senegal river. There they
quickly conquered the people and replaced the Diaobe who had

ruled before. The memory of their reign is not entirely pleasant; they were troublesome and belligerent, proud and quick to violence.

MALICK SY AND BONDU

Bondu was an Islamic kingdom lying at the headwaters of the Senegal river, founded around 1700 in relatively empty territory ceded to Malick Sy by the Soninke ruler of Gadiaga, and later populated by immigrants from the Futa Tooro who were unhappy under the rule of the Deniyanke. There are many versions of this story published in the last century.

Malick Sy was born in Sonyma, in the Futa Tooro. He was a gifted student, and his father sent him away to study the holy texts of Islam in the north. Anticipating his son's future return, he then set aside a ram which he kept in a stall and fattened carefully. After seven years, Malick Sy returned to Sonyma. But that very day, a slave, one of the servants of the Satigui (the ruler of the Futa Tooro), came to the village. As was the custom, he was offered a gift: would he accept a cow? Two cows? An ox? No. What he demanded was the fattened sheep that he had heard was kept by the father of Malick Sy, and nothing else would satisfy him. He was told that the father had sworn to God that he was saving the sheep for his son's return; the Satigui's slave insisted he must be given the sheep. The village leaders went to Malick Sy's father and asked him to give up the sheep. The father asked the son, who told him he should give up the sheep. They did so. The slave had it slaughtered and cooked, and then offered it to the village, including Malick Sy and his father.

After the feast, Malick Sy went to the slave and stabbed him, to avenge the insult done his father through the breach of the oath. Then he told his father what he had done. His father was horrified, fearing the reprisals of the Satigui, and wished to flee.

'If we flee, we shall be caught,' answered Malick Sy. 'Let us try another course.' He led the village leaders to the court of the Satigui and there told how the slave had come and demanded the sheep, despite the oath sworn by the father, and how after they had given him the sheep Malick Sy had killed the slave to avenge his father.

The ruler was furious. 'Because you have faced me,' he pronounced, 'I shall not have you killed, but you must remove yourself. Never let me see you again. Leave this land at once.'

Malick Sy then left Sonyma, and travelled to Jara. There he settled and began to practise his faith. His learning and his piety won him a great reputation. His skills went beyond religion; the king entrusted to him the construction of the wall, the *tata*, intended to protect the town from raiders. When the project was completed, the king offered Malick Sy sheep or cattle or gold. Malick Sy refused all these gifts.

'What should I give you?' asked the king.

'I ask only one favour,' answered Malick Sy. 'Allow me to see the sword from Mecca which was given to your ancestor Daman Gille.'

'It is a sword of kingship,' answered the king. 'I cannot take it out of its sheath.'

Malick Sy was apparently satisfied with this answer, but in fact he simply sought out another means of seeing the sword. The king had a favourite wife, Dongo, who was childless despite many efforts and much assistance from healers and diviners. Malick Sy came to know Dongo, and eventually she asked him for his assistance in getting her a child. He agreed to offer up his prayers on her behalf, but told her that the price for his assistance would be to see the sword from Mecca. She agreed. He prepared amulets for her, and went into a retreat in which he prayed concentratedly. Soon Dongo became pregnant, to her great joy. Her pregnancy came to term, and she was delivered safely of a boy.

After the naming ceremony for the child, Malick Sy came to Dongo and reminded her of her promise. She recognized her obligation, but asked him to wait until the night was troubled with thunderstorms. He agreed. Soon after, the clouds rolled over the horizon and the thunder sounded at dusk.

That night, Malick Sy made his way to Dongo's chamber. She had brought the sword from Mecca into the room. He drew the blade a small way out of its sheath. An intense light filled the room, and a rumbling shook the walls. The king came running to ask Dongo what had happened. The wife concealed Malick Sy and answered that it was only a flash of lightning, and that the stroke seemed to have landed nearby.

A second time, Malick Sy took up the sword. This time he drew it halfway out of the sheath. Again, light filled the room, and again a rumbling shook the ground. The king was not so easily satisfied with his wife's explanations this time, but he finally left her alone.

'You have seen the sword,' said Dongo. 'Surely that is enough?'

'No,' answered Malick Sy. 'I must see the whole blade.' With that, he unsheathed the sword so that it flashed in the dark room like lightning itself and a great roll of thunder made the palace complex shake. The king came running.

'It was the sword from Mecca,' explained his wife. 'It fell from the sheath as I was holding it over our son.'

The next morning Malick Sy went to the king as usual, to greet him and ask after his health. As he approached, the king stared at him.

'Your face is luminous,' stated the king. 'It is as though the sun shone behind your eyes. What has brought this change?'

Malick Sy admitted that he had seen the sword from Mecca. At first the king was furious, and was ready to order his execution. But then Dongo intervened, and explained that she had helped Malick Sy as the price of her – or their – son. At these words the king calmed down. But the portents were still clear. Malick Sy was destined to become a king. So the king ordered Malick Sy to leave the land of Jara and find a territory to the west.

Malick Sy left Jara. He passed through the Kaarta, and was guided by the words of an old man to the mountain of Krina, where he greeted the mountain and prayed, in the name of God, for its favour. Then he travelled on over the hills into the land that would become Bondu. He took service with the Tunka, the ruler, for a while, until he felt ready to ask for a boon. He asked the Tunka for some land, and the Tunka readily granted him a stretch of land: the region was arid and unpopulated.

Malick Sy then prepared charms which he hung on certain trees, and after a time they died. His servants went out and easily knocked over the trees; where the roots had dug into the earth, wells sprang forth. Thus the country acquired its new name: Bondu means the land of wells. The water brought people to the place, and they considered themselves subject to Malick Sy, as it was his power that had produced the water. More people came, and his authority grew.

Eventually he felt strong enough to ask the Tunka to divide their lands. The Tunka agreed, having heard how Malick Sy had brought water and fertility to Bondu, and proposed that they should each depart from their homes at dawn, walking towards the other's residence, and that where they met should be considered the dividing line of their territories. But Malick Sy left his home well before dawn, and hastened towards the Tunka's palace. The next morning, the Tunka was amazed to meet Malick only a short distance from the edge of his town. But he had given his word, and so that point became the border of their two lands. Malick Sy's sons ruled after him; the dynasty was known as the Sisibe.

THE SAHARA

71

THE TUAREG OF
THE SAHARA

The Sahara is not uninhabited, although it counts as one of the harshest environments on earth and there is some question (from historians and demographers) whether the populations of the central Sahara have actually been self-sustaining, or whether the peoples of the desert have maintained their numbers thanks to a constant influx from the edges due to marriage, trade and slave-taking. The oases allow the cultivation of date-palms, but most other foodstuffs are imported. The nomads of the desert have survived through trade and through persistent raids on the more fertile lands to the south. The populations are not at all unified; they are marked by a degree of linguistic diversity (within a larger family) and by intense political rivalry between segments of the same larger groups. But their image has benefited from the mystique of the desert itself, enhanced by particularities such as their matrilineality, unusual within heavily Islamized groups, and the wearing of the veil (dyed a rich indigo) by the men. In recent years, there have been conflicts along the southern edge of the Sahara, as Tuareg and Berber groups claimed more autonomy or political power in the newly independent states. The stories given below are taken from a variety of sources, ranging from a mid-nineteenth-century account to modern transcriptions of oral traditions.

THE FIRST QUEEN

Many years ago, a queen fled from the Maghrib with her entourage. Her name was Tin Hinane, and she was accompanied by a servant named Takamata. The cause of their departure is not given, but probably involved an indiscretion whose consequences the women wished to escape. They came to the middle of the desert, and their food supplies ran out. The servants did what they could to protect their queen, but she was suffering from hunger and the heat and was soon close to death. Takamata went out to see what she might find: she came across some anthills, and hopefully broke them open. She was rewarded: the ants had laid up a stock of grain and other foods. She scooped out her treasure and quickly brought it back to Tin Hinane. This trove enabled the group to regain its strength and continue on, until they came to a village, Abalissa, near Tamanrasset in the heart of the desert. There both Tin Hinane and Takamata gave birth, to one and two daughters respectively, and these three daughters are considered the founding mothers of the Tuareg people of Tamanrasset. Tin Hinane's tomb can still be seen in Abalissa.

CHILDREN OF THE JINNS

A party of merchants was travelling north from the region of Gao with seven Bella slave-girls. They came to the region of Taylalt and there were joined by a holy man. As they travelled on, they came to a valley. The holy man warned them not to camp there, although it might seem a favourable spot, for the valley was the habitation of jinns. But the merchants disregarded his advice. It was the end of the day when they reached the valley, and it promised a secure and comfortable campsite. So they spent the night there. As the trip progressed, however, it became clear that the seven Bella women had all become pregnant and seemed to be inhabited by spirits. The merchants then remembered the holy man's warning, and realized that the women had been visited by the spirits as succubi, and so they abandoned the women at an oasis. The women all gave birth, and their children established the Iwillimiden group of the Tuareg.

THE ORIGIN OF MATRILINEAL
SUCCESSION

A king once was cursed. In consequence, his first wife's child proved to be a jinn who fled the world of humans at birth and joined the other spirits. The father blamed his wife and divorced her. He married again; his wife conceived. Again, she gave birth to a spirit, which vanished. The king divorced her and married again. This continued until he became too old to marry again. All his children had gone to the world of the spirits. He had no heir.

He was worried what might happen after his death; he feared a civil war that would split the people and bring harm to them. So he summoned all his subjects and put to them the question how they should ensure a peaceful transmission of power upon his death. Some suggested one recourse, others something else. Some were ready to put the question to a test of arms, others suggested divination and auguries. At last, an old man asked to speak and was granted leave. He was a holy man who had spent his time in contemplation.

He reminded them of the series of wives, all noble and virtuous, who had passed through the king's bedchamber. He pointed out that such a series of events must have occurred according to the divine will, and asked then why the people were being subjected to this trouble. Why had the king been denied an heir? Certainly, the people needed a ruler, and a ruler of known royal blood. How then to ensure this result? There was only one way, said the holy man. They must look to the son of the king's sister, for there was no question of his royalty. The people agreed to this solution, and so the king's nephew became ruler upon his death.

THE FIRST IHAGGAREN

The Ihaggaren are a Tuareg sub-group based in northern Niger. This story is retold from a recent collection of Tuareg tales.

There was a man of some intelligence and resource who had two wonderful possessions: a sword that could cut through anything: flesh, wood, even stone, and a servant of tremendous strength who had been seen to uproot a tree with his bare hands. The man was not married; he was looking for a wife of rare cleverness and perception.

He was raiding with his companions when they came upon the trail of a travelling group: a family with their servants and camels. The man went to scout out the situation. He slipped over the dunes and spent the day spying on the camp. He soon realized it was one family, and that they had no sons but only a daughter. Their camels were of rare quality. He waited until a servant went out to milk one of the camels. The servant tethered the camel colt to one side and called for help in milking the mother. The man then slipped down from the dunes and joined the servant, standing on the other side of the she-camel and helping to milk her. The servant thought it was his master.

The servant brought the milk to the daughter, and she asked him who had helped him milk the camel. He answered that it must have been her father, although he had not seen the man's face. The daughter sniffed the milk. 'No,' she said. 'The man who helped milk the camel had been riding all day, holding in one hand a wooden stick and in the other a metal spear. There must be raiders somewhere near here.'

The man had heard her words, for he had followed the servant to the tent and then slipped around the back to listen to what passed. He realized that this was the woman he had been seeking, a woman of intelligence and perception. He waited. The woman went to her father and warned him that a party of raiders lay nearby and that they should try to escape. But they could think of no way to slip off without leaving tracks that the raiders would have no trouble finding. When

the woman was alone, the man went into her and revealed that
he was the man she had detected, who had helped to milk the
camel. 'But I have not come to raid your camp,' he said. 'I have
been seeking a woman such as yourself for my bride, and so I
shall do what I can to protect you.' He arranged a stratagem
with her: they hamstrung the male camel, so that he lay on the
ground bellowing and groaning, and then they tethered a young
camel nearby so that it called out for its dam. Then the party
packed up their camp and slipped away in the night. The man
gave the woman his camel-stick, and asked her to drop it after
they had ridden for half a day or more.

The man returned to his companions at dawn and told them
he thought they had missed their chance. The people of the
camp had left. But the companions pointed out the noise of the
camels, and said they should wait until the evening to attack.
When they did so, however, they found an empty campsite,
with two camels bellowing and groaning loudly enough to
deceive them. They butchered the male camel and feasted on
its meat, and then the next day they began following the trail
of the party. In the afternoon, they found the man's camel-stick
in the sand.

'I told you they had left,' said the man. 'I followed them this
far, but still could not find the camp.'

The man waited for three years and then went looking for
his promised bride. But he found no trace of her or her father's
camels. More years went by as he searched across the sands
and through the valleys, and as the seventh year was ending he
finally heard where they were and hastened to join them. But
time had run out for her. Her father had promised her to a
man, and his suite had come to fetch her and bring her to her
wedding tent.

While she sat alone in the tent, a lion passed by and smelt
her presence. It broke through the sides of the tent and carried
her off into the waste. It passed by the man who had finally
located the camp and was watching it from a nearby dune, and
he attacked it. The lion dropped the woman and leaped on the
man; the man used his shield against the mighty paws and
talons and then slashed at the lion's neck with his sword. His

sword was a wonderful blade that cut through anything, even stone; the lion's head fell to the sands. Then the man turned to inspect its prey. He recognized his intended bride, and she him. They spent the night talking and planning how to undo her marriage.

Before the dawn light came, the man arranged the lion's carcass so that it seemed to be standing over its prey. The woman lay beneath the paws, and the head was mounted on a stick, and swayed from side to side. Servants came running from the wedding tent. They had brought food to the bride and found the sides shredded and the lion's track. They stopped when they saw the lion and turned away. Soon, the leaders of the camp arrived, among them the intended groom and the bride's father.

'Go!' called the father. 'There may yet be life in her! Kill the lion!' But the men refused. The father turned to the groom and asked him to try to save his daughter. The groom refused: he was sure the daughter was dead and beyond hope. At that, the man came and offered to attack the lion if he was given a reward.

'What reward do you want?'

'Give me the lion's prey.'

'What would you do with a corpse, a dead woman?'

'Grant me the gift, then I shall attack the lion.'

The men agreed, and the man then went and knocked over the lion's carcass. He raised the woman to her feet and returned her to her father. Her father willingly gave her as a bride to the lion-killer.

Their troubles were not over. As the man and his bride were returning to his home territory, he left her for a moment in the care of his servant while he went to refill their waterbags. When he returned, he found that the servant had seized the woman, who was riding one of the wonderful racing camels that her father bred, and carried her off. The camel's pace and endurance were such that the man could not catch up with them. The servant and his captured bride rode for forty days into the wilderness, without pausing to let the camel eat or drink, and then they rested for a time at an oasis. They then continued further into the desert. The servant settled in a forbidden land, one which even the jinns feared to enter. He took the woman as his bride. She did not dare refuse: the servant had carried off her lover's wonderful sword, and he had, besides, a ferocious dog who would attack and kill anything. But she stopped caring for herself, and her hair became grimy and tangled, her clothes tattered and stained.

Her lover cast about in all directions from their tracks, looking for his lost bride, but he could find no sign of her. Finally, he returned to her father and asked for his help: the servant had escaped thanks to the endurance of his camel, and only with a similar animal might he hope to find their trail. The father gave him a four-year-old she-camel which had been tested for its endurance and courage. Then the man set off.

He rode for forty days over the desert, following the direction his servant had taken. He came to an oasis and met a man living there. He asked for news of his servant and the captured bride, but the man could tell him nothing.

'But perhaps the birds can give a sign,' said the man. 'I have watched them for some time now. They fly north, and return six days later with fine white camel-hair for their nests. If the woman was riding a white camel, perhaps that is the direction you should take.'

The man followed his advice and rode north, following the line taken by the birds. After several days, he saw the signs of a camp nearby. Then he began to move with caution. He crept up over the dunes until he could see the rude camp which the servant had made. He watched until he saw the servant ride off on the racing-camel, accompanied by his monstrous dog. Then the man crept into the camp and found the woman, filthy and unkempt. She had two small children, a boy and a girl, born during this captivity. She recognized him, and greeted him hesitantly. But he was able to restore her spirits, and together they planned how to overcome the servant with his beasts and the marvellous sword. The servant was accustomed to challenge the woman to tie him as tightly as she could with leather thongs made from camel-hide, to test his strength: he would then flex his muscles and the thongs burst apart like thin cotton thread.

The man gave the woman a rope made of goat-hair, and she helped him to dig a pit in which he hid.

The servant returned and found the woman more gay and cheerful than he had seen her in years. She explained that she had become resigned to her lot, and had decided to become a loving wife to him and a good mother to their children. But, she added, she was mortally afraid of his dog, and she was sure that some day it would kill or maim her or one of the children. The servant scoffed at her fears, but agreed to tie up the dog so that it could not come near her while in camp. Then he told her to bring out the thongs and bind him, so he could test his strength.

'You know you will burst the camel-hide,' she said. 'But I have just found an old rope which may be a better test of your strength. It was at the bottom of my sack.'

'Bring it, and lash me to the tree,' ordered the servant, and the woman did so with fervour. She pulled the rope about him as tight as she could, bracing herself against the tree-trunk, and then she tied the knots. The servant strained against the rope. It gave a little, but it did not burst into pieces like the thongs. Then the man came from his hiding place and seized the sword which was hanging nearby.

'Do you know me?' he asked.

'I know you,' said the servant.

'And what do you have to say for yourself today?'

'I say that if it were not for this rope, I would be slicing you up for jerky as we speak.'

'So be it,' said the man, and with one blow he struck off the servant's head. Then, bit by bit, he sliced up the servant's body, and when he had finished he killed the dog.

They left the two children with six milk-camels in the wilderness. They rode back together to his home. The children were clever; they knew where to get water and how to milk the camels. They grew up, and when they were adults the boy married his sister. Their offspring became the Ihaggaren.

ALI GURAN AND HIS NEPHEW
ADELASEQ

These two figures, and their stories, are widespread among all the Tuareg groups of Niger; it is interesting that the opposition of uncle and maternal nephew also marks one of the major historical narratives of the Songhay, the story of Mamar Kassai (the Askia Muhammad) who overthrew Sonni Ali to establish the Ture dynasty. These stories are retold from a recent collection of tales.

Ali Guran feared his sister's children, for he felt they would threaten his power. Accordingly, he killed every child born to her. But at one time she and her slave-woman were both pregnant and gave birth at the same time. The noble mother exchanged her son for that of the slave-woman. Ali Guran took what he thought was his nephew and killed him, but in fact the true nephew survived.

As the child grew, Ali Guran began to suspect that in fact the slave-boy was of his blood, for the child showed unusual intelligence. Once, Ali Guran, his son and his nephew Adelaseq were travelling across the desert. They had a store of food and water with them. Ali Guran told the boys that they must give the desert its share. His son immediately spread out his stores and poured out a part of his water, and threw away some of his dried meat and dates. His nephew simply drew closer to him and began to recount the doings of the men of the camp and the news he had heard of nearby camps: where they had raided, what booty they had taken, how they had treated their camels, where they had found water, until the day was almost over and they had completed their trip. Ali Guran then asked the boys what they had given the desert for its share. His son answered that he had given the desert a portion of his supplies. Adelaseq answered that the desert's share was talk, for by keeping up the conversation they had crossed the desert without noticing the time pass.

Another time, Ali Guran was travelling alone in the desert and was taken captive by another group of Tuareg. He offered them a ransom, and they agreed to let him buy off his life. He told them to ride to his camp and ask for his belt and the draw-string of his trousers. The raiders were puzzled, but agreed. They bound up Ali Guran and left him on the sands, and they rode into his camp. They asked for the belt and the draw-string to his trousers; Ali Guran's son had no idea what they were talking about. But Adelaseq came and told him that he, Adelaseq, was the belt, and the son was the draw-string. He added that clearly the father had been taken captive and they must find a way to rescue him.

He invited the raiders to wait for a meal, and then set the slave-women to work. But instead of grain they pounded sand in their mortars, and the work continued for some time until the raiders all became sleepy and dozed off. Adelaseq then went among them, gathered all their weapons and placed them in a pile in the middle of the camp, in the sun. Then he took the dish of sand and went as though to bring them their meal. But he tossed the sand in their faces and then drew his sword and began striking them. The raiders grasped for their weapons, but found nothing close at hand. Some of them saw the pile and reached for the swords and spears, but the sun had made the weapons so hot that the raiders could not hold them. In this way Adelaseq routed them and drove them from the camp. Then he and Ali Guran's son retraced the raiders' path and freed Ali Guran from his bonds.

Ali Guran then decided that he must kill this clever lad. He sent Adelaseq out to mind the sheep, giving him two raw hides. He told him he could use the one as a sunshade, and he should peg the other one to the ground to dry out. But Adelaseq mistrusted his uncle, and so he wrapped the hide over an ewe. Ali Guran came in the middle of the day and speared the sheep through the hide, thinking he had killed his nephew, but Adelaseq arose from his resting place and told his uncle he had killed a sheep instead.

Another time, Ali Guran, his son and his nephew were out camping together. They were near a waterhole, but the boys did not know where it was. That night, Adelaseq slept some distance from his uncle, fearing a trick or an attempt on his life. In the middle of the night, Ali Guran roused his son and the two of them crept down to the waterhole and drank their fill. They spent the night by the water, drinking, and then slipped back to their camp in the morning. Adelaseq at that time was beginning to feel very thirsty, for he had emptied his own waterskin during the night. He saw his uncle and cousin sleeping, and knew that there must be water in the area. So he took some of the grease from their food – they had a good store of meat – and daubed it on the bottom of their sandals. Then he waited. That night, the uncle and cousin returned to the waterhole and again they drank their fill. They returned to the camp the next morning. But Adelaseq followed their trail by noting where the ants had come to feed on the grease from their sandals, and so he was able to find the waterhole and drink his fill. Then he observed a tall stalk of reeds, and guessed that this served as his uncle's marker to find the waterhole. He cut it down and returned to the camp.

That evening, Ali Guran could not find his way to the waterhole. Adelaseq came and mocked him. 'I understand your tricks,' he said. 'You wished me to die of thirst. But now you are suffering, are you not?' Then he showed them the way to the waterhole. As he was drinking, Ali Guran drew his sword and prepared to strike him, but Adelaseq saw the reflection in the water and was able to dodge the blow. Then he had his own sword out, and beat down his uncle's blade. Ali Guran gave up, muttering that they were united through mothers' wombs and mothers' milk.

Sources and Further Reading

GENERAL

M. G. Adam, *Légendes historiques du pays de Nioro* (Paris: Augustin Challamel, 1904).

Stephen Belcher, *Epic Traditions of Africa* (Bloomington: Indiana University Press, 1999).

Cambridge History of Africa, 8 vols., ed. Oliver D. Fage and Roland Oliver (Cambridge: Cambridge University Press, 1975–).

Harold Courlander, *A Treasury of African Folklore* (New York: Crown Publishers, 1975; reissued New York: Marlowe and Co., 1996).

Luc de Heusch, *The Drunken King*, trans. Roy Willis (1972; repr. Bloomington: Indiana University Press, 1982).

Leo Frobenius, *The Voice of Africa*, trans. Rudolf Blind (2 vols., 1913; repr. in one vol., New York: Arno Press, 1980).

—— *Atlantis: Volksdichtung und Volksmärchen Afrikas*, 12 vols. (Iena: Eugen Diederichs, 1921–8; Nendeln: Kraus Reprint, 1978).

John Iliffe, *Africans: The History of a Continent* (Cambridge: Cambridge University Press, 1995).

H. R. Palmer, *Sudanese Memoirs* (3 vols. in one, 1928; repr. London: Frank Cass, 1967).

Raffaele Pettazzoni, *Miti africani* (Turin: Unione Tipographico, 1948).

Harold Scheub, *Dictionary of African Mythology* (Oxford: Oxford University Press, 2000).

Harry Tegnaeus, *Le Héros civilisateur* (Stockholm: Studia Upsaliensa Africana, 1950).

Unesco General History of Africa, 8 vols. (Paris, London, Berkeley: James Currey and University of California Press).

Alice Werner, *Africa: Myths and Legends* (1933; reprinted London: Senate, 1995).

CHAPTER 1. THE SAN PEOPLES OF SOUTHERN AFRICA

The Battles of Khaggen, retold from J. M. Orpen, 'A Glimpse into the Mythology of the Maluti Bushmen', *Cape Monthly Magazine*, July 1874; reprinted in *Folklore*, 30 (1919), pp. 142–6, 149–51; Wilhelm Bleek and Lucy Lloyd, *Specimens of Bushman Folklore* (London: George Allen, 1911), pp. 17–30. Khaggen Creates an Eland, retold from Dorothea F. Bleek (ed.), *The Mantis and his Friends: Bushman Folklore* (Capetown: Miller, 1923), pp. 1–5, 5–9. Qwanciqutshaa, retold from Orpen, pp. 146–9. The Marking of the Animals, retold from Megan Biesele, *Women Like Meat* (Bloomington: Indiana University Press, 1993), pp. 116–21. The Python Wife, retold from Biesele, pp. 124–33 (three versions).

Mathias Guenther offers a collection of stories in *Bushman Folktales: Oral Traditions of the Nharo of Botswana and the /Xam of the Cape* (Stuttgart: Franz Steiner Verlag, 1989) which combines recently collected material with much older unpublished material from the Bleek and Lloyd archives. An early standard ethnography is Isaac Schapera's *The Khoisan Peoples of South Africa* (London: Routledge and Kegan Paul, 1930), which includes a comparative discussion of mythology. More recent is Elizabeth Marshall Thomas's *The Harmless People* (New York: Vintage Books, 1958–9), to which one might add Marjorie Shostak's *Nisa: The Life and Words of a !Kung Woman* (New York: Vintage, 1983), but either would be only a starting point in a very large bibliography. Megan Biesele's *Women Like Meat* does provide good commentary on the stories given above. A title attempting a new synthesis is *The Bushmen of Southern Africa: A Foraging Society in Transition*, by Andrew Smith, Candy Malherbe, Mathias Guenther and Penny Behrens (Capetown: David Philip; Athens: Ohio University Press, 2000). Penny Miller has put together a nice collection of South African myths (including almost all the major groups besides the Khoi-San), *Myths and Legends of Southern Africa* (Capetown: T. V. Bilpin Publications, 1979). There is also a useful new reference work: Richard B. Lee and Richard Daly, *The Cambridge Encyclopedia of Hunters and Gatherers* (Cambridge: Cambridge University Press, 1999), which covers a number of African groups on pp. 175–229.

CHAPTER 2. PYGMIES OF THE CENTRAL AFRICAN FORESTS

The Creation of Humans, retold from H. Trilles, *Contes et légendes pygmées* (Bruges: Librairie de l'œuvre St Charles, 1931), pp. 78–9. Why Pygmies Live in the Forest, retold from Paul Schebesta, *Among Congo Pygmies*, trans. Gerald Griffin (London: Hutchinson and Co., 1933), p. 166. How the Pygmies Got Fire, retold from Schebesta, pp. 81–2.

There is a good deal of ethnographic literature upon the various groups; one of the most sympathetic accounts is that of Colin Turnbull, *The Forest People* (New York: Simon and Schuster, 1961), although other ethnographers have since questioned his portrayal.

CHAPTER 3. THE SONGHAY HUNTERS OF THE NIGER RIVER

Musa Nyame and the Hira, retold from A. Dupuis-Yakouba, *Les Gow, ou chasseurs du Niger* (Paris: Ernest Leroux, 1911; Nendeln: Kraus Reprint, 1974), pp. 20–39. Kelimabe and Kelikelimabe, retold from Dupuis-Yakouba, pp. 88–149. Fara Makan and Fono, retold from Jean Rouch, *La Chanson de Fara Makan* (Documents presented to the SCOA conference in Niamey, 1978) and A. Prost, 'Légendes Songhay', *Bulletin de l'IFAN*, 18 (1956), pp. 188–201.

Dupuis-Yakouba provides other narratives at the end of Louis Desplagnes, *Le Plateau central nigérien* (Paris: Émile Larose, 1907), pp. 383–450. Leo Frobenius also gives a number of stories in *Dämonen des Sudan*, *Atlantis*, vol. vii. For Songhay political traditions, see Chapter 61.

CHAPTER 4. THE ORIGIN OF HUNTERS' ASSOCIATIONS: SANEN AND KONTRON OF THE MANDEN

First Version, retold from Youssouf Cissé, 'Notes sur les sociétés de chasseurs malinké', *Journal de la société des africanistes*, 34 (1964), pp. 175–226, at p. 177. Second Version, retold from Fodé M. B.

Sidibé, 'Deux récits de chasse Banmana: Ndoronkelen et Bani Nyenema', master's thesis, Université Cheik Anta Diop, Dakar (1984), pp. 164–7. Third Version, retold from Youssouf Cissé, *La Confrérie des chasseurs Malinké et Bambara* (Paris: Nouvelles du Sud/Arsan, 1994), pp. 39–44.

See Leo Frobenius, *Dämonen des Sudan, Atlantis*, vol. vii, and Karim Traore, *Le Jeu et le sérieux* (Cologne: Rüdiger Köppe Verlag, 2000) for a supplementary view of Mande hunters. For the Manden, see also Chapters 64–6.

CHAPTER 5. HOW HUNTERS LEARNED ABOUT MAGIC

The story is retold from Melville and Frances Herskovits, *Dahomean Narrative* (Evanston, Ill.: Northwestern University Press, 1958), pp. 232–5. For other references on the Fon, see notes to Chapter 51.

CHAPTER 6. THE ANIMAL BRIDE I: THE CHANGED SKIN

This story appears widely in hunters' narratives, and is occasionally known by the name of the hunter as given in some Mande versions, Maghan Jan. See the references given for Chapter 7.

CHAPTER 7. THE ANIMAL BRIDE II: SIRANKOMI

The story is retold from multiple versions: Annik Thoyer, *Récits épiques de chasseurs bamanan du Mali* (Paris: L'Harmattan, 1995), pp. 27–98; Gerard Meyer, *Contes du pays malinké* (Paris: Karthala, 1987), pp. 25–9; Leo Frobenius, *Dämonen des Sudan, Atlantis*, vol. vii, pp. 47–50; Mamby Sidibé, *Contes populaires du Mali* (Paris: Présence Africaine, 1982), pp. 19–43.

CHAPTER 8. KHOI-KHOI CATTLE STORIES

The Two Men, retold from Wilhelm Bleek, *Reynard the Fox in South Africa* (London: Trübner, 1864), pp. 83–4. Heitsi-Eibib and the King of Snakes, retold from Jan Knappert, *Myths and Legends of Botswana, Lesotho, and Swaziland* (Leiden: E. J. Brill, 1985), p. 53.

For further references on the Khoi-Khoi, see notes to Chapter 38. On African pastoralism in general, see Andrew B. Smith, *Pastoralism in Africa: Origins and Development Ecology* (London: Hurst, Witwatersrand University Press, 1992).

CHAPTER 9. FULBE STORIES OF CATTLE

Tyamaba, the Great Serpent, retold from Lilyan Kesteloot, Christian Barbey and Siré Mamadou Ndongo (eds.), 'Tyamaba, mythe peul', *Notes africaines*, 185–6 (1985), multiple versions given on pp. 44–68. A Muslim Version from Northern Nigeria, retold from M. D. W. Jeffreys, 'Mythical Origin of Cattle in Africa', *Man*, 113–14 (1946), pp. 140–41. The First Cow: Why Fulbe are Herdsmen, retold from Sheikou Balde, 'L'Origine de la première vache', *Éducation africaine*, 101 (1938), pp. 29–32.

For the political traditions of the Fulani or Fulbe, see notes to Chapter 69.

CHAPTER 10. THE MAASAI OF EAST AFRICA

The Origin of Cattle, retold from A. C. Hollis, *The Masai: Their Language and Folklore* (Oxford: at the Clarendon Press, 1905), pp. 270–71; and Naomi Kipury, *Oral Literature of the Maasai* (Nairobi: Heinemann, 1983), pp. 30–31. Women and the Camps, retold from Hollis, pp. 120–22.

On Maasai history, see Thomas Spear and Richard Waller (eds.), *Being Maasai: Ethnicity and Identity in East Africa* (London: James Currey, 1993), and as a personal statement, Tepilit Ole Saitoti's *The Worlds of a Maasai Warrior: An Autobiography* (Berkeley: University of California Press, 1988).

CHAPTER 11. THE GREAT LAKES I: THE ORIGIN OF CATTLE (RWANDA)

The story is retold from Claudine Vidal, 'De la contradiction sauvage', *L'Homme*, 14 (1974), pp. 5–58; her source was L. Delmas, *Généalogie de la noblesse du Ruanda* (Kagbayi, n.d.); see also A. Coupez and Th. Kamanzi, *Récits historiques Rwanda* (Tervuren: Musée royal de l'Afrique centrale, 1962), pp. 70–84, and Pierre Smith, *Le Récit populaire au Rwanda* (Paris: Classiques africains and Armand Colin, 1975), pp. 284–9. For other stories from Rwanda, see Chapter 29.

CHAPTER 12. THE GREAT LAKES II: THE STORY OF WAMARA (BAHAYA)

The story is retold from P. Césard, 'Comment les Bahaya interprètent leurs origines', *Anthropos*, 22 (1927), pp. 440–65, at pp. 447–52.

For background on the BaHaya kingdoms and culture, see Peter R. Schmidt, *Historical Archaeology: A Structural Approach in an African Culture* (Westport: Greenwood Press, 1978), especially pp. 61 ff.; Peter Seitel's *The Powers of Genre: Interpreting Haya Oral Literature* (New York and London: Oxford University Press, 1999); Mugyabuso Mulokozi, *The African Epic Controversy* (Dar es Salaam: Mkuki na Nyota, 2002), pp. 13–109.

CHAPTER 13. THE CHAGGA OF EAST AFRICA: MURILE

The story was first reported by the Revd J. Raum in 1909, and retold or reprinted by Carl Meinhof, *Afrikanische Märchen* (Iena: Eugen Diederichs, 1921), pp. 71–8, and Alice Werner, *Africa: Myths and Legends*, pp. 70–76.

CHAPTER 14. UTHLAKANYANA, THE ZULU CHILD TRICKSTER

The story is retold from the Revd Henry Callaway, *Nursery Tales, Traditions, and Histories of the Zulus* (Natal: John A. Blair, London: Trübner and Co., 1868), pp. 6–40. Other Zulu stories are given in Chapter 37.

CHAPTER 15. STORIES OF MONI-MAMBU OF THE BAKONGO

The stories are adapted and retold from J. van Wing and Cl. Scholler's *Légendes des Bakongo-Orientaux* (Brussels: Bulens; Louvain: AUCAM, 1940), pp. 11–34. The hero has also been turned into a novel by Guy Menga, *Les Aventures de Moni-Mambou* (Yaoundé: Editions Clé, 1971). For the kingdom of Kongo, see Chapter 40.

CHAPTER 16. TURE, THE ZANDE TRICKSTER

Ture Releases the Waters, retold from E. E. Evans-Pritchard, *The Zande Trickster* (Oxford: at the Clarendon Press, 1967), pp. 38–9. Ture Sets Fire to the Bush, retold from Evans-Pritchard, pp. 39–40. Ture's Wife and the Great Bird Nzanginzanginzi, retold from Evans Pritchard, pp. 40–42. Ture Dances, retold from Evans-Pritchard, pp. 58–9. Ture and his Innards, retold from Evans-Pritchard, pp. 111–13. Ture and his Mother-in-Law, retold from Evans-Pritchard, pp. 144–6.

Evans-Pritchard also published a number of other works on the Zande.

CHAPTER 17. ESHU OF THE YORUBA

Eshu's Knowledge, retold from William Bascom, *Sixteen Cowries* (Bloomington: Indiana University Press, 1980), pp. 101–3. Eshu, Orunmila and the Servant of Death, retold from Wande Abimbola, *Ifa Divination Poetry* (Lagos: Nok Publishers, 1977), pp. 89–93. Eshu

Parts Two Friends, retold from Ulli Beier, *Yoruba Myths* (Cambridge: Cambridge University Press, 1980), pp. 55–6; Pierre Verger, *Notes sur le culte des Orisa et Vodun à Bahia . . .*, Mémoires de l'IFAN, 51 (Dakar: IFAN, 1957), p. 112. Stories about Eshu are widely told and printed; other principal sources would be Harold Courlander, *Tales of Yoruba Gods and Heroes* (New York: Crown Publishers, 1973). Verger's valuable study of *orisa* cults in Brazil and on the west coast of Africa retells many of the well-known stories.

For West African tricksters in general (Eshu, Legba, Ananse), see Robert D. Pelton, *The Trickster in West Africa* (Berkeley: University of California Press, 1980). Leo Frobenius also gives additional early material on Yoruba religion in *Die Atlantische Götterlehre*, *Atlantis*, vol. x, pp. 50–199; for Eshu especially pp. 168–81. Other Yoruba stories are given in Chapter 49.

CHAPTER 18. LEGBA OF THE FON

This story is retold from Melville and Frances Herskovits, *Dahomean Narrative* (Evanston, Ill.: Northwestern University Press, 1958), pp. 142–8. Other Fon stories are given in Chapter 51.

CHAPTER 19. ANANSE THE SPIDER, OF THE ASHANTI

The Story of Nanni, retold from Ludewig Rømer's *A Reliable Account of the Coast of Guinea (1760)*; (ed. and trans. Selena Winsnes, published for the British Academy by Oxford University Press, 2000), pp. 80–83. How Ananse Got the Stories from the Sky-God, first published by R. S. Rattray, *Akan-Ashanti Folktales* (Oxford: at the Clarendon Press, 1930), pp. 54–8; the story has also been collected by Harold Courlander, *The Hat-Shaking Dance and Other Ashanti Tales from Ghana* (New York: Harcourt, Brace, Jovanovich, 1957). The story has been widely retold and reprinted. Ananse and the Corncob, retold from A. W. Cardinall, *Tales Told in Togoland* (1931; repr. London: Oxford University Press, 1970), pp. 15–21. This story is a type ('successive exchanges') which is widespread in Africa: see Denise Paulme's essay on the topic in her collection of essays, *La Mère dévorante* (Paris: Gallimard, 1976). For Ashanti political traditions, see Chapter 52.

CHAPTER 20. EGYPTIAN STORIES

The literature on ancient Egypt is enormous. The corpus of stories, however, is limited, although available in many translations.

The Contending of Horus and Seth, Cheops and the Magicians, The Two Brothers, retold from multiple translations: Miriam Lichtheim, *Ancient Egyptian Literature*, 2 vols. (Berkeley: University of California Press, 1973, 1975); William Kelly Simpson (ed.), *The Literature of Ancient Egypt* (New Haven and London: Yale University Press, 1972); M. V. Seton-Williams, *Egyptian Legends and Stories* (London: The Rubicon Press, 1988); and E. A. Wallis Budge, *Legends of the Egyptian Gods* (New York: Dover Publications; first printed 1912). The Treasure of Rhampsinitus, retold from Herodotus, *The Histories*, trans. Aubrey de Selincourt (Harmondsworth: Penguin, 1954), pp. 147–50.

CHAPTER 21. ETHIOPIA

The story of Solomon and the queen of Sheba is a part of the *Kebra Negast* (the Glory of Kings), a medieval history of the kings of Ethiopia; I have used several versions: the translation of Miguel F. Brooks, *A Modern Translation of the Kebra Nagast* (Lawrenceville, Kan.: Red Sea Press, 1995), pp. 19–45, and two versions in Harold Courlander, *A Treasury of African Folklore*, pp. 524–37 (one from the oral tradition, another from the scholarship of Enno Littmann). The Separation of the Darassa and the Jam-Jamo, retold from A. Jensen, *Im Lande des Gada* (Stuttgart: Strecker und Schröder, 1936), pp. 500–501. How Rule Passed from Women to Men, retold from Jensen, pp. 502–4 (two versions).

CHAPTER 22. THE OROMO OF SOUTHERN ETHIOPIA

The First Humans, retold from A. Jensen, *Im Lande des Gada* (Stuttgart: Strecker und Schröder, 1936), pp. 491–2. The Adamites of the Kingdom of Guma, retold from Enrico Cerulli, *Folk Literature of the Galla*, Harvard African Studies (Cambridge, Mass.: Harvard University Press, 1922), pp. 152–5. The Story of Mohammed Gragn, retold from Jensen, pp. 10–11, and from Hans Jannasch, *Im Schatten des Negus* (Berlin: Die Brüder, 1930), pp. 9–28.

For Oromo history, see Mohammed Hassen, *The Oromo of Ethiopia: A History 1570–1860* (Cambridge: Cambridge University Press, 1990), but this is only one of many studies on specific aspects of Oromo history. Ernesta Cerulli provides ethnography of the region covered by the stories in *Peoples of Southwest Ethiopia and its Borderland* (London: International African Institute, 1956), and Asmarom Legesse offers analysis and evaluation in *Gada: Three Approaches to the Study of African Society* (New York: Free Press, 1973). On religion, and particularly for discussion of the figure of Waqa, see Lambert Bartels, *Oromo Religion: Myths and Rites of the Western Oromo of Ethiopia* (Berlin: Dietrich Reimer Verlag, 1983).

CHAPTER 23. THE SHILLUK OF SOUTHERN SUDAN

Several sources are combined in this account of the career of Nyikang and his sons. The starting point is Diedrich Westermann, *The Shilluk People: Their Language and Folklore* (1912; Westport, Conn.: Negro Universities Press, n.d.), pp. 155 ff. The Revd D. S. Oyler adds some material in his essays, 'Nikawng and the Shilluk Migration', *Sudan Notes and Records*, 1 (1918), pp. 107–15, and 'Nikawng's Place in the Shilluk Religion', ibid., pp. 283–92, and the stories are summarized by Godfrey Lienhardt in 'The Shilluk of the Upper Nile', in C. Darryl Forde (ed.), *African Worlds* (London: Oxford University Press, for the International African Institute, 1954), pp. 138–63. Many of the stories are also given in J. P. Crazzolara, *The Lwoo*, 3 vols. (Verona: Missioni africane, 1950), vol. i, pp. 35 ff.

CHAPTER 24. THE LUO OF SUDAN AND UGANDA

The Origin of Death, retold from B. Onyango-Ogutu and A. A. Roscoe, *Keep My Words* (Nairobi: East African Publishing House, 1974), pp. 43–4. The Spear and the Bead, retold from Otok P'Bitek, *Religion of the Central Luo* (Nairobi: East African Literature Bureau, 1971), p. 20; Onyango-Ogutu and Roscoe, pp. 133–8; J. P. Crazzolara, *The Lwoo*, 3 vols. (Verona: Missioni africane, 1950), pp. 62–6. A Shrine of Baka and Alela, retold from P'Bitek, pp. 60–63.

The most impressive compilation of sources on Luo traditions of origin is that of Crazzolara, which provides an extensive collection of clan traditions of origin for most of the Luo sub-groups. The poet Otok P'Bitek identifies the principal traditions of origin in his *Religion*; B. A. Ogot provides historical background in his *History of the Southern Luo* (Nairobi: East African Publishing House, 1967). Onyango-Ogutu and Roscoe also provide a version of the 'Bead' story, pp. 133 ff.

CHAPTER 25. THE GIKUYU OF KENYA

The story is retold from Jomo Kenyatta, *Facing Mount Kenya* (1938; New York: Vintage Books, n.d.), pp. 5–10. See J. Scoresby Routledge and Katherine Routledge, *With a Prehistoric People: The Akikuyu of British East Africa* (London: Edward Arnold, 1910), pp. 283–4 (a slightly different version); Leonard J. Beecher, 'The Stories of the Kikuyu', *Africa*, 11 (1938), pp. 80–87; and Louis Leakey's 3-volume work, *The Southern Kikuyu before 1903* (New York: Academic Press, 1977), vol. i, pp. 48–9, whose publication was delayed in deference to Kenyatta's book. A modern discussion of Gikuyu oral literature is Wanjiku Mukabi Kabira and Karega wa Mutahi, *Gikuyu Oral Literature* (Nairobi: Heinemann, 1988), and for Gikuyu history, see Godfrey Muriuki, *A History of the Kikuyu, 1500–1900* (Nairobi: Oxford University Press, 1974).

CHAPTER 26. THE SWAHILI OF THE COAST

Liyongo Fumo of Shaha, retold from several versions: Alice Werner, *Africa: Myths and Legends*, pp. 145–54; Jan Knappert, *Epic Poetry in Swahili and Other African Languages* (Leiden: E. J. Brill, 1983), pp. 142–68; Lyndon Harries (ed.), *Swahili Poetry* (Oxford: Clarendon Press, 1962), pp. 48–71. Knappert also gives a selection of the poems attributed to Liyongo, with some suggestions on historical or narrative context, in his *Four Centuries of Swahili Verse* (Nairobi: Heinemann, 1979), pp. 66–101. The Foundation of Kilwa, retold from two versions in G. S. P. Freeman-Grenville (ed. and trans.), *The East African Coast: Select Documents from the First to the Earlier Nineteenth Century* (Oxford: Clarendon Press, 1962), pp. 35–7 and 221–3.

A useful study on the background and history of Swahili language and culture is Derek Nurse and Thomas Spear, *The Swahili: Recon-structing the History and Language of an African Society, 800–1500* (Philadelphia: University of Pennsylvania Press, 1985), which discusses the Shirazi legends, pp. 70–79. A more general study is John Middle-ton, *The World of the Swahili* (New Haven: Yale University Press, 1992).

CHAPTER 27. THE KINGDOM
OF BUNYORO

All the stories are retold from Ruth Fisher, *Twilight Tales of the Black Baganda* (2nd edn., London: Frank Cass, 1970), pp. 69–98.

The introductory essay by Merrick Posnansky in Fisher (pp. xi-xxxvii) is very useful; it offers a comparative synthesis of the stories and excellent background information. John Beattie's *Bunyoro: An African Kingdom* (New York: Holt, Rinehart and Winston, 1960) offers a basic ethnography. An early account of the kingdom, relevant for Bunyoro and Buganda, is John Roscoe, *The Bakitara or Banyoro: The First Part of the Report of the Mackie Ethnological Expedition to Central Africa* (Cambridge: Cambridge University Press, 1923) and *The Banyankole: The Second Part of the Report of the Mackie Ethnological Expedition* (Cambridge: Cambridge University Press, 1923). David William Cohen offers a historiographic analysis of the Kintu legends in *The Historical Tradition of Busoga: Mukama and Kintu* (Oxford: at the Clarendon Press, 1972), while Benjamin Ray looks at the stories for the region in terms of mythology and royal rituals in *Myth, Ritual and Kingship in Buganda* (New York and Oxford: Oxford University Press, 1991).

CHAPTER 28. THE KINGDOM
OF BUGANDA

The most authoritative source for Buganda is the account prepared by a member of the royal house, Sir Apolo Kaggwa, *The Kings of Buganda*, ed. and trans. M. S. M. Kiwanuka (Nairobi: East African Publishing House, 1971), written around 1900. The stories are retold from pp. 1–15.

See also John Roscoe, *The Baganda: An Account of their Native Customs and Beliefs* (London: Macmillan, 1911), and R. R. Atkinson,

'The Traditions of the Early Kings of Buganda: Myth, History, and Structural Analysis', *History in Africa*, 2 (1975), pp. 17–57. See also the additional references given for Bunyoro in the notes to Chapter 27, and the books by Luc de Heusch given in the notes to Chapter 29.

CHAPTER 29. THE KINGDOM OF RWANDA

A Royal Version of the Origin of the Kingdom, retold from A. Coupez and Th. Kamanze, *Récits historiques Rwanda* (Tervuren: Musée royal de l'Afrique centrale, 1962), pp. 61–71. A Popular Version, retold from Fr. Loupias, 'Tradition et légende des Batutsi sur la Création du monde et leur établissement au Ruanda', *Anthropos*, 3 (1908), pp. 1–13.

The kingdom of Rwanda has been very extensively documented, although not all documents have been published. The historical narratives have a great deal of stability from one version to another. Jan Vansina offers a new history of the kingdom, *Le Rwanda ancien* (1980; repr. Paris: Karthala, 2001). For studies of the mythology, see the works of Luc de Heusch: *The Drunken King*, and its sequel, *Rois nés d'un cœur de vache* (Paris: Gallimard, 1982); these two volumes summarize and discuss traditions from all the major kingdoms of the central Bantu-language area (Buganda, Rwanda, Burundi, Kuba, Luba, Kongo, and others), and provide valuable retellings of inaccessible versions. For an introductory ethnography of the kingdom of Rwanda, see J. J. Maquet, 'The Kingdom of Ruanda', in C. Daryll Forde (ed.), *African Worlds* (London: Oxford University Press, for International African Institute, 1954), pp. 164–89.

CHAPTER 30. THE KINGDOM OF BURUNDI

The story is retold from different versions given in Claude Guillet and Pascal Ndayishinguje, *Légendes historiques du Burundi* (Paris: Karthala, and Centre de civilisation burundaise, 1987), pp. 49–103 (different stories).

CHAPTER 31. NSONG'A LIANJA, HERO OF THE MONGO

All episodes are retold from multiple versions. There are more than forty versions of the epic of Lianja available in print. The two principal collections are: E. Boelaert, *Nsong'a Lianja: L'Épopée nationale des Nkundo* (Antwerp: De Sikkel, 1949; Nendeln: Kraus Reprint, 1973), which presents a lengthy composite version, and A. de Rop, *Versions et fragments de l'épopée Mongo* (Brussels: Académie Royale des Sciences d'Outre-Mer, Classe des Sciences Morales et Politiques, NS XLV-1, 1978). For additional textual references, see Stephen Belcher, *Epic Traditions of Africa*, pp. 31–8. Two versions not listed there are by Jan Knappert, *Myths and Legends of the Congo* (Nairobi and London: Heinemann Educational Books, 1971), pp. 75–135, and Mubima Maneniang, *The Lianja Epic* (Nairobi: East African Educational Publishers, 1999). Many Lianja tales are included in Mabel H. Ross and Barbara K. Walker, *'On another day...': Tales Told among the Nkundo* (Hamden, Conn.; Archon Books, 1979); the authors apparently were unaware of the connections of their material with the Lianja tradition.

CHAPTER 32. THE KUBA KINGDOM OF THE BUSHOONG: MBOOM AND WOOT

The story is retold from multiple versions: Luc de Heusch, *The Drunken King*, pp. 88–139, summarizes many narratives; Jan Vansina, *The Children of Woot* (Madison: University of Wisconsin Press, 1978), pp. 47–68; id., 'Initiation Rituals of the Bushong', *Africa*, 25 (1955), pp. 118–53; id., 'Les Croyances religieuses des Kuba', *Zaire*, 12 (1958), pp. 725–8; Emil Torday, *On the Trail of the Bushongo* (1925; repr. New York: Negro Universities Press, 1969), pp. 124–30.

Jan Vansina's classic study, *Kingdoms of the Savanna* (Madison: University of Wisconsin Press, 1966), is a valuable guide to the general history of this and the neighbouring kingdoms and peoples (especially Kongo, Chapter 40, below), and the same author gives us a general ethnography of the Kuba kingdom in *Le Royaume Kuba* (Tervuren: Musée royal de l'Afrique centrale, 1964).

CHAPTER 33. THE FIRST KINGS OF
THE LUBA

The story is retold from multiple versions. The principal source is Harold Womersley, *Legends and History of the Luba* (Los Angeles: Crossroads Press, 1984). Luc de Heusch provides summaries of the variant versions collected in *The Drunken King*, pp. 11–29; Thomas Q. Reefe, in *The Rainbow and the Kings* (Berkeley: University of California Press, 1981), pp. 23–40, also summarizes the story and compares the contents of the different versions.

CHAPTER 34. THE KINGDOMS OF
THE LUNDA

The Kingdom of Mwata Yamvu, retold from Mwata Kazembe XIV, *My Ancestors and my People*, Rhodes Livingstone Communication, 23: Central Bantu Historical Texts II: Historical Traditions of the Eastern Lunda, trans. Ian Cunnison (Lusaka 1961; repr. 1968), pp. 1–17, and E. Labrèque, 'Histoire des Mwata Kazembe, chefs Lunda du Luapula', *Lovania: Tendances du temps*, 16 (1949), pp. 9–23. Peoples of the Luapula River, retold from Ian Cunnison, *The Luapula Peoples of Northern Rhodesia* (Manchester: Manchester University Press, 1959), pp. 34–40. The Kingdom of Mwata Kazembe, retold from Mwata Kazembe XIV, pp. 18–60, and E. Labrèque, 'Histoire des Mwata Kazembe', part 2, *Lovania: Tendances du temps*, 17 (1949), pp. 21–48.

CHAPTER 35. THE BEMBA OF ZAMBIA

The story is retold principally from E. Labrèque, 'La Tribu des Babemba I: Les origines des Babemba', *Anthropos*, 28 (1933), pp. 633–48. Andrew D. Roberts, *A History of the Bemba* (Madison: University of Wisconsin Press, 1973), provides a good summary and discussion of the legends of origin of the Bemba kingdom; Luc de Heusch also summarizes and discusses the traditions in terms of comparative mythology in *The Drunken King*, pp. 228 ff.

CHAPTER 36. THE SHONA OF ZIMBABWE

Creation: the Cult of Mwari and Chaminuka, retold from Michael
Gelfand, *Shona Ritual* (Capetown: Juta, 1962), pp. 31–9. How
Muskwere Became Chief of the Wahungwe, retold from F. W. T.
Posselt, *A Survey of the Native Tribes of Southern Rhodesia* (Salisbury:
Govt. of Southern Rhodesia, 1927), pp. 14–15. The Source of the
Sabi River, retold from Posselt, p. 19. The Power of the Mbira, retold
from several versions given in Leo Frobenius, *Erythräa* (Berlin: Atlantis
Verlag, 1931), pp. 150–52 and 358–60.

Although a wealth of Shona oral historical tradition has been
recorded, much of it remains unpublished; it also appears to cover
principally the recent history of the Shona groups. David Beach's *The
Shona and their Neighbours* (Oxford: Oxford University Press, 1994),
and M. F. C. Bourdillon, *The Shona Peoples* (rev. edn., Harare:
Mambo Press, 1982), are good introductions to the peoples involved
and their history. Paul Berliner, *The Soul of Mbira* (Berkeley: University of California Press, 1978) is an excellent introduction to the world
of the musicians who perform in the spirit-cults of the area. The first
two stories can also be found in Penny Miller, *Myths and Legends of
Southern Africa* (Capetown: T. V. Bilpin Publications, 1979).

CHAPTER 37. THE NGUNI PEOPLES
OF SOUTHERN AFRICA: ZULU,
XHOSA, SWAZI

Creation, retold from multiple sources (see below). Death, retold from
multiple sources (see below). The Different Peoples, retold from Janet
Hodgson, *The God of the Xhosa* (Capetown: Oxford University Press,
1982), pp. 21–2; see also Henry Callaway, *Religious Traditions of the
AmaZulu* (Springvale, Natal: J. A. Blair; London: Trübner and Co.,
1870), pp. 76ff. A Swazi Story of a King, retold from Hilda Kuper,
An African Aristocracy: Rank among the Swazi (London: Oxford
University Press for the International African Institute, 1952), p. 237.

A good general collection of myths from this region is Penny Miller's
Myths and Legends of Southern Africa (Capetown: T. V. Bilpin Publications, 1979); she covers the major ethnic and linguistic groups,
including some Shona stories. Wilhelm Bleek's *Zulu Legends*, ed. J. A.
Engelbrecht (Pretoria: J. L. Van Schaik Ltd., 1952), with material

collected in 1855–6, also summarizes most of the basic stories, pp. 1–7. Almost all the collections of narratives consulted for this region were dominated by animal tales; it would appear that the political upheavals associated with the establishment of the Zulu state at the start of the nineteenth century (or possibly the intrusion of settlers and missionaries from the eighteenth century on) have dissipated what politically oriented myths of origin did exist, and what is left now are historical narratives of the relatively recent past, but almost nothing comparable to the rich traditions of the great lakes region. For religion, see such works as Axel-Ivar Berglund, *Zulu Thought Patterns and Symbolism* (Bloomington: Indiana University Press, 1976), pp. 33ff.; Charles Brownlee, 'A Fragment on Xhosa Religious Beliefs', *Africa*, 14 (1955), pp. 37–53, and Hodgson (above). For the Swazi, one might also consult Hilda Kuper, *The Swazi: A South African Kingdom* (New York: Holt, Rinehart and Winston, 1963); Brian A. Marwick, *The Swazi* (London: Frank Cass, 1966); and J. S. Malan, *Swazi Culture* (Pretoria: Africa Institute of South Africa, 1985).

CHAPTER 38. THE KHOI-KHOI: STORIES OF HEITSI-EIBIB

The stories of Heitsi-Eibib are adapted from the material in Theophilus Hahn, *Tsuni-ǁGoam, the Supreme Being of the Khoi-Khoi* (London: Trübner, 1881), esp. pp. 56–72. See also Wilhelm Bleek, *Reynard the Fox in South Africa* (London: Trübner, 1864), pp. 75–83; Jan Knappert's *Namibia: Land and Peoples, Myths and Fables* (Leiden: E. J. Brill, 1981), pp. 86ff. and also *Myths and Legends of Botswana, Lesotho, and Swaziland* (Leiden: E. J. Brill, 1985), pp. 50ff.

CHAPTER 39. THE YAKA OF THE KWANGO RIVER

The story is retold from Hubert van Roy, *Les Byaambvu du Moyen-Kwango* (Berlin: D. Reimer, 1988; Collectanea Instituti Anthropos, 37), supplemented with M. Plancquaert's *Les Yaka: Essai d'histoire* (Tervuren: Musée royal de l'Afrique centrale, 1971).

I am indebted to a colleague, Arthur Bourgeois, for drawing my attention to this set of traditions, and for guiding my research. For a general history of the region, Jan Vansina's *Kingdoms of the Savanna* (Madison: University of Wisconsin Press, 1966), is a good guide. Plancquaert has also produced a collection, *Soixante mythes sacrés Yaka* (Tervuren: Musée Royal de l'Afrique centrale, 1982), which contains interesting creation narratives but little obvious political material. One might also wish to read L. de Beir's *Religion et magie des Bayaka* (St Augustin: Anthropos Institut St Augustin, 1975).

CHAPTER 40. THE KINGDOM OF KONGO

A colleague, John Thornton, has been very helpful and generous in sharing his expertise and his unpublished translations of seventeenth-century sources, and I would like to express my gratitude to him. I have retold the early versions of the story of Luqueni from his unpublished translations. I also learned a great deal from his essay, 'The Origins and Early History of the Kingdom of Kongo ca. 1350–1550', *International Journal of African Historical Studies*, 34: 1 (2001), pp. 89–120. The third version is retold from a well-known, colonial-era history of the kingdom by a missionary, J. Cuvelier, *L'Ancien Royaume du Congo* (Brussels: L'édition Universelle, 1946); parts of this history were also published in KiKongo, and so have now become the standard version.

The kingdom of Kongo is well documented. Besides John Thornton's *The Kingdom of Kongo: Civil War and Transition 1641–1718* (Madison: University of Wisconsin Press, 1983), a more recent history is that of Anne Hilton, *The Kingdom of Kongo* (Oxford: at the Clarendon Press, 1985). Wyatt MacGaffey has several works on the political and spiritual culture of the BaKongo: *Kongo Political Culture* (Bloomington: Indiana University Press, 2000) and *Religion and Society in Central Africa: The BaKongo of Lower Zaire* (Chicago: University of Chicago Press, 1986). Luc de Heusch also treats the mythological symbolism in *Le Roi de Kongo et les monstres sacrés* (Paris: Gallimard, 2000; Mythes et rites bantous, III).

CHAPTER 41. THE FANG OF GABON AND CAMEROON

Creation, retold from James Fernandez, *Bwiti: An Ethnography of the Religious Imagination in Africa* (Princeton: Princeton University Press, 1982), pp. 54–5, and Jacques Binet, Otto Gollnhofer and Roger

Sillans, 'Textes religieux du Bwiti-Fang et ses confréries prophétiques dans leurs cadres rituels', *Cahiers d'études africaines*, 46 (1972), pp. 197–253, at pp. 221–2. Migrations I: the Separation of the Peoples, retold from Pierre Alexandre, 'Proto-histoire du groupe beti-bulu-fang: Essai de synthèse provisoire', *Cahiers d'études africaines*, 5 (1965), pp. 503–60, esp. pp. 515–17. Migrations II: Ngurangurane, Son of the Crocodile, retold from H. Trilles, *Le Totemisme chez les Fang* (Munster: Bibliothèque Anthropos, 1912), pp. 184ff.

The first stop for any reader interested in the Fang should be Fernandez' excellent and full study, *Bwiti* (see above) which reviews previous scholarship and mixes its observations with vivid descriptions of daily life among a Fang group. For a general description of this ethnic group, see Pierre Alexandre and Jacques Binet, *Le Groupe dit Pahouin (Fang – Boulou – Beti)* (Paris: Presses universitaires de France, 1958).

CHAPTER 42. JEKI LA NJAMBE OF THE DUALA

The story is retold from multiple versions. The best available versions are by Pierre Celestin Tiki a Koulla a Penda, *Les Merveilleux Exploits de Djeki la Njambe*, 2 vols. (Douala: Éditions Collège Libermann, 1987), and Manga Bekombo-Priso (ed. and trans.), *Défis et prodiges: La fantastique histoire de Djèki-la-Njambé* (Paris: Classiques africains, 1993).

On the Jeki tradition, see Ralph Austen's study, *The Elusive Epic* (n.p.: African Studies Association Press, 1995); he gives a comprehensive listing of available versions, with a good analysis. There is also a short discussion in Stephen Belcher, *Epic Traditions of Africa*, pp. 41–4.

CHAPTER 43. THE BAMUN KINGDOM OF CAMEROON

The story is retold principally from Sultan Njoya, *Histoire et coutumes des Bamum*, trans. Henri Martin (Mémoires de l'Institut Français d'Afrique Noire (Centre du Cameroun), 1952), pp. 22–4, with additional material from Eldridge Mohammadou, *Traditions d'origine des peuples du centre et de l'ouest du Cameroun* (Tokyo(?): Institute for the Study of Languages and Cultures of Asia and Africa, 1986), pp. 41–62.

For additional information on the kingdom, see Claude Tardits'
monumental study of the kingdom, *Le Royaume Bamoum* (Paris:
Armand Colin, 1980).

CHAPTER 44. THE IGBO

Ale, retold from Percy Talbot, *Tribes of the Niger Delta* (1932; repr.
London: Frank Cass and Co., 1967), pp. 25–7. Eri and the City of
Nri, retold from Elizabeth Isichei, *Igbo Worlds: An Anthology of Oral
Histories and Historical Descriptions* (Philadelphia: Institute for the
Study of Human Issues, 1978), pp. 21–8 and ff.; M. D. W. Jeffreys,
'The Umundri Tradition of Origin', *African Studies*, 15 (1956),
pp. 119–31; Northcote Thomas, *Anthropological Report on the Ibo-
Speaking Peoples of Nigeria*, 4 vols. (London: Harrison and Sons,
1913; New York: Negro Universities Press, 1969), vol. i, pp. 49ff.
Onojo Oboni of Iddah, retold from Christopher Ofigbo's excellent
Ropes of Sand (Nsukka: published for University Press Limited, in
association with Oxford University Press, 1981), pp. 117ff. See also
Jeffreys, p. 125, and Austin Shelton, 'Onojo Ogboni', *Journal of
American Folklore*, 81 (1968), pp. 243–57.

The Igbo-speaking groups are so diverse that it is rash to offer any
attempt at a synthesis. I have been guided in this enterprise by John
Nwachimereze Oriji's study, *Traditions of Igbo Origin* (New York:
Peter Lang, 1994), which provided an excellent starting point. Particu-
larly useful after him were Ofigbo, *Ropes of Sand*, and Isichei, *Igbo
Worlds*.

CHAPTER 45. THE KINGDOM OF THE
NUPE: TSOEDE

The basic source for the story of Tsoede is also the basic source for
the Nupe kingdom: S. F. Nadel's classic study, *A Black Byzantium:
The Kingdom of Nupe in Nigeria* (London: Oxford University Press
for the International African Institute, 1942), pp. 72ff. Michael Mason
has done a study on the background of Nadel's information, 'The
Tsoede Myth and the Nupe Kinglists: More Political Propaganda?',
History in Africa, 2 (1975), pp. 101–12. Another author to report the
story is Leo Frobenius, in his *The Voice of Africa*, pp. 575ff. Frobenius
offers a great deal more information on Nupe culture and narratives

in *Volkserzählungen und Volksdichtungen aus dem Zentral-Sudan, Atlantis*, vol. ix, including a retelling of the Tsoede story ('Etsu Edegi'), pp. 179–82.

CHAPTER 46. THE JUKUN KINGDOM OF THE KORÓROFA

The stories are retold from Charles Kingsley Meek, *A Sudanese Kingdom: An Ethnographic Study of the Jukun-Speaking Peoples of Nigeria* (London: Trübner, 1931). The Son of Ama: pp. 90–96. Kingship of the Kororofa: pp. 30–31, 36–7, 46–7.

CHAPTER 47. THE BACHAMA AND BATA OF THE UPPER BENUE

The stories are retold from Charles Kingsley Meek, *Tribal Studies in Northern Nigeria*, 2 vols. (London: Trübner, 1931). Nzeanzo: pp. 25–7. The Separation of the Bachama and Bata: pp. 2–3.

CHAPTER 48. THE CITY OF BENIN

The Foundation of Benin, retold from Jacob U. Egharevba, *A Short History of Benin* (3rd edn., Ibadan: Ibadan University Press, 1960), pp. 1–8. Ewuare, retold from Egharevba, pp. 14–21.

Egharevba wrote numerous locally printed volumes on the history and culture of his city; besides his *History* one should consult his *The Origin of Benin* (Benin City: BDNA Museum, 1953). The bibliography on the arts of Benin City is considerable. Isidore Okpewho offers a revisionist view of local oral tradition in his study, *Once Upon a Kingdom: Myth, Hegemony, and Identity* (Bloomington: Indiana University Press, 1998).

CHAPTER 49. THE YORUBA OF
SOUTH-WESTERN NIGERIA

The Orisha, The Creation of the World, Oduduwa, Ife and Oyo, retold from multiple sources (Beier, Courlander, Frobenius, Wyndham below). Moremi, retold from Wyndham, pp. 35–60; Samuel Johnson, *History of the Yorubas* (Lagos: CSS Bookshops, 1921), pp. 147–8. The Migration from the East, retold from Samuel Johnson, pp. 4–5. The Origin of Ifa Divination I, retold from Stephen S. Farrow, *Faith, Fancies and Fetich, or Yoruba Paganism* (1926; repr. New York: Negro Universities Press, 1969), p. 37. The Origin of Ifa Divination II, retold from Johnson, pp. 32–3.

The bibliography on the Yoruba is large. For the myths, good collections are Ulli Beier, *Yoruba Myths* (Cambridge: Cambridge University Press, 1980), and Harold Courlander, *Tales of Yoruba Gods and Heroes* (New York: Crown Publishers, 1973; much of this material is reprinted in his *Treasury of African Folklore* (New York: Crown Publishers, 1975)). Leo Frobenius discusses the Yoruba in the first volume of his early study, *The Voice of Africa*, and again in *Die Atlantische Götterlehre*, vol. x of his wonderful collection, *Atlantis*, which gives much information about the *orisha*. Pierre Verger's study on the transatlantic dimensions of the Ifa and Vodun cults offers a number of stories about the gods: *Notes sur le culte des Orisa et Vodun à Bahia . . .*, Mémoires de l'IFAN, 51 (Dakar: IFAN, 1957). John Wyndham, a colonial administrator, versified the stories in his *Myths of Ife* (London: Erskine MacDonald, 1921), and I have trusted him for some of the details in the story of Moremi. R. E. Dennett's *Nigerian Studies* (London: Frank Cass, 1968; first printed 1910) offers interesting descriptions of the major *orisa*, as does Farrow's *Faith, Fancies and Fetich, or Yoruba Paganism* (see above), which are useful mainly as evidence for the variety of traditions before the publication of Johnson's *History of the Yorubas*. This book deserves some remark. The original manuscript was lost; his brother reconstructed the work and published it after the Revd Johnson's death. It seems to have become the accepted version of the history and theology of the Yorubas, although it is clear that Johnson adapted his material in accordance with his Christian views. That is why a short version of his vision of the origin of the Yorubas is given. While variant traditions have survived, the influence of his literary version has been great. Yoruba historiography is now a fascinating field, and one might start with essays by Robin Law: 'How Truly Traditional is our Traditional History? The Case of Samuel Johnson and the Recording of Yoruba Oral Tradition', *History in Africa*, 11 (1984), pp. 195–211, and 'The Heritage of Oduduwa: Traditional History and Propaganda among the Yoruba', *Journal of African History*, 14 (1973), pp. 207–22, and by Cornelius Adepegba, 'The Descent from Odudua: Claims of Superiority among Some Yoruba Traditional Rulers and the Arts of Ancient Ife', *International Journal of African Historical Studies*, 19 (1986), pp. 77–92, or with Toyin Falola's *Yoruba Gurus: Indigenous Production of Knowledge in Africa* (Trenton: African World Press, 1999).

CHAPTER 50. BORGU AND THE LEGEND OF KISRA

This short account is cobbled together from multiple sources, in particular H. R. Palmer, *Sudanese Memoirs*, vol. ii, pp. 56–63; S. J. Hogben and A. H. M. Kirk-Greene, *The Emirates of Northern Nigeria* (London: Oxford University Press, 1966), pp. 577 ff.; Femi Obafemi, 'History of Borgu', *Image: Quarterly Journal of the Kwara State Council for Arts and Culture*, 1:2 (1974), pp. 25–6; A. B. Mathews, 'The Kisra Legend', *African Studies*, 9:3 (1950), pp. 144–7; Phillip Stevens, 'The Kisra Legend and the Distortion of Historical Tradition', *Journal of African History*, 16: 2 (1975), pp. 185–200; and Paolo de Moraes Farias, 'A Letter from Ki-Toro Mahamman Gaani, King of Busa (Borgu, Northern Nigeria) about the "Kisra" Stories of Origin', *Sudanic Africa*, 3 (1992), pp. 109–32. Leo Frobenius, *The Voice of Africa*, and Charles Kingsley Meek, *A Sudanic Kingdom: An Ethnographic Study of the Jukun-Speaking Peoples of Nigeria* (London: Trübner, 1931), also discuss this legend.

CHAPTER 51. THE FON AND THE KINGDOM OF DAHOMEY

The Creation, Earth and Sky, retold from the several versions given in Melville and Frances Herskovits, *Dahomean Narrative* (Evanston, Ill.: Northwestern University Press, 1958), pp. 125–34. The Allada Dynasty of Abomey, Hwegbadja, the First King, retold Herskovits and Herskovits, pp. 355–67, with information from Emmanuel Karl's *Traditions orales au Dahomey-Bénin* (Niamey: Centre régional de documentation pour la tradition orale, 1974), and from Melville Herskovits, *Dahomey: An Ancient West African Kingdom* (2 vols., New York: J. J. Augustin, 1938).

A more recent study of the kingdom and its traditions is Edna G. Bay, *Wives of the Leopard: Gender, Politics and Culture in the Kingdom of Dahomey* (Charlottesville: University of Virginia Press, 1998); a short ethnographic account is given by P. Mercier, 'The Fon of Dahomey', in Daryll Forde (ed.), *African Worlds* (London: Oxford University Press, for International African Institute, 1954), pp. 210–34. On religion, see Robert D. Pelton, *The Trickster in West Africa* (Berkeley: University of California Press, 1980), and Pierre Verger, *Notes sur le culte des Orisa et Vodun à Bahia*, Mémoires de l'IFAN, 5 (Dakar: IFAN, 1957).

CHAPTER 52. THE AKAN-ASHANTI AND THE BAULE OF THE FOREST

Origins, retold from various sources: Carl Christian Reindorf, *History of the Gold Coast and Asante* (1895; repr. Accra: Ghana Universities Press, 1966), pp. 19–20; A. B. Ellis, *The Tshi-Speaking Peoples of the Gold Coast of West Africa* (1887; repr. Oosterhut: Anthropological Publications, 1970), pp. 335–7. Osei Tutu and the Rise of Ashanti, retold from K. O. Bonsu Kyeretwie, *Ashanti Heroes* (Accra: Waterville Publishing House; London: Oxford University Press, 1964), pp. 1–20. Queen Pokou and the Baule, retold from various sources: J. N. Locou, 'Between History and Legend: The Exodus of the Baule during the XVIII Century', trans. Cherie Maiden, *Afrique-Histoire US*, 2:1 (1984), pp. 37–42; H. Lanrezac, *Le Folklore au Soudan* (Paris: La Revue Indigène, n.d.), pp. 20ff., and 'Légendes Soudanaises', *Revue économique française*, 29 (1907), pp. 607–19; Maurice Delafosse, *Essai de manuel de la langue Agni* (Paris: Librairies africaine et coloniale, 1901), pp. 159–64.

Various works by Eva Meyerowitz offer a good starting point: *The Akan of Ghana: Their Ancient Beliefs* (London: Faber and Faber, 1958), *Akan Traditions of Origin* (London: Faber and Faber, 1952), and *Early History of the Akan States of Ghana* (London: Red Candle Press, 1974). Also very useful was K. O. Bonsu Kyeretwie (see above). Variants on the creation are taken from Ellis (see above). A significant early source is Reindorf (see above); see also the references given for the trickster Ananse in the notes to Chapter 19.

For the Baule, there are various sources (including Kyeretwie, above), which all give much the same story. The Baule may be best known outside Côte d'Ivoire for their art, for which see the catalogue of the exhibition organized by Susan Vogel, *Baule: African Art, Western Eyes* (New Haven: Yale University Press, 1997), which also includes discussion of Queen Pokou.

CHAPTER 53. THE FOUNDING OF GONJA

The Gonja histories are edited in Ivor Wilks, Nehemia Levtzion and Bruce M. Haight, *Chronicles from Gonja: A Tradition of West African Muslim Historiography* (Cambridge: Cambridge University Press, 1986), pp. 44–6, 91–7; a variant on the tradition is given by E. F. Tamakloe in A. W. Cardinall's *Tales Told in Togoland* (1931; repr. London: Oxford University Press, 1970), pp. 237–79.

CHAPTER 54. A DAGOMBA HERO

The basic source for the Dagomba is the account by E. F. Tamakloe, which appears in A. W. Cardinall, *Tales Told in Togoland* (1931; repr. London: Oxford University Press, 1970), pp. 237–79, and was also published separately: *A Brief History of the Dagomba People* (Accra: Government Printing Office, 1931), pp. 3–9. But Leo Frobenius also gives a version in his *Voice of Africa*, pp. 468ff. The story has echoes in Mossi tradition as well.

CHAPTER 55. THE MOSSI OF
BURKINA FASO

The story retold from multiple sources (see below): Frobenius, pp. 256ff.; Delobsom, pp. 2–10; Balima, pp. 66–75.

There are many compilations of Mossi traditions. An early local account is that of Dim Delobsom, *L'Empire du Mogho-Naba* (Paris: Les Éditions Domat-Montchrestien, 1932); less satisfying is Albert Balima's *Légendes et histoire des peuples du Burkina Faso* (Paris: private printing, 1996). Leo Frobenius gives many traditions of the

Mossi kings in *Dichten und Denken im Sudan*, Atlantis, vol. v, pp. 256–303. The French historian Michel Izard has devoted considerable effort to the history of the Mossi kingdoms: *Introduction à l'histoire des royaumes Mossi (= Recherches Voltaiques*, 12, 1970) and *Le Yatenga précolonial* (Paris: Karthala, 1985). An accessible English account of the Mossi people is that of Elliott Skinner, *The Mossi of Burkina Faso* (1964; repr. Prospect Heights, Ill.: Waveland Press, 1989).

CHAPTER 56. THE DOGON OF THE BANDIAGARA ESCARPMENT

Creation: a Popular Version, retold from Marcel Griaule, *Masques Dogon* (Paris: Institut d'ethnologie, 1938, 1994), pp. 44–52. Death and the Dancing Costume, retold from Griaule, *Masques Dogon*, pp. 52–8. Creation: the Esoteric Version, retold from Marcel Griaule, *Dieu d'eau* (1948; repr. Paris: Fayard, 1966), pp. 23–54.

The Dogon of the Bandiagara plateau have been the subject of study since Louis Desplagnes, *Le Plateau central nigérien* (Paris: Émile Larose, 1907); and Leo Frobenius also offered an early description in *Spielmannsgeschichten der Sahel*, Atlantis, vol. vi, pp. 249ff. But the name most closely associated with descriptions of the Dogon is that of Marcel Griaule, in three books: *Masques Dogon* (1938), *Dieu d'eau*, known in English as *Conversations with Ogotemmeli* (London: Oxford University Press for the International African Institute, 1965), and *Le Renard pâle*, which was published posthumously (*The Pale Fox*, trans. Stephen Infantino, Chino Valley, Ariz.: Continuum Foundation, 1986; French version published in 1965). Griaule's team included Germaine Dieterlen, who produced *Les Âmes des Dogons* (Paris: Institut d'ethnologie, 1941) and Michel Leyris, *La Langue secrète des Dogon de Sanga* (Paris: Institut d'ethnologie, 1948). The list might continue. A new generation of anthropologists is now reviewing Griaule's work on the Dogon, as questions have been raised about many of his findings, particularly the results reported in *Conversations with Ogotemmeli* and *The Pale Fox* (see Walter van Beek, 'Dogon Restudied: A Field Evaluation of the Work of Marcel Griaule', *Current Anthropology*, 32 (1991), pp. 139–67, and the responses on the following pages of the same issue). The article about the star Sirius appeared in 1950 (Marcel Griaule and Germaine Dieterlen, 'Un système soudanais de Sirius', *Journal de la Société des Africanistes*, 20

(1950), pp. 273–94). Griaule's account of the myths retold in this section are echoed in the works of his collaborators.

CHAPTER 57. THE SARA AND THE SOW OF LAKE CHAD

The stories of Sow and Loa are retold from the different versions given by Joseph Fortier, *Le Mythe et les contes de Sou* (Paris: Classiques africains and Julliard, 1967): Creation by Loa and Sou, pp. 63ff.; Sou and the Arts, pp. 79–81 and ff.; Sou and the Star Women, pp. 115–17.

The stories about Goulfeil and Makari are retold from Marcel Griaule's study, *Les Saô légendaires* (Paris: Gallimard, 1943): The Foundation of Goulfeil, pp. 83–9; The City of Makari, pp. 121–5.

For the general background on this region, Humphrey Fisher's essay, 'The Eastern Maghrib and the Central Sudan', is very useful reading (in *Cambridge History of Africa*, vol. iii: *From c. 1050 to c. 1600*, ed. Roland Oliver, pp. 232–330), and H. R. Palmer's collection of translated documents, *Sudanese Memoirs*, provides useful primary source material, including discussion of the Sow. See also Gustav Nachtigall, *Sahara and Sudan*, vol. iii: *The Chad Basin and Bagirmi*, trans. Allan G. B. Fisher and Humphrey J. Fisher (1889; repr. London: C. Hurst and Co; Atlantic Highlands, NJ: Humanities Press International, Inc., 1987).

CHAPTER 58. THE KINGDOM OF BAGIRMI

The account is reconstructed from the information given in Viviana Pâques, *Le Roi pecheur et le roi chasseur* (Strasbourg: Travaux de l'Institut d'anthropologie de Strasbourg, 1977).

See also the sources given in the notes to Chapter 57, especially Nachtigall, vol. iii, pp. 211–91.

CHAPTER 59. THE KINGDOMS OF KANEM AND BORNU

The Five Tribes of Kanem, retold from H. R. Palmer, *Sudanese Memoirs*, vol. ii, pp. 83–4. The Saifawa and the Sow, retold from Palmer, vol. ii, pp. 64–8; A. Schultze, *The Sultanate of Bornu*, trans.

P. A. Benton (1913; repr. London: Frank Cass, 1968), pp. 246–50.
The Wars with the Bulala, retold from Palmer, vol. ii, pp. 39–43.

The texts in Palmer are translations of Arabic manuscripts collected
in the region in the nineteenth century. See also Gustav Nachtigall,
Sahara and Sudan, vol. iii: *The Chad Basin and Bagirmi*, trans. Allan
G. B. Fisher and Humphrey J. Fisher (1889; repr. London: C. Hurst
and Co.; Atlantic Highlands, NJ: Humanities Press International Inc.,
1987) and P. A. Benton, *Languages and Peoples of Bornu* (London:
Frank Cass, 1968). For the historical background, see Humphrey
Fisher, 'The Eastern Maghrib and the Central Sudan', in *Cambridge
History of Africa*, vol. iii: *From c. 1050 to c. 1600*, ed. Roland Oliver,
pp. 232–330. For an ethnography of the Kanuri, see Ronald Cohen's
The Kanuri of Bornu (New York: Holt, Rinehart and Winston, 1967).

CHAPTER 60. THE HAUSA

Bayajida and Daura, retold from multiple sources. Bagauda and the
Founding of Kano, retold from 'The Kano Chronicle', in H. R. Palmer,
Sudanese Memoirs, vol. iii, pp. 97ff.

There are numerous versions of the story of Daura. One of the
longest, collected from oral tradition, is the *Histoire du Dawra*
(Niamey: Centre régional de recherche et de documentation pour la
tradition orale, 1970). Another version is given in Palmer, vol. iii,
pp. 132–4, as also in Frobenius, *Volkserzählungen und Volksdichtungen aus dem Zentral-Sudan*, Atlantis, vol. ix, pp. 277ff. W. K. R.
Hallam offers a study, 'The Bayajida Legend in Hausa Folklore',
Journal of African History, 7 (1966), pp. 47–60, which is useful in
presenting the sources, although it may now be dated. M. Hiskett
has presented a number of other Hausa primary sources: 'The *Kitab
al-Farq*: A Work on the Habe Kingdoms Attributed to Uthman Dan
Fodio', *Bulletin of the School of Oriental and African Studies*, 23
(1960), pp. 558–79, and ' "The Song of Bagauda": A Hausa King List
and Homily in Verse', *Bulletin of the School of Oriental and African
Studies*, 27 (1964), pp. 540–67; 28 (1965), pp. 112–35; 28 (1965),
pp. 363–85. For a useful general introduction to Hausa literature,
see Graham Furniss, *Poetry, Prose, and Popular Culture in Hausa*
(Washington, DC: Smithsonian Institution Press, 1966).

CHAPTER 61. THE SONGHAY PEOPLES OF
THE MIDDLE NIGER

Es-Sadi's Account of the Origins of the Songhay Kingdom, retold from Abdourahmane es-Sadi, *Tarikh es-Sudan*, ed. and trans. O. Houdas (Paris: Maisonneuve et Larose, 1913, repr. 1972), pp. 6–12; see also John Hunwick, *Timbuktu and the Songhay Empire* (Leiden: Brill, 1999), pp. 5–8. Mali Bero and the Escape from Mali, retold from multiple versions given in Fatimata Mounkaila, *Le Mythe et l'histoire dans la geste de Zabarkane* (Niamey: Centre d'études linguistique et historique par la tradition orale, 1989), pp. 63–163. Koukamonzon and the Kingdom of Dendi, retold from the version collected by Ahmadou Hampâte Ba, *Koukamonzon* (Niamey: Centre national de recherche en sciences humaines, 1970). Zwa the Hunter, retold from a version collected by Julde (or Dioulde) Laya, *Traditions historiques de l'Anzuru* (Niamey: Centre régional de documentation pour la tradition orale, 1970), pp. 10–29.

A new collection of Songhay traditions is a volume by Hammadou Soumalia, Moussa Hamidou and Dioulé Lya, *Traditions des Songhay de Tera* (Paris: Karthala/Arsan/Centre d'études linguistique et historique par la tradition orale, 1998). On the history and culture of the Songhay, see the works of Jean Rouch, *Contribution à l'histoire des Songhay*, Mémoires de l'IFAN, 29 (Dakar: IFAN, 1953), pp. 138–259, and *La Religion et la magie songhay* (1950; new edn., Brussels: Éditions de l'Université de Bruxelles, 1989); the films of Jean Rouch are also a significant documentation of Songhay culture. Jean-Pierre Olivier de Sardan also offers valuable resources: *Les Sociétés songhay* (Paris: Karthala, 1984) and *Concepts et conceptions Songhay-Zarma: Histoire, culture, société* (Paris: Nubia, 1982). Readers interested in the spirit cults, which link the Songhay with their southern neighbours, the Hausa and the Yoruba, might wish to read Paul Stoller, *Fusion of the Worlds: An Ethnography of Possession among the Songhay of Niger* (Chicago: University of Chicago Press, 1989), and, with Cheryl Olkes, *In Sorcery's Shadow* (Chicago: University of Chicago Press, 1987).

CHAPTER 62. THE CITY OF DJENNE

The first version is retold from Charles Monteil, *Une cité soudanaise: Djenné, métropole du delta central du Niger* (1932; repr. Paris: Éditions Anthropos and the International African Institute, 1971), pp. 34–6, and the second from the rich material collected by Leo Frobenius in *Dämonen des Sudans, Atlantis,* vol. vii, pp. 173–81.

Our sense of the historical importance of the city of Djenne has been increased by recent archaeological work; see, as a starting point, Roderick and Susan McIntosh, 'The Inland Niger Delta before the Empire of Mali: Evidence from Jenne-Jeno', *Journal of African History,* 22 (1981), pp. 1–22.

CHAPTER 63. THE SONINKE

The Legend of Wagadu, retold from multiple versions: Frobenius, *Spielmannsgeschichten der Sahel, Atlantis,* vol. vi, pp. 60–72; Charles Monteil, 'La Légende de Ouagadou et l'origine des Soninke', *Mémoires de l'IFAN,* 23 (1953), pp. 358–409; Germaine Dieterlen and Diarra Sylla, *L'Empire de Ghana* (Paris: Karthala, 1992), pp. 11–60; Oudiary Makan Dantioko, *Soninkara Tarixinu: Récits historiques du pays Soninké* (Niamey: Centre d'études linguistique et historique par la tradition orale, 1985), pp. 102–44. Daman Gille and the Kingdom of Jara, retold from multiple versions: Maurice Delafosse, *Traditions historiques et légendaires du Soudan occidental* (Paris: Publications du Comité de l'Afrique française, 1913), pp. 30–47; Frobenius, *Atlantis,* vol. vi, pp. 76–79; M. G. Adam, *Légendes historiques du pays de Nioro,* pp. 26–38.

There are now many versions available of the story of Wagadu and Jara (or Diara); for a description and general discussion, see Stephen Belcher, *Epic Traditions of Africa,* pp. 76–88. An excellent discussion of Soninke traditional historiography is Mamadou Diawara, *La Graine de la parole* (Stuttgart: Franz Steiner Verlag, 1990).

CHAPTER 64. THE MANINKA AND THE EMPIRE OF MALI

A Ritual Story of Creation, retold from the versions reported by Germaine Dieterlen and others from the reroofing ceremonies of the Kama Blon in Kangaba; see Dieterlen's initial essay, 'Mythe et organis-ation sociale au Soudan français', *Journal de la Société des Africanistes*, 15 (1955), pp. 39–76; Solange de Ganay, *Le Sanctuaire Kama blon de Kangaba* (Paris: Éditions nouvelles du Sud, 1995). Migration from Mecca: the story of Jon Bilal and his sons is taken from a performance of the epic of Sunjata by Kele Monson Diabaté, which has been published by Rex Moser, 'Foregrounding in the Sunjata, the Mande Epic', Ph.D. dissertation, Indiana University (1974), and in multiple versions by Massa Makan Diabaté: *Kala Jata* (Bamako: Éditions pop-ulaires, 1970) and *Le Lion à l'arc* (Paris: Hatier, 1986). The story of Mystery was also published separately by Charles Bird in Richard Dorson (ed.), *African Folklore* (New York: Doubleday, 1972), pp. 443–8. Sunjata and the Empire of Mali, retold from a composite image of the more than forty versions now available. Well known is the prose version of D. T. Niane, *Sunjata: An Epic of Old Mali* (London: Longman, 1965), or John W. Johnson (ed.), *The Epic of Son-Jara* (Bloomington: Indiana University Press, 1986). David Conrad has published a new collection of versions from upper Guinea: *Epic Ancestors of the Sunjata Era* (Madison: African Studies Program/ University of Wisconsin, 2000). For fuller references, see Stephen Belcher, *Epic Traditions of Africa*, pp. 89–114.

On the Sunjata tradition, see also Ralph Austen (ed.), *In Search of Sunjata* (Bloomington: Indiana University Press, 1999). Mande culture is now perhaps inseparable from the notion of its music and per-formers, the *jeliw* or griots; an excellent study of the music is that of Eric Charry, *Mande Music* (Chicago: University of Chicago Press, 2000).

CHAPTER 65. THE BAMANA OF THE MIDDLE NIGER

The Creation, adapted from the account given by Germaine Dieterlen in *Essai sur la religion bamana* (Paris: Presses universitaires de France, 1951), pp. 1–33. The Kulibali Dynasties, retold from M. G. Adam,

Légendes historiques du pays de Nioro, pp. 55–7; Charles Monteil, *Les Bambara du Segou et du Kaarta* (1924; repr. Paris: Maisonneuve et Larose, 1977), pp. 27ff. The Diarras, retold from David C. Conrad, *A State of Intrigue: The Epic of Bamana Segu*, Fontes Historiae Africanae (London: Oxford University Press and the British Academy, 1990), pp. 48–55. Biton Kulibali and the Founding of Segou, retold from many versions: Conrad, pp. 64–88; Lilyan Kesteloot, 'Le Mythe et l'histoire dans la formation de l'empire de Ségou', *Bulletin de l'IFAN*, ser. B, 40: 3 (1978), pp. 578–611.

There are two full versions of the rich epic cycle of Segou: Lilyan Kesteloot's *L'Épopée bambara de Ségou* (2 vols., 1972; repr. Paris: L'Harmattan, 1993), made up of performances by different artists, and David Conrad's version, based on a performance by the gifted Taïrou Banbera which stretched over four days. Frobenius, *Spielmannsgeschichten der Sahel*, *Atlantis*, vol. vi, also gives many of the episodes of the epic cycle. For a discussion and fuller bibliography, see Stephen Belcher, *Epic Traditions of Africa*, pp. 115–41.

CHAPTER 66. THE MANDINKA OF SENEGAMBIA

The Conquest of the Jolof, part of the epic of Sunjata; references are given in notes to Chapter 64. A particularly interesting version is given by Bamba Suso in Gordon Innes (ed.), *Sunjata: Three Mandinka Versions* (London: School of Oriental and African Studies, 1974). See also the collection of narratives made by Donald Wright: *Oral Traditions from the Gambia* (2 vols., Athens: Ohio University Center for International Studies, 1979 and 1980). Niumi and Jarra, retold from Wright, vol. i, pp. 75–87.

There are two recent collections of Gambian Mandinka oral literature: Katrin Pfeiffer, *Mandinka Spoken Art: Folk-Tales, Griot Accounts, and Songs* (Cologne: Rudiger Koppe Verlag, 1997), and Matthew Schaffer, *Djinns, Stars, and Warriors* (Leiden: E. J. Brill, 2003). For additional references, see Stephen Belcher, *Epic Traditions of Africa*, pp. 175–81.

CHAPTER 67. THE SEREER OF SENEGAL

The Guelowar Lineages, retold from Gravrand, *Cosaan* (see below), pp. 243–55; see also Donald Wright, *Oral Traditions from the Gambia* (2 vols., Athens: Ohio University Center for International Studies, 1979 and 1980), vol. i, pp. 150ff; vol. ii, pp. 170ff. Lineage Stories I: the Caxer, retold from Gravrand, pp. 203–5. Lineage Stories II: Sira Badiane, retold from Gravrand, pp. 264–6.

The history and religion of the Sereer have been described by Henri Gravrand in two volumes: *La Civilisation Sereer: Cosaan* (n.p.: Les Nouvelles Éditions africaines, 1983) on history, and *La Civilisation Sereer: Pangool* (n.p.: Les Nouvelles Éditions africaines, 1990), dealing with belief systems.

CHAPTER 68. NJAAJAAN NJAAY AND THE WOLOF

The story is retold from multiple sources. Jean Boulègue's history, *Le Grand Jolof* (Paris: Éditions façades, 1987), pp. 24–7, reprints the earliest account (collected in the eighteenth century). J. L.-B. Bérenger-Féraud gives another in his *Recueil de contes populaires de la Séné-gambie* (Paris: Ernest Leroux, 1885), pp. 191–6. Samba Diop has published a lengthy version: *The Oral History and Literature of the Wolof People of Waalo, Northern Senegal* (Lewiston, Pa.: Edwin Mellen Press, 1995).

For the Wolof, see Boubacar Barry's history, *Le Royaume du Waalo* (Paris: Karthala, 1985), and an excellent collection by Bassirou Dieng, *L'Épopée du Kajoor* (Paris and Dakar: CAEC/Khoudia, 1993) which gives two versions of the king-cycle. There are also two volumes of Wolof tales and myths: Lilyan Kesteloot and Cherif Mbodj, *Contes et mythes wolof* (Dakar: Nouvelles Éditions Africaines, 1983) and Lilyan Kesteloot and Bassirou Dieng, *Du Tieddo au Talibé: Contes et mythes wolof II* (Paris: Présence africaine, 1989); the latter volume contains a discussion of Njaajan Njaay on pp. 183–200.

CHAPTER 69. THE FUTA TOORO

The Origin of the Fulbe: there are numerous accounts (see also the notes to Chapter 9). The variant given here for the Islamic origins is a consensus version, with some details taken in particular from the narrative of M'Baba Diallo in *Tradition historique peule* (Niamey: Centre d'études linguistique et historique par tradition orale, 1974); see also Boubou Hama, *Recherche sur l'histoire des Touareg sahariens et soudanais* (Paris: Présence Africaine, 1967), pp. 66–9. Koli Tengela and the Deniyanke Dynasty, retold from Sire Abbas Soh, *Chroniques du Fouta sénégalais*, ed. and trans. Maurice Delafosse and Henri Gaden (Paris: Leroux, 1913); M. G. Adam, *Légendes historiques du pays de Nioro*; Henri Labouret (ed. and trans.), 'Livre renfermant la généalogie de diverses tribus noires du Soudan', *Annales de l'Académie des Sciences Coloniales*, 3 (1929), pp. 189–225; and Robert Arnaud, *L'Islam et la politique musulmane en Afrique occidentale française* (Paris: Comité de l'Afrique française, 1912), pp. 172–6.

For a general introduction to the history of the Futa Tooro, see David Robinson, *The Holy War of Umar Tal* (Oxford: Clarendon Press, 1985). The bibliography on Fulbe history and oral traditions is considerable; see Stephen Belcher, *Epic Traditions of Africa*, pp. 142–63, for references.

CHAPTER 70. MALICK SY AND BONDU

The story of Malick Sy is well known. It was reported in the late nineteenth century by J. L.-B. Bérenger-Féraud, *Recueil de contes popularies de la Sénégambie* (Paris: Ernest Leroux, 1885; Nendeln: Kraus Reprint, 1970), pp. 141ff., and later from local sources by M. G. Adam, *Légendes historiques du pays de Nioro*, pp. 47–55, and H. Lanrezac in *Le Folklore au Soudan* (Paris: La Revue Indigène, n.d.), pp. 38–9.

CHAPTER 71. THE TUAREG OF
THE SAHARA

The First Queen, retold from Boubou Hama, *Recherche sur l'histoire des Touareg sahariens et soudanais* (Paris: Présence africaine, 1967), p. 124, and from H. T. Norris, *The Tuareg: Their Islamic Legacy and its Diffusion in the Sahel* (Warminster: Aris and Phillips, Ltd., 1975), pp. 14ff. Children of the Jinns, retold from Norris, pp. 101–2; see also Hama, p. 125. The Origin of Matrilineal Succession, retold from Henri Duveyrier, *Les Touareg du Nord* (Paris: Challamel aîné, 1864), p. 398. The First Ihaggaren, retold from Jeannine Drouin, 'L'Origine des Ihaggaran dans la tradition orale des Kel Dinnig', *Littérature orale arabo-berbère*, 12 (1981), pp. 59–101. Ali Guran and his Nephew Adelaseq, adapted from Dominique Casajus, 'Une série de mythes touareg', *Tisuraf* (Paris: Groupe d'études berbères), 3 (1979), pp. 83–98; much the same cycle of stories is given in Mohamed Aghali Zakara and Jeannine Drouin, *Traditions touarègues nigériennes* (Paris: L'Harmattan, 1979), pp. 50–83.

The Tuareg groups of the Sahara have fascinated outsiders for some time, and the literature treating of their customs, traditions and origins is very uneven. There is now also an Islamic overlay on many of their traditions. Henri Lhote provides a good example of an early study of the Tuareg peoples in *Les Touaregs du Hoggar* (2nd edn., Paris: Payot, 1955), as does Lloyd C. Briggs, *Tribes of the Sahara* (Cambridge: Harvard University Press, 1960). But for a comprehensive (indeed, encyclopedic) modern discussion of Tuareg society and material culture, see Johannes and Ida Nicolaisen, *Pastoral Tuareg* (2 vols., New York: Thames and Hudson; Copenhagen: Rhodos International, 1997). Dominique Casajus also offers analysis of Tuareg oral culture in *Gens de parole: Langage, poésie et politique en pays touareg* (Paris: Éditions la Découverte, 2000).

Index